With love, friendship and gratitude to the amazing team behind the Friendly Book Community and to all the wonderful readers/listeners and authors who make it a warm and happy place to be. And to the wonderful members of my own Facebook group, Redland's Readers, who have shown such incredible support for my books and who make me smile every day xx

A WEDDING AT HEDGEHOG HOLLOW

HEDGEHOG HOLLOW BOOK 4

JESSICA REDLAND

Boldwood

First published in Great Britain in 2022 by Boldwood Books Ltd.

Copyright © Jessica Redland, 2022

Cover Design by Debbie Clement Design

Cover Photography: Shutterstock

A CIP catalogue record for this book is available from the British Library.

Paperback ISBN 978-1-80162-414-5

Large Print ISBN 978-1-80162-415-2

Hardback ISBN 978-1-80162-413-8

Ebook ISBN 978-1-80162-416-9

Kindle ISBN 978-1-80162-417-6

Audio CD ISBN 978-1-80162-408-4

MP3 CD ISBN 9978-1-80162-409-1

Digital audio download ISBN 978-1-80162-410-7

Boldwood Books Ltd
23 Bowerdean Street
London SW6 3TN
www.boldwoodbooks.com

Recurring Characters from Family Secrets at Hedgehog Hollow

Samantha Wishaw, aka Sam or Sammie
Former district nurse and tutor at Reddfield TEC. Owner and full-time manager of Hedgehog Hollow

Jonathan Wishaw
Samantha's dad. Veterinary surgeon at Alderson & Son Veterinary Practice

Debs Wishaw
Samantha's estranged mum. Identical twin to Chloe's mum, Louise

Chloe Turner
Samantha's cousin, who married Samantha's ex, James

James Turner
Samantha's ex-boyfriend, now married to her cousin, Chloe

Samuel Turner
Chloe and James's baby

Louise Olsen
Samantha's auntie/Chloe's mum. Identical twin to Samantha's mum, Debs

Simon Olsen
Samantha's uncle/Chloe's dad

Josh Alderson
Samantha's fiancé. Practice owner and veterinary surgeon at Alderson & Son Veterinary Practice

Paul Alderson
Josh's dad and former business partner

Beth Giddings
Paul's girlfriend/Josh's ex-girlfriend

Archie Alderson
Paul and Beth's young son

Lottie Alderson
Paul and Beth's baby daughter

Connie Harbuckle
Josh's mum. Non-identical twin to Lauren. In a relationship with Alex Williams

Lauren Harbuckle
Josh's auntie. Non-identical twin to Connie. Samantha's former boss at Reddfield TEC

Thomas Mickleby
Elderly widower befriended by Samantha. Left Hedgehog Hollow to Samantha in his will on the proviso she run it as a hedgehog rescue centre

Gwendoline Mickleby
Thomas's wife, whose dream it was to run the hedgehog rescue centre

Rich Cooper
Ambulance paramedic. Good friend of Samantha/partner of Dave

Dave Williams
Builder. Good friend of Samantha/partner of Rich

Alex Williams
Dave's uncle. In a relationship with Connie

Hannah Spiers
District nurse. Samantha's best friend

Toby Spiers
Hannah's husband/James's best friend

Amelia Spiers
Hannah and Toby's baby/Samantha's goddaughter

Lewis
Josh's best friend from school

Danny
Lewis's younger brother

Fizz Kinsella
Trainee veterinary nurse. Volunteer at Hedgehog Hollow

Barney Kinsella
Fizz's older brother. Farmer

Natasha Kinsella
Fizz's mum. Runs catering business

Hadrian Kinsella
Fizz's dad. Police sergeant

Phoebe Corbyn
Accountancy student at Reddfield TEC (2nd year). Volunteer book-keeper at Hedgehog Hollow

Zayn Hockley
Animal Care student at Reddfield TEC (2nd year). Volunteer at
Hedgehog Hollow after work experience

Brynn Grimes
In prison for arson attack on Hedgehog Hollow. Cody and Connor's
cousin

Cody Grimes
In prison for arson attack on Hedgehog Hollow. Brynn's cousin,
Connor's older brother

Connor Grimes
In prison for assault on Samantha. Brynn's cousin, Cody's younger
brother

Terry Shepherd
Has brought in several rescue hedgehogs/hoglets and has befriended
Samantha

THE STORY SO FAR...

It's been a busy year packed full of change for Samantha Wishaw, the owner of Hedgehog Hollow, which she inherited from her friend Thomas Mickleby on the proviso she fulfilled his wife Gwendoline's dream of running a hedgehog rescue centre.

Hedgehog Hollow already had several hedgehogs needing attention, but when hoglets started to arrive requiring round-the-clock care, Samantha was concerned she might have taken on too much. After fainting at work, she accepted she couldn't run the rescue centre and work full-time, so she resigned from her tutoring role.

Hedgehogs weren't the only new arrivals. Josh's previously estranged dad, Paul, moved into the farmhouse with his family – girlfriend Beth, young son Archie and newborn baby Lottie. Paul had been diagnosed with Hodgkin lymphoma and after Samantha and Fizz – a rescue centre volunteer – set up several mass testing sessions in the local community, Paul had a stem cell transplant.

When Samantha's cousin Chloe turned up in mid-June with her four-month-old baby Samuel and announced she'd left her husband James, Samantha was shocked to discover a secret that Chloe had kept hidden since her teens. James and Chloe decided to give their marriage another try, but they both knew the road ahead wouldn't be easy.

Samantha's health challenges continued to blight her, triggered by the attacks by the Grimes family. She was diagnosed with post-traumatic stress disorder (PTSD) and secured professional support.

Samantha took on a couple of new volunteers at Hedgehog Hollow from Reddfield TEC where she used to teach: accountancy student Phoebe and animal care student Zayn. She also arranged for a couple of barns to be converted into holiday cottages and for a secure outdoor area to be created to help hedgehogs rehabilitate.

Josh and Samantha decided to get married at the farm on the anniversary of their opening day – 2nd May – on what would have been Gwendoline's eightieth birthday.

Now Samantha is preparing to celebrate her second Christmas at Hedgehog Hollow, but her first as the owner.

1

SAMANTHA

'Oh, my God, Sam! Could you have crammed any more into one day?' Fizz asked, giving me a rather-you-than-me raise of her eyebrows after I'd run through my plans.

I hitched my bag onto my shoulder, grinning at her. 'I probably won't have any voice left and I'll be sloshing with tea by the end of the day, but I'm looking forward to it. Thanks for doing a full day with the hedgehogs.'

'Uni's finished for Christmas and there's nowhere I'd rather be.'

'Give me a call if you need me. I'll have my phone switched off during counselling, but either side of that—'

'I'll call Josh if I need anything,' she interrupted, shooing me towards the door. 'Enjoy your day off. If anyone deserves one, it's you.'

Stepping out of the barn into the farmyard, I breathed in the fresh countryside air. The blue sky was so pale it was almost white, but the lack of colour wasn't from the threat of snow. With four days until Christmas, the weather forecasters had confirmed there was no chance of a white Christmas this year, which was disappointing but also a relief as even a light snowfall could cut Hedgehog Hollow off. We were expecting a house-full on Christmas Day and it would be disappointing if they couldn't make it after all the preparation we'd done to make it such a special day.

The local radio station was playing Christmas songs and I sang along to East 17's 'Stay Another Day' as I steered the jeep along the farm track. I was meeting my friends Rich and Dave in Reddfield for breakfast, followed by some last-minute Christmas shopping, a late-morning counselling session, lunch with my dad, then meeting my friend Terry to help him choose a Christmas jumper for the big day.

My phone rang and Chloe's name flashed up on the dashboard.

'Hi, Chloe,' I said, connecting on hands-free.

'Hi, Sammie. Quick question. I'm heading into town shortly to finish my Christmas shopping and I want to get something to wear on New Year's Eve. Is there a dress code? I've never been to a party in a dairy shed.'

I laughed. 'That makes two of us, but it's anything goes.'

When I'd suggested Josh and I get married at Hedgehog Hollow, I'd imagined hosting the reception in a marquee in one of the fields and had been stunned when he proposed using the dairy shed instead. With a high corrugated iron roof, metal struts, joists and pillars, it struck me as too industrial. We'd asked Dave to take a look when he was on site with the holiday cottage conversions and he shared Josh's vision. The cow stalls had been long since removed, so it was basically an empty shell, but I still couldn't see it. That was when Josh suggested road-testing it with a New Year's Eve party for our friends, family and members of the community who'd been exceptionally supportive of the rescue centre.

Fizz's mum, Natasha, ran a catering and events company and Fizz mentioned she'd had a cancellation of a New Year's Eve engagement party, so I asked if she'd cater for our party instead. She used a barn at her son Barney's farm to store chairs, tables, chocolate fountains, candy carts and a whole pile of other paraphernalia used for events such as weddings. She even had a couple of carriages for hire, pulled by Barney's horses. We signed her up to dress our reception – wherever we held it – and, in the meantime, I was intrigued as to how she'd transform the dairy shed on New Year's Eve.

'What are you wearing?' Chloe asked.

'I might brave another one of Gwendoline's vintage dresses.'

'Will I be able to wear heels?'

'There's a concrete floor and there'll be a wooden dance floor so you'll—'

A loud cry from ten-month-old Samuel interrupted me.

'His majesty's demanding more breakfast,' Chloe said. 'I'd better go. Speak to you soon.'

The call ended and I turned up the radio, smiling to myself. Life was pretty amazing right now. There was so much to look forward to with our plans for Christmas Day, the New Year's Eve party, our wedding and honeymoon. We hadn't booked the latter yet. Our dream destination was an African safari and we'd spent hours researching and discussing it but, much as I told myself it would be the holiday of a lifetime, I couldn't justify wiping out all our savings on the wedding and honeymoon, especially after spending the last of my inheritance from Thomas on converting two of the barns into four holiday cottages. As long as I was with Josh, I'd be happy with a week in Skegness.

This year had been such an emotional rollercoaster and it was incredible looking back and reflecting on how much my life had changed in such a short space of time.

The first eight months had been non-stop, setting up the rescue centre, having the farm refurbished, Josh's family moving in and Chloe turning up out of the blue, having left James. As summer gave way to autumn, life at Hedgehog Hollow seemed to have finally calmed down and settled into a routine. Paul was recovering well and Beth had become such a good friend that I'd asked her to be a bridesmaid, alongside Chloe and Hannah. Chloe visited the farm at least once a month and our relationship seemed to be back on track, as did her relationship with James.

And, best of all, there'd been no further incidents with the Grimes family. They'd put me through hell this year. What started with a demand from cousins Brynn and Cody Grimes for me to hand over the farm to them – as relatives of Gwendoline Mickleby – escalated to vandalism. When they were told they had no legal claim on the property as Gwendoline had legally disinherited her family, they burned down the barn and I nearly died trying to save the hedgehogs. They were sent to prison, which was when Cody's brother Connor and his mate picked up the mantle, breaking their parole and putting them both back behind bars. Although the extended family had adhered to police warnings and stayed away, their hate vendetta had left a lasting impact on me – a PTSD diagnosis – which was why I'd accessed counselling.

My counsellor Lydia, who I was seeing today, focused on issues arising from my lifelong difficult relationship with my mum, alongside the anxieties of my PTSD. This complemented the more targeted work of a psychotherapist specialising in CBT (cognitive behavioural therapy).

I left each counselling or therapy session feeling uplifted and proud of the progress I'd made. Being under stress was one of my main triggers so I'd become better at recognising when I'd taken on too much and had learned how to change my thinking. I hadn't had any episodes since September, but my big test would be the next time I was under significant stress.

* * *

'It sounds like you have a lot of exciting plans for over Christmas and New Year,' said Lydia during our counselling session a little later.

A curvaceous woman in her late fifties with a wavy grey bob, warm grey eyes and pink cheeks, she reminded me a little of my nanna and I'd warmed to her the moment we met.

'What are your thoughts on avoiding stress?' she asked.

'New Year's easy as I've outsourced it all to Fizz's mum, so no stress for me. As for Christmas, most of the presents are already bought and wrapped with a few last bits to get today, so I'm feeling calm and organised about that. I find cooking relaxing, so Christmas dinner for nine adults doesn't faze me, but I've learned to stop trying to do everything by myself. I've got plenty of people on hand to help.'

'That's good. We've talked about your cousin Chloe and how her demands can sometimes be triggering...?'

I smiled. 'She's coming to the New Year's Eve party but I haven't invited her for Christmas Day. It's just Josh's dad's family, his mum and her boyfriend, his Auntie Lauren, my dad, and my friend Terry. No drama expected. Unless Terry's dog Wilbur tries to run off with the turkey.'

She laughed. 'Now that would be a sight to see.'

'Fortunately, he's really well trained. It's my dad we have to watch out for!'

'How do things stand with your mother at the moment?'

My shoulders slumped. 'I'm not sure. I still haven't seen her since the summer, but Chloe says she sometimes asks after me, which is progress. I told you about her gift for my thirtieth, didn't I? She's sent me something for Christmas, too, although I haven't opened it yet.'

I'd been under no illusion that the birthday gifts from previous years presented as being from 'Mum and Dad' were truly from both of them, so I'd been stunned to receive a birthday gift in the post from Mum in October. When I'd phoned her and thanked her for the gorgeous hand-crafted keyring with an embroidered hedgehog on it, we'd had a polite but stilted conversation and it was only afterwards that I discovered from Auntie Louise that Mum had made it herself. Her purchasing a gift from a crafter had felt special enough, but discovering she'd made it herself blew me away. It had felt like a significant step forward. Then nothing.

'She sent me a Christmas card with "daughter" on it,' I added.

'How did that make you feel?'

'Like she was finally acknowledging me as her daughter after years of rejection. There was no gushy verse or anything but to have her specifically choose a daughter card was touching.' I ran my hands through my long dark hair and shook my head. 'Am I reading too much into it?'

Lydia gave me a gentle smile. 'The only person who can explain the motivation behind the choice of card or gift is your mother. Do you have any plans to see her over the festive period?'

'We've invited her to the New Year's Eve party, but I don't think she'll come.'

'What makes you say that?'

I shrugged. 'She's really decisive so, if she was definitely coming, she'd have said so.'

'Has she said she's definitely *not* coming?'

'No. Not yet.'

'How about we talk through some coping strategies for both scenarios?'

Josh had asked me how I felt and I'd been fairly blasé about it; if she came, she came, and I'd have a great time whatever. But as I talked it through with Lydia, it became apparent how much I wanted Mum there and how much I was hoping that the New Year would mean a fresh start for our relationship.

As I left the session and went to meet Dad for lunch, I felt that familiar rush of positivity, but it was tinged with something else. Worry about Mum. Fear that I'd got carried away. I hadn't seen her since the summer. I'd clung to the gifts and cards as signs that things were changing and had held New Year's Eve up as the crunch moment, but that had all been my imagination running away from me. Had I just set myself up for a fall?

Something caught my eye and I took a couple of paces back to gaze into the window of the wedding boutique, my stomach churning. There was something else I hadn't been honest about, to Josh or to myself.

I gazed at the simple but beautiful display in the window of Ivory Sparkles. A mannequin wearing a white gown with silver snowflakes embroidered all over the bodice and sparsely across the net skirt stood next to a white artificial tree decorated with silver and turquoise baubles.

In a little over four months, Josh and I would be saying 'I do'. My wedding day was something I'd dreamed of for so long but, until meeting Josh, had thought would never happen. When we'd set a date, I'd imagined filling the gorgeous planner he'd given me but it remained pretty much empty and it was time to be honest with myself about the reason for that. I'd convinced Josh – and myself – that it was because we'd been so busy with the rescue centre, but that was an excuse.

'Getting some inspiration?'

I spun round at the sound of Dad's voice and hugged him. 'It's a beautiful dress, but maybe not for a May wedding.'

'Have you been in to look?'

I shook my head and steered him away from the boutique and towards the high street. 'My head is too full of Christmas to think weddings. I'll go dress shopping in the New Year.'

'I'm surprised you haven't picked a dress yet. I'd have thought you'd have gone shopping as soon as you set a date.'

'Yeah, well, there's always something going on at the farm.'

I'd tried to keep my voice light, but Dad must have picked up an edge as he stopped walking.

'Is everything okay with you and Josh?'

'Gosh, yes! It's perfect. Why?'

He narrowed his eyes at me. 'So what's stopped you from choosing a dress?'

'Nothing, I... it's...' There was no point hiding it from him as he'd drag it out of me eventually. 'It's Mum. I was hoping we'd spend some time together and maybe...'

I tailed off, feeling daft for holding out hope for something that was never going to happen. I'd been the chief bridesmaid for Hannah and for Chloe and, both times, I'd gone wedding dress shopping with them and their mums. Wasn't it meant to be the ultimate mother and daughter bonding moment?

'You thought she might help you choose?' Dad asked, intuitive as ever. 'Aw, Sammie.'

He drew me into another hug and planted a kiss on the top of my head. 'It would be lovely but I'm not sure either of you are quite ready for that.'

'I know. It's stupid of me.'

'No, it's not. It's understandable.' He stepped back, his brown eyes full of empathy. 'Do you want me to have a word with her?'

I shook my head vigorously. 'Definitely not. If it was going to happen, it needed to happen naturally and it hasn't, so...'

He glanced back towards the boutique. 'I'm happy to be of service if you want to take a look.'

I smiled, a feeling of warmth flowing through me at how amazing my dad was and how he was always there for me. 'You want to be careful. I might take you up on that.'

'It's a genuine offer.'

Linking his arm, I pulled him towards the precinct once more. 'Thank you, but I'd like it to be a surprise on the day when you see me. That's a special moment, too. I'll round up my bridesmaids and we'll do a road trip to The Wedding Emporium in Whitsborough Bay next month.'

Chloe had bought her dress from The Wedding Emporium on Whitsborough Bay's Castle Street. The owner, Ginny, had been so warm and welcoming and carried such a fabulous range of wedding and bridesmaid dresses that I couldn't imagine going anywhere else for mine.

'You know where I am if you change your mind.'

I squeezed his arm. 'Thanks, Dad. You're the best.'

* * *

Over a delicious lunch in a local café, Dad and I had a lovely chat about our plans for Christmas and the New Year. We also talked more about Mum.

'I hate to say it, poppet, but I don't think she'll come to the party.' He squeezed my hand across the table. 'I'd suggest you plan for her not to come and see it as an unexpected bonus if she does.'

An hour and a half later, we hugged goodbye outside the café.

'Promise me you won't let worries about your mum spoil your Christmas,' he said.

'I promise.'

'And you'll crack on with dress hunting and all the other things you need to do in the New Year?'

'I promise that too.'

'Good. My work here is done.'

Laughing, I waved to him as we headed off in different directions. I could always rely on my dad to pick me up.

Walking towards the market square, I spotted Terry waiting on a bench, his head turning from one side to the other.

'Taking it all in?' I asked, sitting down beside him.

'It's right busy. And on a Monday an' all,' he said, shaking his head. 'I've never seen it like this. Mind you, I tend to avoid town for at least a fortnight before Christmas.'

'You didn't have to come in today, you know. You're still welcome on Friday with or without a Christmas jumper.'

'I'm not gonna let the side down.' He stood up and brushed down the back of his wool coat. 'Let's get shopping.'

With a full head of thick silver hair and twinkling brown eyes, I always thought Terry Shepherd looked younger than his eighty years. He lived in Fimberley – one of the local villages – and had brought in several hedgehogs and hoglets since we'd opened. I often joked that he was our best customer and needed a medal for the number of hedgehogs he'd saved but he reckoned it was his gorgeous black and white springer spaniel, Wilbur the 'hog-sniffer', who deserved it.

Terry reminded me so much of Thomas, with a gruff exterior hiding a heart of gold, and an air of loneliness. Our friendship had developed when he'd started dropping by 'just to see how the hedgehogs are doing' and taking me up on the offer of a cup of tea.

When he shared that he'd been Gwendoline's friend, I couldn't help feeling we were meant to be in each other's lives. I loved hearing tales about Gwendoline from when they were at school together and their friendship afterwards and, although he'd never said it, I was convinced he'd been in love with her and wondered if that could have been why he'd never married.

Terry's older sister Marion passed away in October. She was the only family he had left, and I couldn't bear the thought of him spending Christmas alone and grieving. He'd refused my invitation at first, saying he didn't want to encroach on family time, but I'd eventually managed to convince him.

'Are you sure it's okay to bring our Wilbur on Friday?' he asked as we walked towards the precinct. 'I know you've got little 'uns there but he's a right softy around kids.'

'The invitation was for you both and I reckon Archie and Lottie will love him. Can't expect you to leave the hog-sniffer at home on Christmas Day.'

'In that case, I might have to get him one of them festive jumpers too. He is a lad, after all.'

* * *

A couple of hours later, jumpers and final gifts purchased, we settled down at a table in The Owl and Pussycat Tearoom. While we waited for our order to arrive, Terry pulled out his jumper and held it against his chest.

'Do you think they'll like it?'

I grinned at the picture of a grumpy-looking pug on it and the words 'Bah humpug!' Although I knew that he was a big softy like his dog, it was the perfect choice for his gruff exterior.

'They'll love it.'

He folded the jumper and took out the snowman bandana he'd bought for Wilbur.

'That's so cute,' I said. 'I think he'd have been too warm inside in a jumper.'

He stuffed the items back in his bag as our tea and cake arrived.

'I came here once with Gwendoline,' Terry said, looking round as I poured the tea. 'It's changed hands several times since then.'

'When was this?'

'It'd be nigh on sixty years ago, but I can still picture it exactly how it were back then. Mrs Tiller's Tea Parlour.' He had that same wistful expression on his face that he often had when he spoke of Gwendoline.

'Was it a special occasion?' I asked, when I really wanted to ask if it had been a date.

'Her twenty-first birthday, although it were a week after the big day. She wanted to go to the picture house to see *Dr No*. First Bond film, you know. It wasn't at the pictures until a week after her birthday, so the plans shifted.'

He picked up his fork and ate a mouthful of chocolate fudge cake. 'Can't watch a Bond film without thinking about her. She had a thing for Sean Connery. Best Bond ever if you ask me.'

'It's Daniel Craig for me. *Casino Royale* was the first Bond film I ever saw.'

He shook his head. 'He's good but he's not Connery.'

And so the subject of Gwendoline was dropped but we had fun debating the merits of the different actors and films in the James Bond franchise. Sitting there with him, drinking tea, eating cake, and laughing, I was reminded of afternoon teas with Gramps and I loved how Terry reminded me of elements of Gramps and of Thomas but with a strong presence of his own. I couldn't help wondering if Gwendoline had sent him to me.

On Christmas morning, I opened my eyes and stretched out under the warm duvet, excitement flowing through me as I registered what day it was.

What a difference a year could make. This time last year, I'd woken up alone and broken-hearted in the spare room at Rich and Dave's, ostracised from most of my family following a major falling out at Chloe's wedding. And now I was living at Hedgehog Hollow with my gorgeous fiancé, looking forward to our wedding in May, running a hedgehog rescue centre – the most rewarding job ever – and about to host Christmas for nine adults and two babies.

My eyes adjusted to the darkness in the bedroom and rested on the canvas of the wildflower meadow out the back of Hedgehog Hollow that I'd given to my wonderful friend and surrogate granddad, Thomas Mickleby, as a Christmas gift last year.

'Are you awake?' whispered Josh.

I turned over and smiled at him. 'Happy Christmas!'

'Happy Christmas to you too.'

He kissed me and we snuggled together under the duvet.

'Do you hear that?' he said. 'Silence.'

Situated deep in the Yorkshire Wolds countryside, surrounded by fields and reached by a long farm track, the only external noises at Hedgehog Hollow were birdsong, the buzz of insects, the whispering of the trees, and the noisy chomping of hungry hedgehogs. Inside, tranquillity was rare.

'You do realise you've probably just jinxed it?' I said.

'I realised that the minute I said the words. Were you thinking about Thomas just now?'

'I can't believe a whole year has passed since he died, which means he's been out of my life for three times as long as he was in it.'

'Will you be okay today? If you need a cry or you want some space, just say. I know—'

But Josh didn't get to finish his sentence. He *had* jinxed it and his baby half-sister Lottie's wails punctuated the silence and set off her brother Archie. Neither of them were too loud individually but, when they both cried, I swear it became a competition for who could grab their mum's attention first.

I was about to push back the duvet when Josh beat me to it. 'I'll give Beth a hand. You have a quiet moment with Thomas.'

With a light kiss, he left the bedroom and I smiled as I heard him affectionately calling across the landing, 'Archie Alderson, do you *have* to out-screech your sister?'

I returned my gaze to the meadow canvas. 'Happy Christmas, Thomas and Gwendoline,' I whispered. 'We'll raise a toast to you today.'

* * *

Later that morning, I could scarcely see an inch of flooring in the lounge for colourful wrapping paper. I'd billowed out a bin bag to clear it away for the recycling bin, but eighteen-month-old Archie was having too much fun running through it and kicking up the pieces like autumn leaves so there was no chance of that.

'How typical is this?' Beth rolled her eyes at me. 'We spend hours choosing the perfect gifts for him and he's happier playing with the discarded wrapping. He'll probably move onto the empty boxes next.'

'At least you know what to get him next year.'

Our cat Misty-Blue wandered in and joined in the fun, pouncing on the pieces Archie scattered. Lottie, aged just over seven months, sat in her bouncer watching her older brother, kicking her legs as though trying to play too.

Even though Paul wasn't back to full health following his stem cell transplant, looking thin and pale-faced, he was laughing and it warmed my heart to see the happy family together having overcome a horrendous year.

I went into the kitchen to make a round of drinks and Josh joined me after I'd filled the kettle. He slipped his arms round my waist and drew me into a kiss, making my heart race.

I ran my fingers down his Scandi-style Christmas jumper. 'I'm loving this on you. It's surprisingly sexy.'

'You think so? In that case, I'll never take it off.'

'That would defeat the object,' I said, kissing him once more.

'I've got another gift for you,' he said when the kettle clicked and I reluctantly pulled away. 'It's for both of us really, but I wanted to give you it while we're alone. Wait here.'

He'd already thoroughly spoilt me with a pile of amazing presents. I couldn't imagine what he might want to give me without the others around.

He was back moments later with a shiny red A5-sized gift bag. 'Happy Christmas.'

I sat down at the table, opened the bag, rummaged among the tissue paper and pulled out a wooden object.

'It's a Russian doll!' I said, grinning at the large exterior 'doll', which was painted to look like an elephant. 'You remembered!'

It had been such a brief conversation and way back in April before the refurbishment of Hedgehog Hollow was complete. We'd had a lovely day together shopping in York and we'd walked past a gift shop with Russian dolls in the window. I'd said I'd always wanted a set and he'd evidently stored that snippet of information until now, which was so touching.

'This Russian doll is extra special because it's not actually the gift. It's a clue to the gift. Open it up.'

I took the doll apart and reassembled each figure. As I took in the elephant, rhino, buffalo, lion and leopard lined up on the table from largest to smallest, my heart leapt.

'Josh! You didn't!'

He tried to look innocent but his dark eyes were sparkling with excitement.

'Have you booked that African safari for our honeymoon?'

'I know it's a small fortune, but we've done everything we want for now in the farmhouse, so what else are the savings for? Why not use them for our dream honeymoon?'

'Oh, my gosh! You've *really* booked it?'

'We're going on safari in the Serengeti National Park, home to all of the big five.' He pointed to the Russian dolls. 'Followed by a week in Zanzibar.'

I squealed as I threw my arms round him and kissed him. 'I know I should be panicking about the money but I'm too excited. This is the best Christmas gift ever!'

'And I don't want you to worry about the hedgehogs. Between your dad, Fizz, the staff at the practice and other volunteers, we'll have it all covered and you and I can finally have some time alone.'

'I can't wait. Thank you for spoiling me.'

'You deserve to be spoilt.'

'You are, without a shadow of a doubt, the most amazing person I've ever met.'

'Right back at you.'

* * *

Dad and Lauren arrived around late morning, armed with gifts for us and the children, and I burst out laughing when he removed his coat to reveal his Christmas jumper. It was bright red and showed a pair of cute pigs wrapped in blankets.

'That's brilliant, Dad! Couldn't be more perfect for you.'

'I hope you've prepared loads. We don't want the day turning ugly.'

'Don't panic. There's more than enough to go round, even with your insatiable appetite.'

'And I couldn't resist the Christmas theme either,' Lauren said, 'although I'd better warn you that I'm wearing a dress. Don't want anyone to keel over with shock.'

'Oh, I love that!' I cried as she revealed a tunic dress patterned with colourful baubles, snowmen, Christmas trees, gingerbread men and candy canes, worn over black leggings and boots.

She flicked her long blonde hair over her shoulder. 'Couldn't let your dad outdo me in the festive stakes.'

We'd only just started opening the gifts when Josh's mum Connie arrived with her boyfriend Alex, followed shortly after by Terry and Wilbur.

Christmas dinner was exactly how I'd hoped it would be when I'd had the kitchen refurbished. With nine adults and two children round the kitchen table there was a lot of noise, mess and so much love. It was hard to believe that a year ago, Dad was the only one of them who was in my life and that Josh's family had, like mine, been broken.

'Get your grubby mitts off my pigs!' Lauren shouted from across the table as Dad tried to liberate a couple of her pigs in blankets from her plate.

'He used to do that to me every Christmas,' I said. 'He's sneaky. But don't panic because I did extra.'

I removed another dish full of sausages wrapped in bacon from the Aga and placed them down on a mat in the middle of the table, laughing as Dad and Lauren raced to grab some.

Watching them giggling, I wished there was more than friendship between them as they seemed so good together, but they were both adamant that the chemistry wasn't there. Plenty of friendships became more with time, so I wouldn't give up hope just yet. Dad deserved to find someone special after a tough marriage to Mum. To my knowledge, he hadn't dated anyone since they'd separated at the start of the year. Hopefully he'd feel ready to dip his toe into the water next year.

When everyone had finished eating – including Wilbur who'd sussed that if he lay under the table, he'd get a treat from everyone's plate – I checked they all had a drink then stood up and proposed a toast.

'Thank you all for coming today to share in a very special Wishaw family Christmas tradition of witnessing my dad eating twenty pigs in blankets and still managing to polish off a full Christmas dinner. I think we should all applaud that impressive feat.' I paused for laughter and applause. Dad stood up and bowed, cheeks glowing red.

'Sorry, Dad. I couldn't resist. Seriously, though, Josh and I would like to thank you all for sharing our first Christmas Day together. It's my first Christmas with Hedgehog Hollow as my home but, as you all know, it's not my first Christmas Day here. Last Christmas, I had the honour of spending the day with the most wonderful man who was only in my life for a short space of time but he showed me so much friendship and kindness in those months, which changed my life back then and ever since.'

I raised my glass towards the framed photo of Thomas from last year wearing six paper hats, which I'd brought down from my office to place on the table.

'To Thomas! Happy Christmas to you and Gwendoline, wherever you are.' My voice cracked but I smiled as everyone cheered and took a sip of their drink. I had to pretend to take a sip of mine because there was no way I could swallow anything over the lump in my throat. Josh squeezed my hand as I sat back down, feeling suddenly overwhelmed.

'Everyone fancy a break before pudding?' he suggested.

A ripple of agreement went round the table.

'Is it pigs in blankets with custard for Jonathan?' Paul called, making me laugh and easing the pain in my throat.

'I thought you might need a moment,' Josh said after the kitchen emptied.

'Thank you. I did. I do.' Tears pricked my eyes as I glanced at Thomas's smiling image. 'I miss him so much, which seems ridiculous when he's been gone longer than I knew him.'

'It's not how long you know someone, it's the impact they have on you during that time that makes the difference.'

I rested my head against his chest and shed a few tears for Thomas and for the hedgehogs who hadn't made it but who'd all left their footprints on my heart.

I wiped my wet cheeks as I pulled away. 'I needed that. Thank you. Let's get these plates cleared away and get back in the lounge for some more fun.'

'You go. I'll clear away.'

I shook my head. 'We're a team. Always. So we'll do it together.'

* * *

Following dessert and a crazy game of Pictionary full of cheating, Terry said his goodbyes while I prepared a doggy bag. I walked him and Wilbur to the door and he paused with his hand on the handle.

'I was dreading this Christmas without our Marion. You opening up your home like that to a grumpy old man like...' He sounded a little choked up as he tailed off.

'I don't see a grumpy old man, Terry. I see a lovely man who's passionate about animals and is a hedgehog rescuer extraordinaire. In my eyes, that makes you part of the family.'

He smiled warmly as his eyes searched my face. 'I know you're not related to her, but I see so much of Gwendoline in you. You have her kindness and understanding. It's no wonder people gravitate towards you. They did that to Gwendoline.'

'Aw, thank you. That's such a lovely thing to say.' It echoed of what Gramps and Thomas used to say and I felt tears rushing to my eyes once more.

'It's true. You know me, speak as I see. You're a special lass, just like her.'

I'd never hugged Terry before but there was no way I couldn't after a statement like that. He seemed surprised at first, rigid in my arms, but then he relaxed and squeezed me back.

'Thank you,' he whispered, stepping outside. 'Best Christmas in years.'

Wilbur raced past him and ran round in circles on the gravel.

I pulled the door to behind me to keep the heat inside and breathed in the cool fresh air. The low sun peeped through the trees and it wouldn't be long before the baby blue sky faded to darkness, signalling the end of a truly special day.

'Enjoy your doggy bag,' I called as Terry and Wilbur headed towards the farmyard. 'Happy Christmas!'

'Thank you. Happy Christmas to you too!'

Half an hour later, Connie and Alex headed off, Beth took Lottie and Archie up for a sleep, and Paul went for a nap.

'And then there were four,' Josh said, handing round coffees and a tub of chocolates – the law to eat on Christmas Day, no matter how stuffed you are.

As I took my drink, Josh mouthed, 'Now?'

I nodded.

'I've got something I want to show you, Jonathan,' he said to my dad as he removed a cardboard wallet from a drawer in the dresser. 'The signs at the practice are looking a bit shabby so I want to replace them.'

He sat on the sturdy coffee table opposite Dad and removed some A4 pages he'd printed off yesterday. 'This is a quick concept I threw together and I'm no graphic designer, but I wanted to get your initial thoughts on the idea before I take it any further.'

He handed Dad the pages and my heart raced with excitement as I watched Dad's eyes widen and his mouth open. He was clearly too taken aback to say anything.

'It's got your name on it!' Lauren cried. 'Josh?'

'I could hardly keep the name as Alderson & Son Veterinary Practice if Jonathan was my partner.'

Dad clapped his hand over his mouth, shaking his head. Being a partner in a veterinary practice had been his long-held dream.

'What about Paul?' he asked, finally finding his voice. 'I wouldn't want to tread on his toes.'

'I've spoken to Dad and he doesn't want the responsibility of returning as a partner. After what he's been through, his priorities have changed.'

'You're sure he'd be okay?'

'He's given his blessing. So what do you think? Do you like the sound of Alderson & Wishaw Veterinary Practice?'

'Like it? I love it.' Dad stood up and shook Josh's hand then pulled him into an embrace. 'This is what I've always dreamed of. I can't thank you enough for the opportunity.'

'You've earned it. I've worked with some excellent vets but only two phenomenal ones. One of those is upstairs and the other can eat an astonishing number of pigs in blankets.'

'Congratulations, Dad!' I said, hugging him.

'Thank you for doing this for me,' he said.

'Nothing to do with me. As Josh said, you're a phenomenal vet. He'd be daft not to partner with you.'

Josh brought a bottle of champagne and some fresh glasses through, and we toasted the new and improved Alderson & Wishaw Veterinary Practice. I felt quite tearful again – but in a good way – seeing Dad so happy and, ultimately, it was thanks to Thomas. If it hadn't been for meeting him and inheriting Hedgehog Hollow, I wouldn't have gone to Josh's practice to seek support with the hedgehogs, he wouldn't have offered a job to Dad and now a partnership. Thomas Mickleby was the gift that kept on giving.

3

SAMANTHA

'Hi, Sam! How was Christmas?' Fizz asked, running down the barn towards me a few days later, arms outstretched.

'Amazing,' I said, squeezing her tightly. 'How was yours?'

'Awesome. Barney had us all up at the farm and it's always a riot.' Barney was Fizz's older brother who ran what had been their grandparents' farm. I hadn't met him yet, but I'd heard a lot about him.

'I'm liking the red hair.'

'Thank you.' Fizz ran her fingers down her French braids. 'I thought it was more festive than pink.'

'Suits you.' I looked down the barn past her. 'Where's Zayn? I thought you were picking him up.' Zayn had impressed us during a fortnight's work experience back in June and had loved his time with the hedgehogs so had stayed on as a volunteer.

'I did. He's on his phone. He'll be in soon.'

'Great. Phoebe's dropping by to collect the receipts and invoices shortly. I told her she didn't have to do them over the Christmas break but you know Phoebe.'

Fizz smiled. 'Reliable as always.'

I still didn't know what to make of Phoebe. She was an accountancy student in her second year at Reddfield TEC and had been recommended by the accounts tutor Adam when I'd been looking for a volunteer to maintain Hedgehog Hollow's accounts. Fizz and Zayn were open books, constantly chatting about family, friends and hobbies, but I had no sense of who Phoebe was outside of her passion for numbers and a wish to become an accountant. I felt like I overwhelmed her every time I saw her, which was an odd feeling when, coming from a nursing background, I was so used to putting everyone I met at ease.

Her work was superb, though. She was reliable and punctual and always polite. She'd proved herself to be trustworthy, too. I'd given her limited admin rights for online banking so she could keep on top of bill payments for me and I checked the account religiously but she'd given me no cause for concern. She'd saved us money by switching energy supplier and had secured some small grants too, all off her own back. She now pretty much managed all the finances and it was certainly a weight off my mind. Time spent on the accounts was time away from my top priority of caring for hedgehogs and it gave her valuable experience for her CV when she started applying for jobs next year; a perfect arrangement for both of us.

* * *

'Hi, Phoebe,' I called down the barn when she arrived a little later, the pink helmet for her moped tucked under one arm.

'How was Christmas?'

'Quiet but okay.' She glanced nervously towards the table where Fizz and Zayn were busy treating a dog bite on a hedgehog that had just been admitted. 'Sorry. I didn't know you'd have people here.'

'Only Fizz and Zayn,' I said as she came closer.

Fizz looked up and smiled. 'Hi, Phoebe, how's it going?'

'Fine, thank you.' Phoebe twirled a lock of long dark hair round one of her fingers as she shuffled uncomfortably on the spot.

'I don't think you've met Zayn yet but he goes to the TEC,' I said. 'You might have crossed paths.'

Zayn looked up, grinned at her, then focused his attention back on the hedgehog.

Phoebe stared at the top of his head – a mass of ebony corkscrew coils – frowning, then turned back to me. 'No, I don't think we have. The receipts? Sorry. I need to get back.'

I handed her a plastic folder. 'All in there. Thank you.'

'I'll get these back to you quickly. See you later.'

Shoulders hunched, head down, she scuttled out of the barn.

While Fizz and Zayn finished up, I put the kettle on to boil and watched Phoebe from the barn window heading down the track on her pale pink moped. I wished there was something I could do to make her feel more relaxed round me; round any of us. Maybe I was expecting too much but it had been six months now. Although, if Fizz – the world's bubbliest person – couldn't get much out of her, I shouldn't be too hard on myself.

'Have you decided on a name for him?' I asked Fizz and Zayn once they had the new hedgehog settled in his crate.

'Are we still using Christmassy names?' Fizz asked.

'Yeah. Let's stick to Christmas for the rest of December and we'll start a new theme on Friday for the New Year.'

'In that case, can we call him Tinsel?'

'That's a cute name. Tinsel it is.' I added it to his chart. 'I can't believe we're almost at five hundred admissions.'

Tinsel was patient number 498. We'd rehabilitated and released nearly three hundred adult hedgehogs and thirty-one hoglets and, including Tinsel, were currently boarding thirty-four adults and fifty-eight hoglets. Known as 'autumn juveniles', the latter came from a second litter in September or early October. They didn't have enough time to gain the weight they needed to survive through hibernation, so our job was to keep them warm and fed so they'd be a healthy weight for release in the spring. A significant proportion of recent admissions had been autumn juveniles.

When the drinks were ready, Fizz and I sat down on the sofa bed and Zayn pulled up a chair. He shoved a chocolate digestive into his mouth whole.

'Oh, my God, Zayn!' Fizz cried. 'You're such a pig.'

'Party trick,' he said, showering biscuit crumbs onto the floor. He finished eating it. 'Guess how many marshmallows I can get into my mouth at one time.'

I grimaced. 'I don't know. Thirty?'

He grinned and pointed towards the ceiling.

'Thirty-five?' Fizz suggested.

'Forty-two!' he declared proudly.

'That's gross,' I said.

'The Guinness world record is currently fifty-six but I'm improving all the time. One day, I'll be a record breaker.'

I laughed. 'It's good to have goals. Fizz's goal is to become a veterinary nurse, mine is to have enough people booking the holiday cottages to fund this place and Phoebe's is to be an accountant, but I think most marshmallows in the mouth eclipses all of those.' I clapped my hands and Fizz joined in, laughing.

'That reminds me,' Zayn said. 'Phoebe. I'm surprised you'd have her working here.'

'I thought you didn't know each other.'

'We don't, but I know who she is. Not that it's any of my business, like, but it's a bit brave, especially if she's got access to your bank accounts.'

I sat up straight. 'What are you saying?'

'I am on the right person, yeah? Phoebe Corbyn-Grimes?'

My stomach lurched. 'Grimes? Did you just say Grimes?'

'Yeah. Although she maybe doesn't go by her full name. The tosser who torched this place – Cody Grimes – is her stepbrother. So's Connor, who I'm pretty certain got banged up again for vandalism here. Is that right?'

I nodded numbly. She couldn't be related. She just couldn't.

But Zayn was on a roll. 'If I've got this right, Phoebe's dad married

Cody and Connor's mum, making her Corbyn-Grimes, but he died a few years back and... are you okay? You've gone really pale.'

'Oh, shit!' I ran to the table, grabbed my phone and clicked into my banking app. I normally kept a close eye on the accounts but, with the chaos of getting ready for Christmas, a stack of new patients, and the excitement of the honeymoon, I hadn't checked for several days.

I stared at the balance. Shaking, I sank down onto the nearest chair. 'Oh no! It can't have.' But the balance on the screen – £7.86 – told me it had. Feeling like I was in a slow motion, I twisted to face Fizz and Zayn.

'It's gone. It's all gone.'

'What has?' Fizz asked, rushing over to me.

I thrust my phone at her. 'That's the rescue centre account. There was nearly thirty grand in there. It's been emptied.'

4

PHOEBE

My arms shook, my legs felt like jelly, and I was all fingers and thumbs as I tried to tighten the strap on my helmet. With it finally fastened, I clambered onto my moped and accelerated across the farmyard, anxious to get away from Hedgehog Hollow as quickly as possible.

As I headed down the farm track, I had the strongest sensation of being watched. I didn't dare look round to check. I knew how guilty I'd look if I did that.

I chewed on my lip, my heart racing. Why had Zayn had to be there? I recognised him from around college. We'd never spoken, but that didn't mean he didn't know who I was. Reddfield TEC wasn't that big and everyone seemed to know someone who knew someone.

What if he said something to Samantha? She'd sack me the minute she knew and then everything would be ruined. There was so much more I still wanted to do. Had to do. My future depended on it.

I kept staring at the screen. £7.86. It was all I could see, all I could think about.

Fizz said something to Zayn and, moments later, a glass of water was pressed into my hand. My hand shook as I raised the glass to my mouth and gulped it down.

'Could it be a mistake?' Fizz asked, plonking herself down beside me. 'Like a payment for £300 going out as thirty grand instead?'

Her voice lacked conviction but I appreciated her trying. I picked up my phone and scrolled through the recent transactions, my stomach churning at a list of withdrawals ranging from £1,000 to £5,000.

'They're all cheques. I *never* use the cheque book. Phoebe's got it. But... oh, no!' I clapped my hand across my mouth.

'What is it?'

'It's my fault. I wanted to pay all our suppliers before Christmas and most prefer bank transfer but there's one who's really traditional and likes cheques. The invoice was faded and we couldn't read the amount or the payee name so I...' I couldn't bring myself to say the words.

'You signed a blank cheque?' Fizz suggested. I didn't need to look at her to know she was wincing. I could hear it in her voice.

I nodded, fuming with myself for being so careless. I'd tried to phone them but there'd been no answer so Phoebe had said she'd keep trying and send the cheque off when she found out.

'But there's more than one cheque withdrawal,' Zayn said, peering over my shoulder. 'That's...' I scrolled down so he could count. 'Ten cheques.'

'Twenty-nine grand,' Fizz added. 'Shit! You don't think Phoebe...?'

'I wouldn't have. But if she's a Grimes...' I looked up at Zayn. 'You're absolutely sure about that?'

'One hundred per cent. I don't know her personally but it's definitely her.'

I lay my phone down on the table, held my head in my hands and closed my eyes. I wished this was another of my nightmares but this was reality and I needed to think. Someone had obviously forged my signature from that blank cheque and replicated it on the others. Had that person been Phoebe?

I looked up at their concerned expressions. 'I need to phone the bank. Zayn, would you mind cracking on with the crate-cleaning while I do that?'

'Sure.'

'Do you want me to phone my dad?' Fizz asked. I'd met her dad, Sergeant Kinsella, after the younger Grimes brother Connor and his mate vandalised the barn. Sergeant Kinsella took control of the case and advised the extended family of the trouble they'd be in if there were further incidents. I thought it had worked. The past six months had been peaceful but perhaps that was because they'd been plotting this.

'Would I let the police know or would the bank?' I mused, not really expecting Fizz to know the answer but unable to think clearly myself.

'I'm not sure but, if this is the Grimes family again, it's part of a continued campaign of harassment and Dad warned them of the consequences. He'd want to know.'

'Level with me, Fizz. Does Phoebe strike you as the sort who'd steal twenty-nine grand?'

'Honestly? No. She strikes me as too sweet and timid to do anything like that. And doesn't she want to be an accountant? That'll never happen if she's done for theft.'

I was inclined to agree, but as the withdrawals were cheques and she was the one with the cheque book, she had to be involved in some way. She *was* sweet and timid. But didn't criminals manipulate people like that?

'Do you think she could have been coerced by someone else in the family?'

Fizz wrinkled her nose. 'Possibly. I wouldn't put anything past that lot.'

'Me neither.'

'What's more likely is she knows nothing about it. She's been shy and jumpy from day one. Do you think she'd be physically capable of turning up today knowing she'd emptied your bank account?'

It was a good point. I'd given her an out by saying I didn't expect her to do any work on the accounts over Christmas and a guilty person would surely have grabbed at that, but she'd insisted on coming over.

I thought about how she'd behaved this morning – no different to usual – but could it all have been an act to build my trust and throw me off the scent? No. That didn't add up.

I needed some air, so I went round to the back of the farmhouse to phone the bank. Sitting on Thomas's bench looking out over the meadow usually calmed me but not today. Even Misty-Blue jumping up beside me, nudging my arm for a fuss, didn't ease my panic. My stomach was in knots and my hands were still shaking as I progressed through the phone options to connect to an adviser.

'Hello, and welcome to Fellings Bank. You're speaking to Charmaine this morning, how may I help?'

'I've just logged onto my banking app and somebody has been writing fraudulent cheques. There's nothing left…'

* * *

I disconnected the call half an hour later and released a shuddery breath, warm tears cascading down my cold cheeks as I stared across the meadow, cuddling Misty-Blue for comfort.

I'd let Thomas and Gwendoline down so very badly. What was wrong with me? Why was I always so willing to trust people?

I logged onto my banking app again, praying for a miracle, but that sparse £7.86 balance was still taunting me. What was I going to do now?

'What did they say?' Fizz asked when I returned to the barn a little later, no more tears left to cry. Zayn was still cleaning out crates, earbuds in, singing along to something I didn't recognise.

I slumped onto the sofa bed, feeling numb.

'The good news is they've put stops on the rest of my cheques and they've given me an overdraft so no impending payments will bounce.' I couldn't sound positive about it. It seemed insignificant when pitched against the full outcome.

Fizz sat down beside me. 'And the bad news?'

'The worst.' I ran my fingers through my hair and kept them there, clutching my head. 'I can't believe how stupid I've been. I've lost the money, Fizz. They say I willingly gave my cheque book to a third party who wasn't set up as a signatory on the account and, as if that wasn't bad enough, I gave her a blank cheque which was asking for trouble. They claim that was gross negligence on my part and they're not liable to refund me the money.'

'You're kidding!'

'I wish I was. I told them that there was only one blank cheque and the others were forgeries. They said it didn't matter because I'd given the fraudster the opportunity to forge my signature by handing over my cheque book containing a signed blank cheque.'

'Oh, my God! That doesn't sound fair.'

I shrugged. 'I can see their point. I made a mistake – a huge one – and why should they cough up because of it? I can complain to the Financial Ombudsman if I disagree with their decision, although that could take ages and may not get me anywhere. Or I can try to recover the money myself by taking Phoebe and her family to court.'

'They confirmed it was Phoebe?'

'It was several different family members. None of the cheques were made payable to Phoebe, although that doesn't mean she wasn't involved.'

I pictured shy, nervous Phoebe scuttling out of the barn earlier. I couldn't help thinking she was a victim in this too, but was that because I always tried to see the good in people? Was that blinding me to what she was really like?

'I'm so sorry,' Fizz said.

I shrugged, feeling helpless. 'What did your dad say?

'I couldn't get hold of him but I left him a message so I'm sure he'll call back when he's free. Are you going to phone Phoebe?'

I'd gone back and forth on that while I'd been outside but had concluded I might make things worse than they already were. 'I think I'd better wait until we hear from your dad, just in case she is involved.'

'I've finished the crates,' Zayn said, joining us. 'Do you need anything else doing?'

I appreciated the offer but I knew they both had plans and I could use some alone time to work through this mess.

'You both head off. Thanks for your help today.'

Fizz pulled on her coat. 'I'll let you know as soon as I've heard from my dad.'

'Can I ask you both to keep this quiet for now? Especially among your college friends, Zayn. We don't know that Phoebe's involved. If she isn't – and I want to believe she isn't – a rumour like this could ruin her career and I'd hate to cause any problems for her.'

'I won't breathe a word.'

'Try not to worry,' Fizz said. 'I'm sure it'll all work out.'

I nodded and smiled as they left the barn then slumped back on the sofa bed once the door closed. She was sure it would all work out? I wasn't. How could it? Even if I complained to the ombudsman and the conclusion was that I hadn't been negligible and had genuinely been defrauded, how long might it be before the money was recovered? Would the bank have to repay me then chase the Grimes family to recover the money or would I only have any chance of getting it back if the bank could recover it? I'd been too upset to ask further questions on the phone, not that they'd have shared that information even if I'd asked because, according to Fellings Bank, I was stupid and it served me right. Obviously they hadn't said those exact words, but it was how I felt.

In the meantime, the account was empty and, with my inheritance spent, I had nothing left with which to replenish it.

The cottages had been available to let since October half-term and we'd had a few guests. Eventually the income from letting them out would be more than enough to run the rescue centre, but this was a new venture so we weren't anywhere near that point.

I needed to speak to Josh but he was out on call. Dad would be my second choice but he'd gone to the cinema with Lauren so his phone would be on silent. I wondered about calling Chloe but swiftly dismissed that thought. Even though our relationship had improved considerably since the summer and I'd seen her being a lot more thoughtful and considerate of others, Chloe was still Chloe and she had a tendency to engage mouth before brain. I could predict her reaction and even hear her voice in my head: *You gave someone from the Grimes family access to your hefty bank account? Seriously, Sam, what were you thinking?* And she was right, but I couldn't face that conversation because it was only going to make me feel worse than I already did.

The urge to call Phoebe was strong. I longed for her to reassure me she knew nothing about it and would never get involved in something so despicable, but I was going to have to be patient and see what Sergeant Kinsella advised.

Learning forward, I held my head between my hands and released a frustrated squeal. How could I have been so stupid? Not just about the cheque but about taking on Phoebe in the first place without conducting some sort of background checks?

'Hello?'

I looked up at the sound of a woman's voice.

'I knocked but nobody answered.'

Pulling myself together, I stood up, pasted a smile on my face, and strode down the barn towards the woman standing near the entrance holding a plastic crate.

'Sorry. I was miles away. Do you have a hedgehog for me?'

'I found it in my garden and it wasn't moving. Those cute cartoons in our village newsletter said they wouldn't normally be out during the day at this time of year and to watch out if they're smaller than a small loaf of bread. This one's more like a bread bun.'

I'd managed to secure space in most of the village newsletters and on noticeboards running my 'Bed Hogs' campaign, explaining that we had the potential for hundreds of beds available for overwintering hedgehogs. I'd commissioned Devansh Chandra, the Art and Design student from the TEC who'd won the competition to design the logo for Hedgehog Hollow, to create a series of cartoons depicting the indications that a hedgehog – whether adult or autumn juvenile – might need some additional support. I'd suspected his amazing illustrations would have more impact than words and most people bringing in a hedgehog had mentioned the images sticking in their mind.

The woman peeled back a towel to reveal a small hedgehog who, from the elongated shape, looked to be severely dehydrated and extremely underweight.

'Do you want to bring it over to the treatment table?' I asked.

I pulled on a pair of thick gloves and gently lifted the hog onto the scales. He didn't even curl into a ball so he was clearly lacking in energy.

'We've got a boy here and he's only 317 grams, so he's very underweight and wouldn't survive the winter. You've potentially saved his life by bringing him here.'

'Really?' The woman, who appeared to be in her fifties, looked quite tearful. 'Can you make him better?'

'Hopefully, yes. I can't see cuts or parasites on him but that doesn't mean there isn't something going on internally. I'll be able to check that once he's left me a sample. There may be something wrong or it could simply be that he's struggled to find food and water and has grown weaker. We'll give him any meds he needs and keep him here over the winter, helping him gain weight.'

'Will you let me know how he gets on?'

'Are you on social media?'

The woman nodded.

'I do regular updates on all our patients if you follow us and, if you've got a suitable garden, he can be released there in the spring if you leave me your details.'

After leaving her contact information, the woman handed over a ten-pound-note. 'I'm sorry it isn't more. Money's always tight after Christmas.'

'Every penny makes a difference, so thank you very much.'

I waved her off, clutching the note to my chest, tears pricking my eyes. It was very generous of her to give a donation and we really did need every penny right now. But how far would a tenner stretch when I'd just lost twenty-nine grand?

A wave of nausea swept through me and I grabbed at the table, taking a few deep breaths to steady myself. I couldn't think about it and risk triggering an episode. I needed to focus on our new arrival instead, starting with giving him his Christmassy name. Not that I felt remotely festive anymore.

'How about Figgy?' I asked him. 'We'll soon have you fattened up so you look more like a figgy pudding. Let's give you some fluids and get you settled in your new home. And then I need to calmly work out how the heck I'm going to keep this place running without any money. If you have any bright ideas, Figgy, now's the time to speak up.'

I rode straight back to Reddfield after leaving Hedgehog Hollow and pulled up outside the row of garages at Renleigh Court on the outskirts of town. Unlocking the garage owned by my friend and former neighbour Rosemary, I pushed the moped inside, plugged it in to charge, and removed my helmet.

I hated that I had to keep it hidden away here, but my stepmother Tina or one of my stepbrothers, Connor or Cody, would flog it if they knew about it, like they'd done with my bike a few years back. Stolen, they reckoned. Yeah, by them! No way was I letting them get their grubby mitts on my beloved moped, especially when it had been a secret gift from Dad. I had no idea he'd been slipping money to Rosemary to save for it so it had been a hell of a shock when she told me to unlock the garage on my sixteenth birthday, five months after Dad died, because there was a special gift from him inside.

Every time I rode it, I bricked it that one of Tina's mates would spot me and report back to her. I didn't need to worry about news getting back to my stepbrothers at the moment as they were both in prison, along with their cousin Brynn. What a scummy family Dad had married into. There were only two family members I liked – Tina's niece Hayley and her six-year-old daughter Darcie – but I hadn't seen

Hayley in years. I wrote to her and sent her pictures from Darcie but I had no idea if it helped. Jenny and Tina had broken her and I feared she'd never recover.

I hung my helmet on the handlebars and looked round the garage as I rolled my shoulders, feeling the usual pang of guilt that Rosemary could be making some income from the garage if it wasn't for me. Only half of the flats in the three-storey block had garages and, as Rosemary was severely visually impaired, her driving days were long gone. She regularly had offers from neighbours wanting to rent it from her but she always refused, saying she needed the storage space. She didn't. There were some metal shelves at one end holding a random selection of items I'm pretty sure were of no use to her, a few boxes which probably contained junk too, and a wooden folding table and pair of matching chairs for the summer. So really she kept the garage for my moped.

I closed the door behind me and paused for a moment, looking across the car park towards the flats, experiencing the familiar sensation of coming home. But it wasn't my home anymore and hadn't been since Dad made one of the biggest mistakes of his life and married Tina Grimes when I was twelve. It wasn't his fault. He wasn't to know what she was really like. She'd duped us both and he'd realised it too late. I'm convinced he was building up to leaving her before the accident at work but now I'd never know. He wasn't around to ask and Rosemary didn't have any answers.

Since Dad died, I'm not sure how I'd have coped without Rosemary Norris in my life. Actually, I'm not sure how we'd have managed before then either as she'd always been there for Dad and me. We'd rented the flat next door, right until Dad married Tina. Mum had died when I was a baby. She'd been an accountant earning way more money than Dad's income from his shifts at a ready-meals factory so, without her salary, paying the rent and bills was a struggle. Dad needed to hold down three jobs to stay afloat, but that left him in a pickle for childcare. Rosemary was already looking after her two young grandchildren, Matthew and Morgan, and offered to look after me too, assuring Dad that a third child would make little difference.

She'd always felt like my grandma and she often joked about me being her third grandchild. These days, she was the only 'family' I had left. I visited at least three times a week, although I didn't let on to Tina it was that often. She thought I was with friends. No point telling her I didn't have any.

I was fifteen when Dad died. I'd never wanted to worry Rosemary by letting on how bad things were with Tina and the boys, but something snapped during the funeral when I looked round at the 'mourners', who didn't shed a single tear. If anything, they looked smug.

Everyone had been invited back to Tina's house – cheaper than going to the pub – and they all got hammered. I'd never been to a funeral before but I'd seen enough on TV to know that there could be laughter afterwards as people reminisced about the deceased and toasted their memory. There was raucous laughter at Dad's funeral and plenty of toasts, but they weren't to his memory. They were to the great financial position he left Tina in.

'Are you all right?' Rosemary asked, following me as I'd stormed upstairs to my bedroom, unable to bear it any longer.

'My dad's dead but they're acting like they've just won the bloody lottery,' I snapped.

Rosemary winced at the swearword but didn't reprimand me.

'I did pick up that vibe. Where's the money coming from? Life assurance?'

I flung myself down on my bed in the box room. 'Compensation claim. The factory have admitted liability and Tina was named as next of kin on Dad's health forms at work.'

Shortly after I'd started at primary school, Dad was appointed as supervisor at the factory, giving him enough income to drop the other two jobs, and he'd been there ever since, but he often moaned about standards slipping and management making bad decisions.

At the start of the summer, a piece of machinery malfunctioned, resulting in two severed fingers and deep cuts on his left arm. It was seriously grim but he would have recovered and coped. Only he contracted sepsis and it was picked up too late.

The factory was found negligible because the Health and Safety Executive had already ordered them to replace the faulty part which led to Dad's injury and ultimately his death, so they were coughing up. Tina had also put in a compensation claim with the hospital for not picking up the sepsis. She'd likely get that, too.

'Oh!' Rosemary exclaimed. 'And you'll get...?'

'Sod all. Dad had nothing. *She* spent everything he earned and wiped out his savings.'

Rosemary sat down beside me and sighed. 'I'm so sorry, darling girl. It all seems very unfair.'

'I hate it here! I hate *them*! If Dad hadn't married her...'

'The accident was nothing to do with your stepmother. You can't blame her for that.'

I didn't appreciate the stern tone, but then her voice softened. 'My spare room has your name on it if it's too much for you here. You'd be welcome to stay.'

My heart leapt at the thought. Rosemary was prone to the occasional spiky moment, but we'd always rubbed along nicely. Even on her grumpiest days, she was a million times nicer than Tina in a good mood.

'Are you talking the occasional overnighter or do you mean permanently?'

She smiled. 'I don't think you'd want to live with an old lady forever, but you'd be welcome to move in until you're settled in a job and ready to find your own home.'

I flung my arms round her and kissed her cheek. 'Yes, please! When?'

'Whenever you're ready. Although you will have to get permission from Tina. She's your legal guardian.'

Tina hated me. There was no way she'd refuse.

She had a raging hangover from 'celebrating' my dad's death so I waited a couple of days before I tackled the subject of moving out. I'd wanted to get her alone but her younger sister Jenny was there. As always.

I honestly thought she'd have been delighted to be rid of me but I'd misjudged my worth. The child benefit she received for me was small change compared to what she'd get from the compensation claims, but my role as the family servant was priceless. I'd become the cook and cleaner and the lazy cow wasn't willing to lift a finger herself.

I'll never forget the smug look on her face as she took a drag on her spliff. 'Of course, you're very welcome to move out, but wouldn't it be a shame if summat 'appened to that old blind biddy while you're at school? Must be terrifying sensing someone's in your home but being unable to see them.'

I could immediately picture Connor or Cody hiding in Rosemary's flat and shuddered.

'You wouldn't.' But I knew she would.

'Hearing them breathing,' she continued.

'Wondering why your dog hasn't barked,' Jenny added, delight in her tone. 'Scary shit, eh?'

'So do you want a hand packing, sweetheart?' Tina asked, her voice dripping with sarcasm, causing Jenny to cackle like the evil witch she was. 'Your choice.'

'What about when I finish school?' I asked, trying not to sound casual rather than desperate. I had the rest of the term then one full year left of senior school. It wasn't a lifetime, even if it felt like it.

Tina narrowed her eyes at me, her lip curled up in disgust, her voice as cold as ice. 'You can leave when I tell you to leave.'

She took another deep drag of her spliff and blew the smoke in my direction. I held my breath and hoped the weed would chill her enough for her to give me a sensible answer.

Jenny glowered at me. 'I can't believe what an ungrateful brat you are after everything my sister's done for you.'

I bit back a retaliation.

'When you've finished college,' Tina muttered. 'The money stops then so you can piss off and leave us alone.'

'I can go to college?'

Although I hated the idea of living with Tina for another three years, going to college was my dream so that I could get my accounting qualifications and follow in my mum's footsteps. I'd overheard Tina and Dad arguing about it before his accident – another reason I'd suspected (and hoped) their marriage was near the end. Dad was adamant that I'd go to college and Tina wanted me to get a job and 'pay my way'. I'd willed him to win that battle because I was certain that, if I worked, I'd never see a penny of my wages. 'Housekeeping', she'd call it. Bingo, fags and beer money, more like.

Tina flicked some ash into her empty coffee mug. 'Yep, but only because it's shorter hours than a full-time job. Means you can still do your chores.'

'And still look after Darcie,' Jenny said. 'Unless you'd prefer her to be left on her own.'

Darcie, aged three at the time, was Jenny's granddaughter but I spent far more time looking after her than anyone else did, not that I minded because I adored that little girl. It pissed me off that Jenny barely acknowledged her, especially when it was her fault Hayley wasn't around to raise Darcie.

Jenny constantly moaned that becoming a nanna in her late thirties was far too young, but Darcie had been born when Hayley was sixteen and Jenny had started her family young herself, having Hayley when she was twenty.

She might have felt too young to be a grandparent but she didn't look it. Jenny had a face that Rosemary would call 'lived in'. With lank shoulder-length mousy hair, a forehead permanently creased into a frown and a downturned mouth, years of smoking and sitting in the sun had aged her to the point where she could pass for a woman twenty years older.

Tina, two years older than her sister, had been handed the looks in the family and, when I first met her, I thought she was beautiful with her short dark hair, high cheekbones and full lips. Until I discovered how ugly she was inside.

So that was it; my future had been decided for me yet again. I was stuck with Tina because everyone and everything I cared about the most – Rosemary, her guide dog Trixie, and Darcie – would suffer if I didn't and I couldn't risk that. Tina wasn't the sort to issue an empty threat. She *would* do it. At least I could go to college. I would somehow struggle through three more years if that meant getting my accountancy qualifications.

Only three years became four. The year I was due to start my course, it got cancelled. Not enough students. I was offered a place on the business studies course with an accountancy module on it, so I accepted that. The course was good but it wasn't what I wanted so, when they confirmed there was enough demand the following year and I could start over, I had an agonising decision to make: walk away from my dream or face another year with Tina.

I chose my dream and hoped the pay-off would be worth it.

* * *

'Only me!' I called out when I let myself into Rosemary's flat using the key from the miniature safe outside her front door.

'We're in the lounge.'

Rosemary was listening to an audiobook with her gorgeous dark golden retriever guide dog laid by her feet.

'How's my darling girl today?' she asked, pausing the book.

I leaned over and kissed her on the cheek and gave Trixie a scratch behind the ears. 'Perfect, thank you. Is the book good?'

'Brilliant. But I've guessed the killer already.'

'After how many chapters?'

'Three.'

'Tell me the truth. You like guessing the killer more than you like the books, don't you?'

She laughed. 'You know me too well. Would you like to make us both a hot chocolate while I get to the end of this chapter?'

'Sure.'

I heated up a pan of milk in the open-plan kitchen and watched her with her head back against the sofa listening to her story. She was the same height as me – five foot nine – and slender. Her shoulder-length greying blonde hair was pulled back into a neat chignon as always and she was wearing a typically Rosemary outfit of smart trousers, plain blouse, colourful chiffon scarf and a long pendant. She always looked so effortlessly smart and as though, at the age of seventy-four, she was about to stride into a board room and negotiate a killer business deal. She probably could. She had a sharp tongue when she chose and I reckoned she'd probably made a few enemies pre-retirement.

I was certain that me making the hot chocolate just now had nothing to do with her wanting to finish the chapter. She never moaned about it, but the shift over the past year or so from fierce independence and insisting she could manage absolutely everything to casual suggestions that I might like to make the drinks or take the bins out when I left told me her eyesight wasn't the only faculty now letting her down. She tried to disguise it when she moved round the flat, but I was in no doubt that she was struggling with her mobility and I worried every day about her having a fall. My only reassurance was knowing that, if anything did happen, Trixie would bark like mad to alert the neighbours.

Rosemary never asked for anything else from me but I would happily do all of her cooking and cleaning if she let me – the least I could offer after she'd been so kind to Dad and me.

'Perfect timing,' she said as I returned to the lounge and placed a mug of hot chocolate beside her. 'Chapter's just finished. So what have you been up to today?'

'I've been to Hedgehog Hollow again.'

'Oh! How wonderful! Did you stay for longer this time?'

'I was going to. I thought about what you said about getting more involved and got myself all psyched up for it, but there was a boy from college there and I thought he might know who I was so I panicked.'

'And you left?'

'As fast as my moped would go.'

Her forehead scrunched into a deep frown and I knew I'd disappointed her. She didn't like it when people didn't heed her advice.

'Phoebe! You'll never get anywhere in life if you run away from all the situations that scare you.'

I pulled at a loose thread on the sleeve of my top. Run away from all the situations that scared me? She had no idea.

'I'll stay longer next time,' I offered feebly. 'I promise.'

'I should think so too. What's there to be so scared of, anyway?'

Everything! I wanted to take Rosemary's advice of building my confidence by staying longer, asking questions, and perhaps building a friendship with someone who wasn't six or seventy-four but that in itself was the problem. Samantha was warm and welcoming and seemed to want to know everything about me. Fizz was the same. Rosemary had been excited for me when I'd mentioned there was a volunteer who wasn't too much older than me but Fizz was even bubblier than Samantha and had already fired a stack of questions at me, which I'd completely evaded. I couldn't let either of them in. I couldn't go down that road.

'It's just me being silly,' I said, hoping that would placate Rosemary, but she was still frowning. 'Okay! So I'm worried about being found out. I should have been honest with Samantha at the start but how could I? She'd never have given me the job.'

'Do you think this boy will say anything?'

'Probably. I keep expecting my phone to ring and it to be over.'

'I think you should tell her. You said she's a lovely person. I'm sure she'll understand. You're not like *that* family and I'm sure she'll already have seen that.'

'I hope so. It's brilliant work experience and I love what Samantha's doing for the hedgehogs. I wish there were more people in the world like her.'

'And fewer like your stepmother.'

'Exactly.'

Rosemary only knew a small fraction of it.

My heart sank as I approached Tina's house on foot a couple of hours later and spotted Darcie huddled on the doorstep. Her head was buried in the fur of a soft toy and, as I got closer, I could see it was the cerise pink unicorn I'd given her for her birthday in January.

Jenny was obviously here as usual and, if Darcie had been kicked out of the house, Tina and Jenny were either drunk, stoned, or both. So much for them looking after her for the day.

I placed the bag containing our evening meal on the path and crouched down in front of her. 'What are you doing out here, Princess?'

She looked up at me with wide eyes, her grubby cheeks streaked with tears. She was such a pretty little girl with her big brown eyes and black curls and she had the most dazzling smile, but there were too many occasions like now when she had nothing to smile about. I often wished I could transport us both away from all of this.

'Nanna and Great-Aunt Tina are smoking those things that smell funny,' she said.

Weed. Great. 'Have you been out here for long?'

She shrugged. 'I don't know. I think so. I'm cold.'

I wasn't surprised. She wasn't wearing a hat, scarf or gloves, and her coat looked more like a summer jacket.

'Shuffle your bum up, munchkin.'

Giggling at the name, Darcie wiggled her bottom to the edge of the step and I sat down beside her and put my arm round her. I could feel her shivering and mentally added another reason to the long list of why I despised Tina and Jenny.

'Twizzle's cold too. I asked if we could go back inside but they shouted at us.'

I removed my gloves and took her small hands between mine. They felt like blocks of ice and had a blueish tinge to them.

'You can put my gloves on but we need to try and warm your hands up first.' I rubbed them, furious at Tina and Jenny. There was no need to kick her out in the middle of winter but I wasn't feeling brave enough to challenge it. If I took Darcie inside, directly going against their orders, I'd pay for it and they'd likely yell at Darcie too. I wasn't going to inflict that on her.

'Do your hands feel warmer now?'

I slipped my gloves on them when she nodded. 'I know they're a bit big but they'll keep you warm.'

'They're really soft,' she said, giving me a brief flash of that smile.

'They were a Christmas present from my friend Rosemary. They've got a fleecy lining. And I think you need this more than me.' I had my denim jacket on underneath so I slipped off my puffer jacket – also a gift from Rosemary – and wrapped it round her.

'Twizzle's paws are cold,' she said, thrusting her unicorn into my hands. 'But I told her it won't be cold when we go on holiday.'

I raised my eyebrows at her. 'I didn't know you were going away.'

'Nanna and Great-Aunt Tina were talking about it. We're going somewhere called Minica Public.'

'Minica Public? Oh! You mean the Dominican Republic?'

'That's it!'

'Really sorry, Princess, but I don't think you'll be going there,' I said, rubbing Twizzle's turquoise paws. 'It's a long way away and it's *very* expensive. They were probably just talking about how nice it would be to be somewhere warm like that.'

She shrugged. 'I asked if I could look for shells on the beach but they told me I wasn't allowed to listen and sent me out here.'

I handed back Twizzle.

'Will you tell me a story?'

I'd always been drawn to numbers rather than words so making up stories wasn't my thing, but Darcie didn't seem to mind that they were all plagiarised from her favourite animated films.

'What sort of story would you like?'

'One with Twizzle in it.'

'Okay, let me think. A story about a magical unicorn. Once upon a time...'

A few minutes later, the front door was thrust open.

'Where the hell have you been?'

Wincing at Tina's high-pitched nasally squawk, I stood up and brushed the muck off the back of my jeans.

'I went to see Rosemary then to get something for tea.'

'Rosemary? Why do you still bother with that blind old bat?'

She laughed but I didn't join in, which earned me a scowl and the evil eye. If she hadn't been chilled by the weed, it would probably have earned me a lot more.

'Your nanna says you can come back in now, Darc.'

Darcie looked up at Tina, wide-eyed, and nodded.

'Bloody freezing out here,' Tina added and closed the door, muttering something about letting all the heat out.

Yeah, it was freezing but she'd thought nothing of kicking her little great-niece outside dressed in very little while she got stoned again and fantasised about holidaying in the Caribbean.

'What's a blind old bat?' Darcie asked.

'A nasty name to call an elderly lady whose eyesight has nearly gone. Will you promise me you won't ever use it?'

'I promise.'

'Good girl. Should we go inside? You and Twizzle can help me make tea if you like.'

She smiled as she stood up and passed my coat and gloves back to me. 'Thank you for making us warm.'

'You're welcome.' I could have cried when she flung herself against my legs and cuddled me. She was such a lovely little girl and so polite too and I knew that was directly down to all the time she'd spent with me and not from her nanna or great-aunt. My biggest fear was how long she'd stay that way before their influence became too strong and she morphed into one of them. Or they broke her like they'd broken her mum.

* * *

Darcie only managed about five minutes in the kitchen with me before Jenny burst through the door.

'Coat on, Darc. We're going home.'

'But I'm helping Phoebe.'

Jenny glared at her. 'I don't care, young madam. I've said we're going home so that's what we're doing. Coat! Now!'

Darcie looked up at me as though willing me to speak up for her but I knew better than that. Jenny had an even shorter temper than Tina. I wasn't sure which of them I hated the most.

'I'll see you again soon, Darcie.' I wiped her hands with a cloth and removed her apron.

'Hurry up!' Jenny demanded. 'Trigg's outside the house right now and he's gagging for a coffee.'

He was gagging for something. Coffee wasn't it. Trigg was Jenny's boyfriend and he creeped me out. Teeth missing, greasy slicked-back hair, a tattoo of a naked woman on his forearm, and roaming hands. For some weird reason, he was obsessed with aniseed chewing gum and always reeked of the stuff. It made me gag being close to him. No idea what Jenny saw in him, although I'm not sure what he saw in her either. A match made in hell.

Darcie gave me another hug and I wished I could say or do something to let her stay but, as they liked to frequently remind me, my opinion didn't count. It would make things worse if I spoke up, but the poor girl didn't need to hear her nanna and Trigg at it. She was only six years old. Made me feel queasy.

It was a few minutes before the front door closed and I felt anxious as I peeled the potatoes. The only reason Jenny would have paused on the doorstep would have been to feed a pack of lies about me to Tina. It was one of her favourite games. Sure enough, the kitchen door burst open, making me jump and drop the potato peeler onto the chopping board.

'Who the bloody hell do you think you are?' Tina demanded.

As usual, I had no idea what she was talking about. I gulped as I picked up the peeler and continued with the potatoes.

'How dare you argue with *my* sister in *my* house. When she says it's time for Darcie to go home, it's time for Darcie to go home. Got it?'

'But I didn't say anything to her.' I wished I had now.

Tina thumped her fist against the cupboard door. 'Are you calling my sister a liar?'

'No. Sorry.'

'You think you're better than us, don't you?'

I'd learned from experience that most of Tina's questions were rhetorical. Responding would end badly.

'You think you're special 'cos you're at college.' Her words were slurred. I could just about cope with her when she was only stoned, but drunk Tina was vicious.

'Always looking down your nose at the rest of us.' She took a couple of steps closer and I held my breath, waiting for another insult. 'Spoilt fucking brat.'

I wasn't. Nobody could look at what I'd been through and label me 'spoilt'.

'Look at me when I'm talking to you!' she yelled.

I turned to face her, trembling, willing my face not to show any emotion. She played on fear and acted on anger.

'Did you just sneer at me?'

'No! I...'

She grabbed my wrist, her grip so tight that the potato peeler clattered onto the tiled floor.

Her face was so close to mine that I could see the blood vessels in her eyes and smell the drink on her breath. She showered my cheek with spit as she spoke slowly and deliberately. 'Don't you dare sneer at me or my sister ever again or I'll make you sorry you were ever born.'

Most days I was already sorry.

She wrapped her other hand round my forearm and I bit hard on my lip, drawing blood, as she twisted her hands in opposite directions.

'There's more where that came from,' she hissed before storming out of the kitchen and slamming the door.

Blinking back tears and willing myself not to scream, I rushed to the sink and ran cold water over my burning skin.

More where that came from? There usually was.

9

SAMANTHA

A look at new admission Figgy's faeces sample under the microscope revealed nothing untoward internally, which was a relief.

I'd settled him into his crate and was cleaning down the table when a FaceTime request came through from Fizz.

'I've just spoken to my dad. He says he'll come to see you tomorrow but you might want to call Action Fraud in the meantime.'

'Thank you.'

'You look worn out.'

'I feel it.'

'Do you want me to come back?'

'No. I'll be fine. Josh'll be home soon.'

'Okay. I know it's easier said than done but try not to worry. We'll work it out somehow.'

I wasn't sure how, but I appreciated her optimism.

'Dad said it's best not to contact Phoebe and, if she turns up at the farm, do your best to act normal.'

'Okay, thanks. Enjoy your pub crawl. Hope your friend has a good birthday.'

We said our goodbyes and disconnected the call. I hoped Phoebe wouldn't show up. There was no reason for her to do so but, if she did, there was no way I could act 'normal'.

* * *

I managed to keep myself busy for the next couple of hours, posting updates on social media about our more recent admissions and some of our longer-term patients including an update on Gollum, our bald hedgehog. He'd been admitted in early May, two days after we officially opened, with really bad mange. He'd lost several of his spines back then and the rest fell out over the next few weeks and hadn't grown back.

Gollum had been the inspiration for creating 'Hedgehog Dell' behind the barn – a fully enclosed secure hedgehog-friendly garden paradise. Hedgehogs like Gollum who couldn't be released into the wild could explore the garden instead of spending the rest of their lives in a crate, and those who were recuperating longer-term could experience what was known as a soft release, spending time getting back to strength in the garden before being released into the wild.

Darkness fell and so did the rain. The steady patter against the windows was unexpectedly soothing and I felt calmer than I had done all day.

I was giving Gollum a baby oil massage when Josh returned from his callout. My stomach lurched at the thought of telling him what had happened. I knew he wouldn't blame me but that didn't matter because I blamed myself.

'How was it?' I asked as he approached me. His shoulders were dipped and his forehead creased, so it clearly hadn't gone well.

'Disaster. We lost a cow, her calf, and another two calves.'

'Oh no! Why so many?'

'Pure coincidence. Same farmer hasn't lost any for the past three years.'

'I'm so sorry. Are you okay?'

'Gutted, but we did everything right. Just one of those unfortunate things.'

I slipped off my chair and hugged him tightly. I'd longed for a hug all day but it seemed Josh needed one as much as I did.

'I'm going to have to grab a shower,' he said when he released me. 'I stink.'

I forced a smile as I wafted my hand in front of my nose. 'I wasn't going to say anything.'

'I'll be back over shortly and you can tell me all about your day. I need cheering up.'

'I'll put the kettle on.'

Cheering up? That wasn't going to happen.

* * *

Josh slumped back on the sofa bed, running his hands through his damp hair after I'd told him about the latest in the Grimes family vendetta.

'I can't believe they did that. I thought it was over.'

'So did I. That family are clearly intent on destroying me.'

Josh put his arm round me and cuddled me against his side. 'Well, they're not going to succeed.'

'Do you think Phoebe could be involved?'

'Not from what I've seen of her, but who knows? Even if she's innocent of taking the money, she's still guilty of keeping her family connection hidden. That's pretty devious.'

'I've been thinking about that all afternoon and going round in circles. My gut tells me she's not involved and Fizz agrees, but why lie about who she is? What I keep coming back to is that she's only a Grimes through marriage rather than blood so she's hopefully nothing like them. She started her college course before I'd even met Thomas and she's always talked so passionately about her future as an accountant. What if it was just about getting some work experience?'

'She still should have told you.'

'But I wouldn't have given her the job if she had. She'd have realised that.' I shrugged. 'It doesn't really matter. What matters right now is that the account is empty, I don't have any inheritance left, and all our savings have gone into the wedding and honeymoon fund.'

Josh stiffened. 'Don't say it!'

I adjusted position so I could look him in the eye. 'I don't want to, but what other choice is there? I'm not saying cancel the wedding, but maybe we can cut back on the number of guests. And the honeymoon is so expensive. I know we'd lose the deposit...' I knew I didn't sound convincing. Changing any aspect of our wedding and cancelling our dream honeymoon were the last things I wanted to do but I had no idea what else to suggest.

'Answer me this question: how many times do you plan on getting married?'

'Just the once.'

'Me too. Our wedding day is a special day, Sammie, which is going to give us a lifetime of memories. As for the honeymoon, we've both dreamed of going on safari for years and I think we deserve that break. And what would happen if we did cancel? The wedding and honeymoon combined won't cost anywhere near thirty grand so changing our wedding plans and cancelling the honeymoon might ease the financial predicament but it wouldn't solve it. There are other ways to fund Hedgehog Hollow. The practice can help out for a start, and I'm sure your dad will too.'

'But I can't just take that money. It would have to be loans, and how am I going to pay them back? We've got ninety-eight hedgehogs at the moment. Overwintering them all is going to cost a small fortune in food alone and we're only just into winter. That number could double or even triple next month.'

'I'm sure the community will step in if we let people know.'

'But then I'd have to admit what happened and how stupid I've been.'

Josh gave me a gentle squeeze. 'You haven't been stupid. You couldn't have predicted what would happen and the bank weren't fair to suggest you were negligent. I wouldn't be surprised if the Financial Ombudsman doesn't come down on your side so I think we definitely need to complain to them. As for letting the community know what's happened, you don't have to tell them *how* it happened.'

'Maybe not, but they've done so much for us already.' Outraged locals had joined forces to rebuild the barn after the arson attack, they'd supported our Family Fun Day, and they regularly placed food and cleaning products in the various donation bins in the community.

'Which shows how generous they are,' Josh said. 'They love what you do here and they want to help.'

'I guess so, but we'd probably better not spread the word before I've spoken to Fizz's dad. I wouldn't want to jeopardise anything.'

'There's something we can do right now – something which we've been talking about for ages that's going to save us some money.'

'What's that?'

'Get a wish list set up on Amazon and put a link to it on social media. I know you were hesitant about doing it because you'd rather support local businesses, but this is a time of crisis and we can't afford not to give it a go. I'm sure there are things we can do with local businesses down the line but, in the meantime, this is a brilliant way of getting donations of food, gloves and medicine while we're working on recovering the money. I bet it'll be more successful than the donation bins because it's more convenient.'

I nodded slowly, my mind whirring. The donation bins placed at the end of the farm track, in Josh's practice and a few key places round the area including Reddfield Library had been successful but we needed so much more than they provided.

'Okay. I'll set up a wish list after we've eaten.'

'Good. And I'll transfer five grand over from the practice. No protests. I'm not having you worrying about bills you can't pay. Promise me there'll be no more suggestions about touching the wedding fund or cancelling the honeymoon?'

'Okay. No more suggestions for the moment.' Five grand was amazing. It would take the immediate pressure off, but what would happen when that was gone?

'I can't promise you I'll never mention it again,' I added in a small voice.

He hugged me to his side once more and kissed the top of my head. 'I'll take that for now.'

'I wondered if we should cancel Thursday's party, but it's already paid for so there's no point.'

'I know a party is probably the last thing you want right now,' Josh said, 'but I think it's what you need after what's happened today.'

I couldn't imagine laughing and dancing, but maybe I'd feel differently in a couple of days' time after the initial shock had worn off. So many people were looking forward to it and many of them had had a tough year so I didn't want to let them down. I was looking forward to it too. Or I had been.

'There's something else I need you to promise me.' Josh twisted round and took my hand in his. 'Promise me you won't beat yourself up about this. It's *not* your fault. The only people who are to blame are the Grimes family and, if she's involved, Phoebe. You haven't failed the hedgehogs or Thomas and Gwendoline.'

I lowered my eyes as he voiced my biggest worry and he tilted my chin upwards to regain eye contact. He fixed his dark eyes on mine, his expression solemn.

'Repeat after me: this is not my fault.'

'This is not my fault.'

'With a bit of conviction this time.'

'This is *not* my fault,' I said, rolling my eyes at him.

'The Grimes family all belong behind bars and I'm going to help put them there.'

I repeated what he'd said.

'And I am a strong, resilient woman who doesn't let a mild inconvenience like a missing twenty-nine grand stop me from being a badass hedgehog saviour.'

I repeated the final words, smiling at him. 'How do you do it every time?'

'Do what?'

'Lift me when I'm feeling at my lowest?'

'Because I'm a badass Sammie saviour,' he deadpanned, making me laugh. He always did it. Even though he was obviously feeling low about the losses at the dairy farm earlier, he'd managed to stay completely focused on me and make me feel better about myself and positive about the situation. The wish list was a great starting point. I had plenty of stock in at the moment because I'd ordered extra at the start of the month knowing we'd have high winter admissions. The money from Josh's veterinary practice would tide us over and settle any immediate bills and the overdraft from the bank would be a handy back-up. With Josh by my side, giving practical support and solutions, it didn't seem quite so bleak.

10

PHOEBE

'What the bloody hell's this?' Tina curled her lip up in apparent disgust as she let a dollop of mashed potato fall from her fork back onto her plate with a splat.

'Mashed potato.' The moment I said it, I regretted it.

'Are you trying to be clever?'

'No, I...' I gulped. 'I'm sorry. I boiled the potatoes for too long. I thought it would still taste all right.'

'You did, did you? Does it look like it'll taste all right?'

I looked down at the sloppy mess on my plate, my tummy churning. It hadn't looked that bad when I'd dished it up so I'd stupidly thought I could get away with it, but it had since spread across the plate.

'Do you want me to make some instant mash?'

'No. Because the rest of my food will be cold by then,' she snapped. 'I'll have to get a takeaway.'

'Sorry.'

She folded her arms and grinned at me. 'But first, I want to watch you eat yours.'

'I'm not sure.'

'Eat it!' she yelled.

I hastily shovelled in a forkful but the texture was all wrong – like liquid potato with a few lumps in it – and it made me gag.

'Don't you dare puke on my table.'

I gulped down some water. 'I can't eat it.'

'But you thought *I* could.'

'I didn't realise it was this bad. Sorry.'

'Eat some more.' Her light-hearted tone suggested she was joking but I knew she wasn't.

'Please, Tina.'

'Eat. Some. More.'

My tummy gurgled as I raised my fork to my mouth and nibbled at it.

'That's not how you eat!' She leapt off her seat, fork in hand, and strode towards me. '*This* is how you eat!'

I squealed as she yanked my head back by my hair, and spluttered as she shovelled in a large forkful.

'Eat!' she screeched, her eyes wild as they bore into mine.

I somehow managed to swallow that mouthful but there was no way I could eat any more.

'More!' She grabbed another forkful and jabbed it towards my mouth, but I kept my lips clamped shut. No matter how many times she yanked my hair or jabbed the fork at me, I wasn't going to eat any more potato because what she'd do to me when my body rejected it would be a hell of a lot worse than the pain she was inflicting right now.

Her mobile ringing saved me, and I realised it was time for Connor's call from prison.

'Hi, Connor!' Her face softened as she spoke to her precious younger son. 'Will you give me a few seconds, sweetie?'

She glared at me. 'Fuck off up to your bedroom and don't even think about coming down later in search of food.'

I don't think I've ever been grateful to Connor for anything but I could have kissed him right now for his impeccable timing.

'Do you want me to clear the plates away?' I didn't want to be in more trouble later.

'No. Get lost.'

I pushed back my chair and was about to stand up when she caught me across my left cheek with a resounding slap. The pain brought tears to my eyes and I hastily blinked them back.

'That's for cooking me shit and for arguing about it. Now get of my sight.'

I rushed towards the door as she returned to her call, sounding like a completely different person as she adopted the gooey tone she reserved for her sons. 'Sorry about that, sweetie. Just teaching Vinnie's spoilt little brat another valuable life lesson. So how was...'

I didn't hear the rest of the conversation. Dashing up the stairs and into the bathroom, I ran cold water onto my flannel and winced as I held it against my throbbing cheek.

Sitting on the edge of the bath, tears coursed down my cheeks as I adjusted the position of the flannel to ease the worst of the pain. But even after several fresh applications, I could still see the imprint of her fingers reflected in the mirror. There was mashed potato encrusted round my mouth so I gently dabbed that away, wincing at the cuts and puncture marks on and around my lips, chin and cheeks where she'd jabbed me with the fork.

My face was a mess. She was usually more careful than this, but she probably thought she was playing it safe with it being college holidays. Rosemary couldn't see any damage and she knew I'd make excuses not to see my friends because that pattern had already been set back in school. Back when I had friends.

Other than Rosemary's, the only place I went regularly was Hedgehog Hollow and Tina had no idea about that. I'd have to hope Samantha was in no rush to get the receipts back as I couldn't let her see me like this.

I couldn't let anyone know for fear of what Tina would do to Rosemary and Trixie.

11

I stayed in my bedroom the following morning and released a long, shuddery breath when I heard the front door bang closed. When it was the college holidays, I lived for Tuesdays: bingo day.

Glitter Bingo in Reddfield town centre opened at ten and Tina and Jenny aimed to be there for bang on opening. There was a gang of twelve or so who went most weeks and stayed there all day and into the evening, rolling in drunk after eleven. I made sure I was in bed well before then.

I stopped halfway down the stairs, my ears straining. Had they left the TV on? Then I heard a child's giggle. I ran down the rest of the stairs and found Darcie curled up on the sofa with Twizzle the unicorn, absorbed in a cartoon.

'Hey, Darcie, what are you doing here?' I asked, keeping half an eye on the front door in case Jenny or Tina appeared.

'Nanna and Great-Aunt Tina have gone to the bingo.' Her eyes didn't leave the television.

'But you don't usually come here on bingo day.' Jenny usually offloaded her onto an elderly neighbour for the day.

'Dottie's on holiday so Nanna said you could look after me because you were naughty yesterday.'

She looked up at me and I swiftly pulled my hoodie up to cover my cut face.

'What did you do?'

'Nothing much. I'm going to make a cup of tea. Do you want a glass of milk or juice?'

'Milk, please.'

In the kitchen, I shook my head. What was so wrong with them that they saw looking after Darcie as some kind of punishment for my supposed bad behaviour yesterday?

'Did they say anything about your bedtime?' I asked Darcie as I handed her a glass of milk.

She shook her head.

'Did they say they'd be home at their usual time?'

She nodded.

'But they definitely didn't say whether I should take you home and put you to bed?'

'They said you'd feed me. You will, won't you?'

Her eyes widened and the look of fear in them suggested to me that skipping meals was familiar. I'd never picked up on that before. Jenny was as useless in the kitchen as Tina. I was often ordered to make double and was sent round to Jenny's with a meal for her and Darcie before I was allowed to eat my own. Cold.

'Of course I will, Princess. Have you had any breakfast?'

'No.'

'Would you like some cereal or toast?'

'Toast, please. And can Twizzle have some too? She loves strawberry jam.'

'I'll see what I can do.'

I took my mug of tea back into the kitchen and popped a couple of slices of bread into the toaster then took my phone out of my jeans pocket. I tried to avoid texting Tina whenever possible, as the responses were always abusive, but I needed to pre-empt doing the wrong thing with Darcie.

⊠ To Tina
Just checking whether I should settle Darcie here
tonight or take her home and get her settled there

I read the message over and over then reluctantly added 'hope you win big' and a smiley face before sending it.

⊠ From Tina
What do you think?

'I don't know. That's why I'm asking you,' I muttered. I could guarantee that I'd pick the wrong path but, if I responded, I'd be accused of being argumentative. Fortunately, another text arrived.

⊠ From Tina
Jenny says take her home. Don't text me again

Once again, it was a no-win situation. If I texted 'thank you', I'd be accused of pestering her and, if I didn't, I'd be accused of being rude. I braved a 'thanks' then switched my phone to silent and shoved it back in my pocket.

'Toast's ready,' I called to Darcie, 'but you need to eat it at the kitchen table.' She was a messy eater and no way could I risk sticky jam and greasy butter over Tina's sofa – one of the many treats she'd bought herself with Dad's compensation money.

She skipped into the kitchen, placed Twizzle on the table, sat down opposite me and gasped.

'Did you hurt your face?'

I realised too late that I hadn't covered up and self-consciously put one hand up to my cheek. 'Erm, yeah.'

'How?'

'Erm... I slipped in the shower.'

'When I broke my arm, Nanna said it was my fault because I'd put too many bubbles in the bath. Did you put too many bubbles in the shower?'

'Something like that. Eat your toast before it gets cold. It's nicer warm.'

She took a bite and chewed then smiled at me. 'It's lovely warm. It's always cold when I get it.'

If only never giving Darcie warm toast was the worst thing Jenny had ever done. I feared that, one day soon, there'd be unexplained bruises or a black eye. The broken arm incident a year ago had terrified me but Darcie's story matched Jenny's; that she'd slipped in the bath after pouring in too much washing-up liquid (cheaper than bubble bath).

I kept my eye on her as much as I could, but I was already worried sick about what would happen to her when I got my accountancy diploma and could finally escape from Tina's clutches. I repeatedly told myself that all teachers were trained in safeguarding so somebody would notice if Jenny turned on Darcie.

But if Jenny was as careful as Tina, there'd be no obvious physical signs and the emotional ones could easily be missed.

After all, nobody had noticed mine.

'These flats are pretty,' Darcie said, stopping at the edge of the car park later that morning, hand in mine, looking up at Renleigh Court.

I'd loved living there, but they were 1960s-built boxes that I'd never have described as 'pretty'. As I looked up, I realised why she'd said that. Even though it was only lunchtime, it was a dull, dark day so each of the flats overlooking the car park had either a lit Christmas tree or some fairy lights in the window. There were red, yellow, blue and green lanterns strung across the entrance and more fairy lights in the tall conifer tree in the garden.

'It *is* pretty,' I agreed, setting off walking again. 'I used to live here when I was a little girl.'

'Why don't you now?'

'My dad married your great-aunt and moved in with her so that's where I live now, but my friend Rosemary still lives here and I thought you might like to visit her today.'

'Why?'

'What's your favourite animal?'

'Unicorn.'

I smiled. 'And your second favourite?'

'Dog.'

'My friend Rosemary doesn't have a unicorn but she has a very lovely golden retriever called Trixie.'

'Is that a girl?'

'Yes, and she's a very special dog because she's a guide dog. Do you know what that means?'

'It's a dog that helps people who can't see properly. One came to school assembly.'

'Can you remember what they said about stroking guide dogs?'

'You shouldn't stroke them while they're working.'

'That's right. They've got a job to do and it can distract them and place their owner in danger. Because we're going into Rosemary's home, Trixie might be relaxing rather than working but we need to ask Rosemary first before stroking her dog. Is that all right?'

'I'm excited,' she said, grinning at me and squeezing my hand.

I was excited too, but nervous. Rosemary had repeatedly asked me when she'd get a chance to meet Darcie and I was sick of using the same excuses: *she's with her nanna today, she's got a cold, she's going on a playdate.* I was sure Rosemary knew I was fibbing. Truth was, I was 100 per cent certain Jenny wouldn't let me take Darcie to visit Rosemary because she never let me take her anywhere except the scabby playground on our estate. I'd need to ask Darcie to keep quiet about our visit.

* * *

'That little girl is an absolute delight,' Rosemary said, joining me in the kitchen as I finished washing up the dishes after lunch.

'She's lovely, isn't she?' I smiled at her lying on the carpet on her stomach with one arm round Trixie and the other round Twizzle. Rosemary had told her that Trixie was 'off duty' and had pointed towards a basket filled with dog toys. I thought Darcie might get bored after a few minutes, but she'd played right up until food was ready. I'd never heard her giggle so much, which made me both happy and sad.

'She says you've hurt your face,' Rosemary said.

'What? Yeah, erm, nothing to worry about. I spilled some shampoo while I was washing my hair and I slipped on it and bashed my cheek against the tiles.' If she could see my face, she'd know I was lying. But she could hear my voice and, even though I tried to sound casual, I don't think I'd have been convinced, so there was no way Rosemary was going to buy it.

'She says you've got cuts round your mouth too.'

'It's nothing.' I couldn't think of a plausible explanation for those. 'How come you were discussing me?'

'We weren't. Darcie spotted I had a plaster on my finger and she asked what I'd done. I told her it was a paper cut that kept bleeding and she volunteered that you were hurt too but you weren't wearing a plaster.' She leaned against the door frame. 'Is there something you want to tell me?'

I'd thought about telling her so many times, but doing so would place her in danger. Tina had frequently made that clear after the initial threat. It didn't matter that Connor, Cody and their cousin Brynn were all banged up. She and Jenny had plenty of thugs they could call on to do their dirty work and I couldn't take that risk.

'No. Just a bit clumsy.'

'You know that offer of a room here never went away.'

'Thanks, but I'm fine. It's not perfect. We're never going to be besties but it's only until I finish college and get a job.' I'd once read that a lie sounded more convincing if you mixed in some truth. I hoped me admitting to life with Tina not being perfect was enough truth for Rosemary.

'You would tell me if they weren't treating you right, wouldn't you?'

'You don't need to worry about me.'

'Darling girl, I'll *always* worry about you.'

She put her arms out and I wiped my hands on a tea towel and hugged her. 'I'm fine at Tina's.'

If only that were true. If only I could stay with Rosemary instead. My life was full of 'if only...' If only Dad hadn't died. If only he hadn't had that accident. If only he hadn't married Tina. If only he hadn't had that win on the premium bonds. If only Mum hadn't been killed in a hit and run.

And, on my darkest days, if only the car that hit her had been a second quicker and had killed me in my pram too.

Around mid-morning the day after the theft, I spotted a police patrol car coming along the farm track.

In the farmyard, Misty-Blue ran up to me. Her gentle purrs comforted me as I cuddled her against my chest.

Fizz's dad, Sergeant Kinsella was accompanied by PC Sunning who'd I'd met a few times previously, each time in connection with the Grimes family.

'In the nicest possible way, I was hoping I wouldn't see you again,' PC Sunning said when he exited the car.

'Same here. But it looks like they're up to no good again. Same players, different game.'

'You've had no trouble at the farm, though?' Sergeant Kinsella asked.

'Nothing that I'm aware of.'

Inside the barn, Misty-Blue went to explore while we settled round the treatment table.

PC Sunning took out a notepad. 'Let's take a full statement. Start with when you discovered the money was missing and we'll work back from there.'

Despite Josh's reassurances, I still felt stupid when I explained about the blank cheques, but neither man flinched. I felt a little less tearful relaying the story now, having already been through it with the bank, Action Fraud, Josh and my dad who'd driven over last night and insisted on transferring money into the business account.

'And you didn't know that Phoebe Corbyn was connected to the family?' PC Sunning asked.

'No idea.'

'Did Fizz pass the message not to speak to her?' Sergeant Kinsella asked.

'Yes, so I haven't been in touch and she hasn't either, which is just as well because I don't know how I'd have reacted. She's only eighteen and she strikes me as a bit...' I searched for the right word '...fragile. If she's got nothing to do with this – and I really want that to be the case – then I didn't want to sound like I was accusing her of anything. And if she is involved, I didn't want to let her know we were onto her.'

'You did the right thing,' Sergeant Kinsella said. 'I think we'll pay Ms Corbyn a visit and hopefully catch Mrs Grimes there too. You said you had a list of the payees for the cheques.'

'I printed it off.' I handed them a piece of A4. 'There's Brynn, Cody and Connor on there. I don't know who the rest of these people are but they nearly all have the surname Grimes so presumably they're family.'

Sergeant Kinsella and PC Sunning exchanged knowing looks.

'We recognise most of them,' PC Sunning said, folding the list into four. 'Anything else you'd like to add?'

'No more information, but I do have questions. What's the likelihood of me ever seeing this money again?'

Sergeant Kinsella nodded towards the folded list on the table. 'As you can probably tell from that, they're not exactly criminal masterminds. There's a clear money trail there. As to whether they still have that money is another matter.'

'You think they'll have spent it already?'

'Or moved it on.'

'That doesn't mean we'll never recover some of it,' PC Sunning added, 'but it's not going to be a speedy process.'

I hadn't missed the use of the word 'some'.

'Is there a possibility I'll not get any of it back?'

'That is a possibility, yes,' Sergeant Kinsella said. 'We'll do what we can for you.'

I waved them off a few minutes later, returned to the table and sat with my head between my hands. With the bank saying no to me, I'd been clinging on to the hope that the police would somehow be able to recover the funds in the same way they might recover a stolen car or jewellery, but I was going to have to face reality. There was no way I'd get everything back and there was a strong likelihood I'd get nothing.

I ran a finger across my left cheekbone, which had needed stitches after Connor Grimes and his mate pelted me with a box full of eggs. The scar was barely visible and I could no longer feel it but I knew it was there, forever reminding me what they were capable of.

Once again, the Grimes family had taken what was mine. They might not be criminal masterminds, but they knew how to cause pain and damage.

With a mew, Misty-Blue jumped onto the table and nudged at my arm. I pulled her to my chest and nuzzled into her grey striped fur, drawing comfort from her warmth.

I thought about the evening of the assault when they'd chased my beloved cat. Even though the subsequent attack on me brought on terrifying PTSD episodes, I hadn't let them break me then and I hadn't let them break me after the arson attack.

'They're not going to break me this time either,' I said, conviction in my voice.

It was only money. This time, no animals died, no buildings were destroyed, and no people got hurt. I'd get that money back somehow. I could engage a lettings agency to try to get the holiday cottages booked up quicker. It wasn't what we'd planned but income generation was paramount right now. I could probably generate a stack more support from the community as Josh suggested, and the local newspaper would definitely respond well to a story like ours. I couldn't risk interfering with the police investigation so I'd get in touch with a lettings agency first and then prepare an action plan of everything I could do to try to secure donations when Sergeant Kinsella gave the go-ahead to contact the paper.

Determination flowed through me. I had this. Bullies could not and would not win.

14

'There's a police car outside your house!' Darcie declared as we walked along Trench Street towards Tina's house after visiting Rosemary.

'So there is.'

Police cars had been a familiar sight outside the house ever since Dad and I moved in but there hadn't been any visits since Connor was sent back to prison. The thought popped into my head that they might be there to give some 'bad' news about the boys or Tina, and I added my excited butterflies to my ever-growing list of reasons to hate Tina. I didn't want to be the sort of person who was excited about another person dying. Like Tina was when Dad went.

One policeman was at the door and another had his hands cupped round his eyes, peering into the lounge.

I stopped at the edge of the path and cleared my throat. 'Are you looking for Tina Grimes?'

They both turned my way. 'Are you Phoebe Grimes?' asked the one by the door.

'Phoebe Corbyn.' Dad had wanted me to go as Corbyn-Grimes but had never got round to completing any official paperwork, thank God. 'Tina's my stepmother.'

'And who's this?' he asked, crouching down and smiling at Darcie.

'I'm Darcie, I'm six years old, and this is Twizzle.' She thrust her unicorn towards him.

'Twizzle's a beautiful unicorn. My daughter would love her.'

'You should buy her one. How old is she?'

The policeman laughed. 'Twenty-six, but she loves unicorns now just as much as she did when she was your age.'

He straightened up. 'Could we come in and have a word with you, Phoebe?'

'Okay.' I fumbled with the key in the lock, suddenly nervous. What if it was about Rosemary instead? Although if it was, the police wouldn't come to tell me. I wasn't family. Not in name anyway.

'What should I do with Darcie?' I asked once everyone was inside.

'Is there a room she can play in?'

'I can get her settled in my bedroom. Is that okay?'

With their consent, I took a bottle of blackcurrant juice out of my shopping bag and ushered Darcie and Twizzle upstairs. We'd called via her house to collect her felt tips and a colouring book, so I laid them on my bedroom floor.

'Will you be a good girl and have your drink and do some colouring while I talk to the policemen?'

'Okay.'

I felt shaky as I descended the stairs. 'She's settled.'

'Darcie, was it?' the other policeman asked. 'What relation is she to you?'

'I call her my little sister but we're not blood-related. It's complicated.'

'We're used to complicated. Go on...'

'Tina Grimes is my stepmother. Her sister Jenny Grimes is Darcie's nanna. Darcie's mum is... she's poorly. She's not around.'

'Would that be Hayley Grimes?'

'Yeah. So I suppose Darcie's really my step-second cousin but I don't think that's a thing. Little sister's easier.'

'I'm Sergeant Kinsella and this is PC Sunning,' the man with the unicorn-loving daughter said. 'Do you mind if we sit down?'

'That's fine. Was it Tina you wanted, because she's at the bingo? Glitter Bingo in Reddfield.'

'Actually, it was you we wanted to speak to first.'

'Me?' I sat down on the armchair while they both perched on the sofa. 'Is everything okay? Has something happened to Rosemary?' I needed to know she was okay.

'We don't know a Rosemary. This concerns Hedgehog Hollow. I believe you've been volunteering there.'

'Oh, my God! Has something happened to Samantha or the hedgehogs?'

Sergeant Kinsella frowned. 'What makes you ask that?'

'My family hate her. Well, they're not really my family. My dad married Tina and he's dead now and...' I was aware I was rambling. 'My oldest stepbrother Cody and his cousin Brynn went to prison for burning down the barn and then my other stepbrother Connor got sent back to prison for some stuff they did there. They think the farm should be theirs.'

'And what do you think about that?' the other policeman asked. 'Do you think they should have the farm?'

'God, no! They don't even want it, really. They don't care about it or their great-aunt who used to run it. All they want is the money.'

'And what is it you do at Hedgehog Hollow?'

'I look after the bank account. I pay the bills and apply for grants.'

'And how did you end up volunteering at Hedgehog Hollow?'

'I'm studying for my accountancy diploma at Reddfield TEC and Samantha was looking for a volunteer to do the accounts at the rescue centre. My tutor, Adam, recommended me. It's great work experience.'

'Let me check I'm understanding this correctly,' Sergeant Kinsella said. 'Your stepfamily hate Samantha Wishaw and they've caused her no end of problems this year, but Ms Wishaw took you on to do her accounts knowing about your connection to the Grimes family.'

My tummy sank and I nibbled on my nail. 'I didn't tell her. I knew some work experience would be great on my CV but, when Adam told me it was at Hedgehog Hollow, I was sure Samantha wouldn't want me to work there if she knew who I lived with so I never said. I didn't tell Tina, either.'

The two men exchanged glances.

'What's going on?' I asked. 'Have I done something wrong?'

Sergeant Kinsella fixed his eyes on mine. 'You're telling me that Tina Grimes doesn't know you've been volunteering at Hedgehog Hollow for the past six months or so.'

'I didn't dare tell her. She'd either try to stop me or she'd make me do something bad.'

'Like what?'

I shrugged. 'I dunno. More vandalism. Steal some supplies. Mess with some meds. I wouldn't put anything past her.'

'Would you do anything like that?'

'No way! If she ever found out and told me to do something bad, I'd stop working there. But she doesn't...' I tailed away as they exchanged looks and the butterflies in my tummy did a giant loop-the-loop. 'Has she found out? Has she done something? Please say no.'

'A substantial sum of money has gone missing from the Hedgehog Hollow account.'

My throat felt very dry and I struggled to force out the words. 'How much?'

'All of it.'

I clapped my hand over my mouth, feeling sick and dizzy. 'No! That's not possible. There was nearly thirty grand in there.'

'We know.'

'How?'

'Cheques.'

'But that's impossible. The cheque book's locked in a tin under a loose floorboard in my bedroom and I have the only key.' I removed the cover from my mobile phone to reveal a small silver key. 'My phone's always with me.'

Sergeant Kinsella stood up. 'Will you show me this tin?'

'It's the box room at the front of the house. Darcie's in there.'

I gripped onto the banister, forcing my legs to carry me up the stairs. Tina couldn't have. She didn't know about Hedgehog Hollow and, even if she knew, how could she know about the cheque book or where to find it?

'Darcie, would you and Twizzle mind sitting on my bed for a minute?' I asked.

She obediently stood up and scrambled onto my bed with the unicorn. I fell to my knees and pulled back the faded blue carpet, lifted the floorboard, removed the small metal money tin and gave it a shake. My tummy sank even further.

'It feels empty.'

I handed it to the sergeant along with the key.

'Other than the cheque book, what should be in here?' he asked.

'My mum's wedding and engagement rings and some money I've been saving from tutoring maths.' Something else I hadn't told Tina about.

I held my breath as he turned the key and opened the lid.

'Anything?'

He showed me the empty tin and a sob escaped as I slumped back against the wall. This was a nightmare.

'What's wrong, Phoebe?' Darcie asked, her voice small and frightened.

I scrambled to my feet and sat on the bed, putting my arms out for a cuddle. 'Some things that are important to me have gone missing, but the police will help me try to find them.'

'I need to ask you a few more questions.' Sergeant Kinsella placed the empty tin on my bedside drawers. 'I'll see you downstairs shortly.'

'Do you like my picture?' Darcie asked.

I looked down at the dark-haired princess riding a unicorn.

'Very beautiful.'

'She looks like you and you both look like Snow White. So pretty.'

A lump caught in my throat. Dad used to call me Snow White because of my porcelain skin, pink cheeks and raven hair. My prize possession had been a soft toy Snow White, which Mum had bought for me shortly after I'd been born. It went 'missing' off my bed about a year after Dad married Tina. Among her many negative qualities was jealousy. She couldn't bear any reminders of my dad's happy marriage to Mum. I swear it was one of the reasons why she couldn't bear me.

'I wish I looked like a Disney princess,' Darcie said, her eyes downcast.

'But you do! Have you seen *The Princess and the Frog*?'

She shook her head.

'There's a beautiful princess in that called Tiana. Look!' I searched for a picture on my phone and passed her it.

Her eyes lit up as she studied the image then grabbed me in a bear hug.

I kissed the top of her head. 'Let me speak to the policemen again then then we'll see if we can find *The Princess and the Frog* and watch it together.'

On the landing, I took a few deep breaths to compose myself. Snow White. It seemed such a long time since I'd been called that. I hardly ever looked in the mirror because I didn't recognise the haunted girl staring back at me. The frequent insults from Tina and Jenny didn't help: *pasty, gaunt, chalky.* They joked that I looked like a ghost or that I was anaemic. I'd learned to hate how I looked but a passing comment from a six-year-old had just lifted me.

'Does Samantha know who I am?' I tentatively asked Sergeant Kinsella when I returned to the lounge.

'Yes.'

My tummy did a somersault and I struggled to force my words out. 'And does she think I took the money?'

PC Sunning unfolded a sheet of A4 and handed it to me, evading the question. 'You see the names on this list with asterisks next to them? Can you tell us who they are?'

Returning to the chair, I scanned down the list of ten names. Tina, Jenny, Connor, Cody, Brynn and Hayley were all on the list without asterisks.

'Darcie Flynn is Hayley's daughter, upstairs. Flynn was her dad's surname. Barry and Vera Grimes are Tina and Jenny's parents.

Maureen Grimes is an auntie. Barry's sister, I think. I haven't seen her since my dad married Tina.'

I handed back the paper. 'Are these the people who took the money?'

'We can't say, but thanks for your help in identifying them all.'

'Will you be able to get the money back?'

'We don't know,' Sergeant Kinsella said. 'But we'll try.'

I remembered my conversation with Darcie yesterday about the Dominican Republic and my tummy lurched. 'What if they've spent it already? What if they've booked a Caribbean holiday?'

The sergeant took out his notepad. 'I think you'd better tell us what you know.'

15

SAMANTHA

An unfamiliar number showed up on my phone around mid-afternoon.

'Hello? Hedgehog Hollow Rescue Centre.'

'Hello,' a man said. 'Do you come out and collect hedgehogs?'

'Sometimes. What's the problem?'

'Bit of a strange one, this. I'm the landlord of The Black Swan in Umplesthorpe and there's a hedgehog in the beer garden but I think there's something seriously wrong with it. Hedgehogs aren't huge, are they?'

'A fully-grown healthy hedgehog is bigger than you might expect.'

'This one's the size of a football. And it's on its back.'

'The size of a football? Really?'

'No exaggeration. I'd bring it to you, but I won't make it back for opening time if I do.'

'It's fine. I'll be with you in about twenty minutes. Could you keep the hedgehog somewhere safe and warm in the meantime? A box or a crate with some towels or newspaper in the bottom would be great.'

'How do I pick it up?'

'Thick gardening gloves or a towel.'

'Okay. I'll see you soon.'

* * *

The landlord, Mick, wasn't exaggerating about the hedgehog being the size of a football. Its legs were splayed out and I suspected the reason Mick had found it on its back was that it had become so big it couldn't walk anymore.

'What's wrong with it?' he asked as we peered into the crisp box.

I pulled on my gloves and lifted the hedgehog up. It was much lighter than it looked, which confirmed my diagnosis.

'It's balloon syndrome. I've read about it and I've seen photos but I've never seen a real case. The poor little thing.'

'What's balloon syndrome?'

'Hedgehogs have a fair bit of space under their skin to enable them to curl up into a ball but, on a rare occasion, they might experience an injury – usually blunt-force trauma by being hit by something – which causes some lung damage. Instead of breathing in air and breathing it out again, this specific type of lung damage means the hog retains the air so they quite literally blow up like a balloon, like our little friend here.'

It was a bit more complicated than that, but I didn't think Mick would appreciate the technical explanation, especially when he was trying to get ready to open the pub. I placed the hedgehog – a male – back among the bar towels.

'Will he survive?'

'Hopefully. The first thing we need to do – and this is going to sound really grim – is to pop him, like we'd do with a balloon. Obviously we're not going to stick a pin in him, but we'll sedate him and the air will be removed. We'll see what damage there is to his lungs and start him on some antibiotics to keep infections away while they heal.'

I picked up the box. 'I'll take him to the vet to be popped. Balloon syndrome's rare and this is my first case so I'd rather they do the deflating.'

'Just when you think you've seen it all!' Mick smiled at me. 'Do I owe you any money for treatment?'

'No. Hedgehogs are wild animals so it's not the responsibility of the finder to pay, although Hedgehog Hollow's a charity so donations are always welcome.' *Especially now that the bank account is empty.* 'We've just set up a wish list on Amazon if you or any of your customers wanted to support. The link's on our Facebook page.'

'I'll check that out. Have fun popping the hedgehog.' He laughed. 'That seems so wrong.'

'I know! It's certainly different.'

I secured the box in the back of my jeep and drove to Josh and Dad's veterinary practice.

* * *

Josh was tied up in surgery but Dad had a cancellation, so it was perfect timing for him to see to my latest patient.

'Balloon syndrome,' he said as soon as he saw him.

'Have you treated it before?'

'Once, years ago. It's shocking to see, isn't it?'

'I've seen photos but seeing a live case is something else.'

Dad picked him up for a visual inspection. 'Does he have a name?'

I bit my lip. 'We're still using Christmassy names until the end of the year and one came to mind and wouldn't go away. Don't judge me, but I've called him Bauble.'

The sides of Dad's mouth twitched. 'I shouldn't laugh, but that *is* funny. Hi, Bauble. We're going to make you better.' He placed him back in the box. 'We'll start with an X-ray to see what damage there is to his lungs and take it from there.'

Seeing the X-ray a little later was the most surreal thing – a small body with a huge dome of air surrounding him. There didn't appear to be any serious damage to his lungs, which was good as it meant that the injury was from a small tear which should heal fairly easily.

It was the most fascinating procedure I'd ever observed. The air wasn't in one giant dome but in four smaller compartments sectioned off by connective tissue under his skin. Dad needed to make four small incisions to deflate each one and it was exactly like watching a balloon deflating as the air left Bauble and he returned to a healthy size.

'The tear in Bauble's lungs needs to heal,' Dad said. 'Breathing in through that is what's inflated him so, if I close up these four incisions, he'll start inflating again. We'll keep him here with the incisions open until we're sure the tear has healed, and then we can close them. The antibiotics will stave off any infection, but he looks pretty healthy to me otherwise.'

'Thanks, Dad. That was amazing to watch.'

'Absolute pleasure. Something different to take your mind off things, eh?'

'Gosh, yes. It couldn't have come at a better time. The police stopped by earlier and they were going to visit Phoebe this afternoon, so I guess I'll know soon whether she was involved or not.'

'How are you feeling about the money side of things?'

'Still anxious. I spoke to a holiday lettings agency this morning so that ball's rolling. I've also got an action plan for fundraising on the back of the theft, but I can't jeopardise the investigation by cracking on with it. I'll pay you that money back as soon as I can.'

'Like I said last night, you can consider it a gift.'

'I can't. You're about to buy into the practice and what's left is your house deposit, so I *will* pay you back as soon as I've built up enough funds and I won't take no for an answer.'

'I've got no plans to move out of Lauren's yet, so there's no rush.'

'I'd better let you get back to your other patients.' I hugged Dad and took one last look at Bauble laid out on the table with a tiny oxygen mask over his face helping him breathe as he came round from his anaesthetic. 'See you both soon.'

As I drove away from the practice in the direction of Hedgehog Hollow, a surge of determination swept through me. The work we did at Hedgehog Hollow was invaluable in helping secure the survival of a gorgeous but vulnerable species and I was going to let nothing stand in the way of me playing my part. I'd already wasted too much time on the problems caused by the Grimes family, and it ended here. I couldn't do anything about the days spent in hospital after the arson attack, the hours devoted to cleaning up and replacing items after each spate of vandalism, or the lost time from the PTSD episodes, but I was damned if I was going to devote any time to worrying and getting upset about the latest thing they'd done to me. Josh and Dad had given me enough funds to see us through, the wish list would hopefully generate some supplies, and the cottages would soon be bringing in an income. I had this covered. They *wouldn't* win and I *would* enjoy my New Year's Eve party because I deserved to.

16

After the police left, Darcie and I watched *The Princess and the Frog*, cuddled together on the sofa. I couldn't concentrate on the film. My phone lay on the sofa arm beside me and, every time it lit up with a notification, my eyes were drawn to it wondering if it would be a message from Samantha demanding an explanation, or an abusive text from Tina or Jenny accusing me of setting the police on them. That's how they'd both see it. It would be my fault they'd been found out rather than their fault for stealing the money in the first place.

Although it was my fault, really. I'd been selfish. I'd wanted the work experience so badly to help me get a job and leave the Grimes family for good that I hadn't paused to think about what might happen if Samantha found out or, worse, if Tina found out. I'd convinced myself there was no reason either party would discover the truth so I'd ignored it.

And now look at what had happened! I felt sick. Samantha would be bricking it about how she was going to feed the hedgehogs or pay the bills. I'd have given her all my savings. I'd even have sold Mum's rings, but everything was gone.

I'd never told Tina about the tutoring because she'd have made me hand over my pay. I'd thought about opening a bank account but, even if I'd opted for paperless statements, there'd have been post from the bank like a debit card and PIN. She'd have questioned why I needed a bank account when I had no money of my own and would have forced the truth from me. I'd genuinely thought the tin would be safe. Turns out nothing was safe in Tina's home.

Samantha hadn't tried to contact me. Can't say I blamed her. She probably hated me. Couldn't blame her for that either.

Darcie and I had eaten a decent meal with Rosemary so, midway through the film, I made grated cheese sandwiches for tea. She sat cross-legged on the floor while she ate, glued to the screen, captivated by a princess who looked like her. She'd only recently got into Disney princesses, expanding her love from fairies and unicorns. I wished I had some money so I could buy her a Tiana doll and a beautiful green and lemon costume. She didn't have any dressing-up clothes, which didn't seem right. When I was a little girl, I'd loved dressing up. I didn't care that they were hand-me-downs from Rosemary's granddaughter, Morgan; all I cared about was being in that magical world of make-believe. Little did I know back then that the darker side of the fairy tales I loved would become my reality and that I'd stop being my dad's Snow White and turn into a real-life Cinderella with a wicked step-mother and two ugly brothers.

'That was awesome!' Darcie cried, flinging herself onto the sofa and cuddling up to me when the film ended. 'Can we watch it again?'

I smiled down at her sparkling eyes and my worries temporarily lifted knowing I'd made a little girl very happy.

'Not tonight, Princess Tiana, but we'll watch it again soon. We need to get your stuff packed up and get you back to your house for a bath and bedtime.'

Darcie was upstairs retrieving her colouring book and felt tips when there was a knock on the door. I peeked through the curtains and spotted a police car and the same two policeman from earlier.

'We wanted to update you,' Sergeant Kinsella said when I opened the door. 'Can we come in?'

'Sure.'

I stepped back, feeling weary.

'Where's Darcie?' he asked when he sat down.

'Upstairs getting her things. We were heading round to her house for her bath and bedtime.'

'We've arrested Tina Grimes and Jenny Grimes,' the sergeant said. 'They won't be home tonight.'

My tummy did a somersault. 'Oh. Did they admit to stealing the money?'

'We can't go into any details,' PC Sunning said. 'We just wanted to let you know that neither of them will be home tonight. You're eighteen?'

'Yeah.'

'Jenny Grimes has given permission for you to look after her grand-daughter Darcie overnight, but we need to make sure you're comfortable with that.'

'It's fine. I've known her since she was a baby and, to be honest, I've spent more time looking after her than...' I stopped myself from dropping Jenny in it, although the police could probably guess where I was going with that. 'I'm used to having Darcie overnight.'

'You'll be staying at Jenny Grimes's house tonight?' PC Sunning confirmed. 'Can you confirm the address?'

'Seventeen Butler Street.' It was only a five-minute walk away.

PC Sunning scribbled it down. 'Thanks for that.'

'What would have happened if I'd refused to have Darcie? I never would, but what if I had?'

'We'd have needed to involve Social Services and she'd have gone into emergency foster care overnight.'

I pictured Darcie frightened and alone in a stranger's bedroom, clinging onto Twizzle, tears streaking her face.

'She's definitely fine with me. I'd do anything for her.' I gulped down the lump in my throat.

'I'm ready!' Darcie skipped into the lounge with her grubby pink backpack on her back and Twizzle tucked under one arm. She stopped when she saw the policemen. 'We watched *The Princess and the Frog* earlier. Have you seen it?'

The two men looked at each other and shrugged.

'You should watch it,' Darcie told them. 'It's awesome. I'm Princess Tiana but I'm not a frog because I've got a magical unicorn.'

'Magical unicorns are the best,' Sergeant Kinsella said. 'Especially pink ones with turquoise hooves like Twizzle.'

She giggled. 'You remembered his name!'

'I have to remember lots of things for my job.' He winked at her then stood up and addressed me. 'Do you have plans for tomorrow?'

Darcie beat me to it. 'Phoebe takes me to the playground after bingo day because Nanna doesn't get up until really late and she has a poorly head and shouts a lot, which is silly because shouting must make her head hurt even more.'

I gave her a gentle smile as I ruffled her hair. 'I'll be with Darcie tomorrow day and tomorrow night if needed. As I said earlier, she's like a little sister to me, aren't you Princess?'

She grinned up at me and stretched out her arms. I picked her up and kissed her cheek, wishing I could keep her forever and never send her back to Jenny.

'Could we have a private word with you?' Sergeant Kinsella asked.

I lowered Darcie onto the sofa. 'You wait here while I say goodbye to the policemen.'

She waved Twizzle at them. 'Bye!'

'Bye Darcie, bye Twizzle,' they chorused.

I closed the lounge door behind me as they both stepped outside onto the path.

'We wanted to ask how you got that bruise on your cheek and the bruises and cuts round your mouth,' Sergeant Kinsella said.

I looked down at the ground, unable to look him in the eye while I lied. 'I fell.'

'She slipped in the shower,' Darcie called through the door. That girl had amazing hearing.

'Is this true?'

'Erm, yeah, yesterday. I slipped on some shampoo and face-planted the tiles.' I still couldn't look him in the eye. My dad had always taught me to respect the police and to tell the truth. 'I'm really clumsy.'

Next moment, Darcie burst through the door. 'She is! She's always covered in bruises. Look at her arm.' Before I had a chance to react, she'd pulled up the sleeve of my long-sleeved T-shirt.

I yanked it down and looked up, hoping I'd been quick enough, but the expression of empathy in the sergeant's eyes told me I hadn't been. I nibbled on my thumbnail, dreading the line of questioning.

'I've got an idea,' he said. 'After you've been to the playground tomorrow, why don't you both come down to the police station? We can show you round and I might be able to rustle up some chocolate biscuits. What do you say, Darcie?'

'Yes, please!' She tugged on my sleeve. 'Can we, Phoebe?'

'Sure. What time?'

'Should we say eleven?'

I nodded, weariness taking hold once more. 'We'll be there.'

It was past nine and Darcie had been asleep for over an hour with Twizzle tucked under her arm. She'd asked me to tell her a story about princesses and frogs and magical unicorns and, even though my brain ached, I managed to cobble something together, which she loved.

She asked if I could stay in her room until she fell asleep. No problem. There wasn't anywhere else I'd rather be than making sure she was safe.

With the curtains drawn and her lamp switched off, the only light came from a purple unicorn-shaped nightlight, which I'd bought her for Christmas last year. When it came to Darcie's birthday and Christmas, I had to lie and say Rosemary loaned me the money for her gifts and I was going to pay her back when I got a job. I'd half-expected Tina to demand I 'borrow' more so I could buy her gifts too but she never did, probably because she didn't want to give me presents in return.

I sat with my back against her wardrobe door, slowly pushed up my left sleeve, and gazed down at my arm. Silent tears trickled down my cheeks and, when I couldn't bear the sight anymore – even in the dim light – I pulled my sleeve back down and used it to wipe my cheeks.

Someone knew now. The secret I'd kept for five long years was out. I'd kept my promise. I hadn't told anyone. But tomorrow I'd have to and I had no idea where that would lead.

From the barn window the following morning, I spotted Fizz's bright blue mini convertible coming along the farm track, closely followed by a white van. I washed my hands and left the barn to greet them.

'I felt like I was being chased,' Fizz joked as she got out of her car and the van pulled into the yard. 'Expecting a delivery?'

'No.'

'Delivery for Hedgehog Hollow Rescue Centre,' a courier said, jumping down from the driver's side.

'That's us.'

'I've got quite a few boxes. Where do you want them?'

'In the barn, please.' I caught Fizz's eye and shrugged. Josh must have ordered something and not told me.

I gasped as I watched the courier load several large cardboard boxes onto a trolley and wheel them into the entrance.

'Thanks,' I said. 'Enjoy your day.'

'I'm not finished yet. Another three loads, I think.'

'You're kidding? You're sure they're all for me?'

'They've all got the rescue centre on them.'

I darted into the barn, followed by Fizz, and ripped the first box open. It contained two forty-pouch boxes of cat food and a 2kg bag of dry kitten food. A gift receipt read:

For the hedgehogs. Belated Happy Christmas and bon appetite! From the Clarkson Family in Great Tilbury xx

I moved the box aside as the courier brought in the next trolley-load. Fizz opened another package, revealing several boxes of kitten food and a pack of disposable gloves. There was another gift receipt:

Keep up the great work! Polly Hanson, North Emmerby.

'I don't believe it!' I stared in amazement at the growing mound of boxes. 'We only put the link on Facebook on Monday night and we never breathed a word about the stolen money, but look at all this!'

Fizz looked as stunned as me.

By the time the courier left, we had twenty-two boxes of assorted sizes stacked up and it took two hours to unpack them and take photos of the goods and messages so we could thank our generous supporters.

Mick, the landlord at The Black Swan, had sent a generous donation and several other donors mentioned the pub. The Black Swan's Facebook page showed a photo of Bauble, which Mick must have taken before I arrived, and a link to our wish list encouraging the pub's followers to give generously. There were a stack of likes, shares and comments.

'That's awesome!' Fizz exclaimed as we scrolled down the feed.

'I recognise quite a few names from the deliveries. Looks like a lot of this is down to Mick. What a star.'

There was a wonderful mix of food, medicine, hand sanitiser, cleaning equipment, and medical kit like microscope slides and syringes.

'I can't get over how generous people have been after only one day,' I said. 'And especially just after Christmas. I thought everyone would be spent-up.'

'Hey! Don't cry.' Fizz rushed over to hug me.

'I can't help it. They're happy tears. I'm just so overwhelmed. First they rebuilt the barn, then we had all that support on the Family Fun Day and now this! There's so much love out there for the hedgehogs.'

I stepped back and wiped my eyes.

Fizz placed a hand on each of my shoulders. 'The love isn't just for the hedgehogs, Sam. This is for you, too. You're devoting your life to saving vulnerable animals and you've been into schools and villages educating people. You've inspired the community and this is their way of thanking you.'

'You're setting me off again!' I cried, grabbing a couple of tissues. 'Thank you.'

'Cup of tea?' she asked.

'Gosh, yes. I think we've earned it unpacking that lot.'

'And I need hear all about Bauble.'

While Fizz prepared the drinks, I flicked through the photos of the gift messages on my phone, a lump welling in my throat once more. This was why people like the Grimes family wouldn't break us. Because the world was also full of kind and generous people who cared.

18

PHOEBE

It was icy-cold on Wednesday morning, but nothing was going to keep Darcie from the playground. She squealed as I chased her upstairs and helped pull on a long-sleeved top, a jumper and a cardigan. The sleeves on them were all too short and a quick glance at the 'age four to five' label explained why. It was lucky she was so slim or she'd have been bursting out of the seams. I'd toyed so often with spending some of my tutoring earnings on clothes for Darcie, but Jenny would have noticed and demanded to know where the money came from. I felt guilty for not helping when I could have afforded to. Now it was too late and I wished I had splurged on her.

I found a Peppa Pig scarf and wrapped it round her neck. I thought she might complain that she was too old for it, but she didn't seem bothered, although she refused to wear the hat saying it dug into her head. Age three to four. No wonder. There were a pair of gloves that were too small too, but I found some larger fingerless ones, presumably Jenny's, which would give her some protection.

An overnight frost crunched under our feet as we walked to the playground. It was deserted, which wasn't surprising. Set back on the edge of the estate, it had once been sheltered by a high-rise block of flats but, after the council had them demolished, there was nothing to give protection against a biting wind that seemed to whip across the playground, even in the height of summer. My eyes and nose were already streaming and so were Darcie's.

It wasn't the most inspiring playground – a set of baby and child swings, a fairly tame slide, a witch's hat, and a dolphin and penguin on springs – but it was functional. So many names had been scratched into the once colourful metal equipment that there was virtually no paint left and one of the baby swings had been vandalised a couple of years ago and never replaced.

Darcie loved it, although I often wondered if that was because she had nothing to compare it to. I knew there were much better playgrounds round Reddfield but Jenny refused to let me take Darcie, saying it was too expensive on the bus. I'd mentioned that under-fives travelled free but got such a mouthful about arguing back that it hadn't been worth trying again, especially now that she was old enough to have to pay.

Darcie slid down the slide a few times, squealing with delight, and I giggled as she pulled silly faces at me. This was how it should be: just the two of us together having fun.

She ran over to the swings but, as I pushed her, I had the strongest sensation of being watched. I glanced over my shoulder but couldn't see anyone. There was an open green area and a row of bushes, maybe about a metre high. They'd shed their leaves but were dense in parts so, if someone was hiding behind them, I wouldn't be able to see them.

'Push me higher!'

I did as she instructed, but a shudder ran through me and I checked behind me again. Still nothing. I shook my head. I was on edge because of my appointment at the police station and not knowing when Tina and Jenny might be released. That was all.

A twig cracked and I spun round, heart thumping. A couple of birds shot from the bushes, as though someone had spooked them.

I stopped pushing. 'I think it's probably time we headed home, Princess.'

'I haven't been on the witch's hat yet. Or the bouncers. Please can we stay a bit longer?'

I'd never been able to resist those big brown eyes. 'Not much longer. It's cold.' I glanced over my shoulder again. Nothing. I hated this.

Darcie jumped off the swing and ran over to the penguin bouncer and suddenly I knew we weren't alone. I could smell the aniseed before he spoke.

'I hope you've got nowt to do with our Jen and Tina being banged up last night.'

I stiffened and sidestepped away from him, keeping my eyes fixed on Darcie. 'I don't know anything, Trigg.'

'Not what I 'eard.'

My heart raced as he stepped closer. Darcie had stopped rocking and was staring at us, frowning.

'I 'eard the filth was at Tina's place for hours yesterday,' Trigg continued.

I sidestepped away from him again and gave Darcie a reassuring wave and smile.

Trigg stepped closer. 'What've you been sayin'?'

I spun round to face him and couldn't fail to notice the smart new bomber jacket. Another purchase with Samantha's money? His greasy hair was slicked back and I could see flakes of dandruff on his shoulders.

'Nothing,' I muttered.

'Bullshit!'

He grabbed my forearm, catching me right where Tina had burned my skin.

'Get off me!'

But he tightened his grip and I gasped as the pain seared through me. I didn't want Darcie to see but she'd thankfully clambered off the rocker and had her back to me as she headed towards the slide.

'You told them your mam's been stealing money.'

'She's *not* my mam and I knew nothing about it until the police showed up. Let. Me. Go!'

He released my arm and I was about to run towards Darcie when he grabbed it again and yanked it up my back. I bit back a scream, not wanting to scare her.

'I've heard a rumour you're expected down the nick later.'

'You heard wrong.'

'Good.'

He released my arm and shoved me aside. I desperately wanted to rub it, but I refused to let him see how much he'd hurt me.

'How's your mate doin'?'

Darcie had reached the top of the slide. She waved to me and I waved back.

'What mate?'

'Old biddy. Blind. Shame if anything ever happened to her. Or her dog.' He narrowed his eyes at me and I felt the full force of his threat.

'You don't know where she lives.'

'I know everything! Laters.'

Darcie was on her way to the witch's hat now and Trigg called across to her. 'See ya later, Darc!'

She turned but she didn't respond.

'Nice kid, that one,' he hissed, nudging me hard. 'But kids can be so clumsy, falling down the stairs and shit like that.' He laughed as he thrust his hands in his pockets. 'Just sayin'.'

I shuddered from head to foot as he sauntered out of the playground, his maniacal laughter travelling back to me on the wind. He suddenly turned and shouted, 'Renleigh Court. Number one. Told you I know everything.'

I sat down heavily on the nearby bench, my legs too shaky to hold me up. The threat to Rosemary and Trixie wasn't a new one, but there'd never been a suggestion of hurting Darcie. Surely Jenny would never condone that. I hugged my arms round myself. I knew first-hand what Jenny was capable of. Would Darcie being her flesh and blood make any difference? The poor kid had no clothes that fit and was never taken anywhere except this scabby playground or the beer garden in the local pub. It didn't exactly scream caring grandparent. She was passed from one person to another and, if it wasn't for having free school meals and whatever I cooked her, I'm not convinced she'd be fed properly.

Darcie ran over to me, clambered onto the bench, and cuddled up against me. 'I'm cold. We can go home now. Can we watch *The Princess and the Frog* again?'

'If you like.'

My legs still felt shaky when I stood up but, confident that Trigg had gone, we set off.

'When are we going to the police station?' Darcie asked.

I wanted to go so badly. I wanted it all to end, but it was too risky. Even if they took Darcie into protection, what would happen to Rosemary and Trixie? I couldn't do it.

'Erm... we're not.'

'But the policeman said he'd give me some chocolate biscuits.'

'I know. I'm sorry.' I dug in the pocket of my jeans and scowled at the few coins resting in my palm. 'We'll go to the shop before we go home. I might not have enough money but, if I do, I'll get you some chocolate biscuits or some sweets. Is that okay?'

'Thank you. But if you don't have enough money to buy them, you won't take them, will you? I don't like it when Nanna does that. My teacher Miss Kelly says it's wrong to take things without paying for them.'

I stopped and crouched down beside her. 'Miss Kelly's right. Stealing's very wrong. But it's probably not a good idea to say that to your nanna.'

She nodded solemnly. 'I know. She shouts at me and says she'll rip Twizzle's tail and horn off if I ever say it again. He won't be magical if he doesn't have his horn, will he?'

'I don't know. I don't think so. Best not take that chance.'

Hand in hand, we continued in the direction of the shop.

'I don't like Trigg,' Darcie said. 'He smells funny.'

'Does he come round often?'

'Most nights. Nanna and Trigg tickle each other and she screams a lot and he makes funny sounds like a cow mooing. I don't like it. I hide under my duvet.'

'Best place to be,' I said, cringing for her. 'You know you said your nanna shouts at you? Is that all she does?'

'Sometimes she snaps my crayons or she throws my toys down the stairs then tells me off if they get broken.'

'Has she ever hurt you?'

'She hurts my arm sometimes when we walk home from school and she says I'm dawdling. I like to look at the pretty flowers or kick the leaves and she pulls me like this.'

She yanked at my arm to demonstrate, although I already had a clear picture in my head.

'Anything else?'

'No. It's a secret.'

'What's a secret?'

'What Nanna did.'

I stopped walking and crouched down beside her once more. 'You can tell me, Princess. I won't tell her you have.'

She looked around us, her eyes wide. 'Can I whisper?'

'If you want.'

She cupped her hand round her mouth and whispered in my ear. 'Nanna and Trigg were tickling each other and she made me wait in the garden but I needed a wee and they wouldn't let me in so I weed in my pants. Nanna was really angry.'

'What did she do?' I asked, the words catching in my throat as my heart thumped rapidly.

'She chased me upstairs and pulled my pants off and rubbed them in my face. They were wet and smelly and I didn't like it. I tried to run away but she pushed me towards the toilet and I slipped and broke my arm.'

Tears rushed to my eyes as I cuddled her tightly. 'You didn't fall in the bath because there were too many bubbles?'

'No. But Nanna told me I had to say that or I'd be sent to prison because I was a dirty girl who'd weed my pants.'

Her arms crept round my neck and she kissed my cheek and I knew at that moment that I had to tell the police. Darcie was only six, but she'd already been on the receiving end of a broken arm thanks to Jenny's foul temper. She'd taken that first step down a slippery slope of aggression and lack of control and I'd seen that escalate with me. I would *not* let her do that to Darcie.

I stood up and took Darcie's hand. 'You're safe with me, okay? Let's see what we can afford in the shop.'

'Ooh! There's five pence!' She bent down and picked it up off the path. 'We might be able to buy some chocolate biscuits now.'

'You little superstar. That five pence could make all the difference.'

But the thing that could make the biggest difference was me. I loved that little girl with all my heart – which was just as well because nobody else seemed to – and I'd do everything in my power to protect her. I just needed to find a way to meet with Sergeant Kinsella which didn't involve me going to the police station or him coming to the house.

'Jacket potato, beans and cheese for the beautiful Princess Tiana,' I said, putting a plate down in front of Darcie shortly after 5 p.m.

'Where's yours?'

'I'm not very hungry.'

'You didn't eat your sandwich, either.'

'Are you the food police?' I ruffled her hair. 'I had a biscuit, remember? And I might have snuck a few more when you weren't looking.'

Thanks to that five pence she'd found on the path, we just had enough money to buy a packet of chocolate digestives, but I'd struggled to eat one and keep it down. I knew if I ate anything else, I'd be sick. My tummy had been churning all day and I felt weak with worry at what might happen if and when Tina and Jenny were released.

Between mouthfuls, Darcie chattered about her teacher who she adored. I'd always hated the way Jenny and Tina zoned out of everything she said and took care to give her my undivided attention, but I couldn't help drifting off myself today. My eyes flicked from the clock on the kitchen wall to the door to my phone. It had been more than twenty-four hours now. Wasn't that the maximum time someone could be held? The police would need to charge Jenny and Tina or release them. *Please let them be charged.*

'I've had plenty,' Darcie said, pushing her plate aside. 'It was very yummy. Thank you.'

I was about to reach for her plate when a key turning in the front door froze me to the spot. Oh, God! Jenny was back.

There was a bang followed by a giggle and squelchy sounds like people kissing.

'Shouldn't have had that last drink,' Jenny slurred. 'I'm so pissed right now.'

'Does that mean we can—?'

'Nanna!' Darcie cried, jumping down from her chair and running through the lounge, saving us from whatever Trigg had been about to say. Something gross, no doubt.

'You're here! I thought you'd be at Tina's.' Jenny's tone was full of disgust and her lip curled as she looked down at Darcie, cuddling against her leg. She obviously wasn't pleased to see her granddaughter, although that wasn't surprising as her priority on release had been to get hammered and to hook up with Trigg.

Jenny looked over at me as I hovered in the doorway between the kitchen and the lounge, not daring to speak in case I said the wrong thing or choose the wrong tone of voice. Jenny didn't speak either. She swayed on the spot, swatted Darcie away, muttering something about sticky fingers, but her eyes didn't stop boring into me.

'You're home, then?' I cringed at making such as obvious statement when I couldn't bear the silence any longer.

'No thanks to you.'

'I didn't do anything.'

'No. You never do. Little Miss Bloody Perfect, aren't ya?'

'Is Tina home too?'

'Yep. And there's steam coming out of her ears. So go on. Piss off and let her deal with you. As for you...' She scowled down at Darcie. 'Bed!'

'But it's really early.'

'Are you arguing with me, young madam?'

She raised her hand. I thought for a moment that she was going to hit Darcie and prepared to sprint across the room to stop her, but she pulled a bobble out of her hair instead and shook it loose. 'Urgh. I stink of that bloody police cell.'

'You smell good to me, babe,' Trigg said, looking her up and down.

She pouted at him. Urgh!

'You still here?' she snapped at Darcie.

'Can I just...?' She glanced towards the kitchen and I knew what she wanted: Twizzle.

'No, you can't! Upstairs. Now!'

I caught Darcie's eye and gave her a subtle thumbs-up then indicated with a flick of my head that she'd better do as she was told and get upstairs.

'Do you want me to wash up before I go?'

'No! Just get out! I've got stuff to do.'

'Are you calling me "stuff"?' Trigg pushed her down onto the sofa and lay on top of her. Seriously? I hadn't even left the house. Her granddaughter had just this second gone upstairs. The pair of them were disgusting.

I pulled on my denim jacket and draped my coat over my arm, covering Twizzle. Grabbing my bag, I grimaced as I shuffled past the sofa, trying to avert my gaze from the grinding. But that meant I didn't see Trigg reach out. I squealed as he grabbed my arm.

'No filth today, I hear. Let's keep it that way. Or you know what'll 'appen.'

I yanked my arm free and closed the lounge door behind me, hoping it would muffle some of the sound for Darcie.

Darcie was sitting at the top of the stairs. I held my forefinger to my mouth. 'Shhh.'

She nodded then smiled as I produced Twizzle from under my coat. I beckoned her to me but mouthed the word 'quiet'. She crept down the stairs, retrieved Twizzle, and hurled herself at me, wrapping her arms round my neck and her legs round my waist like a koala.

'Promise me you'll go to bed,' I whispered.

'I'm not tired yet,' she whispered back.

'It doesn't matter. You don't have to go to sleep. Just get ready for bed and stay there. Please.'

'Okay.' She kissed my cheek then scampered back up the stairs clinging onto her unicorn.

'See you soon,' I mouthed as I waved to her before turning and reluctantly leaving Darcie alone with her criminal of a nanna who clearly didn't care. She hadn't even said hello to her. I hoped Darcie understood the severity of the situation and stayed in her bedroom all evening. I wasn't going to sleep tonight for worrying about her.

* * *

It was only a five-minute walk back to Tina's but I was in no rush to see her, especially after Jenny's heads-up. I walked as slowly as I could, taking detours up side streets to prolong the journey but my cheeks were numb with cold and I could barely feel my feet after only fifteen minutes. I was going to have to suck it up.

I stood on the path under the lamp post looking up at 31 Trench Street. The lounge curtains were drawn but there was a strip of light showing where they hadn't been pulled together. And my bedroom light was on. My heart sank. I definitely hadn't left it on when I left the house yesterday, which could only mean one thing. Tina was either in my room or she had been. What did she want? She'd already taken my mum's rings and all my money.

I tugged my turquoise beanie further down over my ears in a desperate bid to warm up while I psyched myself up to go inside. Suddenly Tina appeared at my bedroom window and sneered as she spotted me.

I turned my key in the lock and pushed open the door but the chain was on and the door only opened about five centimetres.

'Tina!' I called. 'The chain's on.'

'I know!' she yelled down the stairs.

'Can you take it off so I can come in?'

'No!'

I heard the sound of her running down the stairs, then jumped back as her flushed face appeared between the narrow gap.

'Bet you were hoping we'd get charged. Well, we didn't. They let us go.'

'But what about the money?'

'A gift from the hedgehog lady as compensation for stealing our family's farm.'

'They believed that?'

'Our word against hers.'

I wanted to accuse her of lying, but I knew better than that. 'Can I come in?'

'No. Spoilt brats who dob on their families to the pigs don't deserve a warm bed for the night.' She shivered. 'It's a bitter one, too. Shame, that.'

She slammed the door shut.

'Tina!' I banged on the door.

'Sod off!'

'Where am I supposed to go?'

'Don't know and don't care. I've put up with your shit for years and I've had enough. You're not my problem anymore. You can come back and collect your crap tomorrow but, for tonight, you're on your own.'

'But it's freezing. Can I get some more clothes?'

'I'll throw you some down.'

Moments later, my bedroom window opened. 'Here!'

I caught the bundle she tossed at me and opened it out. It was what was left of my favourite navy blue hoodie; a Christmas gift from Rosemary a year ago. The hood part was dangling from a couple of centimetres of material, a chunk of one of the sleeves had been cut off, and the torso had been cut into shreds.

'As you can probably imagine, Jenny and I were pretty pissed off when we got out of that cell. She went to the pub to release her frustration and I found another way to relieve mine.'

'You've destroyed all my things?'

'Not yet, but that was a lot of hours banged up. I might feel frustrated again later and need to release my anger.'

When Tina waved, I realised we were being watched by several neighbours, hanging out of their windows or standing on their drives. I wanted the ground to swallow me whole.

'Bit of excitement for you tonight,' Tina continued, raising her voice to play to her audience. 'Wondering if you'll have any possessions left intact by the morning. You can come back tomorrow at eleven when I've gone out. Not a minute sooner.'

There was no point fighting her. I'd rather she take out her anger on my belongings than me. I turned to leave.

'Oh! Phoebe!' she called. 'If you go to the pigs, we'll know. If you turn up at that blind old bat's place, we'll know. I hope you've got some good mates.' With a cackle, she slammed the window shut.

Good mates? Nope. None. We'd drifted apart during the final couple of years at school. When I started college, I didn't have the confidence to make new friends and what was the point if I had? I couldn't offer them anything. I had nothing interesting to talk about, I had no time to go out with them, and there was no way I could invite anyone round to Tina's.

I stuffed my shredded hoodie into my backpack and shivered as I pulled my zip right to the top of my coat. There was only one place I could think of to go. It would still be freezing cold, but there'd be no biting wind and it would be dry but I was going to have to wait until much later before I could go there.

* * *

Shortly after midnight, I sidled alongside the garages at Renleigh Court and cautiously opened Rosemary's. If someone was watching, they couldn't accuse me of disobeying Tina's orders. This wasn't staying with Rosemary in a warm, cosy flat.

I cautiously lifted the garage door, grateful it was squeak-free, slipped inside, and lowered it. I activated the torch on my phone and shone it around, searching for anything that might give warmth and comfort.

I opened out the wooden table, placed my backpack in the middle of it, and opened both the chairs. I could sit on one and put my feet up on the other.

The metal shelves at the far end of the garage contained a random mix of things – a toolbox, a box of crime paperbacks and sudoku puzzles, and a badminton racket – that Rosemary had no use for anymore. Sighing, I removed a large orange bucket. That was going to have to be my makeshift toilet. I'd managed to slip into the toilets in a pub earlier, feeling paranoid that I'd get caught and be ordered to buy a drink for using their facilities. I'd have happily bought several drinks and stayed where it was warm if I'd had any money but I had 2p to my name, so I'd walked miles round the streets of Reddfield instead, growing steadily colder and more weary.

I'd stopped at one point, shed my coat and denim jacket, and pulled on my shredded hoodie. There was enough material remaining to give me a bit of extra warmth. And warmth was what I needed right now. I could see a couple of electric fans but no heater. Maybe just as well. With my luck, if there'd been a heater, I'd probably burn the garage down or get carbon monoxide poisoning.

I found a couple of dust sheets in a carrier bag. They were stiff with splodges of paint but, folded over, they'd give me some protection.

I shuffled the table and chairs closer to the double electric point on the wall and unplugged my moped. I switched on the laptop I had on loan from college, which I always kept with me for fear of my step-family flogging it. It was old and battered and probably not worth anything, but I swear Tina would sell her granny for a bag of weed. Using the dim light emitting from the screen, I plugged in the laptop and phone chargers.

Tina had probably destroyed all my stuff by now, leaving me with only the clothes I was wearing and the contents of my backpack but, aside from Mum's rings, I still had the most important stuff. The hard drive on the laptop held all my college work along with scans of photos from my childhood and Mum and Dad's wedding photos. They were also sent to two different email accounts, stored in a Dropbox, in the cloud and on a USB. The latter was hidden in a freezer bag, taped behind the shelves at the back of the garage for safekeeping, along with a Pandora bracelet that Rosemary had given me for my sixteenth birthday. Tina wasn't going to take away my memories or my future.

I set the photo album on my laptop to scroll and settled back in the chair with the dust sheets folded over me. Tears trickled down my cheeks as I watched. Dad and I hadn't had much, but my childhood had been happy. We did things together that cost nothing like autumn walks through the park, kicking the leaves, and hours spent at the playground near the flats.

As my eyes grew heavy and exhaustion took me, the last thing on my mind was Darcie and how much she'd missed out on. Jenny never took her anywhere and Hayley would have done her best, but she'd developed severe agoraphobia and couldn't leave the house. So it was all down to me.

I should have done more. I *would* do more. I'd defy Jenny and take Darcie to the big adventure playground, even if it meant piggybacking her across town because I had no bus fare. I'd endure the beatings if it meant that little girl enjoyed her childhood. I got them anyway. Might as well get them for a good reason.

At least Darcie was warm tonight. I just hoped she was safe.

When I looked out the bedroom early on Thursday morning – New Year's Eve – I thought it had snowed but, when Josh and I wandered over to the barn at 6.15 a.m., it became apparent it was a heavy frost.

'It's freezing,' I said, my breath hanging in the air like a cloud.

He put his arm round my waist as we crunched our way over to the barn. 'Don't think about it.'

'Think about what?'

'I know you too well. You're thinking about all the autumn juveniles out in the wild in these temperatures and worrying if they've survived the night.'

'I can't help it. I wish we could save them all, but I know that's impossible.'

'I know it's hard to let it go, but you have to. There are nearly sixty autumn juveniles currently snug in their crates in the barn. None of them would have survived if you hadn't set this place up, and most of them wouldn't have been admitted if it hadn't been for your Bed Hogs campaign.'

We reached the barn door and I hugged Josh before I unlocked it. 'Thanks for always knowing what to say. I know it's silly to worry.'

He cupped my chin and gently kissed me. 'It's not silly. It's caring.'

It would have been a beautiful moment, but we were both shivering so I bundled us inside, relishing the warmth of the barn.

Our morning routine was always the same – an hour in the barn before breakfast, cleaning out the crates and laying down fresh news-paper and fleecy blankets, cleaning the food bowls, checking the weights of the hogs, and issuing any medication. If there'd been any new admissions the day before, checking on them would be the priority.

Mistletoe had arrived yesterday in a bad way after a dog walker found her tangled in some chicken wire which had been dumped in a field along with a fridge, mattress and an old lawnmower. It was surprising that she hadn't severed a limb trying to escape but she had some nasty infected cuts and abrasions as well as being dehydrated and hungry.

I was aware of Josh watching me as I tentatively opened Mistletoe's crate, releasing the breath I'd been holding when she moved. After eight months running the rescue centre, I still felt a frisson of nerves as I checked the crates, worried that we might have lost a hedgehog during the night. The most recent admissions usually made me the most nervous and I always psyched myself up for a really ill admission not making it through to morning, but nothing prepared me for the shock of losing a hedgehog I'd have said was healthy and ready for release.

'You can talk to me any time it's getting to you, you know,' Josh said as we worked. 'Never worry about saying the same thing. It's better to keep repeating the conversation than bottling it up.'

'Thank you. I really appreciate it.'

'I wish I could save every animal that comes into the practice. Losing an animal on the operating table or euthanising one never gets any easier. Did I tell you I cried after the first dozen or so who died?'

I stopped what I was doing, tears pricking my eyes at the thought of him being upset. 'No. Aw, Josh.'

'It was a combination of letting go of a beautiful animal and seeing the client so heartbroken, but Dad was there for me. I'll never forget

what he said to me: *The day I don't feel anything is the day I need to retire.*
Vets, doctors, nurses, badass hedgehog rescuers, we all do what we do
because we care, but that means we feel and we worry. It's about
finding a balance and, for the sake of our mental health, celebrating
every patient we make better or save, and not dwelling on those we
can't. And here's someone who's looking so much better.' He held up
Figgy. 'He's looking a lot more rounded today. Let's see what you weigh,
little fella.'

Figgy had already gained several grams and had lost that awful,
emaciated appearance in the space of a few days. Josh was right about
celebrating what we could do and Figgy was a case in point. He
wouldn't have made it to the New Year without our help, and the
woman who'd found him wouldn't have brought him in without my
Bed Hogs campaign in the village newsletter. Everything we did really
did matter.

* * *

'Last day of the year,' Josh said, as we settled at the kitchen table a little
later with bowls of cereal. 'Will you be glad to see the back of it?'

I pondered for a moment. 'I'm not sure. Like most years, there've
been ups and downs, but they've been more extreme.'

'And, of course, the highest high was meeting me.'

'Oh, I'm not so sure about that. Meeting you was one of the low
points. As was meeting you the second time. And the third and fourth.'
I blew him a kiss across the table. 'But the fifth time I saw the real you
and fell in love. That was a definite high. Although you nearly messed
it up by running out and leaving twenty pounds on the table.'

Josh's cheeks coloured and he scrunched up his face. 'I'm beginning
to wish I hadn't started this conversation. Can we please forget about
the twenty pounds for services rendered disaster?'

'Nah! It's a great story. One to tell our kids.'

His expression softened. 'What did you just say?'

'One to tell...' I clapped my hand to my chest, my eyes wide as I registered my words. 'Oh, my gosh! That just came out.'

'And how do you feel saying it?'

'Okay. It felt natural.'

'No anxiety?'

'Not this time.'

Josh rushed round to my side of the table, hugged me and tenderly kissed me. We'd had a moment over the summer when I'd thought I didn't want children and was worried I might lose Josh if he did. The concern came from the difficult relationship I had with my mum and fear of projecting that onto my own children. I knew it was irrational, but that fear was part of me and wasn't going to simply vanish. Josh insisted he loved me and chose to be with me, no matter what decision I made about parenthood.

'Do you think the counselling is helping?' he asked, returning to his chair.

'Definitely. Making some progress with Mum in the summer helped too, although I'm starting to think that was simply a moment in time when she needed someone on her side and I was the only person around.'

'It was more than that, Sammie. She was proud of you.'

I shrugged. 'I thought so too, but I haven't seen her since. We haven't spoken. Although she made my birthday and Christmas gifts. That has to mean something.'

Her Christmas gift was a vintage-style necklace with embroidered wildflowers on the pendant, all of which I recognised as flowers that grew in our meadow – perfect for wearing with Gwendoline's dresses.

'I agree. You don't spend hours embroidering gifts for someone you don't care about. It's going to take time and patience, but you've got that in spades. One of the gazillion reasons I love you so much.'

He finished the last of his cereal and put the bowl into the dishwasher. 'I'd best head to work and see how Bauble's doing. I'll bring him home tonight and he can join the other hedgehogs for their New Year's Eve party. Or should that be their Hogmanay?'

'No!' I started giggling. 'You did *not* just say that.'

'I can't believe we haven't thought of it before now.'

'We? Don't involve me in it. You're not even a dad yet and you're already rolling with the bad dad jokes.'

'Not even a dad yet,' he repeated. 'You've just done it again.'

I grinned at him. 'No anxiety. Thanks to a brilliant counsellor, a great therapist, and the most amazing fiancé who has never put any pressure on me.'

'And I never will. If we have children at some point in the future, it has to 100 per cent feel right for you. If it's 99.9 per cent, we don't do it and the only babies we look after are the spiky ones in the barn.'

We kissed, slowly and tenderly, only pulling apart when we heard Beth coming down the stairs with Archie, encouraging him with each step.

'I'm not ready to try for a family immediately,' I said, 'but I'm not averse to seeing the New Year in with a bit of practice.'

'I think we should cancel the party after all.'

Laughing, I kissed him again.

'Ooh, are we interrupting?' Beth said, coming into the kitchen with Archie.

'No. I've got to get to work.' Josh grabbed his packed lunch, bid us goodbye, and left.

'It's good to see you two smiling,' Beth said when the front door closed.

'It's been a tough few days, but we can't change what's happened so we just have to make the most of it.'

'That was how Paul viewed things with his cancer diagnosis, especially after the treatment didn't work. We couldn't change it, but we could make the most of the time we had together.'

'How is he? I'm sorry I've barely seen you since the theft.'

'He's doing well. He's having a lie-in today because he's determined to see the New Year in, eager to send this year packing.'

'I'm not surprised. I bet you are, too.'

She placed a wriggling Archie in his highchair. 'I'll be glad to put the cancer stuff behind us because that's been tough, and my fall didn't help. But we had Lottie, Paul reconnected with Josh, and we've got you, so lots of light in the darkness.'

'Here's hoping there'll be fewer dark things next year because I'm—'

A cry from upstairs interrupted me. 'You see to Lottie. I'll sort Archie's breakfast.'

Thanking me, she ran up the stairs and I smiled at Archie.

'What's your hair doing today?' His dark hair was sticking up in the middle. As I smoothed it down, a feeling of contentment flowing through me. I spent so much time helping out with Archie and Lottie but I'd never imagined how it might feel if I was a mother doing this with my own babies until now. The idea definitely didn't fill me with fear like it had in the summer or even a few months ago.

I loved hearing Beth's children laugh and didn't even mind them crying because it made the house feel alive. I adored the moments when Archie chattered incessantly and the joy at recognising maybe one word in twenty. It was fun playing with them in the bath and reading them stories occasionally.

One day in the not too distant future, Paul would be fit and well enough to leave. Josh hadn't said anything to his dad yet, but he'd arranged for Dave to project-manage the refurbishment of Alder Lea – the house at the veterinary practice – starting next month, with the intention of offering it to the family. Whether they accepted his offer or not, they'd be moving on eventually and the farmhouse was going to feel empty without them. It had already proved itself to be the ideal family home that Thomas and Gwendoline had anticipated, and I couldn't imagine there only being Josh and me living here.

* * *

Over in the barn, I opened my laptop and checked for reactions on social media. Bauble had generated more comments, likes and shares than any other post. I'd only uploaded a couple of photos so far, but I'd taken a video of him before he was deflated. I'd film another once he was healed and share them together, as before and after pictures were more powerful in conveying the difference a rescue centre could make.

After responding to comments, I checked my emails and my stomach did a backflip when I spotted one from Phoebe with the subject line of 'sorry'.

To: Hedgehog Hollow Rescue Centre
From: Phoebe Corbyn
Subject: Sorry
Hi Samantha
I could say sorry a million times and it wouldn't be enough but I am really, truly sorry for what my stepfamily have done to you. I didn't steal the money. I didn't know anything about it until the police turned up but I know it's my fault. I should have told you who I was but I was scared you wouldn't let me do the accounts if I did and I really wanted the work experience so I could get a good job and move out.
I didn't tell Tina I was working at Hedgehog Hollow and I still don't know how she found out. I want you to know that I didn't leave the cheque book lying around. It was locked in a tin and hidden under a floorboard and I had the only key. I'm so sorry but I thought it was safe.
I know there's no way you'll want me to work with you again but I need to get your receipts and a few other bits back to you. Do you want me to drop them off or would you like me to post them? If you want me to post them, can I wait until I get back to college as I don't have any stamps or envelopes left and I don't have any money to buy more?
I'd have given you my savings and sold my mum's wedding and engagement rings but they were in the tin with the cheque book and everything's gone. Sorry.
I don't expect you to ever forgive me. When I get a job, I promise I **WILL** pay you back. I'm really sorry but it might take a long time.
Sorry again.
Phoebe

My heart broke for Phoebe as I read through her email a couple more times. How many times could she write 'sorry' in the space of a few hundred words? She did the same when speaking. I'd already heard from the police that she hadn't been involved, which had been immensely reassuring, but it was good to hear it from her too and I appreciated her recognising that she might not have stolen the money, but she had enabled it by hiding her Grimes connection.

'What's got you so engrossed?'

I hadn't even heard Fizz arrive. 'I wasn't expecting to see you today. I thought you were going bowling with your friends.'

'They all cried off for various reasons but it's all good as I'm rubbish at ten-pin bowling and didn't want to go anyway. What are you looking at?'

'Email from Phoebe.'

She joined me at the table and read over my shoulder as she unwound a colourful chunky hand-knitted scarf.

'Obviously I'm not going to take a penny from her and it sounds like she's flat broke anyway. She didn't take the money so she can't be expected to repay any of it. What I need to decide is whether my message is something along the lines of apology accepted, line in the sand, post my stuff back when college returns, or whether I ask her to come to the farm. I wouldn't have thought she'd want to see me, but the fact that she's given that as an option – and offered it before mentioning posting my things back – makes me wonder if that's what she really wants.'

Fizz plonked herself down on the chair adjacent to mine. 'You could be right. She says she doesn't expect your forgiveness, but maybe she'd like it and coming to the farm is a way of getting that. She knows how lovely you are. She knows you're not going to tear a strip off her. How about a cuppa while you decide?'

'You read my mind.'

I rubbed my forehead, trying to work out what was best for me in this situation. I'd been told so often that I always put others first and should be kinder to myself. In this case, seeing her was probably best for Phoebe but I suspected it was also the best thing for me. It wasn't in my nature to dismiss her with a you're-not-forgiven message, especially when she wasn't the thief. I did feel wary about seeing her again, but she was only eighteen and she'd recognised her mistake. If I said no to the chance to meet, it would probably cause me more pain worrying about the impact that would have on her than any discomfort I'd be caused by seeing her again.

'I'm going to ask her to come to the farm,' I said when Fizz handed me a mug of tea. 'It'll have taken guts to write that email. Look at the time stamp. She sent it at 2.17 this morning so she was wide awake in the early hours thinking about it. I need to let her explain and we'll take it from there.'

'Sounds like the right decision to me. I don't think you'd forgive yourself if you didn't do that.'

'That's what I was thinking.' I glanced at the email again. 'I hate that bit about her savings and her mum's rings. Was twenty-nine grand not enough for them?'

Fizz slurped on her tea. 'I've heard too many tales from Dad over the years not to know how low people can stoop. Probably one of the reasons why I wanted to work with animals instead. Speaking of my dad, have you had an update?'

'Not since they were arrested, so I have no idea if they've been charged or released.'

'He'll be across later to help Mum set up for the party. He'll probably update you then.'

'I have this horrible gut feeling it's going to be bad news, they don't have enough to charge them, and I'm going to have to go through the civil courts if I want to pursue it.'

'Would you do that?'

'I don't know that it's worth it. If I lose, there's court fees to pay and they don't come cheap. It's like flushing another few grand down the toilet and that's money we don't have. If I win, what happens? Likelihood is they've spent it already and, even if that's on assets, they won't fetch much if sold. Imagine all that stress and time for a payment plan of a tenner a month.'

'I hear you.' Fizz took her mug over to the crates so she could meet Mistletoe while I typed in a response to Phoebe. It took me about forty minutes of playing with the wording, with some helpful suggestions from Fizz, before I felt like I had the tone right.

To: Phoebe Corbyn
From: Hedgehog Hollow Rescue Centre
Subject: RE: Sorry
Hi Phoebe
Thanks for your email. I know it will have taken guts to write and send it. The police advised me you weren't involved, which is what my instinct had already told me.
You're right that you should have let me know about your connection to the Grimes family, but there was no way you could have predicted what would happen, especially when you believed your stepfamily didn't know you were volunteering here.
I think it would be good for both of us if you did come to the farm and we can talk it through. It's the New Year's Eve party tonight so I'm tied up getting ready for that today. Tomorrow I'll be up early to see to the hogs. There'll be some family staying but I don't have any firm plans other than tidying up after the party so you're welcome to come over tomorrow or at the weekend if you prefer.
Best wishes
Samantha

I rolled my stiff shoulders after I sent it. 'Ball's in her court now. Hopefully she won't chicken out and post my things back to me instead.'

'I don't think she will. If that was her plan, she wouldn't have sent the email. She might come across as nervous and apologetic, but I think our Phoebe is made of strong stuff when it comes to what's right and what's wrong.'

'Unlike her stepfamily.'

21

My bones ached as I wandered aimlessly round Reddfield after my night in Rosemary's garage. I hadn't known bones could ache. A combination of the cold and trying to sleep on a hard wooden chair had taken its toll.

I'd slept a little, exhaustion finally taking me, and was packed up and out of there by six before people were up and about. At some point in the early hours, I'd concluded that whoever was making sure I didn't stay with Rosemary couldn't live in Renleigh Court because, if they did, they'd have seen me with my moped, they'd have reported back, the garage would have been broken into, and my prize possession would have been long gone. Of course, it was possible that the being watched thing was only to scare me, but I'd never forgive myself if I was complacent and something happened to Rosemary or Trixie.

Digging my phone out of my pocket, I glanced at the time. I felt like I'd been walking for hours but it was only 7.02 a.m. I should have guessed from the darkness. I had four long hours still to kill before I could return to Trench Street and see if any of my belongings had survived the night. No way was I going to turn up even a minute before eleven and face Tina's wrath for ignoring her instructions.

In the centre of town, I passed a bakery and the smell of fresh bread and croissants made me feel light-headed with hunger. My tummy was so empty it hurt. I wished I'd eaten more than half a digestive yesterday. I paused by the window, saliva filling my mouth as I watched a woman with dark hair pulled back into a bun placing pastry-laden trays on a sloped shelf in the window. She wore a pale lemon dress with a brown tabard over it. I squinted my eyes to read the name on her badge. Carolyn. Same as my mum. Carolyn Eloise Corbyn was such a pretty name.

Bakery Carolyn looked up and gave me a smile so full of warmth that tears rushed to my eyes. If a complete stranger could look at me like that, why couldn't the people who were meant to be my family?

My tummy released a loud gurgle. I needed to stop torturing myself. Readjusting my backpack, I set off down the precinct.

'Hey, honey!'

I turned at the woman's voice. Bakery Carolyn was standing in the doorway, smiling. I looked around me to see whether she was calling to someone else.

She laughed lightly. 'Yes, you in the turquoise hat. Come here.' Her voice was as warm as her smile so I took a few steps closer.

'Are you hungry?'

I nodded. 'But I haven't got any money.' I reached into my pocket and produced the two pence coin. 'Just this.'

'Aw, honey, I don't want your money. You sit on that bench for a moment and I'll be right back.'

I sank down onto the green bench opposite the bakery but the icy-cold metal made me gasp and I leapt up and perched on the edge instead with my backpack on the pavement between my feet.

Carolyn emerged from the bakery with a brown paper carrier bag in one hand and a large takeaway cup in the other.

The bag felt heavy. 'This is all for me?'

'A few samples for you to try with your cup of tea.'

I peered inside the bag and could see at least four separate paper bags. 'Thank you. That's really kind.'

'You're welcome. Ooh, customer.'

I looked up as a huge, bearded man clad in biker leathers entered the bakery.

'Enjoy your food, honey.' With another beaming smile, she followed the man.

'Carolyn,' I called.

'Yes?'

'Do you have a charity box?'

'Yes. It's for a local children's charity.'

I held out the two pence. 'Could you put this in it? I know it's not much, but...' I shrugged.

Her eyes sparkled and she swallowed as she took the coin. 'Thank you. When you don't have anything, every penny can make a difference.' She smiled at me again then disappeared into the shop.

Even though I was desperate to devour whatever she'd given me, I felt uncomfortable about sitting outside the bakery while I did that, so I headed down a leafy side street where I found a wooden bench in front of a church. It was covered in frost, so I perched again as I opened the bag. The smell of fresh pastry was overpowering and I could almost taste it before I'd even removed the croissant from the bag.

Not knowing where my next meal might come from, I tried to eat slowly and savour every mouthful, but it was so warm and fluffy and buttery that it was gone in no time. There was a pain au chocolat, some sort of pasty – cheese by the smell of it – a ham and salad baguette, and a piece of flapjack. At the bottom was a bottle of water.

I raised the pain au chocolat to my mouth then stopped and dropped it back in the bag. Tina had kicked me out and had stolen my savings so I might need that tomorrow.

I carefully arranged the food in my backpack, taking care not to squash anything. Tea in hand, I set off on another aimless wander as the sky gradually lightened and the day began.

* * *

At ten past eleven, I stood in front of Tina's house. The lounge curtains were drawn and I couldn't see any lights on upstairs.

I placed my key in the lock and heaved a sigh of relief when it turned. I wouldn't have put it past Tina to have changed the locks. I gently pushed the door open, relieved that she hadn't done the trick with the chain either.

Her thick new coat was gone from the pegs by the door so hopefully she had gone out like she'd said. Best get upstairs and assess the damage.

I'd only just put my foot on the first stair when I froze. The television was on in the lounge. Heart thudding, I slowly opened the door, willing it to have been left on by mistake because I couldn't face Tina. I just wanted to get what was left of my stuff and leave.

'Hi, Phoebe.'

'Darcie!' She was curled up on the sofa wearing her pyjamas, with a grubby-looking cream blanket over her legs.

'Will you watch TV with me and Twizzle?'

'Where's your nanna and Great-Aunt Tina?'

'Gone.'

'Gone where?'

She shrugged. 'They put a letter on the table.'

'For me?'

'Yes. Can I have some juice, please? Nanna said you'd give me some, but I've been waiting for ages and I'm really thirsty.'

'Yeah, sure.' I glanced round the room, frowning. 'You're sure they're not here?'

'A taxi came and they had suitcases.'

'Shit!'

Darcie giggled. 'You said a naughty word.'

'Yeah, I'm sorry. Forget I said it! Sorry. I'm just...' I couldn't even formulate a sentence. Had they done a flit?

I dashed into the kitchen and immediately spotted the 'letter' – a piece of cardboard ripped off a cereal box covered in Tina's almost incoherent scrawl.

Phebe

Off to Carrybeen for new year. You can stay here with Darc til we get back but then your gone, spoilt bratt. Have fun. Or dont. Like we care! Lol

The letter might be littered with typos – and she still hadn't learned how to spell my name, although I suspected she did that deliberately to wind me up – but every word was clear to me. They'd gone on holiday with the money stolen from Hedgehog Hollow and left Darcie behind. And if they'd gone to the Caribbean, we weren't talking for a long weekend. A week? Fortnight?

'Can you put the TV on mute for a minute, Princess?' I asked Darcie.

'Did you get my juice?'

'Sorry. Not yet. I'll do that in a second, but I need to ask you a few things first. Did they say they were leaving for their holidays?'

'Yes. They had big suitcases and I thought I was going but they said I can't 'cause I don't have a pass...' She scrunched up her face. 'I can't remember the word.'

'Passport. Did they say how long they'd be?'

She shook her head.

'Did they say if they'd be back before you return to school?'

When that was met with a shrug, I asked, 'What about your birthday? Will they be back for that?' Darcie would turn seven on 12th January.

'No. They said they'd be back after my birthday.'

'Are you sure?'

'Yes, because I cried and Nanna shouted at me and so did Great-Aunt Tina. Nanna threw Twizzle outside and said she'd stamp on her if I didn't stop making so much noise and waking the neighbours which was silly because they were shouting louder than I was crying.'

Her words jolted me. 'You said waking the neighbours. So what time was this?'

'I dunno. Really early. Nanna woke me up and there weren't any lights on in the houses when we walked here.'

'Was it still dark when they left? Proper dark like night-time?'

'Yes. It was still bedtime. They said I could sleep on the sofa but I didn't have my unicorn light and Great-Aunt Tina said I could leave the big light on but it was too bright and they told me to stop making a fuss. Nanna put the kitchen light on and left the door open a bit so I wasn't scared.'

'And then they left you alone?'

'Yes, but I wasn't scared because the light was on and they said you'd be back soon to look after me.'

It had been dark when I looked in the bakery window just after seven and had only just started to get lighter by the time I'd finished my croissant, which meant they'd definitely left her alone since at least seven.

'The little hand on the clock was nearly at the two and the big hand was at the number ten,' Darcie added. 'Can I have my juice now? I'm so thirsty.'

I cuddled her to my side and kissed the top of her head. 'Of course you can, Princess. I'll get you it now.'

In the kitchen, I rested my hands on the worktop and took a few deep gulps. This was too much. They'd left a six-year-old all alone in an empty house on a rough estate since 1.50 a.m. when they had no way of knowing whether I'd turn up at eleven, three, midnight or at all. What sort of irresponsible monsters were they?

I poured Darcie some juice then made toast with jam when she said she hadn't eaten either. While she tucked in, I dug out my phone and searched for the number for the local police station. I couldn't go down there and I couldn't risk the police coming to the house in case they were seen, but there was no way I wasn't reporting this. If the police couldn't do Tina and Jenny for theft, neglect was worth a try.

My mind whirred as I waited for the call to be answered. Darcie had mentioned the Dominican Republic a few days ago, so presumably that's where they'd gone. I'd bet my life that they were on a plane right now, well into their flight, knowing that I wouldn't dare come to the house before eleven and wouldn't discover what they'd done until it was too late.

'Reddfield Police Station,' a man said. 'How may I help?'

'Can I speak to Sergeant Kinsella please?'

'He's not available today. Can anyone else help?'

'Is PC Sunning in?'

'Just a moment.'

I picked some dirt out of my nails when the line went silent. I felt grubby and longed for a bath, but this was more important.

'Hello, sorry about the wait. He's in the station, but I can't track him down at the moment. Can I ask him to call you back?'

'No, it's okay. I'll try again later. Thank you.'

I hung up. It wasn't worth leaving a message. What if Trigg had friends at the station?

'Did they say anything about money for food?' I asked Darcie.

'I don't think so.'

'Did your nanna bring a suitcase with your stuff in it?'

'Yeah. It's over there.' She pointed to a scruffy navy suitcase in the corner of the room. 'That's why I thought I was going on holiday but it was so I could stay here with you.'

I held my breath as I lay the suitcase flat and unzipped it. *Please let there be some money in there.* I nearly squealed with excitement when the first thing I saw was an envelope with the word 'FOOD' written on it in capital letters. But the excitement was short-lived. Twenty quid. How was I supposed to feed us both for a fortnight with twenty quid? Although the money wouldn't have been meant for me; just Darcie. Even twenty quid just for her would be a struggle.

Returning to the kitchen, I checked the table, the worktops, the breadbin, the fridge magnets – anywhere I could think where Tina might have left some money for me – but there was nothing. I bet the pair of them had laughed their heads off about letting me starve.

I flung open the cupboard doors where we kept the tins. I could see baked beans, spaghetti, ravioli and soup so all wasn't lost. There were also a couple of bags of dried pasta.

'What's your favourite meal at the moment?' I called to Darcie. I crossed my fingers it hadn't changed.

'Pasta,' she called back. 'With lots of cheese.'

Phew! I'd likely empty Tina's cupboards over the next couple of weeks and probably Jenny's too, but what did they expect? Darcie got free school meals so at least she'd get something filling and healthy from Tuesday.

I checked the fridge. No cheese.

'Darcie, can you pull some clothes on and brush your teeth, please? We need to go to the supermarket.'

It was only when we left the house ten minutes later that I realised I'd been so preoccupied with trying to work out what we could eat that I hadn't even been up to my bedroom to see what Tina had trashed. A lovely treat to look forward to after our budget shopping trip.

'My dad's here,' Fizz said after we'd eaten lunch in the barn.

I peered out of the window as Sergeant Kinsella exited a shiny black 4x4 wearing jeans and a sweater. I'd never seen him out of uniform. My stomach lurched as he strode across the farmyard. *Please let there be good news!*

While Fizz put the kettle on, I welcomed him at the door. 'Sergeant Kinsella. Good to see you.'

'I'm off duty today, so feel free to call me Hadrian. Can I come in?'

'Yes, of course.' I stepped back.

'Hi, Dad!' Fizz called down the barn. 'Coffee?'

'Love one, thanks.'

I led him over to the treatment table.

'I'm going away for a couple of days from tomorrow so I wanted to give you an update before I go,' he said, sitting down. Neither his tone of voice nor his expression gave anything away but my gut told me it was bad news.

'I'm not going to like this, am I?'

Fizz handed us drinks and sat down as Hadrian shook his head.

'I wish I had better news for you, but we had to release Tina and Jenny Grimes without charge.'

'Dad!'

'Fizz, you know better than anyone that it doesn't always go the way it should.' He sounded weary and I could imagine how frustrating that part of the job was.

'Can I ask why?'

'Do you want the off-the-record version as a family friend or the official version as a police sergeant?'

'Off-the-record, please.'

'Their solicitor insisted the cheques were a gift from you because you felt bad that their beloved auntie had left her home to you when you were a stranger and they were family.'

I shook my head, scarcely able to believe the nerve of them. Beloved auntie? Generations of that family had tried to bleed Thomas and Gwendoline dry and, when they'd refused to hand over any more money, the hate mail had started. When clearing out the farmhouse, I'd found bundles of letters full of abuse and threats which had continued long after Gwendoline passed away.

'They even showed us an email they claimed was from you saying you hoped they had a good time spending the money.'

'Er, not from Sam,' Fizz said, scowling.

Hadrian sighed. 'Their solicitor suggested that nobody would be foolish enough to steal money and leave such a clear paper trail and therefore it was obvious the money was a gift. As we said before, they're not criminal masterminds and Mike – PC Sunning – and I are convinced they *would* be that daft.'

'Everything they've said is lies,' I said. 'I should have known they'd have a clever answer worked out. What about the harassment?'

'Their solicitor wouldn't accept that because he said the money was a gift from you so there was no logic behind a charge of harassment. There wasn't the time for us to gather enough evidence to charge them, so we had to release them. I'm sorry.'

I ran my fingers through my hair and let out a frustrated sigh. 'It's not your fault. Thanks for trying. So what happens now?'

'They've been told not to leave the area and we'll keep building a case.'

'How realistic is it you'll be able to charge them down the line?'

'Not very. It's their word against yours. We know they're lying, but that's hard to prove.'

'Especially when I had a family member working for me and gave her a cheque book with my signature in.'

Hadrian grimaced. 'And especially when they claimed you knew Phoebe was Tina Grimes's stepdaughter and that you'd taken her on as a favour to the family, also linked to the guilt about the farmhouse.'

'For God's sake, Dad!' Fizz cried. 'They're taking the piss! I suppose they tried to claim that Sam had asked them to pelt her with eggs or burn the barn down.'

'We threw that at them, but their solicitor closed down that line of questioning. Not relevant, he said.'

'Dad!'

'It's okay, Fizz,' I said, placing my hand on her arm. 'We knew it was a long shot and it sounds like their solicitor was on the ball.'

'Keep me posted if they get in touch or anything out of the ordinary happens,' Hadrian said.

'Would years of hate mail to their *beloved* Auntie Gwendoline help things? And evidence of them being legally disinherited by Gwendoline and her husband Thomas?'

'That would all be very helpful.'

'I'll get onto my solicitor, Mr Jeffreys, next week and arrange for copies to be sent to the station.'

'Thank you. Anything else I should know?'

'Phoebe emailed me...' I showed him her email and my response and he agreed it was fine for me to meet with her as she wasn't a person of interest in the case, but suggested I quiz her about any conversations she might have had with the family after they were released from the cells, just in case they'd gloated. It wouldn't be viable evidence, but it might help build a fuller picture.

'I'd better head off and help your mum pack the van,' Hadrian said to Fizz.

She hugged him. 'Sorry for giving you a hard time, Dad. I know you tried your best.'

He squeezed her and laughed. 'I'm glad you give me a hard time. You were brought up to know right from wrong and this situation is wrong, but our hands are tied.'

I walked Hadrian to the door. 'Thanks for trying.'

'I really wish it had been a different outcome, but we won't give up. With families like theirs, it takes patience. They usually get off on a few things but something finally sticks and we'll keep searching for that thing.' He nodded his head towards the outside, presumably wanting to say something in private.

'I won't keep you long because it's bitter out here,' he said when I'd closed the door and stepped away from the barn. 'I just wanted to thank you for letting Fizz volunteer here. She's in her element and it's good to see her so happy again. Has she told you what happened with her partner?'

'Nadine? Yes. I don't know all the details but I know how and why it ended.'

On Fizz's twenty-fifth birthday, Nadine had declared that she was now at an age where she needed to act like a grown-up, stop wearing unicorn-themed clothes, and dye her hair a 'normal' colour. She'd bought her a wardrobe full of 'sensible' clothes and booked a salon appointment. Fizz came out of the salon with bright red hair and that was the end of their relationship.

'Natasha and I were always a bit worried about her relationship with Nadine. We thought she was too controlling, but we never said anything because Fizz seemed to be happy with her. Neither of us liked being right about Nadine, but we were relieved when it ended. Fizz was her usual feisty self for about a week but then she seemed to lose her sparkle. She kept saying how much she missed Nadine and maybe it was time to ditch the coloured hair, the unicorns and the sequins.'

'But that's Fizz!'

'Too right, it is. Even her brother Barney, who used to take the mickey out of her for the unicorn thing kept telling her to stay true to herself. We thought she was going to cave and beg Nadine to try again, and then she had her lottery win and everyone wanted a piece of her, including Nadine. It was the best thing Nadine could ever have done because it woke Fizz up to what she was really like. She's had a tough time working out who her true friends are and who's trying to get her to pick up the bill each night. But, since she started working here, we've seen her growing in confidence and she's always talking about things you've said and done that have inspired her. You've been such a positive influence on her so, on behalf of Natasha and me, I wanted to say thank you for being there for our little girl and giving her a safe space where it's all about kindness and animals and nothing to do with her hair colour, dress sense, or sexuality.' His voice cracked as he said his final sentence and I longed to hug him but managed to stop myself. Probably not appropriate for the sergeant handling my case.

'I think she's amazing,' I said. 'Credit to you and Natasha for raising a daughter who feels comfortable being herself. You say I've inspired her, but it works both ways. I honestly couldn't have run this place without her. You deserve to be so proud.'

'We are. Thank you.'

I waved as he pulled out of the farmyard and onto the track, thinking about what he'd just said about his daughter. Fizz had once told me she'd struggled with friendships at school, labelled as 'the weird, quirky one'. Now she seemed to know everyone but didn't have a best friend or even a small group she regularly spent time with. When she wasn't at university, she spent more time at Hedgehog Hollow than anywhere else. Was it possible that, despite having so many friends and acquaintances, Fizz was actually lonely and this was her sanctuary from that?

A cold wind bit my cheeks, making me shiver as I dashed for the warmth of the barn.

'Everything all right?' Fizz called.

'Everything's great. Your dad just wanted to thank me for taking you on as a volunteer as he says it's made you very happy which makes him and your mum happy.'

'Aw, what's he like, the big softie? But he's right. Hedgehog Hollow is my happy place.'

'Mine, too.' And no matter what the Grimes family did to destroy things, it always would be.

Fizz sang to herself as she cleaned the mugs. I was delighted that Hedgehog Hollow was her happy place, but I hoped it wasn't her only one. She was always so bright and cheerful that it had never entered my head that all might not be well outside of work. I hoped that the New Year would bring her happiness and maybe love. As far as I knew, she hadn't dated anyone since Nadine and it might well be time to try again.

Doing the supermarket shop was one of my many tasks as Tina's minion. She'd give me the cash and demand the change and a receipt the moment I walked through the door. I'd hold my breath while she peered into the bags, prodding a few things, but it was rare that I messed up. I knew which branded products she favoured and which needed to be supermarket own-label, and I'd learned a hard lesson in never 'insulting' her by buying from the own-label basic-range. *What's this shite you're trying to poison me with?* I kept my eye out for multi-buy bargains, knowing she was a sucker for a good deal, and I'd learned to read her mood so I knew when to slip in a sweet treat for her and when it was likely to be pelted at me instead. *Are you trying to make me fat?*

Today's shopping experience had been an eye-opener. I had no idea how cheaply the basic-range essentials could be bought, so I felt encouraged that we'd manage a fortnight on the teeniest of budgets.

'Where's the currybean?' Darcie asked as we walked along Trench Street with the shopping.

'The Caribbean is the other side of the Atlantic, off the coast of South America.'

'Where's that?'

'It's south from us and... why don't I show you on my phone after lunch?'

'Okay. Will they be there now?'

'No. It's a long flight. Maybe twelve hours. I don't know what time they set off but, let's say it was six o'clock this morning which would be about an hour before you usually get up, they'd get there at six o'clock tonight which would be just after your tea and a little before your bath time.'

'A whole day in the sky?'

'Pretty much.'

'Sounds boring.' She squeezed my hand a little tighter. 'I'm glad I'm staying with you instead.'

'Me too.'

Even though I was disgusted with them for leaving her behind and would never forgive them for leaving her in the house on her own like that, I was relieved they hadn't taken her. I could imagine them leaving her all alone in a hotel room in a strange country while they were out partying. They'd spend their days passed out on their sunbeds, leaving Darcie to go in the pool or sea unsupervised, despite being a non-swimmer because' neither of them could be arsed to take her to the pool or pay for lessons. I'd offered but was given a gob-full about thinking I knew best. Thing is, despite my age, I *did* know best when it came to Darcie. Rosemary said I'd always been exceptionally mature for my age, but I'd had to be. Life had made me grow up fast and, even though I called her my little sister, the truth was I'd been more like Darcie's mum since I was twelve.

Despite them probably being halfway over the Atlantic by now, I still felt nervous approaching Tina's house, as though expecting to find them inside and discovering it had been some weird test. I'd never understood their sense of humour, if it could be called that. Long before Dad's accident, I came home from school one day in a good mood after acing a maths test and Tina decided I was too upbeat so it would be 'fun' to deflate me by telling me Dad had been hit by a bus. Who'd do something like that, especially after the way my mum died?

She only told me it was a 'joke' when she spotted Dad walking up the street and Tina and Jenny fell about in hysterics. I would have told Dad, but I was warned about the serious consequences if I did. They knew some people at Dad's factory who could cause serious problems for him – stuff could be planted, rumours started, reputations destroyed.

Darcie liked the look of the baguette Carolyn from the bakery had made, so I cut it in half and we ate that and half the pain au chocolat each, which I heated in the oven. Darcie had never tasted one before and couldn't stop thanking me for giving her something that was 'so delicious the unicorns must have invented it'. I loved her childish innocence and wished she'd been born into a family who'd nurture it instead of wearing her down and turning her into a clone of them.

When I'd done the washing-up, I couldn't put it off any longer. It was time to investigate my bedroom. At Darcie's request, I put *The Princess and the Frog* on again and asked her to stay put. If my room was as bad as I expected, I didn't want her to see it because there was no reasonable explanation I could give her for Tina's behaviour.

At the bottom of the stairs, I took three deep breaths then ran up to the top. My bedroom door was closed and the butterflies in my tummy fluttered like crazy as I reached out and pushed it open.

The contents of my wardrobe and drawers were strewn all over the floor and bed. I picked up a couple of shredded long-sleeved T-shirts, revealing a damaged hoodie underneath. Early indications were that nothing had survived her shredding frenzy.

I didn't own many paperback books, preferring to read from an app on my phone, but the handful I owned were ripped into pieces and scattered across my floor. My make-up palettes looked like they'd been stamped on as the lids were smashed and there were chunks of eyeshadow trodden into the carpet. Hair bobbles had been cut in half, pencils snapped and photos ripped.

I slumped onto the edge of my bed, taking it all in. She'd done the maximum damage and I'd have expected to cry or scream or feel rage flowing through me, but I had nothing. I felt numb. Empty.

And I realised that I'd felt that way for a long time and somehow what I was looking at right now had been inevitable. She'd destroyed my confidence, my happiness, my family, and probably my career, so of course she'd want to destroy all of my possessions, too.

Tina and Jenny sucked the happiness from everyone they encountered. They'd done it to me, to Dad, to Darcie's mum Hayley and they were going to do it to Darcie. I had to stop them.

I picked up my phone and dialled the police station. 'Can I speak to PC Sunning?' I asked.

'He's not in the station at the moment.' I recognised the same man's voice from earlier.

'Do you know when he'll be back?'

'Difficult to say. Can someone else help?'

'No, thanks. I specifically need him. I'll try again later.'

I hung up, took one last look at my room and shook my head. Might as well get clearing.

* * *

By the time Darcie called up the stairs to say the film had ended, I'd filled two carrier bags with ripped books and papers for recycling, two bin bags with shredded clothes which I'd take to the textiles recycling bin in the supermarket car park, and another bin bag full of rubbish.

Tina must have got bored with the scissors by the time she'd got to my drawers because the contents of those hadn't been shredded. Some items of underwear were covered in make-up but that should come out in the wash, and there were a few short-sleeved T-shirts unscathed. I'd hoped some of the cut items could be repaired, but they were beyond saving. Luckily, she hadn't thought to check the laundry basket in the bathroom or the airing cupboard, so I had just about enough clothes to see me through a week. Not great, but better than I'd initially thought.

'Where's all your stuff gone?' Darcie asked, scrunching up her face as she entered my bedroom.

'It was time for a clear-out.'

'But it looks so empty.'

I didn't know how to respond to that, so I avoided it. 'Do you want to share one of those flapjacks with me?'

She gave an excited squeal – which I translated as a yes – and raced down the stairs.

There'd be no buses running tomorrow with it being New Year's Day, but we could catch one across town on Saturday and spend a few hours at the adventure playground. Who was here to stop us? The only problem was the bus fare.

'Do you want to play a game?' I asked Darcie. 'It's called Treasure Hunt.'

Her eyes lit up. 'Ooh! Can Twizzle join in?'

'If she wants. We want to find some money so we can go on a magical, mystical adventure on Saturday.'

'Where?'

'I'd better not say because, if we can't find enough money, we might not be able to go. We'll start together. I'm going to lift up the big cushions on the sofa and chair and I want you to peek under them and, if you find any coins, grab them. Then I'm going to lift up the sofa and chair and I want you to look underneath.'

I made a game of it, alternating between a pirate-voice and a deep, dramatic voiceover, which had Darcie in fits of giggles. Every time we found a coin, we'd bounce up and down, cheering loudly.

We looked in coat pockets and under beds and found plenty of coins but it was mainly small change which didn't add up to much.

'£1.78,' I muttered, feeling deflated.

'Is it enough?'

'No.'

Her disappointed face was unbearable. 'I'm tired.'

'How about I keep looking and you colour in a picture to send to your mummy?'

'Okay. I'll find a fairy and colour her dress orange.'

'Good idea.' Orange was Hayley's favourite colour. Darcie's dad Idris had played basketball and it was his team's colour. I could clearly picture her wearing his vest the day I found her... I shook my head, trying to push aside that memory.

A rummage through the kitchen drawers added 57p to our haul but would £2.35 even cover a return fare for Darcie, never mind mine? I dug my phone out to check fares and my tummy churned when I spotted an email from Samantha. She'd replied! Would it be a good response or a bad one?

Dad had always said it was important to take responsibility for mistakes. Even though the idea of seeing Samantha face to face terrified me, I hoped she'd let me apologise in person. If she forgave me, I needed to see that on her face rather than just read her words and, if she didn't, I needed to take that in person and learn from it.

I chewed on my lip as I scanned down her message. She didn't sound off, although she might be saving that for when she saw me. Which created another problem. I'd sent the message expecting to ride my moped to Hedgehog Hollow, but now I had Darcie. Even if I'd had a second helmet, which I didn't, I'd never have been so irresponsible as to make my first ever pillion passenger a child. I wasn't sure that was even legal.

If I emailed Samantha back and asked if we could delay it, she'd think I wasn't sorry and that I didn't care. She might tell me not to bother and then it would hang round me for life. It had to be tomorrow or over the weekend as she'd suggested but the only way we could get there was by taxi. I'd probably need thirty quid, maybe more, for the return journey.

I wished I hadn't said anything to Darcie about the magical, mystical adventure now. Darcie loved animals, so I could potentially make out that seeing the hedgehogs was the adventure but we were struggling to find enough loose change for bus fare to the playground so there was no chance of finding enough money for the taxi. We'd only searched downstairs, though. What if...?

'I'm just going upstairs for a bit,' I told Darcie. 'You stay here and finish that picture for your mummy, then we can colour a picture together when I come back down.'

Darcie nodded as she carefully coloured in the fairy's bodice with a bright orange felt tip.

Tina had left her bed unmade and her curtains half-closed. There were fitted wardrobes on either side of the bed, with mirrored sliding doors which had been left open. A pile of discarded summer clothes lay in a heap on the floor.

I hadn't ventured into Tina's room since Dad died. She'd hated me going in there when he was alive but, with him gone, it was strictly off-limits. When we moved in after they married, she'd got Dad to paint the walls baby pink. Deep pink curtains and bedding had made it more like a little girl's room than a married couple's and I was convinced it had been a test to see how far she had him wrapped round her finger. The day after he died, she had Connor and Cody painting the walls a sunshine yellow – completely at odds with her personality – muttering about how much she hated pink.

There was a dressing table opposite the bed where decorative wooden boxes and china pots stood among the thick dust. Taking care not to dislodge anything and give away that I'd been in there, I opened each lid hoping to find coins – or maybe even my mum's rings – but without success.

I tried her drawers, under her bed, and in her wardrobes. Nothing. I was about to give up when something in the bottom of the left-hand wardrobe glinted in the light. Hoping it was a coin, I crouched down and reached out for it but over-balanced. I put my hand out to save myself and the carpet beneath my palm dipped. I pressed my palm up and down a few times. Definitely a loose floorboard, like the one in my bedroom which I'd kept my coin tin hidden under.

Kneeling down, I raised the edge of the carpet and, sure enough, the floorboard came up easily, revealing a plastic carrier bag. I was about to lift it out when something stopped me. Maybe I've watched too many crime series or maybe I just didn't trust Tina, but I picked up one of her discarded vest tops, wrapped it over my hand, and lifted out the heavy bag.

'Shit the bed!'

My heart thumped as I stared in amazement at the contents. There were fifteen to twenty thick rolls of ten and twenty pound notes, each secured with an elastic band. A clear plastic freezer bag was full of small sealable bags, another contained cigarette papers, and there was a set of digital scales. I couldn't see any drugs, but this had to be evidence of dealing.

I sat back against the bed, nervously nibbling the skin around my nails, then took out my phone again.

'PC Sunning, please,' I said when the same man answered.

'You've just missed him.'

'No!'

'Have you called for him already? If it's important, I'm sure someone else can help.'

'It isn't. Well, it is, but... I'll try him next week.'

I released a frustrated squeal as I hung up.

Those rolls of money were teasing me. I couldn't even begin to imagine how much was there, but there had to be several thousand pounds. Here was me scrabbling around to scrape together bus fare, buying the cheapest cheese, and worrying about how I was going to feed two people for a fortnight, and there was a fortune right here. But it wasn't my fortune. They wouldn't miss the loose change but I bet they knew exactly how much money was in those bundles. And it was tainted money. Illegal. I couldn't.

Snapping a few photos, I returned the bag to the hidey-hole. The shiny thing at the back of the wardrobe turned out to be a button. Typical.

Mission unsuccessful, I closed Tina's door and paused outside Connor's bedroom. If there was a hidey-hole in my bedroom in the bottom of my wardrobe and another in Tina's room, could there be one in Connor's? When I'd found the loose floorboard in my room, it had never entered my head that Tina already knew about it but if she was the one who'd created it – and a matching one in her room – it explained how she'd found my tin, although God knows what had made her snoop there in the first place. Unless she'd been planning to use it to hide another stash.

Connor's room smelt of old socks, mould, and something else rancid, probably emanating from his bed. Tina had never stripped the covers after he was done for assaulting Samantha and sent back to prison, but I was forbidden from going in his room so I couldn't do it either.

Gagging, I pulled my T-shirt over my nose. The layout of the room was the same as Tina's but the dimensions were smaller. In the wardrobe furthest from the window, I found a loose floorboard and removed another carrier bag. This one contained even more rolls of money than Tina's, more sealable bags, and several small bags containing weed or tablets.

I took some more photos and hastily put everything away, taking care not to touch anything directly, then returned to my bedroom and sat cross-legged on the floor, my mind racing as I scrolled through the photos.

So my stepfamily could add drug dealing to their growing list of charms. Could I get that added to the growing list of offences? The stolen money hadn't stuck, or had it? For all I knew, they'd been bailed pending further investigation but had skipped the country. Now we had drug dealing, neglect, theft of my mum's rings, and... I pushed up one sleeve after the other and gazed down at the patchwork of scars, thinking about Sergeant Kinsella's concerned expression when he'd asked about my face. Surely something would stick, especially when I showed them my arms and the folder on my laptop labelled 'one day'.

'Wow, Natasha! This is amazing!'

I'd been under strict instructions to stay away from the dairy shed while Natasha, Hadrian, Fizz and a few others were working as she'd warned me that the mid-point in the preparations often looked worse than the start and could panic the host.

'Thank you. Glad you like it.'

'Told you she was good,' Fizz gushed, putting her arm round her mum's waist, clearly proud and rightly so.

I hadn't particularly picked up on the family resemblance before. Natasha was taller and slimmer with dark hair, but now that they were standing together, I could see they both had the same heart-shaped face, the same eye shape even if the colour was different, and the same beautiful smile.

'Can you imagine how it might look for your wedding now?' Natasha asked.

'Completely!'

As the holiday cottages refurbishment drew to a close, Dave and his team had patched holes and replaced a few rusty corrugated panels. Several days of cleaning and a lick of black paint on the pillars had made a massive difference but I'd still not been able to see it as a wedding venue. Until now. What a transformation!

Natasha could accommodate pretty much any colour scheme and we'd chosen 'every colour of the rainbow'. Round paper lanterns and stars dangled from the joists at different heights and colourful fairy lights were wrapped round the pillars, the designs alternating between hearts and miniature lanterns.

Bill Davis, our neighbour who farmed the land at Hedgehog Hollow, had dropped off dozens of hay bales to be used for seating. Near the entrance of the barn, hay bales were positioned either side of wooden tables. Some were draped in colourful blankets while others were left exposed to give a more rustic look. On the right, trestle tables were set up ready for the buffet and, on the left, there was a 'help your-self' bar with bottles and cans of beer, lager, wine and soft drinks chilling in old tin baths packed with ice.

Natasha had also set up a 'Smores Station' where guests could toast marshmallows over a fire pit and squash them between chocolate biscuits, as well as a popcorn station and a pink and white striped 'Candy Cart' full of jars of old-school sweets.

At the far end of the barn, there was a dance floor where the DJ was currently setting up, with more hay bale seats and tables flanking it.

Between the eating area and the dance floor, hay bales had been arranged like sofas with colourful throws and scatter cushions to create more comfortable relaxing areas.

'Who stole the cow shed and replaced it with this?'

I turned round and smiled at Josh. 'You were right about this place. Isn't it stunning?'

'Better than I imagined.'

'Is there anything else you need?' Natasha asked.

'I don't think so.'

'In that case, I'll leave you to admire your refurbished cow shed and we'll be back later with the food.'

'And I'll be back later *for* the food,' Fizz chirped, giving me a hug before leaving with her parents.

'How are you feeling?' Josh asked. 'Still thinking we should have cancelled?'

'Definitely not. They'd have won if we'd cancelled, and I'd have started the New Year feeling guilty that I'd ruined everyone's New Year's Eve plans and that I'd caved to the Grimes family.'

Josh placed his arms round my waist and pulled me to him for a tender kiss. 'And do you still think we should hire a marquee for our wedding?'

'No. You were right about that too. This is perfect, but it's got me thinking. We'll see how tonight goes, but we have the potential to make more revenue from running events here. We're getting a licence for weddings so we could hold more of those after ours or parties or other events. I'm sure Natasha would be interested in a collaboration, where we provide the venue and she decorates and caters.'

'I think you're a genius. With that running alongside the holiday lets, there should be more than enough income to keep those hedgehogs warm and well.'

'We'd need to give it a name. The Dairy Barn or The Cow Shed doesn't sound very glam for a wedding. I'd like some connection to the farm or hedgehogs, but I don't know what would work.'

Our two-bedroom holiday cottage had amazing views of the wildflower meadow, so we'd named it Meadow View. The adjoining four-bedroom one was called Mickleby Mews, using Thomas and Gwendoline's surname. The other two holiday cottages were identical three-bedroom ones called Snuffles' Den and Quilly's Cottage after two of our five patients from before the arson attack. A broken leg had meant Mr Snuffles stayed with us for a long time before a successful release, but Quilly sadly perished in the fire. The cottage was a lovely way to honour his memory.

'I'm sure we'll think of something apt,' he assured me. 'Thinking caps on. Ooh, I've got one. Room With a Moo!'

'Oh, my gosh! That's nearly as bad as your Hogmanay comment.' I couldn't help laughing, though. 'We'll keep working on it. In the meantime, we'd better go and get ourselves ready.'

'Before we do, Bauble's in the barn. I thought you'd like to say hello before I settle him into his crate.'

* * *

Even after Bauble had been deflated at the practice, he hadn't looked right – a funny shape with his skin hanging off him – but now he looked like a real hedgehog.

'We did another X-ray and the tear in his lungs has repaired itself so we can let his puncture wounds heal now and he should be well on his way to recovery. Also, my boot is full of food, cleaning stuff and boxes of gloves.'

'You've been shopping?'

'No. It's from the donation bins. One of my clients today works at the library and she brought the contents of theirs with her, so I emptied the practice ones and the ones at the end of the track were full too.'

'People are so generous. With that and the wish list donations...'

'You don't need to worry about the hedgehogs. It'll all work out. I'll unpack the jeep, you settle Bauble, then we'll get ready to see in the New Year in style. In Gollum's Barn.'

'I hope you're kidding.'

'But he's our only permanent resident and, yeah, that's maybe not the best branding, is it?'

'Naming it after a bald hedgehog called Gollum doesn't shout *book me for your wedding!* I prefer Room With a Moo. Keep thinking!'

25

SAMANTHA

As Josh and I made our way over to the dairy shed at 7.15 p.m. ready for a half seven start, my phone buzzed:

✉ From Chloe
HOT TIP: When you have a party starting at 7.30pm, tell us to come at 7 instead and we might be on time! We were running late as usual then Samuel had a nappy explosion so we had to wash and change him and are now even later but we're on our way now. We have a surprise for you. And it's not the contents of Samuel's nappy! Xx

✉ To Chloe
Sounds intriguing! The surprise, not the nappy explosion! Drive safely and see you soon xx

'What do you think the surprise will be?' Josh asked after I read him Chloe's text.

'Knowing Chloe, it could be anything.'

'Another baby?' he suggested.

'It's possible. She's never mentioned having more, although I've never directly asked her about it.'

I hadn't wanted to tackle the subject of Chloe having more children while I was working through my own thoughts about motherhood with my counsellor.

It felt too soon for a second baby. Chloe and James had only got back together in August and she'd been diagnosed with post-natal depression so there was that to consider, as well as the unknown of how James's testicular cancer treatment had affected his fertility.

A group of locals arrived and we paused our conversation as we welcomed them, then Dad arrived with Lauren, Connie and Alex, followed shortly after by Rich and Dave.

'You don't think it could be that my mum's changed her mind about coming tonight?' I asked Josh when they'd all moved away to grab drinks and secure seats.

Mum hadn't directly given me a no, but Auntie Louise had told me she wasn't coming. Auntie Louise, Uncle Simon and Chloe and family were staying over and I'd allocated them Snuffles' Den, meaning a third bedroom for Mum if she changed her mind.

'Promise me you won't get your hopes up. Remember what you discussed with Lydia.'

I squeezed Josh's hand. 'Easier said than done.'

My heart soared as I spotted Auntie Louise and Uncle Simon approaching the barn, then plummeted when Mum wasn't with them.

'Your mum says Happy New Year,' Auntie Louise said, hugging me. 'She's had a lecture from me. I thought she was moving forward and I'm disappointed in her.'

'Maybe she just fancies a quiet night in on her own,' I responded, trying to sound blasé about it. 'Some people don't like New Year's Eve.'

'That's what I said,' Uncle Simon added, ever the diplomat. 'Did Chloe tell you they're running late?'

'Yes, she texted.'

Dad joined us and, after hugs and kisses, he guided them over to the sofa area he'd bagged.

'Are you okay?' Josh asked, his eyes soft with concern.

I ran my fingers over the embroidered pendant worn with a soft grey vintage chiffon cocktail dress.

'Yes. It's just that, when Chloe said she had a surprise...'

He put his arm round me and kissed the top of my head. 'I bet she'd be mortified that you thought that. It's probably something daft like she's had her hair cut short or she's started wearing glasses.'

Josh had never been a Chloe fan. Not many people were. She was wary round strangers and that came across as being cold, but now we knew why. I'd enjoyed watching a friendship slowly develop between them and I loved how he could see the positive changes in Chloe since the summer.

'You're probably right,' I agreed.

Paul and Beth arrived with Archie and Lottie in a double buggy.

'You look really well,' I told Paul.

'I feel well. A day of bed rest helped. I might not last till midnight, but I'm going to give it my best shot.'

My best friend Hannah and her husband Toby were next with their daughter Amelia, and the guests kept on coming after that. I felt like I was in a receiving line at a wedding as Josh and I greeted everyone, thanked them for coming, and accepted their compliments about the dairy shed's transformation. Before we knew it, we really would be in a wedding receiving line. I couldn't wait.

After twenty minutes, we decided we'd done our bit at the door and it was time to mingle. The shed was alive with laughter, chatter and music. I sipped on a glass of wine and smiled as I looked around.

Fizz, a natural with children as well as animals, was on the dance floor with Amelia in her arms and had several small children following her around in a sort of freestyle conga. Rich was chatting to Dad, Uncle Simon and Alex and whatever tale he was relaying had them clutching their stomachs with laughter.

'Sorry we're late,' Chloe cried, hurling herself at me for a hug.

'It's fine. Great to see you. Where are the boys?'

'James wanted to set up the travel cot so he didn't need to faff with it after a few drinks, but I couldn't wait to see you so he sent me over.'

'Drink?' I asked.

'Ooh, yes please.'

We wandered over to the bar area. 'It's help yourself. Beer, lager, wine and soft drinks.'

She poured a large glass of rosé wine – definitely not pregnant, then.

'I'm dying to tell you the surprise, but I promised James I'd wait for him.'

A few more arrivals distracted me so, while I gave them my attention, Chloe went in search of our family.

James finally appeared with Samuel, just as the DJ announced that the buffet was ready if anyone was hungry. Chloe grabbed his hand and pulled him into the queue, so I was clearly going to need to wait a bit longer.

It was about an hour later before Chloe rounded up Josh and me and pulled us over to where James was feeding Samuel a bottle.

'We have to tell you our surprise,' she said when we sat down. 'We've accepted an offer on our house today.'

I did a double take. 'Oh my gosh! I didn't even know it was on the market.'

'It wasn't,' James said. 'We were thinking about it for the New Year, but we found a house we loved and one of Chloe's preschool colleagues is buying ours. She was buying one in the same style round the corner and it fell through so it was perfect timing.'

'So we put an offer in on the house we wanted and that's been accepted too,' Chloe said, eyes sparkling with excitement.

'Speedy! So where are you moving to?'

They exchanged grins. 'Bentonbray!' Chloe declared.

My eyes widened and I felt Josh squeeze my leg. 'Bentonbray? As in the village near here?'

Chloe nodded. 'After I stayed here in the summer, I realised how much I hated our house, particularly being surrounded by other houses. I loved the peace and quiet at Hedgehog Hollow and those gorgeous views, but I'm not sure I could live somewhere as remote as this permanently. Bentonbray's the perfect compromise. It's a big village so it's got amenities, including a good school for Samuel, but the house we're buying is on the outskirts, surrounded by open fields.'

James looked adoringly at her. 'It's going to be the fresh start we need. Chloe's going to hand in her notice and see if she can get a preschool job locally and I'll still be able to commute to York by train, but from Claybridge station instead of Whitsborough Bay. Same length drive, but half the train journey.'

'Sounds amazing. Congratulations!'

'Yeah, congratulations!' Josh said. 'That's some surprise.'

As I hugged Chloe and James and toasted their exciting news, I felt a little out of sorts and couldn't quite fathom why. Chloe moving so close was a great idea. Wasn't it?

26

Darcie wanted to stay up past midnight but only made it to nine o'clock before her eyes were drooping and she admitted defeat. She didn't even ask me for a bedtime story, which told me how shattered she was. Hardly surprising when she'd been dragged out of bed in the early hours.

'I need my light,' she murmured after she clambered into my bed.

'I'm so sorry, Princess. I didn't think about it. How about this?'

I wandered across the landing, switched the bathroom light on and left the door ajar.

Darcie was either happy with that solution or too shattered to debate it, so she settled down to sleep. She drifted off quickly and I watched her for a while, curled up with her arms round Twizzle, occasionally smacking her lips together. She'd been so good all day, as always, and I genuinely couldn't get my head round why Jenny and Tina treated her like such an inconvenience.

When I was sure that Darcie was in a deep sleep, I crept downstairs and put the TV on with the volume low, but I didn't watch it. Too much to worry about. I was annoyed with myself for not thinking about sleeping arrangements until it was too late. I should have gone round to Jenny's earlier to collect the nightlight and Darcie's bedding because she had mine, which meant I had none. Usually when she stayed over, she brought her duvet and pillow and I slept on the floor with mine. At least the house was warm, unlike Rosemary's garage. I'd manage.

I pulled the throw Darcie had been using over me, my mind still racing about where to find some money. We'd go to Jenny's house tomorrow and pick up the nightlight, bedding and anything else that Darcie might want, and we'd do our treasure hunt there too, although we'd probably only find loose change again. I was going to have to sell my Pandora bracelet. It would break Rosemary's heart – and mine – but I was running out of options. I glanced up towards the ceiling and quickly dismissed that thought. No way was I touching their drugs money.

I watched the time change on my phone from 11.59 to 0.00 and I heard cheering and the explosion of fireworks outside.

'Happy New Year,' I muttered to myself. It seemed such a pointless thing to say when the year ahead for me, once again, was already shaping up to be just as crap as the last few.

I was desperate to move out and escape from Tina and Jenny. I often fantasised about passing my exams with top grades, securing an entry-level accountancy job, and moving into a place of my own. I'd only be able to afford to rent a tiny bedsit, but that didn't matter. What mattered was being away from this family. But all that was now in jeopardy. Tina wanted me out when she returned and I doubted even a couple of weeks in the Caribbean would have relaxed her enough to change her mind.

Was having no home worse than living with Tina? I shuddered as I imagined living on the streets. I'd been lucky last night as I had somewhere to go, but even hidden away in Rosemary's garage I'd jumped at every noise, my heart pounding. While I'd wandered round town in the dark last night and again this morning, I'd been on high alert, wary of everyone. I was streetwise enough to know that people like Carolyn from the bakery were rare and that I'd spend most of my time worrying about when I'd eat again. It would be the end of college and my career. Would it be worth it? I wasn't sure it would. The only thing that had got me through all these years was knowing that my studies would secure me a job and a life without the Grimes family. If that was taken away from me, what had it all been for? I might as well have been dead.

I couldn't let Tina take my future from me. Rosemary would take me in, no question. Would Tina be evil enough to keep the threats going if I did go there? I wouldn't put it past her. So I'd need to beg and plead with her when she returned to let me stay. I already did all the shopping, cooking, washing and cleaning. I wasn't sure what else I could do round the house, but there had to be something.

Although, if they could get arrested and slung into prison, my life would be very different. For the first time in years, I might actually have a good year. Was I brave enough to report to the police everything I'd found and everything I'd experienced? I had until Monday to decide.

27

'The New Year's approaching, so grab your loved ones and let's start the countdown,' the DJ announced. 'Ten, nine...'

I beamed at Josh as we joined in the countdown, standing in the middle of the crowded dance floor.

'... two, one, Happy New Year!'

Josh kissed and hugged me and, while an obscure techno dance version of 'Auld Lang Syne' played, I hugged my family and friends. My face ached from smiling so much. Josh had been so right about not cancelling. Tonight had been amazing and just what I'd needed. Because so few people knew what had happened – and they were all sworn to secrecy – I'd been able to switch off and forget about it for a few hours.

'We can't set off our own New Year fireworks, so here's Katy Perry singing about some,' the DJ said, playing a speedier dance version of 'Firework' and everyone jumped up and down to the chorus, waving their arms in the air.

'I need a drink,' I told Josh when the track ended. Wiping my hot forehead with my arm, I made my way towards the bar and gratefully glugged down a glass of water.

'Happy New Year, Samantha.'

I whipped round, my heart thumping. 'Mum?'

She stood a couple of feet away from me, wringing her hands and looking like she might bolt for the door at any moment.

'I can go if you want,' she offered, evidently misinterpreting my shocked expression and silence as displeasure at her arrival.

'Gosh, no! Of course not! I'm just surprised to see you. Happy New Year!'

A combination of too much wine and the high I felt from such a good evening propelled me forward and I hugged her. She felt rigid in my arms and I prepared to step back and apologise, then she relaxed and patted my back. It was awkward but it was a response. Progress.

'Can I get you a drink?' I asked, stepping away and sweeping my arm across the selection of drinks. Natasha had kept the tin baths topped up with fresh ice across the evening, so all the drinks remained perfectly chilled.

'White wine, please.'

She took several gulps when I passed her a large glass so I swiftly topped it up and she didn't object. It had obviously taken guts for her to show up and, as far as I was concerned, it was better late than never.

'I'm glad you came.'

She looked uncertain. 'Really? I wasn't sure if I should. We haven't seen each other since the summer.'

'I know. I'm sorry. It always seems so busy here. I haven't made it over to Whitsborough Bay.'

'I wasn't having a go.' She lowered her eyes and ran her finger round the rim of her glass. 'I could have come across with Louise or Chloe, but—'

'Auntie Debs!' Chloe staggered over and flung herself at Mum, causing Mum to slop her drink over her hands. 'You missed midnight.'

'I know. I'm sorry.' Mum extricated herself from Chloe's hold and shook the wine off her hand.

'Come and dance!' Chloe demanded, grabbing her hand.

'No! You know I don't dance.'

'You should.' The track changed and Chloe squealed. 'You love this song. I know you do.'

No way was Chloe going to take no for an answer, yanking Mum's arm.

'You know she won't leave you alone,' I said, laughing at Mum's pleading expression. 'You might as well just go with it.'

I poured myself a glass of wine, followed them towards the back of the barn and sat on one of the haystacks watching.

'I'm parched,' Dad said, plonking down beside me as he swigged from a bottle of lager.

'Have you seen who Chloe's dancing with?' I said, nodding in her direction.

Dad's face was a picture, eyes wide, jaw open. 'When...?'

'Just now.'

'Well, I never.'

'No, me neither. It's encouraging, though.'

He squeezed my hand. 'Very. Happy New Year, poppet.'

'Happy New Year, Dad.'

Auntie Louise and Uncle Simon had joined Mum and Chloe and they were all swaying together, singing at the tops of their voices. It was a far cry from last New Year when we weren't speaking. My life had changed beyond all recognition across the past twelve months and the year ahead was going to see major changes too – best of all being marrying the man of my dreams.

Hopefully this year would see the Grimes family finally out of my life. Could it be the year to see Mum in my life? We'd never have the close mother/daughter bond that Chloe and Auntie Louise had. It wasn't possible or realistic after how she'd treated me, but I would like to have a relationship. I wanted my mum to be there on my wedding day and, if Josh and I did have children – an idea with which I felt increasingly comfortable – I wanted them to know their grandmother and that wasn't going to happen if we hadn't moved forward.

* * *

Several guests had left after seeing the New Year in and there were only about thirty left by the time one o'clock arrived and the music slowed down to ballads for the last half hour.

Josh led me onto the dance floor and held me close. 'Have you enjoyed tonight?' he asked as we shuffled together.

'It's been amazing. And I can't believe Mum came. She's asked if we can have some time alone tomorrow... I mean later today.'

'That sounds promising.'

'I'm trying not to think about it. It could be an apology, it could be a goodbye, or anything in between.'

He gently squeezed me. 'I'm here for you whatever it is.'

'Tell you what I'm also trying not to think about. Chloe and James moving to Bentonbray.'

'Yeah! Where did that spring from?'

'I don't know. And I don't know how I feel about it. She's my cousin and one of my closest friends and I should be delighted she's going to be just down the road, but...' I tailed off, not quite sure what the end of the sentence should be.

'But after everything she's put you through, it's a little bit too close for comfort?' Josh suggested.

'That could be it.'

'And, even though she's made brilliant progress, Chloe courts drama and now that's going to be on your doorstep.'

I sighed, thinking about her dramatic arrival and refusal to talk about it in June. 'You're probably right. Oh, gosh, I feel so mean and nasty thinking like that. She's trying hard.'

Josh tilted my face to his and tenderly kissed me. 'Nobody could ever call you mean and nasty. And, yes, she is trying hard. But she's also trying. I like Chloe, but in small doses. You might need to establish some parameters, or you could find yourself embroiled in the middle of every single drama and I know what you're like. You'll be there for her and risk making yourself ill again.'

I tightened my hold. I hadn't been able to work out why I hadn't squealed with excitement at the thought of living so close to my cousin again and Josh had nailed it. Since leaving Whitsborough Bay, I'd moved on and found a new life, made new friends, established new routines. Chloe struggled to make new friends and had always clung onto me, jealous of my friendships or muscling in on them. With her moving to the area, things might be about to change and it was rare that I was selfish, but I didn't want them to change. I loved my life how it was. I'd just have to hope that Chloe's recent journey of self-discovery included letting go of that neediness or our recently repaired relationship might crumble once more.

It might be New Year's Day and a day off work for most, but it was business as usual at the rescue centre. Josh and I had cleaned out the crates first thing, although not quite as early as we usually did, and now I was relaxing on Thomas's bench with tea in my favourite hedgehog mug.

The blue sky and gentle sun were most welcome after several icy-cold days, although it was definitely still winter, so a thick coat, hat, scarf and gloves were essential.

'Can I join you?'

I looked up and smiled at Mum. 'Yes, but pull your coat under you. The bench is a little bit damp.'

The silence between us wasn't uncomfortable. She wanted to speak and I wasn't going to distract her from finding the right words by firing questions at her.

'I'm sorry I made Chloe and James late to your party,' she said. 'I hope that didn't cause any problems.'

I frowned. 'I don't follow. How did you make them late?'

'I thought Chloe would have said.'

'She said they were running late anyway and then she had to change Samuel.'

'No. It was my fault. Louise told me off. She does that a lot these days, although she usually has good cause. She must have told Chloe because, ten minutes later, they turned up and tried to persuade me to come.'

I loved that Chloe had done that for me. Each time she'd visited Hedgehog Hollow, she'd asked if there'd been any progress with Mum and she knew how much it meant to me to try to establish some sort of ongoing connection.

'I'm not good at being told what to do,' Mum continued. 'Or being told I'm wrong. But I calmed down after they left and decided that I should finally make this New Year a proper new start. So I got changed and drove over and I made it to the end of your farm track and...' She paused and sighed. 'And I turned round again.'

'You went home?'

'Yes. Drove here then went straight home and, as soon as I got there, I knew I'd made a mistake but I couldn't face the journey again. Then Chloe texted me and said I had loads of time to make it before midnight. She kept texting and, by the tenth one, I decided I had nothing to lose so I drove back and sat in the farmyard for an hour, trying to psyche myself up to coming in. I kept looking at the clock, ticking closer to midnight, and a final text came through from Chloe and I knew that was it. Go home and give up or come inside. I missed the countdown. I was still trying to make myself take those final few steps.'

Mum had always come across as so strong, confident and opinionated that it was difficult to imagine her dithering so much, but there was no reason for her to make it up.

'Why was it so hard for you?' I asked, keeping my voice gentle. 'It's not like you'd have been gate-crashing. You were an invited guest.'

'I know, but I don't understand why you'd want me here. This isn't me going for the sympathy vote. I genuinely don't understand, Samantha. I've been a terrible mother from day one and the things I've put you through... I honestly have no idea how you've turned out the way you have.'

I didn't think this was a good moment to sing Dad's praises.

Without him looking out for me and repeatedly leaping to my defence, things could have been very different.

'How's your PTSD?' she asked, seemingly changing the subject.

'Improving. I still have moments but I can deal with them better now.'

'Can it be cured?'

'Treated rather than cured. Some people might find their symptoms disappear but there's no guarantee that they will never have an episode again so it would be misleading to say it can be fully cured.'

'But treatment does improve things?'

'Definitely, and I'm proof of that, but I wouldn't be where I am now without professional help.'

'And it doesn't matter if the trauma was from a long time ago?'

'No. It's never too late to start therapy.'

She didn't respond so I took a few sips of my tea to give her time to process the information. She had no idea that I knew she'd been raped and that the way she'd treated me directly stemmed from the fallout from that. I was worried how she'd react if I revealed what I knew, so it was best to stay quiet. It had to come from her when she was ready.

'I think I have PTSD,' she said eventually. 'Something happened to me a long time ago that still haunts me now and I'm sick of it controlling my life.'

'You're going to get some help?'

'Yes. I don't usually make New Year's resolutions, but this is mine. It's been too long.'

'I think that's a great resolution to make. Results take time, though, so don't panic if it feels like you're not getting anywhere at first.'

Her leap from a conversation about being a bad mother to asking about my PTSD now made sense to me because I knew about her trauma, but it wouldn't have made sense to someone who didn't, so I was going to need to plead ignorance to avoid suspicion.

'Is how you've been with me connected to what happened to you in the past?' I asked.

'I'm not telling you what happened,' she snapped and my stomach sank at the familiarity of the loud voice, creased forehead and flashing eyes.

'Sorry.'

She inhaled deeply. 'No. I'm sorry. It was an obvious question and I had no right to snap at you when I'm the one who brought up the subject.' She stood up and rolled her shoulders, looking ahead towards the meadow.

Minutes ticked past before she turned to me, her eyes shining with tears. 'Do they make you relive what happened?'

'They need to understand what the trauma was so you will need to talk about it, but it's all done in a safe space at your pace.'

Her lip wobbled. 'I'm scared.'

I didn't care that we weren't tactile. She was my mum and she needed a hug – a proper one rather than the alcohol-induced one like last night. I'd come so close to hugging her in the summer when Chloe's secret came out and Mum had clearly been devastated that she hadn't known the full story, but I'd held back for fear of rejection. I wasn't going to hold back now. I knew how it felt to be haunted by PTSD and it had been part of my life for less than a year. Mum had battled alone with this for over three decades. Admitting it to herself and resolving to get help took tremendous courage.

Unlike last night, she didn't feel rigid in my arms. She didn't awkwardly pat my back. Instead, she melted into my hug and held me tightly. I could feel her shaking and pushed down the lump in my throat.

'I was scared too, but look at it this way: what's more scary? Continuing to let your life be controlled by something that happened to you in the past or talking about it to a trained professional, knowing that they'll be able to help you regain control of your life?'

'The first one.'

'You've got this, Mum. And you have people who care about you, who are here to support you. Including me.'

I'd told Rosemary that I'd visit her today to wish her a Happy New Year in person, but I couldn't risk it.

'Happy New Year!' I said down the phone around mid-morning, my voice sounding nasal.

'Happy New Year, darling girl! You don't sound very well.'

'I'm full of cold.' I hated myself for lying. 'Sore throat. Achy.'

'Aw, no! Have you had some paracetamol?'

'Yeah, and some hot blackcurrant. I might feel better later...'

'No! Don't you even think about it. You stay wrapped up in bed and Trixie and I will look forward to seeing you again when you're feeling better.'

Although she sounded concerned for me, I knew she was concerned for herself too. Any hint of a sniffle and I'd be sent away. Rosemary didn't cope well with illness. When her eyesight started to deteriorate, she often joked about her 'dodgy eyes' but I never once heard her complain; she just got on with it. By contrast, if she ever caught a cold, she acted like she had pneumonia and would work herself into such a state about it. I think she managed to cope with her visual impairment because she had to, but anything else that might stop her in her tracks and take a shred of that fiercely guarded independence away and she was a wreck.

'I'm so sorry,' I said. 'I really wanted to see you.' At least that part wasn't a lie. I fake coughed. 'Did you do anything last night?' I coughed again.

'Hang up the phone and we'll speak when you're well. Take care of yourself, darling girl.'

'I will. Thank you.'

I disconnected the call and tossed my phone onto the sofa beside me. I'd hated that but it had to be done for Rosemary's safety. I wanted to talk to her, to hear her gentle voice, to feel her warmth, but I was scared I'd break down and tell her what was happening or that she'd recognise my coughs were fake and my voice wasn't husky.

'I'm ready!' Darcie burst into the room with her arms flung wide as though she'd just delivered the performance of her life on stage.

'Good girl. Pop your shoes and coat on and we'll go to your house to see what else we need.'

'Can we go to the playground after?'

'Maybe this afternoon. I want to bring your stuff back here first rather than lug it around with us.'

* * *

I pushed open the door at 17 Butler Street and squealed as a man ran down the stairs towards us.

'Trigg!' I clapped my hand over my racing heart. 'What are you doing here?'

'Jen asked me to water the plants,' he said, sneering at me. 'Enjoying babysitting duties?'

'I'm not a baby!' Darcie declared, planting her hands on her hips.

I gently placed a hand over her mouth to stop her saying anything else. I didn't trust Trigg and could imagine him thinking nothing of smacking her if he thought she was being gobby.

'Darcie's no bother,' I said.

'Not what I've heard.' He took a sudden step towards us and she sank back against me.

He released a crazy laugh, like I'd seen gangsters do in movies before shooting someone.

'Hope you're doing as you're told and staying away from the filth,' he growled. 'And that blind woman and her dog.' He did the *you're being watched* thing with his fingers then laughed again, shoving into me as he left the garden and strode off down the street.

'I don't like him,' Darcie whispered.

'Neither do I. Come on, let's forget about him and get your stuff.'

I'd emptied her suitcase and brought it with me. It was on wheels, so it would be easier than trying to carry everything. We added in more clothes, her unicorn nightlight with her pillow wrapped round it for protection, and a few books and toys to keep her occupied. I rolled up her duvet and shoved it into a bin bag.

'Fancy another treasure hunt?' I asked her after I'd tossed the bin bag down the stairs and carried the case down.

'Oo-argh!' she cried, holding an imaginary cutlass in the air.

I tried to make it a fun game once again as we ran round downstairs making pirate calls, cheering each time we discovered treasure, but we only found 63p. Added to the money from Tina's, we were 2p short of £3. I tried hard not to show my disappointment, but Darcie wasn't daft.

'We don't have enough to go on a magical, mystical adventure, do we?'

I shoved the coins in my pocket and shrugged. 'No, but there may be something we can do tomorrow to get some.' I closed my eyes for a moment, my tummy dropping at the thought of taking my bracelet to be pawned. 'We'll have to go into Reddfield to do it and we don't have enough money for the bus so we'll need to walk there but we can get the bus back. Do you think you could manage that?'

She answered with a cuddle and I stroked her hair.

'I love you, Phoebe,' she whispered and I had to swallow hard on the lump in my throat.

'I love you too, Darcie.'

And that was the rub. Every time I thought about getting away from the Grimes family, I thought about my life without Darcie in it. I knew the only way I could ever be happy was to get away from Tina, Jenny and the rest of them, but I couldn't imagine feeling truly happy without that little girl.

'Should we go back and get something to eat?' I asked.

'Do you have any pan chocolates?'

I smiled at her mispronunciation. 'I'm afraid not, but I'll buy you one tomorrow when we go into town.' It was an indulgence on our limited budget but she was worth it. I'd forfeit something.

'I didn't think your nanna had any plants,' I said as we prepared to leave. She hated anyone giving her flowers, saying she never managed to keep them alive longer than a day, so I assumed she'd hate plants too. Although that could have been an excuse from Trigg. He might be pissed off that he hadn't been invited on holiday and had been searching for things to steal before we'd disturbed him. I hoped not. If he came back later and nicked Jenny's stuff, I was bound to get the blame.

'She's got loads,' Darcie said. 'But they're all in Mummy's bedroom and I'm not allowed in there. I don't like it in there anyway. It's too warm and bright and I don't like the shiny wallpaper.'

Oh. My. God! I ran up the stairs.

'You won't be allowed in either!' Darcie cried as I flung open the back bedroom door, my jaw dropping open in shock. No way!

'I'll be down in a minute,' I called to her, as I took several photos of the grow house. Or should that be grow room? I hadn't seen that one coming.

I glanced up at the loft hatch on the landing and opened it with the metal hook on the wall. I didn't even need to pull down the folding ladder as, the moment the hatch opened, I squinted from the light and felt the heat.

I was about to close the hatch but couldn't resist the opportunity to take photos. The more evidence I had, the better. But what if Trigg returned?

'Darcie? Can you put the chain on the door?' I called. It would buy us some time if he came back.

'Done it, but I'm bored now. Can I watch TV?'

'Yes. Good plan. I'll be a bit longer.'

I pulled down the ladder, climbed it and took several more photos. The attic was packed full of cannabis plants, probably about four or five times the number that fit into the bedroom. What had initially appeared to be small scale had just escalated. I had no idea how many plants there were or what their street value was, but there was now absolutely no doubt that Jenny and Tina were drug dealers and Trigg was part of it.

Satisfied I had enough decent photos to convey the size of the operation, I closed up the hatch and shut the back bedroom door. I was about to head downstairs when I wondered about the hidey holes. The sisters lived in identical semi-detached houses. Could they have identical hidey holes?

The answer to that was yes. The wardrobes had been ripped out of what had been Hayley's bedroom to make way for the plants but the hole in Jenny's wardrobe contained maybe three times as many rolls of money as Tina's two stashes combined.

Heart thudding, I looked in Darcie's room and found a hidey-hole matching mine, containing a carrier bag full of small tablets of varying sizes and colours with different images or letters stamped into them. I gulped as I spotted a pale blue tablet with a hashtag on it inside a circle. During the October half-term break, a few students from the sixth form had been hospitalised after taking ecstasy matching that description and one of them had died.

I took more photos, ensuring I captured that pale blue tablet. Picking up a pencil crayon off Darcie's carpet, I flicked some of the bags aside and my heart plummeted to the floor as my eyes rested on a bag of bright yellow tablets with a bee stamped on them and I remembered what Hayley had told me about how her fiancé Idris died.

I felt sick as I stared at the colourful tablets. It wasn't just a bit of weed – not that that wasn't bad enough – but they were peddling drugs that had killed people.

I took photos of the bee tablets then bundled everything back under the floorboard. I was way out of my depth here. I had to report this and I had to do it now. I could never forgive myself if I left it alone for fear of repercussions on me and somebody else fell ill or died. It wasn't about getting Tina and Jenny into trouble anymore; it was so much bigger than that. I had to do this right. I had to get the police to raid the house today because I couldn't risk Trigg returning and removing everything.

If only Sergeant Kinsella and PC Sunning were contactable. I didn't trust anyone else. I gasped as something struck me. Fizz's surname was Kinsella. It had stuck in my mind because I'd read a few books from an author called Sophie Kinsella and I'd nearly asked her if she was related when I found out.

None of my friends from school had bothered with Facebook. They reckoned it was for old people and anyone our age on Facebook was a saddo but after we'd drifted apart, I'd set up an account. I liked seeing the updates Samantha posted of the hedgehogs. I remembered her posting a photo of her, her dad, Josh and Fizz a couple of weeks ago, wishing their supporters a happy Christmas and I'm sure they were all tagged in. I logged in and frantically scrolled through the feed. There she was: Fizz Kinsella. I didn't have a phone number for her but I could message her:

✉ To Fizz
Long shot. I urgently need to get hold of Sergeant Kinsella. Are you related?

I sent the message and stared at the screen, willing her to reply, hoping she wouldn't ignore my message after what had happened.

✉ From Fizz
He's my dad. Why do you need him? Are you okay?

▣ To Fizz
It's complicated but it really is urgent. Can you
ask him to call me?

I added my phone number. Moments later, my phone rang.

'Sergeant Kinsella?'

'No, it's Fizz. I'm not going to ask my dad to call you unless I know it really is urgent.' She didn't sound mad, just concerned.

'It is! You have to believe me! I didn't steal the money. I knew nothing about it.' I could scarcely catch my breath as it tumbled out in one long jumbled sentence. 'My stepmother and her sister did but they didn't get charged and they've gone on holiday and left me alone with Darcie who's only six and we came to her house to get some things and I found cannabis plants and a stack of ecstasy and rolls of cash and I'm scared and Jenny's boyfriend might return and move the stuff and I can't let that happen 'cause a kid from the sixth form took one and died and so did Hayley's fiancé and—'

'Stop!' Fizz cried. 'Slow down. Breathe. Start from the beginning.'

30

SAMANTHA

I was walking along the side of the farmhouse on my way to the barn when Fizz sprinted across the farmyard towards me.

'I've just spoken to Phoebe,' she cried. 'You're not going to believe this!'

I didn't think it was possible for my opinion of the Grimes family to sink any lower until I'd listened to Fizz's update over drinks in the barn. It was one shocking revelation after another. They'd already racked up charges of arson, vandalism and assault, we knew they were guilty of theft and fraud even if the charges hadn't yet stuck, and now there was evidence of neglect, abandonment and drug dealing.

'Where's Phoebe now?' I asked, my stomach on spin cycle thinking about her. 'Is she okay?'

'I'm not sure where she is but she's fine. Or as fine as you can be in this situation. By the sounds of it, she's doing her best to stay strong for Darcie and not worry or scare her.'

I sank back on the sofa bed, shaking my head, my heart breaking for the pair of them. I'd never heard her mention Darcie before, although she hadn't revealed anything about her life outside of college. It sounded like she'd been Darcie's main caregiver. How had an eighteen-year-old managed that alongside her studies, her work at Hedgehog Hollow and the demands from her stepfamily?

'Is there anything I can do?' I asked.

'I don't know at the moment. Dad was halfway to Harrogate and on the hands-free. He was going to pull over and call Phoebe back and get the ball rolling. He'll have loads to coordinate so I'm not likely to get a speedy update.'

'Is your dad going to cancel his holiday?'

Fizz shrugged. 'It's possible. He's super protective of this place and not just because I work here. He says Gwendoline was one of the nicest women he's ever met. He was gutted she never got to set up the centre here like she dreamed of but he loves how you did it and that I'm involved now.'

Shortly after I met Fizz, she brought in the most amazing photos showing that my grandparents and hers had been friends, having met through a mutual friendship with Gwendoline. I'd met Gwendoline, 'the hedgehog lady', when I was young while staying with Nanna and Gramps and had only remembered that when looking through some old photos with Thomas. To discover that Fizz had also met Gwendoline when she was little made me feel like she'd been destined to be part of Team Hedgehog Hollow.

'Mum'll understand if he does need to cancel,' Fizz continued. 'She's brilliant like that. She knows it's important to him that justice is done. Besides, it was only a couple of nights locally. They can reschedule.'

'How are you feeling? It must have been a shock for you hearing all that from Phoebe.'

'You can say that again. I can't bear thinking of them hurting Phoebe. No wonder she was so jumpy. I keep thinking that, if I'd made more effort to talk to her, maybe she'd have opened up sooner and it wouldn't have got to the point where the money was stolen because they'd already have been locked up.'

'You can't think like that, Fizz. Safeguarding has been a major part of my career but I missed it with Phoebe. I know what to watch out for and, looking back, I see the signs, but I know I can't blame myself and you mustn't either. If her college tutors who spent five days a week with her didn't notice anything, we certainly weren't going to. What's important is that it's out in the open now and it can be dealt with.'

Fizz gave me a grateful smile.

We sat in silence for a moment. I'd tried so hard to engage with Phoebe and so had Fizz. We'd experienced moments where she became animated – usually when talking about her career plans – but she'd quickly shut down. I didn't like to speculate, but I wondered now whether she'd deliberately avoided getting close to us because she'd been worried we'd ask too many questions and open doors she didn't want opening.

I wanted to reach out to her and tell her I was on her side and offer her whatever she needed: someone to talk to, a hot meal, somewhere to stay. I stared at my phone, wondering about the best way forward.

'Are you going to call her?' Fizz asked.

'I want to but I don't want to distract her. She's got Darcie to look after and she might be on the phone to the police. I think I'll send her a text to say we're here for her.'

'That's probably the best for now.'

✉ To Phoebe

I've just spoken to Fizz and wanted you to know we're here for you. Let's draw a line in the sand about the money and focus on you and Darcie. If you need anything, including a place to stay, please let me know. Hope you're both okay. Call me when you can

I wasn't sure when she'd see the text but at least I'd made contact and she knew I wasn't angry with her. I was surprised when a response came straight back.

✉ From Phoebe

Thank you. That means such a lot. They're sending
an unmarked car for Darcie and me so we can be out
of the house when they raid it. Should be here
soon. I'm not sure what will happen to us. They're
calling a social worker to meet us at the police
station. I'm scared they'll take Darcie away. She'd
be devastated and so would I. If you know anyone
who can stop that happening, I could really use
their help

Family law wasn't my area of expertise but my time as a district
nurse had given me some knowledge of child protection services,
fostering and adoption. I knew that the social worker's first priority
would be the safety of the child. From what Fizz had relayed about the
situation, Phoebe had taken the role of responsible adult – despite not
being an adult herself for most of that time – since Darcie was a baby
and being with her was safer than being with her blood relations.

The next focus would be on what was best for the child. With
Phoebe now eighteen and officially an adult, it wasn't an impossibility
that what was best for Darcie was to keep the two of them together. In a
text of less than a hundred words, it was obvious that Darcie was
Phoebe's number one priority and that they had a strong bond. If
Phoebe wanted to go down a fostering route – something I suspect
would never have entered her head until now – this would all help her
case.

And I knew what else would help.

⊠ To Phoebe
I'll get down to the police station as soon as I
can. Please tell the social worker that I'm coming
and that I'm here to support you and Darcie. Stay
strong. We'll help you though this

⊠ From Phoebe

THANK YOU!!!!!

I was in the middle of relaying the text conversation to Fizz when there was a knock and a young auburn-haired woman wearing a smart dress and high heels poked her head round the barn door.

'Can someone help me with a hedgehog?' she asked, disappearing without waiting for an answer.

Fizz and I each grabbed thick gloves and she picked up a pre-prepared crate as we followed the woman into the farmyard.

'Sorry. I've got a car full of children and I didn't want to leave them.'

I peered into the car and saw an auburn-haired boy aged about six in the front seat and a toddler and baby in the back, both asleep.

The boy waved at me. 'We found a hedgehog!' he called through the closed window.

'Shh!' said the woman, who I assumed was his mum. 'You'll wake up Georgia and Poppy.'

She turned to me. 'We're on our way to my parents' for New Year's lunch and we saw a hedgehog in the middle of the road. It has a squashed foot.' She reached for the door handle then hesitated. 'Please don't judge me but I had nothing else to put it in. This was Dylan's suggestion.'

She opened the passenger side door and I couldn't help but laugh at the sight of a hedgehog curled up in a potty on the boy's knee.

'It was my idea!' he declared proudly.

'Are you Dylan?' I asked.

'Yes. And this is Mrs Pricklypants.'

'I'm sorry,' his mum said, resignation in her tone. 'Feel free to change it, especially if it's a boy.'

'It's fun. We'll go for Mr Pricklypants if it's a boy.'

The hedgehog was small, so very likely an autumn juvenile, and its front paw was indeed damaged, although there was no sign of blood, suggesting this might not be a recent injury.

'I'm going to pick Mrs Pricklypants up and transfer her to our crate so we can take her into the rescue centre and make her better.'

'Will her leg fall off?' he asked. 'That would be mint.'

'Dylan!' his mum hissed as I made the transfer into the crate, noting that our patient was female, so no name change needed.

The mum grimaced as she looked at me. 'I'm really sorry. He's going through a bit of a gruesome phase. He's obsessed with blood and guts.'

'I think a lot of kids go through that, don't they? Fizz, can you take our new patient inside and give Josh a call and ask him to come over?'

'Will do.'

While Fizz returned to the barn, I crouched down beside the car. 'A leg falling off probably wouldn't be mint for the hedgehog, but thank you for bringing her in. The potty was a great idea.'

I thanked her and said goodbye. Josh was coming out of the farmhouse as I crossed the yard, with Misty-Blue weaving between his legs.

'Fizz said to come over. Everything okay?' he asked when he joined me.

'We've just a female autumn juvenile admitted. She has a mangled foot but it doesn't look fresh. I haven't inspected her yet but I need to get down to Reddfield police station. They've got Phoebe.'

'They've arrested her?'

'No. Long story.'

We stepped inside the barn and headed towards the treatment table where Fizz had already started a chart for Mrs Pricklypants and was weighing her. I couldn't help noticing the scales. Underweight. But I didn't have time to get distracted. I had to leave this one to them.

'The Grimes family are even worse than we thought,' I told Josh. 'Fizz will give you more detail when you've sorted Mrs Pricklypants – don't ask – but Tina and Jenny Grimes have disappeared to the Caribbean using the money they stole from us and have left Phoebe in charge of Jenny's granddaughter Darcie, who's only six. She's just discovered that they're both drug dealers and there's cannabis growing in one of the houses. Fizz's dad is coordinating raids right now and Phoebe's on her way to Reddfield police station to give evidence, but she's worried they'll take Darcie away and I want to help. But there's the hedgehog and my family are still here and—'

'And Phoebe needs you,' he said gently. 'Go!'

'Are you sure? It's a lot to dump on you.'

'You're not dumping it on me. We're a team. I've got Fizz to help and we've got a farm full of family. I'm sure everyone will muck in with whatever needs doing.' He hugged me. 'But take care of you and those anxiety levels.'

'I will. I don't know what's going to happen with Social Services but, if Phoebe and Darcie need a place to stay...'

Josh didn't miss a beat. 'There's plenty of room at the inn. Ring me if you need anything.'

'You're the best. And thank you, Fizz. If your dad calls, can you let him know I've gone to the station and that we can help look after them? I know it's probably not his area, but...'

'I'll tell him. See you later. Give Phoebe my love.'

Halfway down the farm track, a wave of panic swept through me and I had to stop for a moment to catch my breath. *It'll be okay. Anything you're going through right now is nothing compared to what Phoebe must be experiencing. You can be strong for her. You know you can.* I put the jeep back into gear, and set off once again.

31

'Is this the magical mystical adventure?' Darcie asked as we sat in the back of the unmarked police car – a big silver one with leather seats. I'd never been in a posh car like this before, although I'd probably only been in a handful of cars in my lifetime. Neither Tina nor Jenny owned one and I wasn't sure either of them could even drive. Their sons would 'borrow' a car if they needed one.

'Not yet,' I told her, squeezing her hand. 'You know how those nice policemen invited us to look round the police station the other day and we couldn't go? Well, we're going to do that now, although might not get a grand tour. We'll probably go into a room and some people will ask us some questions.'

'Will we still get chocolate biscuits like the policeman promised?'

'I don't know, Princess. I hope so.'

The female police constable in the front passenger seat, who'd introduced herself as PC Griegson, turned round and smiled at Darcie. 'Are chocolate biscuits your favourite?'

'Yes. But I like Jammie Dodgers too.'

'Now you're talking! They're my favourites. I don't like chocolate.'

Darcie looked stunned. 'Everybody likes chocolate!'

'When I was a little girl, I ate too many Easter eggs in one day and it made me very poorly so I've never been able to eat chocolate since. So never eat all your Easter eggs in one day.'

'I only get one.' Darcie looked up at me and smiled gratefully. Jenny told me off for spoiling her, but there was no way I was going to let her go without. Easter eggs hardly broke the bank. Now that I knew how much money they had, it disgusted me even more that they'd never so much as bothered with a token 99p purchase. I thought about all those Christmases when Darcie had barely received any gifts, the clothes that were too small for her, me never being allowed to take her anywhere because it was supposedly too expensive. What a joke!

I watched out of the window, my heart racing. I knew I'd 100 per cent done the right thing but it didn't stop me feeling sick. Could they be raiding the houses right now? There'd been a patrol car stationed outside Jenny's house when we were picked up and another outside Tina's when we stopped by to collect the rest of Darcie's belongings and what was left of mine.

We were taken into the police station through a back entrance, which was comforting in case Trigg had somebody watching the front door. Darcie clung onto my hand as I wheeled her suitcase behind us, a carrier bag containing her nightlight hooked over my arm with a couple of other carrier bags. PC Griegson had accompanied us into Tina's house and suggested we pack anything we might want as it was unlikely we'd return for some time. Hopefully never! I'd left the bedding behind and squashed Darcie's other things into her case. Thanks to Tina's scissors frenzy, what was left of my belongings had fit into my backpack and two carrier bags.

The policeman who'd been driving left us and PC Griegson led us into a room with a table and four chairs in it.

'Do you want to put your case and bags in the corner?' she suggested. 'I'll go on a chocolate biscuit hunt and be back soon.'

'What's that red button for?' Darcie asked, pointing to a panic button on the wall as she clambered onto one of the chairs.

'Some of the people who get brought into this room aren't very nice and they might try to fight with the police officers. That button's for them to get some help if that happens.'

Her eyes widened. 'It's bad to fight. Two boys in year five had a fight in the playground at school and...'

I nodded and smiled but I'd zoned out again. I hated myself for it, but my mind couldn't rest. What was going to happen to us and, more importantly, what was going to happen to Darcie? Tina and Jenny both terrified me, but the fear of losing Darcie was different. It was an emotional one which made my heart ache and I'd never felt this scared before.

'The greedy boys have eaten them all,' PC Griegson said when she returned a little later, 'but the vending machine had these. Hope you like Kit Kats.'

She placed a couple of soft drinks and Kit Kats on the table. Darcie thanked her and eagerly unwrapped hers.

'How much do I owe you?' I asked, hating that she was out of pocket for us but secretly hoping she'd waive it.

'Nothing. It's on me. There's a woman in reception for you, Phoebe. She says her name's Samantha Wishaw and you work with her. Is that right?'

I nodded. 'Can I see her?'

'I'll let her through. I just wanted to make sure she was...' Her eyes flicked to Darcie and I understood her point.

'Samantha's a friend.' I wasn't sure if that was strictly accurate, but she'd offered her help and she was here, so that had to signify something.

When the door opened five minutes later and Samantha rushed in with her arms outstretched, I burst into tears. We'd never hugged before but it felt natural. The past few days had been horrendous but now I wasn't alone.

'Phoebe?' Darcie sounded uncertain as she tugged on my coat. I sniffed and wiped my eyes before crouching down beside her.

'Yes, Princess?'

'Why are you crying?'

How could I even begin to answer that question?

'Some things have made me sad recently but it's going to be all right now.'

She thrust her unicorn at me. 'Twizzle will make you better.'

'Aw, thank you for that,' I said, cuddling the unicorn. 'But do you know what makes me even better than Twizzle hugs? Darcie hugs!'

She flung her arms round my neck and squeezed me.

'This is Darcie, my favourite person in the whole world,' I said, looking up at Samantha.

'And Twizzle,' Darcie added.

'Yes, and Twizzle the magical unicorn.'

Samantha smiled at them. 'It's lovely to meet you both. My name's Samantha and I love unicorns nearly as much as I love hedgehogs.'

Darcie gasped. 'I love hedgehogs too!'

'I'm very happy to hear that because do you know what I do for my job? I run a rescue centre where people bring hedgehogs that are poorly or have been hurt and I try to make them better.'

'Like a hospital?'

'Exactly like a hospital. In fact, some people who run hedgehog rescue centres call them hogspitals but I don't do that because I find it really hard to say.'

Darcie tried to say the word and giggled as she stumbled over it several times.

'See what I mean!' Samantha said. 'We also get lots of baby hedge-hogs to look after at certain times of the year and do you know what we call baby hedgehogs? Hoglets. Isn't that sweet?'

'That's sooo cute. What's a baby unicorn called? Phoebe doesn't know.'

'My friend Fizz says they're called sparkles or shimmers.'

'Oooh, magical!'

Darcie's eyes shone with excitement while mine sparkled with tears again. To Darcie, Samantha was a complete stranger. She had no idea what our connection was because she knew nothing of my work at Hedgehog Hollow but, in the space of a few minutes, Samantha had already given her more focus and attention than I'd seen from Jenny or Tina in her lifetime. She'd shown how easy it was to have a two-minute conversation about unicorns. Why couldn't they have done that instead of constantly telling her to be quiet?

'I'm so sorry about...' I started but Samantha shook her head.

'Line in the sand, remember? We can talk about it later if you want, but let's focus on you two for now.' She took a colouring book and a packet of crayons out of her bag and placed them on the table. 'Do you like colouring in, Darcie?'

'I love it!'

'Do you want to colour in a pretty picture for me while I talk to Phoebe?'

Darcie settled onto one of the chairs, opened the crayons and flicked through the book.

There wasn't anywhere we could go that was completely out of earshot, but we shuffled over to the side of the room.

'What's happening?' Samantha asked, her voice low.

'They need to interview me and we're waiting for a social worker. That's all I know so far.'

Her eyes flicked to Darcie's suitcase and my bags in the corner of the room. 'You can stay at Hedgehog Hollow. Tonight, tomorrow, as long as you need.'

'I can't do that. Not after what I did.'

'Did you steal the money?' she asked, her voice gentle.

'No, but—'

'Did you give Tina the cheque book?'

'No!'

She gave me a reassuring smile. 'Then you did nothing wrong.' She glanced in Darcie's direction again. 'Neither of you did, and it's about time somebody had your back. That person's me. Actually, it's more than me. It's Josh and Fizz and our families. We'll do whatever we can to help.'

'Can you help me keep Darcie?'

'I don't know, but I promise I'll try my best.'

A few days ago, my priority for the future had been getting away from Tina, getting my qualifications and getting a job, but all that had changed. Darcie was top of my list and we had to stay together. I was prepared to fight the police and Social Services and whoever said I couldn't have her because, from the moment I first saw her six and a half years ago, I'd cared for and protected her like nobody else. She was my family and I'd do whatever it took to keep us together.

32

PHOEBE

Six and a half years ago

'Are you excited?' Rosemary asked as she brushed my long hair ready for plaiting. I could do plaits myself, but I knew Rosemary enjoyed it, especially since her daughter Andrea and her children had moved to London.

Rosemary missed Matthew and Morgan loads. I didn't. They were four and two years older than me and I used to love playing with them when we were younger but they'd turned nasty when they started senior school. I'd never told Rosemary that. She adored her grand-children.

'I'm nervous,' I said. 'What if they don't like me?'

'Impossible!' she declared. 'You, Phoebe Corbyn, are the loveliest young lady I have ever met. Smile and be yourself and I'm sure your dad's new girlfriend and her family will love you just as much as I do.'

'Do you think Dad will marry Tina?'

'They've only just started dating!'

'But he's very happy and he says he loves her.'

'Does he? Oh. Well, some people do fall in love very quickly. My Sydney and I did.'

Rosemary's husband Sydney had a heart attack just after I turned four. My only memory was of a tall blond-haired man letting me stand on his feet while he danced me round the room, making me giggle. He'd tried it with Morgan, but she didn't like it.

I used to wish Dad and Rosemary would get married. I'd said that to Rosemary when I was younger and she'd laughed so much she got the hiccups. She said she was old enough to be Dad's mum.

Rosemary finished plaiting my hair and spun me round to face her. 'Beautiful!'

'Morgan's beautiful. I'm not.' I hadn't meant to say that but it just slipped out. Morgan often gazed adoringly at her reflection and told me that some girls were beautiful like her and others were battered with the ugly stick, like me.

I pictured her with her long blonde wavy hair, dark blue eyes and long eyelashes. Even though I didn't like her anymore, she was still the prettiest girl I'd ever seen. Her hair was never bushy like mine and she didn't need braces like me to make her teeth straight.

'Don't say things like that, darling girl.' Rosemary placed her hands on my shoulders and marched me into her bedroom, stopping in front of a long mirror on her wardrobe door. 'Look at you! You and Morgan may look completely different but you're both beautiful young women. Never forget that.'

I gazed at my reflection and smiled at Rosemary peering over my shoulder. 'Thank you for making Morgan's dress fit.'

Andrea was always buying Morgan new clothes which got handed down to me when Morgan declared them 'last season'. Some of them hadn't even been worn! Morgan thought it was funny that I got her cast-offs, but it didn't bother me.

I was slim with no curves – another reason for Morgan to poke fun at me – but Rosemary was brilliant at sewing, so she took most of the clothes in for me, although she had something wrong with her eyes and had told me she probably wouldn't be able to sew for much longer.

There was a knock on the door. 'That'll be your dad,' Rosemary said, leaving the room.

I stayed where I was, twisting and turning. My hair did look smoother and shinier today and the mint green dress with pink roses on it was so pretty.

Dad had always taught me to be nice to other people and said that true beauty was what was on the inside. Morgan might be pretty on the outside but she was ugly on the inside. I'd seen her picking on other kids too. I decided that, if inner and outer beauty were added together, I must be prettier than Morgan.

* * *

'How many people will be there?' I asked Dad as we walked towards Tina's estate. It was about half an hour from our home in Renleigh Court, but I didn't mind the walk. Dad had never had a car so I was used to walking everywhere. I thought he might buy one now after winning £15,000 on the premium bonds but he said it was an 'unnecessary luxury' and he wanted to spoil me for a bit first.

'About twenty-five,' Dad said. 'It's mainly family but I think there are some friends going too.'

It was Easter Sunday but also Tina's sister Jenny's thirty-eighth birthday. Jenny, who lived on the same estate, was having a barbeque in her garden to celebrate, which gave me a chance to meet everyone at the same time. This was another reason why I thought Dad might marry Tina. He'd had girlfriends before but I'd never met their families. I hadn't even met most of the girlfriends. Tina was obviously very special.

I wanted them to like me so badly that I'd been revising the names and ages Dad had told me. I was most excited about meeting the baby. Dad said she was called Darcie and she was only three months old. I loved babies.

'Do you think Hayley will let me hold baby Darcie?' I asked.

'If you ask her nicely and tell her you've done it before, I'm sure she will.'

We arrived at Jenny's house. Music was coming from the back garden and I could hear people laughing and smell sausages and burgers cooking. Dad led me down the side of the house and through a metal gate.

'You'll be fine,' he said, as I grabbed his hand, butterflies swarming in my tummy at all the strangers scattered across the lawn. 'They'll love you.'

'Vinnie!' A tall woman with short, dark hair wearing tight jeans, a low-cut top and giant hoop earrings ran across the grass and planted a big kiss on Dad's lips.

I nearly died of embarrassment when he responded and they did a proper smooch in front of me. She even squeezed his bum.

'This is my daughter, Phoebe,' Dad said when they finally came up for air.

Tina looked me up and down and I could have sworn she was about to say something nasty because that was the look that Morgan used to give me all the time, but then she smiled and reached for my hand. 'I've been looking forward to meeting you so much, Phoebe. Let me introduce you to my boys.'

Half an hour later, I'd been introduced to everyone except the one person I desperately wanted to meet.

'Excuse me,' I said to Tina and Jenny's mum, Vera. 'Do you know where the baby is?'

'Hayley's baby? She'll be with Hayley in her bedroom.'

'Can I go up and see her?'

'That's up to our Jenny. Oi! Jenny!'

Jenny looked over and blew a cloud of smoke in the air. I didn't like her. I'd given her some flowers as a birthday gift and she'd curled her lip up at them. Tina had nudged her and told her I'd bought them with my own pocket money and weren't they beautiful. She'd given me a fake smile as she agreed, but she hadn't thanked me.

'What?' she snapped, scowling as she stubbed out her cigarette on the garden path.

'Can the kid go up to see Hayley and the baby?'

'I suppose so. Tina wants to make an announcement first. She can find her after that.'

'Thank you,' I said to Vera.

'You're a polite little thing, aren't you?'

I didn't know if I was meant to answer that, so I smiled and nodded.

A loud two-fingered whistle silenced everyone. Tina stood in the middle of the garden holding a bottle of lager and beckoned Jenny over.

'As you all know, it's our Jenny's birthday today. Thirty-eight today, so happy birthday to my little sister.' She swigged her drink and smiled at Jenny. 'We don't normally do parties but we decided to have a do for both our birthdays this year. It's my fortieth on the 14th June so keep that free, but it's gonna be a bit different to today 'cause it's not just my birthday. Vinnie asked me to marry him and I said yes and we thought when better to do it than my fortieth.'

My jaw dropped as Dad joined her. They were getting married in June? That was only two months away! And why hadn't he told me first? I wasn't sure I liked hearing such big news at the same time as everyone else.

'And I'm gonna be bridesmaid,' Jenny announced.

'And me!' Tina's oldest son Cody quipped, earning a clip across the ear from Jenny.

I tried to catch Dad's eye to see if I'd be a bridesmaid – a dream come true – but he was too busy gazing adoringly at Tina and, next thing, they had their tongues down each other's throats again. I shuddered. I hoped they wouldn't keep doing that when they were married.

People had gathered round Dad and Tina to say congratulations. I hung back, waiting for Dad to find me when he was ready. And I waited and waited.

'I'd go in and see the baby if I was you,' Vera said. 'I think your dad's got other things on his mind.'

I looked up the garden and they were at it again. Yuck!

There were a few people in the kitchen but none of them paid any attention to me. I passed through to the empty lounge which was dark and cool and smelled of stale cigarette smoke and something sweet I didn't recognise. I could hear a baby crying so I opened the door into the hall and raced up the stairs. The sound was coming from the bedroom at the back of the house.

'Please stop crying!' The woman sounded tearful. 'I've fed you and changed you and you've had a sleep. I don't know what else you want me to do!'

Someone had left the bathroom light on and I could hear the hum of the fan over the baby's cries.

The bedroom door was ajar and I could see a woman pacing up and down by the bed while the distressed baby lay in the middle of the duvet. The curtains were drawn and there were no lights on so I couldn't get a good look at either of them.

'Do you want me to try?' I asked.

She stopped pacing. 'Who are you?'

'I'm Phoebe. My dad's marrying Tina.'

'Marrying? Since when?'

'They just announced it.'

'No way!' She shook her head. 'I'm Hayley, by the way. You know about babies?'

'I sometimes help with our neighbour's baby.'

'Knock yourself out. Nothing seems to work for me, but that's the story of my sad little life.' Her voice cracked and she sank onto the bed, crying.

I didn't know what would work with Hayley, but I had an idea how to stop Darcie crying. I picked her up and carried her into the bathroom, gently rocking her. She paused for a moment, looking up at me with curious brown eyes, then wailed again.

'What's all the noise, Darcie?' I asked in a low sing-song voice. 'Who's a beautiful little girl? I love your hair. And what a pretty dress you're wearing.'

I carried her over to the window and opened it a smidge to let a bit of air in as she felt quite hot to me. The fan continued to whirr and I stood as close as I could to it.

Five minutes later, the cries had stopped.

'How did you do that?'

I turned to face Hayley and tried not to react. Dad had told me she was nearly seventeen, but it was still a shock to see someone so young, knowing she was already a mum. Her cheeks were red and streaked from her tears, and her long dark hair was messier than mine when I woke up each morning, but she was still really pretty. She obviously took after her auntie rather than her mum.

'Babies like certain noises. Things like fans and hoovers and car engines can help soothe them. And she might have been a bit hot, too.'

'Too hot?' She smacked her palm against her forehead. 'Why didn't I think of that?'

'Would you like her back?'

'Are your arms aching?'

'No. I could cuddle her forever. I love babies.'

Hayley sighed. 'You're the only one in this house who does, then.' She returned to the bedroom and I wasn't sure if I should follow or not so I stayed by the fan.

'Your dad and Tina are really getting married?' she called.

I took that as an invitation to join her. She'd opened the curtains a little way, letting some light and a gentle breeze into the room.

'You can sit on the bed if you like.'

I plumped a pillow with one hand and settled against the head-board with Darcie snuggled on my lap.

'They're getting married on Tina's fortieth birthday in June. Your mum's going to be a bridesmaid.'

She wrinkled her nose as though the thought of her mum in a bridesmaid dress grossed her out. 'Are you going to be?'

I shrugged, disappointment flowing through me. 'I don't know. Nobody's asked me.'

'How old are you?'

'Twelve.'

'Where's your mum?'

'She was killed in a hit and run when I was a baby.'

'Shit! Seriously?'

I nodded. 'My dad says your boyfriend died too.'

She sank onto the other end of the bed. 'He was my fiancé. He was on his stag do and he took something he shouldn't have and it killed him.'

I didn't know what that meant and Hayley must have spotted my confused look.

'Drugs. Idris didn't do drugs. Hated them. But somebody either talked him into taking "E" or slipped him it without him knowing. It killed him. Don't do drugs.' She shouted the last part. Darcie jumped and I thought she was going to cry again.

'I won't.'

'Good. It's a waste of money and life.' She ran her hands through her hair. 'So will you be moving in with Auntie Tina?'

I hadn't thought of that but we'd probably have to. There were only two bedrooms in our flat, which wasn't enough for Dad and Tina, Connor and me. Tina's oldest boy Cody had already moved out and was living with his girlfriend.

'Nobody talked to you about that either?' Hayley suggested when I didn't respond. 'Bloody typical. I hope your dad knows what he's doing.'

'He says he loves Tina.'

'Is your dad loaded?'

'No.'

'Really? No flashy job? Big inheritance? Lottery win?'

'He won some money on the premium bonds just before Christmas.'

'Bingo!'

'It wasn't that much. Well, it was for us, but it won't stretch far.'

'In that case, I'm sure they're madly and deeply in love.'

I couldn't tell if she was being sarcastic or not so I focused on Darcie, stroking her soft black hair and her pudgy cheeks.

'You're a baby whisperer.' Hayley sounded impressed. 'I wish I could pay you to be here all the time to help me with her.'

'I've got school.'

'Shame.'

'I don't mind looking after her on weekends sometimes.'

'Why would you want to give up your weekend looking after someone else's baby?'

'Because she's cute.'

Hayley seemed to accept that, which was lucky because I don't think she'd have understood it if I'd given her the real reason. Every time I was round a baby, I felt this overwhelming need to protect it and keep it safe.

I'd said that to Rosemary and she'd wondered if it was because of mum. People who'd seen the accident said she'd pushed my pram out of the way before the car hit her, protecting me at the very end. Rosemary thought I was trying to protect the babies but also play the part of being a mum; something my own mum hadn't had a chance to do. I wasn't sure. It sounded very complicated to me.

33

PHOEBE

Four and a half years ago

Two years later, Jenny's fortieth birthday fell on a Monday but that didn't stop her spending all day celebrating. She didn't work so she was down the local pub from opening time with her boyfriend, Tina, and Dad, who was between shifts.

Before he met Tina, I'd never seen Dad drunk. Now it was a regular thing. The four of them were always down the pub when he wasn't working and he got a right grump on if I said anything.

Everything changed after they got married. Tina had been divorced twice and said she wanted to do it 'right' this time, so we didn't move in until after the wedding. She probably knew we'd see through her if we had and it would all be over.

She'd been really friendly to me before then, even though she never asked me to be her bridesmaid. I'd wanted to be so desperately but Dad wouldn't interfere because he said it was her decision and I had to respect it.

As soon as we moved in, it started. It was like a switch had been flicked and Fake Tina was replaced by Real Tina who was mean and vindictive, just like her sister. She was clever with it, never making snide comments, putting me down or barking orders when Dad was around. When he was home, it was all pet names: *Ooh, would you be a love and make me a cuppa? You couldn't do the washing-up for once tonight could you, sweetheart?* For once? I *always* did the washing-up and the cleaning.

Dad was besotted with her, so I'm not sure he'd have noticed even if she had snapped at me in front of him. Even though Dad was the one who worked long shifts while Tina did sod all each day, he'd be the one massaging her shoulders or feet on an evening. She had him decorating the house whenever he had a spare moment, which meant he never got to spend any time with me. It had always been just the two of us before Tina came along and it hurt that he didn't seem to want to spend time with me anymore.

I spent more time with Hayley and baby Darcie than I did with Dad and that's where I headed straight from school this evening while the adults were down the pub celebrating. It was my usual evening for visiting anyway. I went round every Monday and Wednesday to take Darcie out for a walk in her buggy then back to Tina's for tea so Hayley could spend a couple of hours with her boyfriend Joel.

Hayley worked on weekends, so Darcie spent Friday night until Sunday afternoon at Tina's house, in theory being looked after by the whole family but in reality only being looked after by me. I didn't mind. Dad nearly always worked a weekend shift and the rest of them never spoke to me unless it was to issue an order, so it was nice to have someone to talk to, even if she couldn't talk back.

Hayley must have been waiting for me because the front door flew open as soon as I walked up the path and she didn't look impressed. 'You're late!'

'Sorry! I needed to speak to one of my teachers.'

She glanced up and down the street as she tightened the belt on her red satin robe.

'Help me with the buggy,' she said, stepping back from the door. Darcie was already strapped in.

'Hello, Princess,' I said, bending down. Darcie giggled as I tickled her tummy.

'Hurry! My, erm... Joel will be here any minute.'

I grabbed the bottom bar and helped Hayley lift the buggy out onto the path.

'Can I say hello to Joel today?'

'No! He's shy. I've told you before. He doesn't like meeting people. Off you go! And no returning within the next two hours. I'll text you when he's gone.'

'Okay. See you later.'

She took another look up and down the street then closed the door. I was tempted to loiter so I could see what her boyfriend looked like but I knew it would upset her, so I pushed Darcie in the direction of the park.

I didn't understand Hayley's relationship with Joel. I didn't know anything about him other than his name. She always did her hair when he was coming round and applied full make-up, but she never seemed excited about seeing him. I'd mentioned it to her and asked her if it was because she'd loved Idris so much that it was hard to be happy with someone else. She said, 'Something like that.' I suggested that it might be better to be single for a while if she wasn't ready for a new man. She laughed and muttered something about wishing her life was that simple.

I'd also once asked her why she was never dressed when Joel was due. 'Are you *really* that naïve?' she'd responded. I still hadn't lived that one down.

* * *

Two hours passed and there'd been no text. Then two and a half. I texted Hayley to ask if the coast was clear but she didn't reply.

Another fifteen minutes passed and I had a horrible feeling in my gut that I couldn't place. I put Darcie's coat on, strapped her in her buggy and pushed her round to Butler Street.

The downstairs was in darkness but I could see a dim light upstairs – probably the landing light.

'Hayley?' I called up the stairs. 'We're back. Hayley?'

Music drifted down and I recognised it as the song Hayley and Idris had chosen for their first dance at their wedding. When I dropped Darcie back on a Sunday afternoon, she was usually listening to it and had told me why it was her favourite track.

Her bedroom was full of photos of Idris or the two of them together. It was so sad that he'd never met his baby girl and that Darcie would never know her daddy. I often thought it was one of the reasons I cared about Darcie so much; because I knew what it was like to have had a parent taken away before you got to know them.

I left Darcie strapped in her buggy and my heart thumped with each step. The song ended then started again.

'Hayley? Are you okay?'

As I reached the top of the stairs, I could see that her bedroom door was open and the room was dimly lit by a bedside light. I pushed the door open a little further. The duvet was in a rumpled heap in the middle of the bed but there was no sign of Hayley. I tried the bathroom and even peeked in Jenny's and Darcie's rooms, but all the rooms were empty.

I was about to go down when I heard a noise from Hayley's bedroom. My heart thumped as I stepped back inside and peered behind the door. Hayley was on the floor with her back against the wall, hugging her legs, her body shaking with sobs.

'Hayley? What happened?' I crouched beside her.

She didn't answer; just sobbed louder.

'Is it Joel? Is it over?'

She raised her head and I gasped. Her left eye was bruised and so badly swollen she could hardly open it and there were streaks of mascara down her cheeks.

'Did Joel do that?'

No answer.

'Have you put any ice on it?'

I took the silence as a no and ran downstairs, pasting a smile on my face for Darcie.

'I just need to get something for your mummy,' I told her, wheeling the buggy into the lounge. 'Can you watch some cartoons while I do that?'

She smiled as I put the TV on and left her strapped in her buggy for safety while I rummaged in the freezer. The ice cube trays were empty but there was a bag of frozen peas.

I thought Hayley might object, telling me to stop fussing over her, but she let me hold the bag against her eye, wincing as it made contact.

'I hope you've dumped him,' I said after a while.

'I can't.'

'Why not? If I had a boyfriend who thumped me, I'd dump him.'

'It's not that simple,' she muttered, the tears starting to flow. She momentarily released her legs and I winced at angry red welts across both her arms.

'He did that too?' I dropped the bag of peas as I reached for one of her arms but she hastily wrapped them round her legs again.

'You should go.'

'I'm not leaving you like this. I think we should call the police.'

'No!'

'But look what he's done to you! What if he comes back? What if he hits you again or hurts Darcie?'

She seemed to suddenly remember her daughter. 'Oh, my God! Where is she?'

'Watching telly. She's fine. It's you I'm worried about.'

She stared at me for a moment, shaking her head. 'Why? Why do you care? Why do you spend endless hours looking after a toddler who isn't even related to you? Don't you have friends or a boyfriend you'd rather be spending time with?'

I shrugged. 'I've got friends and I hang out with them when I'm not with Darcie but I love being with her. I always wanted a little sister.'

'She's better off with you than with me.'

'Don't say that. You're a good mum.'

'You wouldn't think that if you knew what I do while you're looking after her.' She grabbed the bag of peas and pressed them against her eye.

I sat back against her bed. 'Try me.'

She stared at me again, as though weighing up whether she could trust me. Then she sighed. 'I don't have a boyfriend. There is no Joel.'

'Then who do you see on Mondays and Wednesdays?'

'Whoever's booked in.'

Her jaw tensed as she waited for my reaction. The going-out hair and make-up but staying in a satin robe. The insistence we leave the house until she'd texted to say the coast was clear. It all made sense now.

'Is that what you do on a weekend, too?'

'Yep. My weekends are fun-filled and action-packed.' Her voice dripped with sarcasm.

Hayley could be sarcastic with me and a bit snappy at times but I liked her and thought of her as a big sister. When I dropped Darcie off, I usually stayed to chat. She never made me feel like I was in the way or that there was something she'd rather be doing.

She wasn't a bad mum. She was gentle and attentive towards Darcie. With her working on weekends, I'd thought she was the only role model in the family, but this wasn't the sort of work I'd expected.

'When did it start?' I asked.

Her bottom lip wobbled. 'You'll hate me if I tell you.'

'You've just told me what your job is and I'm still here, aren't I?'

Twenty minutes later, with Darcie bathed and ready for bed, we sat on the sofa with mugs of tea, Darcie tucked in beside Hayley while she watched more cartoons.

'My family are...' She sighed and shook her head. 'You're not daft. You know what my family are. Waste of space, every last one of 'em. My grandparents taught Mum and Auntie Tina that you don't need to bother at school because qualifications are only needed to get a job, and you don't need to get a job when you can live off benefits and nick what the benefits don't cover. I didn't like the way they looked at life. I wanted to be the first one in the family to get qualifications and a proper job but they all hated that. Told me I was stuck-up, thinking I was better than them. Mum would make studying impossible by playing loud music or inventing jobs for me to do and often my homework would *accidentally* get damaged. So when I hit your age and started with my GCSEs, I went to the library after school and on weekends but I had to lie to Mum about it. Says a lot about my family that she'd have been ashamed of me for studying but proud of me if I'd been out shoplifting and sleeping around.'

I knew what she meant about the studying thing. 'Tina's always having a dig at me for doing my homework. She says she left school with no qualifications and it never did her any harm. As if she'd ever be my role model!'

Hayley managed a weak smile. 'Ignore her. Keep studying, pass your exams, and get the hell out of there as soon as you can.'

'What about Dad?'

She shrugged. 'Not your problem. It might sound harsh but he made his choice. It wasn't your choice so don't stay because of him.'

She was right, although it didn't make me feel any better.

'So I was pretty much living at the library and that's where I met Idris. He was volunteering there. He was three years older than me and at college.' She hugged Darcie closer and stroked the little girl's hair as tears pooled in her eyes. 'He was the most beautiful man I'd ever seen. I was trying to get a book down from a high shelf and he helped me, our hands touched, and that was it. We knew instantly we'd met the one but my family hated him.'

'Why?'

'Because, like me, he studied and worked and they don't trust people like that. *Ideas above his station, that one*, Mum would say. His parents were just as bad. I came from a council estate so I automatically wasn't good enough for their son. When we announced our engagement, they said it was me or their financial support. He chose me so they kicked him out and cut him off.'

'Wow! That's harsh.'

'It isn't even the start of it. They blamed me for...' She glanced down at Darcie and lowered her voice to a whisper, 'for his death and refused to ever meet Darcie. Accused me of sleeping around and that Darcie wasn't even his. I tried to tell them that Idris was my first and only, but they didn't believe me. Looked at where I was from, who my family were, and refused to see beyond their prejudices. Thing is, Darcie's the spit of him. If they'd ever laid eyes on her, they'd know that.'

'They've *never* seen her?' I whispered.

She kissed Darcie's head. 'No, and they're missing out on so much, but what can I do? I used to send them photos, hoping they'd recognise Idris in her and accept she was his, but they returned them unopened. They've moved down south somewhere and I don't even have an address now.'

'So how did you end up...?'

'I lost the plot when Idris died. Not only had my whole future been snatched away but it made sod all sense. Drugs! A stupid bright yellow tablet with a bee on it, for fuck's sake. Idris *hated* drugs. This was a man who'd never smoked, only drank occasionally, ate well, and exercised regularly. He was all about clean living.'

'I'm so sorry.'

'Me too. Such a waste of everything. So his parents turned on me and, deep down, I knew that was unfair because drugs weren't my world either, but they said some nasty things and I believed them. I couldn't eat or sleep. I managed to convince myself that he'd been murdered and whoever did it was coming for me too. I couldn't pay the rent without Idris's wages, so I faced eviction, and then Mum and Auntie Tina showed up and they were lovely. Sorted everything out that I'd let slip. Mum said I could move back home and she'd take care of me and the baby when she arrived. I didn't want to come home but what choice did I have? She promised she'd changed and it seemed like she had. That first month at home wasn't the disaster I expected.'

She winced as she repositioned the peas. 'Then it started. The Idris-bashing. Constant snide comments and digs and I realised this was how it would be for the rest of my life if I stayed with her. A few months after Darcie was born – probably round about the time I met you – I knew I had to get out. I wasn't a priority for a council house because I already had somewhere to stay, so the only way I was going to be able to get out was to get a job with decent pay. But how does someone with average GCSEs and no work experience get decent pay?'

Darcie had fallen asleep on Hayley's knee and she stroked the little girl's hair back from her forehead. 'I'm not proud of myself. It's not what I want for me or this one but I feel trapped now. The pay's good. It's not forever. I'll have enough saved eventually to start over properly. I could maybe go to college. Do Idris proud. He'd have hated this.'

As more tears tracked down her cheeks, I wiped my own away. 'Then stop doing it.'

'I can't.'

'Even after someone bust your eye?'

'It was a one-off. Most of my clients are regulars and they treat me well – lonely old men who've lost their wives and sometimes just want someone to talk to, men who lack confidence with women and want a teacher. The client tonight was new and I thought I knew better. He won't be back, but it's always going to be a risk.'

I was only fourteen, still at school, and had never even kissed anyone so I wasn't the person to offer advice on anyone's career choice or anything connected with sex, but this couldn't be the way.

'What does your mum say about it?' There was no way she didn't know what was going on in her own home.

'She went mad at first, but Mum is only motivated by one thing: money. As soon as she discovered how much I'd earned, she was suddenly all for it and pretty much took over. We needed to do it from here, Darcie needed to be taken care of by you or Dottie down the road, and she'd vet the clients. For a significant share of my earnings, of course.'

'So your mum's your pimp?'

'Ssh! Don't ever let her hear you say that. She's my PA. She still hates it but, you know, good money and all that. And she won't let anyone call when Darcie's in the house. That's good of her.'

I wasn't sure whether Hayley was trying to convince me or herself.

34

SAMANTHA

Present day

I glanced in the rear-view mirror at Phoebe and Darcie, fast asleep in the back of the jeep as we drove back from the police station on New Year's Day.

Phoebe had insisted on sitting in the less comfortable middle seat so she could hold Darcie's hand. They looked so peaceful, hands clasped, heads together, clearly exhausted from the ordeal. I felt drained myself, so it had to have taken its toll on them.

The on-call social worker, Jackie Laine, was behind us, making a detour on her way home to retrieve the car seat she'd loaned me. We'd been at the police station for hours. Phoebe had wanted me to accompany her while she made her statement as she was keen that I know the full story and didn't think she could face going through it twice.

Sergeant Kinsella had delayed his minibreak, as Fizz suspected, so he led the discussion, accompanied by PC Griegson.

Hearing what that family had put Phoebe through was both shocking and heart-breaking. I had to battle to stay strong and not cry because this was about Phoebe, not me. But when she'd pushed up the sleeves on her long-sleeved T-shirt, I couldn't keep the sobs back. Her arms were a patchwork of scars caused by cigarette burns, scalds and scratches and I vividly remembered her washing her hands in the barn one day and spaying water on her denim jacket but refusing to take it off. Now I knew what she'd been hiding.

When she produced her laptop and started scrolling through four years' worth of photos showing bruises, bites and burns, I had to step out for some air. Who could inflict physical pain like that on another person? She'd saved the images under a file called 'one day'. Praying it would stop *one day*. Hoping she'd escape *one day*. Longing for justice *one day*. How did a young girl find the strength to go from each day to the next like that?

Until today, all I'd seen of Phoebe was an extremely capable but nervous, timid young girl. During those conversations with the police and Jackie, I saw a strong, determined woman demonstrating maturity way beyond her years. Phoebe wasted no time laying her cards on the table with Jackie, and I was in awe of how confidently she spoke even though I knew she had to be terrified.

'I know I'm not related to Darcie by blood but that doesn't mean I'm not her family. I've spent more time looking after her over the past six and a half years than any of her blood relatives, including her mum. Darcie's my little sister, I love her, and I'll do anything to protect her. You have to promise me you'll let me keep looking after her and not send her off to live with strangers.'

Jackie gave her a warm smile. 'Thank you for that, Phoebe. I can't promise you anything until we've talked some more and I've spent some time with Darcie, but I can reassure you that we're all about doing what's best for her. My priority is to keep Darcie safe. I've spoken with Sergeant Kinsella and it's clear that the home environment is not a safe space for either of you so what I'd like to explore with you both is where you're going to live.'

And that's how Hedgehog Hollow had become their home for the foreseeable future. We had plenty of room and we had plenty of love to give; something it seemed they'd both been starved of, except from each other.

* * *

'You look shattered,' Josh said as we curled up on the sofa with mugs of hot chocolate late that evening.

'I am. Not quite the relaxing start to the New Year we were expecting.'

'No. Definitely not. Do you think they'll both be okay?'

'Not at first but I think that, by giving them a home here, we've given them a fighting chance of getting there. I think Darcie will just go with it. She's young, used to moving between different houses, and Phoebe has been her main caregiver so it's not a huge adjustment for her. But Phoebe has a heck of a lot to deal with. She's putting a brave face on it now, but I can guarantee they've left more than physical scars on her.'

'I hope they lock them up and throw away the key.'

'Me too. You know what's funny? The stolen money seems so insignificant compared to all of this. I don't care about justice for us anymore, but I do want justice for Phoebe and Darcie.'

35

PHOEBE

I woke up to the sound of knocking and it took me a moment to remember where I was.

'It's only me,' Samantha called through the door. 'Are you awake?'

I rubbed my eyes. 'Yeah. Come in.'

The door opened and she stepped into the bedroom. 'I've brought you some tea.'

I took the mug from her, gulping back a wave of emotion. I couldn't remember the last time anybody had made me a drink.

'Thank you. Where's Darcie?'

'In the kitchen with Twizzle and Josh having breakfast. She's only been up for about fifteen minutes. Come downstairs when you're ready. No rush.'

'I'll get dressed then come down.'

'Okay. See you shortly and we can chat about what you and Darcie would like to do today. We can take a walk round the farm, there are really good playgrounds in Great Tilbury and Bentonbray, or we could take a drive out to the coast. Whatever you feel like.' With another smile, she left.

I lay back against the pillows, feeling all choked up. Samantha had listed three things off the top of her head that we could to today and

Darcie had never done any of them. The closest she'd come to a beach was playing in the sandpit at school.

It was unbelievable to think that Samantha had offered us rooms in her home, just like that. Nobody had needed to ask her. I'd lied to her, I'd run off every time she'd tried to have a conversation with me, and her bank account had been emptied because of me, but she'd taken Darcie and me in without hesitation. Two nights ago, I'd slept in Rosemary's garage and...

I sat bolt upright. Rosemary! I'd told the police about the threats Tina and Trigg had made but I'd got so wrapped up in making sure Darcie wasn't taken away from me that I hadn't asked what they were going to do. Trigg would hear about the raids, he'd be fuming and, with Darcie and me gone, he'd want to make someone pay.

'Come on!' I cried, as her landline rang out. Ring after agonising ring but no answer. I called her mobile, my heart racing, but it went to voicemail.

'Hi, Rosemary, it's me. Can you call me back as soon as you pick this up? It's urgent. Thanks.' I hadn't wanted to say too much and scare her but I suspected my high-pitched voice would be enough to cause her alarm.

She never left the flat without her phone but she often forgot to turn it off silent. No answer didn't mean Trigg had got to her.

'Are you okay?' Samantha asked when I rushed into the kitchen after getting dressed, staring at the screen.

'I can't get hold of Rosemary. I'm worried something might have happened to her.'

'I'll phone my dad.' I looked up at the sound of Fizz's voice.

'Fizz heard that there was a fellow unicorn fan staying with us and she couldn't wait to meet her,' Samantha said, pulling out a chair for me as Fizz left the kitchen with her phone pressed against her ear.

'Look what Fizz gave me!' Darcie cried as I sank onto the chair. 'It's Twizzle's boyfriend. He's called Tango.'

The soft blue unicorn was a little bigger than her pink one. 'He's lovely. That was very kind of Fizz. Did you say thank you?'

'Yes.'

Samantha handed me a glass of orange juice. 'She did. She was very polite. What can I get you for breakfast?' She ran through a stack of options but I couldn't eat anything until I knew Rosemary was okay.

Fizz returned to the kitchen. 'They're sending a patrol car to her flat. Dad says try not to worry. They picked Trigg up last night and he kicked off so he spent the night in the cells. He's still there now.'

Samantha gently placed her hand on my shoulder. 'How about we don't make plans to go anywhere today until we know how Rosemary is?'

I nodded, grateful to her for understanding. I couldn't shake the bad feeling in my gut. They might have picked up Trigg last night, but what had he been doing before then? I couldn't rest until I'd spoken to her. I called her again but it was still voicemail. There was nothing I could do except sit and wait and hope.

Darcie had finished her breakfast and was desperate to meet the hedgehogs, so Samantha told her to get dressed and they'd go over to see Josh in the barn while Fizz and I waited for an update from Sergeant Kinsella.

The pair of them left the farmhouse a little later with Misty-Blue, Darcie quizzing Samantha about how many hedgehogs she had and what all their names were. Darcie was smitten with the cat already. Any concerns I'd had about her settling in at the farm had disappeared last night as I'd watched her rolling round on the lounge floor playing with the cat, giggling as it purred.

'I'm really sorry about everything you've been through,' Fizz said when the front door closed behind them. 'How are you feeling?'

'I've kept quiet about how they treated me for so long. It doesn't feel real that people know now.'

'My dad and his team will push as hard as they can to get justice for you and Darcie.'

'It's not just us. That family have hurt so many people, destroyed so many lives. I can't even be—'

Fizz's phone ringing silenced me and she handed it over. 'It's my dad, so you might as well answer.'

'Hi, Sergeant Kinsella, it's Phoebe.'

'Hi, Phoebe. A couple of my officers are at Renleigh Court right now. There's nobody home but a neighbour let them into the building. There's no sign of a break-in. They noticed a key safe outside Mrs Norris's flat. Do you know if it's in use?'

'Yes. The code's 3675.'

'And you genuinely believe she could be at risk?'

'She's severely visually impaired and she has a morning routine. She should have been back way before now so, yes, I think Trigg or someone else has got to her.' I could barely get the words out for fear of what might have happened.

'Leave it with me. I'll call you back once they've accessed the flat.'

'She's got a guide dog. They might have hurt Trixie.'

'I'll let my officers know. Try not to panic.'

When the call ended, Fizz sat beside me and squeezed my hand. 'We'll know soon.'

I felt drained. And the worst thing was that it wasn't anywhere near over yet. It would all kick off when Tina and Jenny got back from the Caribbean and I'd probably have to give evidence in court. There were no guarantees over Darcie's future either. There was no way Social Services would let her go back to Jenny or Tina but being with Hayley wasn't an option. Jackie Laine said they wanted what was best for Darcie. Me! I was best for Darcie. Would they need Hayley's permission? She'd trusted me with her daughter for years and had always said I was a better 'mum' than she was, but what was her state of mind at the moment? Was she even capable of making such a huge decision about her daughter?

36

PHOEBE

Three years ago

'Come to the playground, Mummy,' Darcie said, tugging at the bottom of Hayley's cardigan on the afternoon of New Year's Eve. 'Please.'

Hayley stood by her bedroom window, staring at the grey sky, and didn't even look down at her daughter.

'Phoebe's taking you,' she said, her voice flat and lifeless.

'But I want you to take me. Please, Mummy.'

'I don't want to. Phoebe?' She glanced briefly at me, her eyes pleading with me to help her.

'Your mummy wants to stay inside but we'll have fun. I can tell you a story on the way, if you like. Why don't you go downstairs and see if you can put your boots on by yourself. If not, I'll be down in a minute to help.'

She left the room and I looked at Hayley, still gazing into space. When I'd first met her, I'd been struck by how young she looked but now it was the opposite. She was only twenty-one but I swear she looked twice that age. Her forehead was creased with worry lines and there were dark bags under her red-rimmed eyes. Her once glossy hair was lifeless, like her eyes.

'Do you need anything before we go out?'

She wrapped her cardigan a little tighter across her body, her shoulder blades protruding through the thin material. 'Black coffee.'

'Okay. Give me a sec.'

Black coffee. It was all I ever saw her consume these days.

* * *

'Does your mummy ever eat with you?' I asked Darcie as we walked to the playground after delivering Hayley her drink.

'Mummy doesn't eat.'

'What? Never?'

'Nanna shouts at her about it. She says she'll turn into a wreck sick. What does that mean?'

'Nothing for you to worry about, Princess,' I said, unable to find the words to begin to explain anorexia to a nearly four-year-old. 'How about that story?'

As I pushed Darcie on the swings a little later, I couldn't stop thinking about Hayley and how much she'd changed this past year. The time I spent with her when I brought Darcie back to the house after she'd had clients over had gradually diminished to the point where I just handed over Darcie, gave her a hug, and left. It was like Hayley couldn't bear to look at me anymore.

I'd overheard Jenny moaning to Tina that she'd lost a few regular clients with complaints that Hayley was distant and disinterested. She never left the house, instead spending her days standing by her bedroom window or lying on her bed, lost in her own world. She didn't seem to have any friends, she'd pushed me away, and she barely glanced at Darcie. I'd tried to talk to Jenny about it but that had earned me a few bruises and a stark warning to keep my nose out of other people's business. Still worried, I'd tried Tina but I came off badly there too.

'Can I go on the penguin?' Darcie asked, bringing my attention back to her.

I helped her off the swing and into the penguin rocker. My phone beeped:

✉ From Hayley
I've got a chance of some work. Can Darcie stay
with you tonight?

✉ To Hayley
OK. Can I come back and pack a bag for her?

✉ From Hayley
Not now. I'll leave one in the hall. You can pick
it up at 4 but don't come in. I'll be busy

'Your mummy needs to work tonight,' I told Darcie. 'You're going to stay with me and we'll pick up a bag later.'

We were walking to Tina's when another text came through:

✉ From Hayley
The bag's in the hall ready but definitely don't
come earlier than 4. Tell Darcie I love her x

✉ To Hayley
Darcie says she loves you too and she sends lots of
big kisses xxx

* * *

I could hear loud music and screeches of laughter as Darcie and I approached Tina's house. Tina and Jenny and a few bingo buddies were in the lounge, drinking cocktails. It was their New Year's Eve tradition to get wasted then head down the local pub to see the New Year in.

I poked my head round the door to let them know that I was back and had Darcie with me. Darcie ran up to Jenny and tried to clamber onto her knee.

'I've got a drink in my hand, Darc!' she snapped as the blue liquid slopped over the glass. She dismissed us both with a wave of her hand.

We headed upstairs and sat on my bed, looking through some books we'd borrowed from the library.

We'd been home about an hour when Tina screeched my name.

'Wait here, Princess,' I said to Darcie.

Tina was standing in the hall. 'We're out of vodka. There's a bottle round our Jenny's. Go and get it. It's on the side in the kitchen next to the fridge.'

It was just after two and Hayley had specifically said I wasn't to collect Darcie's overnight bag until after four, but I'd rather chance it with Hayley than answer back to Tina.

'Okay. I'll be as quick as I can. Can you keep an eye on Darcie?'

'Tell her to stay up there.'

I pulled my shoes and coat on and told Darcie to stay in my bedroom and I'd be back soon. Keen not to leave her unsupervised for long, I sprinted round to Jenny's and slowly, ever so quietly, turned my key in the lock and edged open the door.

Darcie's bag was in the hall, as promised. I cocked my head and listened. I could hear faint music. There were no other sounds, which was a relief as I hadn't wanted to arrive in the middle of something.

I slipped into the kitchen but there was no bottle of vodka next to the fridge. There was no way I could turn up without it and I had no money to go to the shop and buy one, not that I'd get served even if I did; something which frustrated the hell out of Tina and Jenny.

I opened one cupboard after another, scanning the shelves, hoping. Nothing.

Panic welled inside me as I stood by the kitchen table, looking

round the kitchen. I could *not* go back empty-handed. I flinched as
something splashed onto my forehead and glanced up as another water
droplet dripped from the ceiling. The bathroom was right above me.

Heart racing, I dashed up the stairs. The bath was full and overflowing onto the floorboards but there was no sign of Hayley. I grabbed
the chain for the plug, turned the taps off and tossed some towels onto
the wet floor.

'Hayley?'

Her bedroom door was closed. I knocked gently and listened in
case she had a client with her, although I couldn't believe she would
have if she'd just run a bath.

'Hayley? Can I come in?'

No response.

I took a deep breath and tentatively pushed open the door. I recognised her wedding song playing softly. The curtains were closed and
there were no lights on, but the landing light illuminated Hayley lying
on the bed.

'Hayley!' I hissed. 'Are you awake?'

There was no response, so I stepped into the room and flicked on
her bedside lamp, knocking over a bottle. Vodka. No wonder I couldn't
find it.

Hayley was on her side facing away from me, dressed only in Idris's
basketball vest. Her skin was so pale against the bright orange that it
appeared almost translucent and her protruding shoulder blades and
spine clearly conveyed her weight loss.

'Hayley!'

I gave her a gentle shake, wincing at how cold her skin felt. I
repeated her name and shook her a little harder. She rolled over
towards me and I reeled back. Her pale arms were covered in thin red
welts and streaks of blood.

'Oh, my God! What have you done?'

I grabbed her wrist and felt a faint pulse, watched the slow rise and
fall of her chest, and gulped down my fear as I dialled 999. *Please don't
let me be too late.*

37

SAMANTHA

Present day

'He looks like a football!' Darcie exclaimed as I showed her the photos of Bauble the hedgehog before he was deflated. 'What happened to him?'

'He was very poorly but my dad did an operation on him and he's doing really well now. My dad and Josh are amazing vets.'

Darcie looked at Josh adoringly. If I'd introduced him last night as Father Christmas, I don't think I'd have got a better reaction than I did when I said he was a vet. Although she told me she'd never had pets, visited a farm or a zoo, Darcie adored animals, which was obvious from her reaction to Misty-Blue and the hedgehogs. She'd declared that she wanted to be a vet too and asked Josh if he'd give her a job. He'd laughed and said maybe when she was older but he was sure we could find a little job for her in the rescue centre in the meantime.

'Hedgehogs are my third most favourite animal,' she said after we'd finished the tour and introduced her to a few of our patients. 'Unicorns are still my favourite and then dogs.' Misty-Blue weaved round her ankles, making her giggle. 'But now I love cats too! What's my job here?'

'We're getting lots of hedgehogs brought in at the moment who need to stay with us over the winter and we like to have some crates prepared ready for them. If I show you what to do, would you like to prepare ten crates for me so the hedgehogs have somewhere nice and snug to sleep?'

Darcie nodded enthusiastically but we only got as far as counting out the crates when I spotted a car pulling into the farmyard.

'We might have a new hedgehog,' I told her. 'Can you stay here with Josh while I go outside?'

'Can I come with you?'

'I'd love to say yes but sometimes the hedgehogs who arrive can be badly hurt and it's very sad to see that, even when you're used to it like Josh and me, so I'd rather you stayed here.'

She nodded, her face suddenly very serious. 'I hope the hedgehog's all right.'

'Me too, sweetie.'

'Why don't I show you what to do with the crates?' Josh said, reaching for her hand.

I was relieved when she smiled again. If she was going to stay at Hedgehog Hollow longer term, we wouldn't be able to shelter her completely from the harsh realities of not being able to save all the hedgehogs, but there was no need to expose her to it quite so early on.

There was a mud-spattered mountain bike attached to the back of the car and a man dressed in Lycra got out as I approached.

'I found some hedgehogs,' he said, opening the back door. 'I was mountain biking and they were in the middle of a trail.'

He held out a large open toolbox with four small autumn juveniles in the bottom and another on its own in one of the tool compartments. 'I had nothing to put them in. That one on its own is dead. I didn't know whether I should leave it there or bring them all in.'

'Bringing them all is fine, thanks. We can deal with it. Any sign of their mum?'

'I passed a squashed one a few minutes before I found them so it could have been their mum, but I couldn't say for sure.'

'It probably was. Thanks so much for bringing them in.' I pulled on my gloves and transferred all five into the carry crate.

'Will the others survive?' he asked.

'Difficult to say. We'll do our best. If you're on Facebook, I'll post an update later.'

'Great. I'll watch out for that.'

As soon as I returned to the barn, Darcie ran over to me. 'Do you have some hedgehogs?'

'I have four little ones but they may be very poorly, so Josh and I need to give them our full concentration. You can come back and continue with your really important job later but I'll need Josh to take you back to the farmhouse to Phoebe and Fizz for the moment. If you take Misty-Blue with you, Josh will show you where we keep her toys.'

She nodded. 'If I fall over and hurt myself, Phoebe kisses my hurt better. Will you give the little hedgehogs some kisses from me to make them better?'

'I will. That's lovely of you.'

I plugged in a couple of heat pads, my priority being to warm the hedgehogs and get some subcutaneous fluids inside them – fluids injected under the skin which would be slowly absorbed into the blood and body to rehydrate them. The fifth hedgehog was definitely gone, so I left him in the carry crate for now to focus on the other four.

They must have been born particularly late for them all to be out together like that. Presumably their mum had been showing them how to forage for food when she'd met her fate, poor thing, and they'd been left struggling to fend for themselves.

There were two boys and two girls and they weighed between 263 and 309 grams each, which was way too small to survive over the winter. They were cold, dehydrated and hungry but none of them appeared to have any injuries or external problems. I'd need to wait until they ate and pooped before I could rule out internal parasites.

I'd put out dishes of water and was preparing some food when Josh returned.

'Was Darcie okay?' I asked.

'She's a smart kid. She seemed to understand what was going on. What have we got here?'

I filled Josh in on my initial observations and weights. 'The smallest one hasn't taken a drink yet but she's moving so hopefully she will do soon. Any news on Rosemary?'

'No sign of a break-in, but no answer. Phoebe's given the police the code to a key safe and is waiting to hear back.'

'I hope Rosemary's okay. If anything's happened to her, I think Phoebe will blame herself.'

I picked up the smallest hedgehog and placed her closer to a water dish but she made no attempt to lap it up, so I dipped my gloved finger into the water and lightly rubbed it across her mouth. I held my breath, anxious to see her lap up the droplet, and released a shaky breath when she did. I repeated it a few times and then she dipped her head and lapped up some water of her own accord.

'Do we have names?' Josh asked a little later while they all tucked into soft food, the noisy slurps and smacking of lips making us smile.

'We haven't got a new theme yet so I thought Darcie might like to pick one and do the honours with naming them.'

'She'll love that. As these four all seem okay for the moment, do you want me to bring her back so she can see them eating?'

'Yeah, I think we're safe for now.'

They were back moments later, panting.

'She was so desperate to see them, she raced me over here,' Josh said, bending over by the entrance with his hands on his thighs, trying to catch his breath. 'And she's fast!'

'I won the running race at sports day,' Darcie announced, joining me at the table. 'Awww, they're so dinky and cute! What are they called?'

'We haven't named them yet. We usually have a theme but we need a new one and thought you might like to choose a theme and names.'

'What's a theme?'

'Something all the names have in common. For example, our most recent theme was Christmas and before that we've had Disney characters, characters from films and books...'

'Have you had unicorns?'

'Not yet. I can't think of any unicorn names off the top of my head but, if you can think of four names, we can definitely go for unicorns.'

'You can call a unicorn whatever you want. The girls can be Sparkle and Shimmer like baby unicorns.'

'Beautiful. Which one's which?'

'The smallest one is Shimmer.'

'What about the boys?' Josh asked, joining us at the table.

She screwed up her face. 'Boys are harder. We can call this one Magic. And this one... erm... I know! Horny!'

Josh and I exchanged glances. His eyes sparkled and his lips twitched and he had to turn away with his hand over his mouth.

'That's an interesting name,' I said, fighting hard not to laugh myself as I watched Josh's shoulders bouncing up and down.

'It's because they have horns.'

'Of course! I see your logic. Magic and Horny it is then.'

'Can I go to the toilet?' she asked when she'd finished blowing each of them a kiss preceded by a whisper of their new name.

'Yes, there's one at the back there.'

'I'm so sorry,' Josh said, wiping his eyes when the door closed behind her. 'That was too funny.'

'It was the last thing I expected her to say, but he's stuck with it now. We have Horny the hedgehog.'

'At least she didn't add "Mike" onto the end of Magic's name.'

We were still giggling when Phoebe and Fizz burst into the barn.

'She's hurt!' Phoebe cried before dissolving into tears.

Fizz shook her head. 'My dad called. Rosemary's been beaten up.'

'Oh no! Phoebe! I'm so sorry.' I drew her into a hug, devastated for her that she had yet another trauma to deal with.

'They're taking her to hospital,' Fizz continued. 'But her dog's hurt and they need an emergency vet. I told Dad to send them to your practice, Josh. They're on their way now. I hope that was okay.'

'Definitely. I'll meet them there.'

'I need to see Rosemary,' Phoebe said, stepping back from me and wiping her eyes with her sleeve.

'I'd take you, but...' I glanced towards our four new admissions as Darcie emerged from the toilet. 'And we've got Darcie to think about.'

'I could do a detour and drop Phoebe at the hospital,' Josh suggested.

Phoebe shook her head. 'You need to get to Trixie.' She kept her voice low, no doubt not wanting to scare Darcie.

'I'll take you to the hospital,' Fizz said. 'I can stay with you too.'

'Why are you going to the hospital?' Darcie asked.

Phoebe crouched down next to her. 'Remember my friend Rosemary? She had a fall and hurt herself. I want to make sure she's okay.'

'Can I come and play with Trixie?'

'Not today. Can you be a good girl and stay with Samantha while Fizz takes me to the hospital?'

'I've named the hedgehogs.'

'Will you tell me all about them when I get back?'

They hugged then Phoebe, Josh and Fizz left the barn.

'Where's Josh going?' Darcie asked.

'He needs to be an emergency vet so it's just the two of us for now.'

We had no idea what had happened to Trixie and there was no way I was going to scare Darcie by saying she was the patient.

'Do you want me to teach you some more things about hedgehogs?'

'Yes, please.'

We sat at the treatment table.

'We'll watch the hedgehogs and you can ask me any questions you want.'

She pondered for a moment. 'Why do they have prickles?'

'That's a great starting question. They're called spines...'

Over the next hour or so, I answered Darcie's questions in between checking samples from our new admissions under the microscope.

The external inspection had revealed nothing but, as was often the case, the insides told a different story. All four of them had internal parasites and needed treatment. Just as well the cyclist had found them.

'Shimmer, Sparkle, Magic and Horny all have poorly tummies,' I told Darcie so I need to give them some medicine to make them better.

'I'll blow them another kiss.'

My heart melted watching her do that. What a lovely, kind little girl she was and presumably that was all down to Phoebe.

'Will Rosemary get some medicine?'

'Probably.'

'I'll blow her a kiss too. Where's the hospital?'

I took a moment to get my bearings and pointed to the back of the barn. 'Roughly in that direction.'

'Mwah! To Rosemary.' She blew the kiss in the direction I'd indicated.

I hoped it would be enough to save Rosemary and Trixie.

Sergeant Kinsella was waiting for us in the entrance lobby at Reddfield Hospital. One look at the grim expression on his face and I feared the worst.

'She's not...?' I couldn't finish that sentence.

'No. Nothing like that. She's stable. I wanted to catch you before you go in to warn you that she doesn't look good but the doctors have said there are no broken bones and no internal damage. She's badly bruised, though.'

'Has she said anything?' Fizz asked.

'Not yet. We want Phoebe to be with her if possible so she feels more comfortable. My officers say she doesn't have family in the area.'

'Her son Roger is in Canada and barely speaks to her and her daughter Andrea is in London. Do they know?'

'Not yet, but our colleagues in London can go round to the daughter's house.'

'I've got Andrea's phone number but they don't get on very well either. I'd rather ask Rosemary's permission before anyone makes contact. Is that all right?'

'You know best.'

'Can I see her?'

I followed Sergeant Kinsella along the corridor with Fizz right behind us.

'This is a good friend of Rosemary Norris,' he said to a nurse when we entered the ward.

She smiled at me. 'Are you Phoebe? She's been asking after you.'

Even though Sergeant Kinsella had warned me, it was a shock to see Rosemary lying on the bed hooked up to a drip. One side of her face was so badly bruised it was nearly black and there were bruises and cuts on her arms. I closed my eyes and shuddered. I couldn't bear to think of her trying to fight off an attacker she couldn't see.

'Rosemary?' I said gently, edging closer to the bed. 'It's Phoebe. Are you awake?'

Her hand twitched. 'Phoebe?'

'I'm right here.' I grasped the hand without the drip with both of mine as I sank onto the bedside chair. 'I'm here with Sergeant Kinsella. Can you remember what happened?'

'I took Trixie out for a quick walk but it was colder than I'd expected. I decided to warm up with a shower and I heard Trixie bark. She *never* barks but I knew I hadn't imagined it. I pulled on my robe and went into the lounge. Something felt wrong. I could sense somebody in there.'

My tummy twisted at her words describing exactly what Tina had threatened; the terrifying idea of knowing someone was in her home but being unable to see them.

'Did they speak?' Sergeant Kinsella asked.

'Not at first. I called out, asking if there was anyone there and there was silence but I could hear breathing and it wasn't Trixie. I called for her and she didn't come. Where is she?' She tried to sit up but winced in pain.

'She's being checked over by a vet.' I looked at Sergeant Kinsella for help as I had no idea what had happened to Trixie.

'She's safe,' he said. 'We'll update you as soon as we know more. What happened next?'

'I kept shouting for Trixie and that's when he laughed and grabbed my arm. I told him he could take whatever he wanted but not to hurt my dog. He said it was too late for that.' She tried to sit up again. 'Are you sure she's okay? I don't need protecting. I just need to know.'

I recognised the assertive tone and nodded at Sergeant Kinsella to go ahead. Rosemary needed the truth.

'Trixie has a gash on her side but, as I understand it, it isn't deep. My officers think he gave her something to knock her out but we don't know anything more than that.'

She took a few deep breaths as she sank back into her pillows. 'Thank you for being honest with me.'

'Did he say anything else?' I asked.

'No.'

'Did you recognise his voice?' Sergeant Kinsella asked.

'No. He had a local accent but he wasn't someone I know.'

'Anything else you can tell us, Mrs Norris? Did you get a sense of his size when he grabbed your arm? Feel what he was wearing?'

'He wasn't much taller than me. Maybe five ten or eleven. I would think average build. Not sure about the clothes.'

It wasn't much to go on, but it was a match for Trigg so far.

'Oh, and there was this smell. Aniseed.'

I turned to Sergeant Kinsella. 'It's Trigg. He's always eating aniseed chewing gum. Reeks of it.'

'I'll radio the station and see if they found any on him.'

I squeezed Rosemary's hand as he left the ward. 'Are you in pain?'

'Not really. They gave me something. You know the man who did this?'

I gulped, wishing I didn't have to say the words out loud. 'He's Jenny's boyfriend and... erm... well, it's my fault he went after you.'

'How can it be your fault?'

The same nurse who'd welcomed me appeared before I could answer, which was just as well as I had no idea where to start.

'Mrs Norris needs some rest. It's visiting time at two this afternoon if you want to come back then.'

'Okay. Thanks.' I squeezed Rosemary's hand again. 'I'd better go.'

'When you come back, I want to know what's been going on.' The words were strong but her voice was weak.

'It's a long story,' I said, hoping to dismiss it.

'And I'm not going anywhere anytime soon, so a long story's exactly what I need.'

She sounded more determined but I wasn't going to jeopardise her recovery by giving her the horror story of my life. I stood up and slipped my hand from hers. 'Oh, Sergeant Kinsella was wondering about letting Roger and Andrea know. I don't have a number for Roger but—'

'No point. Roger won't care and Andrea will jump on the next train here then spend all her time complaining about how inconvenient it was to be here for me. I don't need any more drama.'

'If you're sure?'

'I couldn't be more sure. If you let them know, I'll never forgive you.'

She meant it too. Rosemary could be extremely stubborn and, if she made her mind up about something, there was no changing it. If she didn't want her children to know, I wasn't going to go behind her back.

* * *

Fizz was waiting in the lobby but there was no sign of her dad.

'How was she?' she asked.

'Covered in bruises but surprisingly okay. She's more worried about Trixie than herself but I don't think it's hit her yet.'

'Poor woman. What do you want to do now?'

'She needs to rest but I can come back for visiting hour at two.'

Fizz glanced at her phone. 'We've got two and a half hours to kill. I've spoken to Samantha and she's going to give Darcie a farm tour so there's no need to rush back. Do you want to go somewhere for lunch?'

I shook my head, feeling embarrassed. 'I can't. I don't have any money.'

'Who said anything about you paying? My treat and if you say anything about paying me back, I'll be mortally offended and we can't be friends.'

Friends? Fizz wanted to be my friend? It felt like a long time since I'd had one of those.

'Thank you. I've got a request, though.'

'Name it!'

'Can we talk about anything except my messy, chaotic life?'

Fizz grinned at me. 'Deal. I can tell you about mine instead. Have you been to April's Tea Parlour in Great Tilbury?'

'I've never been to Great Tilbury.'

'Then that's where we're going.'

She linked my arm and we stepped out into the cool air. Sergeant Kinsella was on his phone and paused the call so Fizz could tell him where we were heading.

'Do you like cats?' she asked me as we belted up in her car.

'Yes.'

'Then we'll go to my cottage afterwards and I can introduce you to Jinks, the world's laziest cat.'

'Do you live in Great Tilbury?'

'Yep. I had a small lottery win last year.'

As we drove towards April's, Fizz told me about her lottery win and how it had enabled her to buy her cottage, a car, and enrol on her university course. I couldn't help thinking about Dad's win on the premium bonds. Fizz's windfall had been good for her but Dad's had brought the Grimes family into our lives. How different would things have been if he'd never won it? It wouldn't have saved his life. He'd have still had his accident. I wouldn't have been used as a punch bag but I wouldn't have met Darcie and I couldn't imagine life without her.

My thoughts turned to Hayley. I was sure she'd want me to look after Darcie permanently but was she well enough to declare that? And would Social Services agree to it if she did?

Even if we got over that hurdle, there were a million practical questions like how was I going to afford it and where would we live? Would I need to pack in my studies so I could take Darcie to school and back?

A gentle nudge from Fizz made me jump.

'You've zoned out, haven't you?'

'Sorry. It's not you.'

'I know. You've got a lot on your mind. I'll shut up and let you think.'

'No, don't. My head hurts from thinking. Tell me about Jinks, the lazy cat.'

'So, he's a stray. My brother Barney found him on his farm...'

She kept glancing across and smiling as she spoke. She had such a beautiful smile. In all the times I'd visited Hedgehog Hollow when Fizz had been there, I'd barely looked at her, too anxious to get back to Tina's to do whatever she demanded of me, but today I saw her properly for the first time.

'We're here. Great Tilbury. Isn't it pretty?'

I wasn't looking out of the window. I was too busy looking at Fizz. My heart began to race and I tore my gaze away. *Stop it. That's the last thing you need on top of everything else that's happening.*

After parking the car in front of a row of shops, she pushed open the door of a double-fronted café. A sudden gust of wind whipped my hair across my face and made me gasp.

'You've got a leaf in your hair,' Fizz said.

I batted at my hair but I couldn't feel it.

'Let me.' As she removed the leaf, the palm of her hand gently grazed my cheek and I felt a zip of electricity shoot through my body.

'All good now,' she said smiling at me again.

All good? Far from it. The last time I felt like this, I acted on it and it was a disaster. No way I was going to risk the friendship and support I had at Hedgehog Hollow. I was only reacting because she was being nice to me and, after what I'd been through, I was grateful for any shred of kindness.

And I'd keep trying to convince myself that was all it was.

Dad and Lauren came round on Sunday morning to prepare a traditional roast lunch for everyone. He'd brought apple pie and custard for
dessert and a unicorn cupcake for Darcie, which made him an instant
hit.

After lunch, Phoebe sat on the lounge floor with Darcie and entertained Archie and Lottie while Paul and Beth cleared the kitchen.
When Darcie asked if she could cuddle Lottie, Phoebe demonstrated
how to hold her and encouraged Darcie with ways of keeping Lottie
engaged. She was a natural with children.

Josh, beside me on the sofa, squeezed my hand. I knew he'd
picked up my thoughts: how relaxed and happy Phoebe could be in
the right environment and how the financial worries of Hedgehog
Hollow were inconsequential when compared to the future of
these two.

'We have a couple of hours of daylight left,' I said. 'Would anyone
like to go to the playground at Great Tilbury?'

Darcie's and Lauren's hands shot into the air. 'Me!'

'You're very welcome to come, Lauren,' I said, laughing. 'As long as I
don't have to push you on the swings.'

'I'll push you!' Darcie grinned at her.

'Thank you very much, Darcie. You're on!' She held up her hand and Darcie high-fived her, giggling.

'A spot of fresh air sounds good,' Dad said. 'I'll pass on the swings but I could be tempted by a roundabout.'

* * *

'He's going to regret it,' Lauren muttered under her breath as we watched Dad climb the steps to the top of the slide.

'I've got my phone ready to video it. Do you reckon he's going to get stuck?'

'I guarantee it.'

Sure enough, Dad sat down at the top, egged on by Darcie, and tried to push off but didn't move. He shot us a panicked look.

'Oh no, Jonathan! Are you wedged?' Lauren called, her laughter stopping her from sounding the least bit concerned.

'Yes! I can't budge.'

'Come on!' Darcie summoned him down the slide with a wave of her hand. 'You don't have to be scared!'

'I'm not scared!'

I glanced across at Phoebe and Beth, who were pushing Archie and Lottie on the baby swings, both of them laughing at Dad.

'I think he might need a shove,' I said to Lauren. 'Or he'll never live this down.'

Still laughing, she went to Dad's aid and, with a lot of huffing and puffing, finally managed to push him free from the top. We all cheered and clapped when he finally made it to the bottom. He took an exaggerated bow then ran over to me, cheeks burning, and pointed to the camera.

'Thanks for the support. Such a caring daughter.'

'Absolute pleasure. Any time.'

He hugged me to his side and we watched the girls. 'I'm so proud of you,' he whispered. 'And I'm here if you want any help or a sounding board.'

'Thank you. I'll probably take you up on that lots of times.'

'Make sure you do.' When he released me, he called Lauren over. 'I've had enough humiliation for one afternoon and I think I've earned a pint. Fancy heading home and going to the pub?'

'Sounds good to me.'

They said their goodbyes and it touched me to see Darcie jumping up for hugs. It was lovely how she'd instantly taken to my family, although I couldn't help wondering if it was symptomatic of being starved of attention from anyone other than Phoebe.

'Are you ready to go home yet?' I asked Darcie.

She shook her head. 'Please can I play a bit longer?'

'Ten more minutes and then we'll need to take you home.'

She stiffened. 'Home?' The word was barely a whisper but it was full of fear and I realised immediately that she thought I meant Jenny's house.

I crouched down in front of her. 'Hedgehog Hollow. That's your home now.'

The relief on her face was obvious. She put her arms round my neck, kissed my cheek, then ran off to the slide. No child should be afraid of their home.

'Samantha?'

I turned at the sound of a woman's voice. 'Jeanette? Hi. Happy New Year!'

Jeanette was a community leader in nearby Fimberley where Terry lived. She'd been exceptionally supportive in helping make the village hedgehog-friendly.

'Happy New Year to you too! I'm just visiting my daughter and I thought it was you I could see. I hope you don't think I'm gossiping but I heard you'd started fostering.'

I knew Jeanette well enough by now to know the question wasn't gossip-driven and she'd have a point to her enquiry.

'Not quite. We have a couple of friends in need staying with us.'

'Is that them at the swings?'

'Yes.' Phoebe was laughing as Darcie attempted to push her, resulting in the swing spinning rather than swinging.

'How old's the little one?'

'Nearly seven.'

'My granddaughters are nine and eleven and my daughter's been doing a big clear-out of clothes. Would you like them?'

'That would be amazing. They didn't come with much and we've not had a chance to go shopping yet.'

'Give me five minutes and I'll bring them over. Sorry we don't have anything for the older girl.'

'It's kind of you to help Darcie. We'll get Phoebe kitted out soon enough.'

I pointed out my car and opened the boot when Jeanette, her daughter and two granddaughters appeared five minutes later carrying seven full bin bags and two cardboard boxes between them.

'Wow! That's loads! Thank you so much.'

Jeanette's daughter introduced herself as Carolyn as she placed the boxes in my boot. 'These contain some games, toys and books that my two are finished with. The bags have a range of sizes so some stuff might be no good. Just pass anything you don't want onto charity.'

'I can't thank you enough. This is such a help when money's so tight after...' I stopped myself from saying 'the theft' just in time and added 'Christmas' instead.

I called Phoebe and Darcie over so they could thank Carolyn.

'It's a bit chilly so I'll take the girls back in the house,' Jeanette said, waving goodbye as she crossed the road.

Phoebe and Darcie ran over but Phoebe stopped before she reached the jeep, eyes wide as she stared at Carolyn.

I glanced at Carolyn, who looked equally surprised.

'We meet again,' she said, smiling at Phoebe. 'How are you, honey?'

'Better now. Thank you so much for the food. That was really kind.'

'You looked like you needed it.'

'I was so hungry.' She looked at me. 'The morning after I'd slept in... you know where... Carolyn gave me some food from her bakery. We shared some of it, didn't we Darcie?'

'The pan chocolate? I loved that! Can we have another?'

Carolyn crouched down in front of Darcie. 'I'm sure that can be arranged, honey. I hear you're staying at Hedgehog Hollow.'

'I'm going to make the poorly hedgehogs better.'

'I bet you are. I've got two girls who are a little bit older than you. You see all those bags and boxes in the boot? They contain clothes that don't fit them and things they don't play with anymore and we thought you might like them.'

'All for me?' Darcie exclaimed, staring at the boot-full.

'All for you.'

Darcie stroked one of the bags, her eyes wide with amazement. 'Thank you so much,' she cried.

'I'll leave you to it.' Carolyn smiled warmly at Phoebe. 'Take care, honey.'

'Thank you,' Phoebe whispered, her hand clapped over her mouth, looking on the verge of tears.

'Five more minutes on the playground, Darcie,' I said. 'Then we'll go home and look through the bags. Can you tell Beth, please?'

'Okay.' She sprinted across the playground to where Beth, holding Lottie against her hip, was gently rocking Archie on a wooden boat.

'Are you o—?'

I didn't even manage to finish the question before Phoebe burst into tears.

'What's wrong?'

'We don't even know her,' she sobbed, 'but she gave me a bag of food and now she's just given Darcie a bigger pile of stuff than she's owned in her entire life.'

'She's obviously a lovely, caring person.'

'Your family and Josh's family have been so nice to us and they don't know us either. And you and Josh...' She struggled to form the words as tears spilled down her cheeks.

I hugged her to me. 'In my experience, there are far more kind people in the world than there are nasty ones and you've been unlucky so far, but your luck has just changed. We won't let anything else bad happen to you.'

As she sobbed on my shoulder, I fought back my own tears. Nobody should have had to go through what she'd been through.

* * *

Back at the farmhouse a little later, after much excitement and giggling, we finally had everything from the bin bags sorted into three piles: fit now, grow into and to donate to charity.

When we opened the boxes, we found a sparkly pink drawstring bag full of My Little Pony unicorn figures and Darcie squealed so loudly that Josh, preparing sandwiches for tea, came rushing from the kitchen to check everyone was okay.

'Don't panic,' I assured him. 'Darcie has discovered a bag of unicorns.'

'Can I show them to Lottie and Archie?' she asked.

'Go on. Should we look at the rest later?'

She nodded and ran out of the room, clutching the bag, and Josh returned to the kitchen chuckling to himself.

'I bought her one of those once,' Phoebe said. 'It was purple and grey and it went missing. She cried for days. Jenny said she was careless with her things and that's why it wasn't worth spending money on her. I swear Jenny will have thrown it in the bin because she couldn't bear to see Darcie happy.'

'That's awful.'

'She is awful.' Her expression darkened. 'I'm dreading going back there tonight.'

We'd arranged to meet Hadrian – Sergeant Kinsella – at Jenny's house after evening visiting time at the hospital so that we could pick up Darcie's final belongings, including her school uniform and shoes which Phoebe had realised she hadn't collected in their rush to leave the house before the raid.

'You don't have to go. I can drop you off at the hospital and meet Sergeant Kinsella at the house without you.'

She pondered for a moment and I could tell she was tempted, but she shook her head. 'No. I want to do it. I can face Jenny's house. It's Tina's I don't want to return to and, as she destroyed all my stuff, there's nothing left for me to collect.'

'We'll go shopping tomorrow and get you some new clothes.'

'Oh, I wasn't hinting for—'

'I know you weren't, but I want to get them. Can't have my accountant wearing the same two T-shirts on rotation, can I?'

Her eyes lit up. 'I can keep my job?'

'Of course you can. There's not a lot of money to work with, but there are still bills to pay.' I kicked myself as her head dipped. 'You have to know that I don't blame you for any of this. Do you hear me, Phoebe? None of this is your fault.'

I looked up at Samantha and shook my head. 'It's all my fault. I should have told you who I was.'

'And we both know that I wouldn't have had you working here if you had. Look, I understand why you didn't tell me.'

'I wasn't trying to deceive you. I just really wanted the work experience. My mum was an accountant. It's all I've ever wanted to be.'

'I know and, from what I've seen so far, you'll be brilliant at it.'

My shoulders sank. 'Yeah, well, we'll never find out for sure.'

Samantha stretched out her legs and leaned back against the wall. 'What do you mean?'

'I'm not going to be able to finish college. I've got Darcie to think about now so I need a job and will have to hope I can find one which fits round getting her to and from school each day, and we need to find somewhere to live and I need to...'

Samantha's hand on my arm stopped me mid-flow.

'Back up a bit. You don't need to leave college, especially when you're so close to qualifying. You only have two terms left.'

'But Darcie...'

'Will get taken to school and picked up by me, Josh, my dad, Lauren, Connie or Beth. They've all offered their help and they mean it. As for finding somewhere to live, Josh and I have discussed it and you can both stay here as long as you want.'

'But I can't pay you for food or fuel.'

'You can. And I don't mean with money. You can pay me by fulfilling your potential and making me so proud of you for over-coming adversity and coming out on top. You can pay me by contin-uing to demonstrate to that unicorn-loving little girl that there are people in the world who care for others even if they're not related by blood. Those things mean more than money ever could.'

I stared at Samantha, struggling to take it all in. It was so different from the life I'd had that I felt quite overwhelmed.

'I'll pay you back when I start working.'

She shook her head. 'You'll do no such thing. We want to do this for you. And do you know what struck me earlier? I'm glad that you didn't tell me about your connection to the Grimes family.'

'Why?'

'Because I'm a firm believer in everything happening for a reason. You're an adult. I'm not going to insult you by pretending the money didn't matter and won't cause us a problem but we live in an amazing community where strangers show extraordinary kindness as you've just seen today with Carolyn.' She pointed towards the piles of clothes. 'When we can share what happened, I'm confident they'll come forward with donations and we'll be back on our feet again. And I know a brilliant accountant in training who can work her magic with finding grants too. So Hedgehog Hollow *will* recover from this and I'd do it all again knowing that the fallout from it is getting you and Darcie away from that horrific family.'

I'd spent years training myself not to cry, not to show any weakness, not to let them break me and now it was like six years of tears were bursting through the dam together.

'Sorry,' I whispered. 'I keep crying on you.'

'Don't be. It'll probably do you good to let it all out. I'll fetch you some tissues and a glass of water. You take your time.'

* * *

'Are you sure you want to do this?' Samantha asked as we pulled up outside 17 Butler Street that evening. 'You can wait here if you want.'

I stared out of the window. 'No, I'm fine. She's not here and we got most of Darcie's stuff before so I won't be inside for long.'

Despite my words, I still felt the same sense of dread wash over me which I always felt when approaching Jenny's or Tina's houses. *She's not here. She can't hurt you.*

I left Samantha talking to Sergeant Kinsella, grabbed Darcie's school shoes and a pair of trainers from a shoe rack by the door, took them upstairs, and placed them in the bottom of Samantha's suitcase. I added Darcie's uniform, bookbag and a few bits we'd missed in our haste.

I wheeled the case along the landing and paused by the back bedroom – Hayley's room turned grow room. The door was ajar and, heart thudding, I shoved it open with one finger.

The plants had gone, as had the lighting and heating system. Some of the lengths of 'shiny wallpaper' Darcie hated had either been ripped down or had fallen to the floor, revealing orange paint; the colour of Idris's basketball shirt. That day I'd found Hayley came flooding back to me, prickling my body with goose bumps.

Shuddering, I slammed the door shut, grabbed the case, ran down the stairs and into the front garden.

'Phoebe?'

I turned to face Samantha. 'I'm fine. It was just seeing Hayley's room again. It brought back bad memories.'

Sergeant Kinsella stepped out of the house. 'Everything all right?'

'All good,' Samantha said. 'Do you need anything else from us?'

He shook his head. 'I'll keep you posted.'

Samantha loaded the case into the boot and we drove away. That was it. Last time I'd ever need to visit either of those houses again. Time for a fresh start.

'Do you want to talk about Hayley?' Samantha prompted. 'I'm a good listener.'

She'd already proved that several times over and I could use someone to help me make sense of it all. Jenny and Tina point blank refused to speak to me about what happened that New Year's Eve.

'I met Hayley the same day I met Tina, Jenny and the rest of the Grimes family...'

Samantha listened without interrupting as I told her what I knew of Hayley's story from her desire to better herself to the day I found her unconscious.

'I can't help thinking that if Tina hadn't sent me to Jenny's for the vodka and I'd waited until four o'clock to get Darcie's bag, I'd have been too late. It's probably the only thing I'll ever be grateful to Tina for.'

'It must have been a heck of a shock finding her like that.'

'The worst. I didn't know what to do. I put some more clothes on her to try and warm her up and all I could think was *what if she stops breathing?* Jenny and Tina arrived and Jenny was in a right state, sobbing and begging Hayley to wake up. It's the only time I'd ever seen her upset. Darcie was in the hall crying, wanting to know what was wrong with Mummy, so I needed to placate her.' It had been so difficult trying to be calm and reassuring with flashing blue lights outside and ambulance crew racing up the stairs, when all I wanted to do was scream.

'She never returned home. She was in hospital for ages and then she was transferred to The Oaks. It's a sort of hospital-retreat-care facility near Hull for people struggling with their mental health. She's anorexic, she self-harms, she's clinically depressed, she's often on suicide watch...' I shook my head, picturing her shrunken eyes and wild hair the one and only time I'd visited.

'It could have been so different if Idris hadn't been given that tablet. And do you know what the worst thing is? I think it came from a batch Jenny and Tina were dealing.'

Samantha gasped and shot me a sideways look. 'Seriously?'

'Hayley said it was bright yellow and stamped with a bee. I found a bag of those in Jenny's house. It could be coincidence, but I doubt it.'

'Does Sergeant Kinsella know?'

'Yeah. When you were with Jackie at the police station, I showed him the photos and told him about Idris. He was going to look into it. Hayley told me they'd found a second tablet in Idris's pocket so Sergeant Kinsella said they'd have analysed it and would be able to compare them.'

'So you're saying Jenny could be responsible for Idris's death?'

'Idris's and nearly Hayley's.'

'That poor girl.'

'I liked Hayley. She didn't deserve any of this.'

I'd never know whether she'd intended to take her own life that day. The bath puzzled me. Had she intended to sink under the water and into oblivion or perhaps take that self-harming razor blade to her wrists? Hayley's insistence that I didn't collect Darcie's bag until a specific time made me wonder if that was the time when she knew it would all be over. If that was the case – and I strongly believed it was – it was so heart-breaking that she'd felt she had nothing to live for, not even that beautiful little girl.

'It's hard to imagine what she must have been going through and how desperate she must have been,' Samantha agreed. 'Did she spend much time with Darcie?'

'She used to but that last six months was like she was going through the motions. Like she was there but not really there.'

Everything was Jenny's and Tina's fault. I just hoped Sergeant Kinsella and his team would be able to bring a strong enough case for them all to pay for the heartbreak and chaos they'd caused.

41

Over the week that followed, the temperature gradually dropped and I woke up on Saturday morning to a thick blanket of snow. I stepped closer to the bedroom window, mesmerised by the huge flakes tumbling to the ground.

Josh joined me, wrapping his arms round my waist. 'That's a lot of snow.'

'Darcie's got her birthday wish. She's going to be so excited.'

'Not as excited as me! I can't remember the last time I built a snowman.'

Darcie would turn seven on Tuesday and, as it was apparent that nobody except Phoebe had ever made a fuss of her on her birthday before, we'd decided to celebrate today with the whole day ahead of us instead of cramming something in after school.

We'd asked if she wanted a party but she said no because she didn't have many friends. I was more upset about that than she seemed to be. Her special request was to build a snowman and go sledging as she'd done neither of those things before.

Darcie had eagerly checked my weather app all week, willing that snowflake icon to stay put, and Josh had bought a few plastic sledges in anticipation.

'Why have you got three?' Phoebe had asked.

'One for Darcie, one for Archie and one for you,' he responded.

She stared at him, wide-eyed, tears pooling in her eyes, then threw herself at him for a hug. 'I've never been on a sledge. Thank you.'

My heart broke every day for Phoebe as I discovered more about her and her past. Most of the time, she displayed maturity way beyond her years and I had to remind myself that she was twelve years younger than me. But there were moments where I caught glimpses of an innocent young child, such as her delight at the thought of going sledging for the first time.

Josh and I had spent several evenings discussing what the future held for Phoebe and Darcie and the part we played in it. I'd also had several lengthy discussions with her social worker Jackie.

Darcie's mother Hayley had met Jackie several times and had consented to Phoebe being the main caregiver, with a view to legally adopting Darcie. She'd made good progress recently but couldn't imagine herself recovering enough to be able to take on the responsibility. She also didn't think it was right to split up Phoebe and Darcie when their bond was so strong and she barely knew her daughter.

Unfortunately, it wasn't as simple as getting Hayley's approval. Jackie needed to proceed with care because Hayley's mental health put a question mark over her decision-making ability. Phoebe's age was a potential issue too. Although classed as an adult, many local authorities required the carer to be twenty-one and she was only just approaching nineteen.

Jackie had confidence in Phoebe and Darcie's relationship and the support available from Josh and me, so her recommendation was a fostering adoption placement which gave Hayley the time and support to reconsider before an adoption was made permanent and also gave Phoebe thinking time. After all, it was a huge commitment to adopt Darcie and move from a sisterly to a parental role.

After much discussion, Josh and I concluded the best approach was a private fostering arrangement. It meant Phoebe would receive no financial support from Social Services but the process would be quicker, easier and with a guarantee of Phoebe and Darcie staying together. Going down that route, she'd still have regular visits from Jackie and support as she moved towards adoption.

Phoebe was worried about causing us further financial problems but it was a no-brainer as far as we were concerned. If private fostering was the best way to keep them together, we'd find the money. Their happiness and security as a family unit would be worth every penny.

* * *

After Josh and I had seen to the hedgehogs and had breakfast, he drove over to Reddfield to collect Rosemary and Trixie. Bill Davis, the neighbouring farmer who rented our fields, had already been up the farm track and along the road in his tractor with a mini snowplough attachment to ensure we weren't cut off. I hadn't met Rosemary yet so was excited about meeting the woman who'd been like a grandmother to Phoebe.

Rosemary had spent three nights in hospital and Phoebe had visited every day. Through Phoebe, we'd offered her the opportunity to stay at Hedgehog Hollow while she recuperated, but she'd already made arrangements to stay with a long-term friend called Celia. She'd told Phoebe that she would have gone back to Renleigh Court but Celia was lonely after losing her husband last year so Rosemary had decided to keep her company. Phoebe seemed to accept that, but I wasn't convinced. In my time as a district nurse, I'd worked with patients who'd been mugged or attacked in their own home like Rosemary and I'd seen how much of a struggle it could be to feel safe after such a violation. It was likely far worse for her as her severe visual impairment would have meant her home was even more of a safe haven and Trigg being there, moving her things, watching her, would have taken that safety away and made her feel vulnerable. Phoebe told me that Rosemary could see shapes and light so I could imagine how easy it would be for her mind to conjure up shapes and shadows when there was nobody there. But I was conscious I was speculating. I hadn't met Rosemary yet. Everything I knew about her came from Phoebe, so it wasn't my place to interfere with any decisions she might make or challenge how she handled this situation.

Trixie's wounds had thankfully been superficial and she'd recovered from whatever Trigg had knocked her out with. It was such a relief when Josh confirmed she hadn't been poisoned.

Cries of, 'It's snowing!' echoed round the farmhouse, announcing that Darcie was awake. Moments later, she thundered down the stairs.

'Can we build a snowman?'

'We can, but you need some breakfast first.'

Phoebe joined us as I was taking Darcie's porridge out of the microwave.

'Happy almost birthday!' she said, giving Darcie a hug. 'The weather app was right. Are you excited?'

'I wanted to go outside but Samantha said breakfast and warm clothes first.'

'Samantha's right. Good job there were some wellies with those clothes you were given. You're going to need them today.'

I placed Darcie's bowl in front of her and added a squirt of golden syrup.

'And so are you,' I said to Phoebe.

'But I don't have any.'

'You do now. Fizz dropped these off.' I passed her a bag.

'Are these brand new?' she said, taking out the pair of navy wellington boots with cerise pink spots on them.

'No, although they look it, don't they? Fizz is involved with the Young Farmers' Club and they run a wellies exchange thing because the members usually grow out of them way before they're past their best. She said these had been donated recently but nobody needed any in that size so she thought of you.'

'That's so sweet of her.'

'Fizz is lovely like that.'

'Is she coming over today?'

'No, she's doing something with some friends, I think.'

Phoebe looked disappointed. 'Okay. I'll thank her later.'

Josh returned with Rosemary and Trixie while Phoebe and Darcie were still getting dressed. She looked exactly as I'd imagined – smartly dressed, standing tall, with an air of confidence about her – but her bruised face was a stark reminder of the trauma she'd been through.

Meeting Trixie was love at first sight for me. She was the most beautiful golden retriever with auburn colouring on her back and sides. As soon as Rosemary was settled on the sofa and had removed Trixie's harness, I stroked her ears and back and smiled as she responded eagerly to a fuss from me then settled on the floor, her head resting against Rosemary's leg.

My early impressions of Rosemary weren't quite so positive.

'It's great to have you here today,' I said. 'The girls are so excited about seeing you.'

'Josh tells me they didn't know I was coming.' Her voice was cold and I sensed her disapproval.

'That's right. They've had such a tough time that we didn't want to get their hopes up in case the snow scuppered the plans.'

'Yes, well, I'm here, aren't I? Can't say I approve of you lying to them.'

'It wasn't a lie.'

'It wasn't the truth.'

Josh arriving with drinks saved me from responding, although I'm not sure what I'd have said.

'Why on earth do you live in the middle of nowhere?' Rosemary asked. 'Those poor girls must be bored to tears.'

Josh raised his eyebrows and glanced across at me as he placed Rosemary's drink on a table beside her, explaining to her where it was.

'And I don't appreciate you all keeping me in the dark about what's been going on,' Rosemary added. 'Why are the girls even here in the first place? They should be with someone who cares about them.'

Josh sat beside me and squeezed my hand.

'They *are* with people who care and, as for telling you what's been going on, that's up to Phoebe as and when she's ready.' I tried hard not to sound defensive.

'So you're not going to tell me?'

'It's not my place to tell.'

'Has Rosemary told you her problem?' Josh interjected before it turned into an argument.

'Not yet.'

Rosemary released a heavy sigh. 'I've got an unexpected situation. Celia is allergic to dogs. She's never been round them so she had no idea she had an allergy. She's said she'll pump herself full of antihistamines and live with it but I can't ask her to do that so we need to move out. I called my daughter Andrea when I got out of hospital and, as I knew she would, she got hysterical about it. She's convinced I can't cope on my own and even suggested it was my fault that man broke in.'

'Aw, Rosemary, that's not very fair.'

'You're telling me! She's already demanded I get myself on the next train down to London to live with her, while in the next breath muttering that they don't have the room in their enormous five-bedroom mansion and that my presence will be immensely inconvenient to them. Talk about feeling wanted.'

I could hear the bitterness in her voice. 'That's not very nice.'

'She's my daughter but, God forgive me for saying it, she's not a very nice person. She's always resented—'

The sound of Phoebe and Darcie racing down the stairs silenced Rosemary and she whispered, 'I'll tell you later.'

'Trixie!' Darcie squealed. 'Can I stroke her?'

'Yes, darling girl,' Rosemary said. 'Her harness is off so she's not working.'

'I didn't know you were coming today!' Phoebe hugged her.

'Samantha and Josh apparently decided to keep it a secret.'

Josh squeezed my hand again. Phoebe hadn't warned me that Rosemary was so feisty. Unless she was only that way with me.

'Are you going to build a snowman with us?' Darcie asked.

Rosemary laughed, softening her features at last. 'I think my snowman building days are over, but I look forward to seeing what you make.'

Darcie frowned. 'I thought you couldn't see anything.'

'I can see shapes and light but everything's fuzzy. However, I used to be able to see clearly so I know what a snowman should look like, and now my hands can see for me. I can touch him and I can imagine him in here.' She tapped her temple. 'I'll be able to see just as clearly as you.'

Darcie's frown deepened. 'When I close my eyes, I can picture unicorn friends for Twizzle and Tango. Is it like that?'

Rosemary smiled. 'Very much like that.'

'I'm glad you'll still be able to see him. He's going to be the best snowman ever.'

Rosemary was like a different person chatting to Darcie and Phoebe, compared to how she'd been with me. What had I done to ruffle her feathers?

* * *

With a break in the snowfall around mid-morning, we all ventured outside, including Rosemary and Trixie. Darcie wanted to build the snowman in the field at the front of the farm to welcome visitors so Josh put out a deckchair for Rosemary and draped a couple of blankets over her for warmth.

I was going to keep Rosemary company, even though I couldn't help feeling apprehensive about what else she might say, but Darcie wanted me to help roll the snowballs. I didn't need to be asked twice.

It was a joy to see Darcie and Phoebe having so much fun, chasing each other round, squealing and laughing as though they didn't have a care in the world. This was how it should be.

Trixie clearly loved the snow too, bouncing about and burrowing her paws into it. I made a small barely compacted snowball and tossed it in her direction. She jumped up and broke it with her nose so that became a game for a while. Misty-Blue joined us and batted a few flakes with her paw but seemed less impressed by snow than Trixie and soon returned to the farmhouse, presumably to find somewhere warm to settle.

What amazed me the most about the experience was that Darcie kept a running commentary going for Rosemary about what we were all doing. I caught Phoebe's eye while Darcie was describing Trixie's face and body when the dog jumped for the snowballs.

'Did you teach her to do that?' I asked Phoebe.

'No. That's completely her. She's amazing, isn't she?'

'You both are.' And they really were. As I'd anticipated, Darcie's transition into life at Hedgehog Hollow had been smooth, but so had Phoebe's. We'd gone through a lot of tissues while she released her grief and expressed her gratitude but she'd shown considerable strength of character as she made decision after decision about their future.

'He's ready!' Darcie announced a little later. 'Rosemary needs to touch him.'

I guided Rosemary over to the snowman.

'Because you couldn't help to make him, you get to name him,' Darcie told her. 'But you need to touch him first so you can see him and pick the right name.'

'That's very kind of you, darling girl. Thank you.'

I placed Rosemary's hand against the snowman's face and Darcie explained where she needed to move her hand and what she'd find when she did. It was as though she'd been communicating with someone who was visually impaired all her life but Phoebe had told me she'd only spent one day in Rosemary's company just after Christmas.

'He's very tall,' Rosemary said, 'and he has a crooked smile and both those things remind me of my wonderful husband. Would you mind if we call him Sydney?'

Darcie clapped her gloved hands together. 'Sydney the snowman! Can we make another one?'

'I'm getting a bit cold now, so I think I'll head inside,' I said. 'Josh?'

'I'm happy to make another.'

'Me too,' Phoebe added.

'Can we make snow hedgehogs?' Darcie asked.

Josh wiped his sweaty brow, laughing. 'That sounds like a challenge but we can certainly give it our best shot.'

'I'm a little cold too so I'll join you inside.' Rosemary reattached Trixie's harness and we made our way back into the farmhouse for a warming cup of tea.

'You were telling me about your daughter,' I reminded her when we'd settled in the lounge with our drinks, hoping a conversation about her daughter would deflect her from further digs at me and my home.

'Oh yes! Andrea. She didn't approve of Renleigh Court. It only has two bedrooms so she had to share with her brother, which was fine when they were little and in bunk beds, but we appreciated it wasn't ideal when they were older so we put up a stud wall, not that she liked that. I lost count of how many times she told us how ashamed she was of where she lived. She became obsessed with bettering herself and she did well. She studied hard, got a good job, married well and now she has the big family property she's always longed for in which she now thinks I should see out my days.'

'But you're not going to move there?'

'Of course not!' she snapped. 'Weren't you listening to me earlier? Would you move in with someone when they'd made out it would be an immense inconvenience?'

I wasn't sure whether or not that was a rhetorical question so, stung from being snapped at again, I remained silent.

'It's not an option for me, anyway,' she said, softening her tone. 'Contrary to what Andrea might believe, there's plenty of life left in me yet but there wouldn't be if I moved to London. I love my daughter but, most of the time, I don't like her very much. A couple of hours in her company is more than enough and, of course, she couldn't have made it more plain that she doesn't want me if she'd hung out a flag declaring it. I shall stay here. A severe visual impairment does *not* mean I'm incapable of looking after myself.'

I didn't doubt that for a moment.

Rosemary sighed once more. 'Having said that, I *am* struggling with the idea of returning to Renleigh Court. What was once the home I loved so much is the scene of a crime and I know I'm not going to be able to settle. I've decided to sell the flat and do the one thing Sydney and I always said we'd do when we retired. I'm going to buy a small bungalow in a pretty village where I can smell the trees and flowers and hear the birds. I have an enormous favour to ask of you.'

'You'd like to stay here in the meantime?' From her attitude towards me so far, I wasn't keen on the idea and hoped I'd managed to keep the doubt out of my voice.

'My goodness, Samantha, that would be far too much to ask of a complete stranger and I have no desire to live so far from civilisation.'

That was me told!

'I was going to ask if you and Josh would be my eyes and my voice of reason, making sure I don't get conned into buying a mouldy shed next to a landfill.'

'We'd be happy to help,' I said, smiling as I spoke so she wouldn't hear my irritation at another dig. 'Josh was born and bred in the area so he knows all the villages. I'm sure we'll help you find somewhere suitable. What will you do about somewhere to stay in the meantime?'

'I've booked into a B&B for a fortnight starting tomorrow and I'll take it from there.'

The sense of relief made me feel guilty, but adding another adult and a dog into the mix would have been far from ideal. Paul was still on the long road to recovery and I couldn't face having someone in my home who was quite so snappy with me. I'd had my fill of that with Chloe in the summer.

'Should I get my laptop and do a search on what's available at the moment?'

'That would be wonderful, thank you.'

I ran upstairs, retrieved my laptop from my office, and sat beside

Rosemary as I logged onto a property search site.

'Do you have a particular village in mind?'

'No. I don't know the area very well.'

'How many bedrooms?

'It'll need to be three.'

'Three?'

'Yes. The girls will need a bedroom each and I'm not going through the stud wall debacle I had with Andrea.'

Butterflies swarmed in my stomach. 'You want Phoebe and Darcie to move in with you?'

'Of course! Where else would they go?' She crossed her legs, angling her body in my direction. 'You surely don't think they'd stay here?'

I could feel the stress levels rising with the negative emphasis she placed on the word 'here' and fought to remain calm.

'They both love it here.'

'Yes, well, they would say that when they thought it was the only option. I invited Phoebe to live with me after her darling father passed away and she would have done back then if she'd had Tina's consent. I still don't know what's happened with that family but I'm pretty certain that what Tina thinks is no longer relevant, which means Phoebe *can* move in now and I can't very well abandon young Darcie, can I?'

'But they've had a lot of upheaval recently and...' I tailed off, unsure where I was heading with that statement.

Rosemary had thrown me into a tailspin. Every conversation Josh and I had had with Phoebe had involved staying at Hedgehog Hollow long-term but Rosemary was right about it being the only option she'd had available.

'You sound upset,' Rosemary declared.

'No. I'm not... It's just that...' I shrugged. 'We love having them here and hadn't thought about them moving out, but we only want what's best for Phoebe and Darcie.'

'And so do I.'

Each word was emphasised and I couldn't help feeling that I'd been put back in my place. Rosemary had known Phoebe all her life and I knew Phoebe thought of her like a grandmother. But Darcie didn't know her. She'd met her once. I shook my head, admonishing myself. This wasn't a competition with points awarded for how many hours the girls had spent in our company. They seemed so happy and settled here, though.

'As I told Andrea,' Rosemary added, 'I'm more than capable of looking after myself along with anyone else who requires my support. Besides, Phoebe is like family to me whereas, until a week ago, she was simply your unpaid employee.'

Ouch! That was below the belt and *definitely* me put in my place. From feeling empathy towards her about the situation with her daughter, I had a strong sense that it was very much fifty-fifty as to who caused the conflict, maybe even higher in Rosemary's favour.

'And what budget are we looking at?' I asked, focusing my eyes back on the screen and trying to keep my voice bright while my stomach churned.

I entered the property search parameters and talked Rosemary through my findings, but I couldn't shake the feeling that Jenny and Tina returning to the UK on Thursday wasn't the only thing we had to be worried about. I was convinced that, surrogate family or not, moving in with Rosemary was not right for Phoebe and Darcie.

There were practical considerations like how Rosemary would get Darcie to school in Reddfield and there'd be financial implications. Would Rosemary be able to afford to raise them both without support from Social Services?

But the biggest concern of all was Rosemary's health. Her age and visual impairment didn't worry me because neither of those things would hamper her ability to provide a stable, caring home for them, but Phoebe had shared her worries about Rosemary's reduced mobility and I'd noticed some difficulties already today. I could foresee a scenario where Phoebe wasn't just caring for Darcie; she was caring for Rosemary, too. That seemed an awful lot for one teenager to handle on her own.

42

PHOEBE

Samantha came out to see how we were getting on. I glanced up from adding sticks to the snow hedgehog's back and noticed Josh frown at her and mouth, 'Are you all right?' to which she responded, 'Tell you later.'

She hadn't been over to the barn so it wasn't anything to do with the hedgehogs. I hoped Rosemary hadn't said anything to upset her. I loved Rosemary but she could be blunt and a little spiky round people she didn't know. I probably should have warned Samantha.

'So, are there some spectacular snowhogs for me to see?' Samantha asked, with what struck me as forced jollity, although I'm not sure I'd have picked up on that if it hadn't been for witnessing her exchange with Josh.

'Snowhogs?' Darcie giggled. 'We made a family of snowhogs. mummy, daddy and three hoglets. We tried to make a unicorn but it didn't work.'

'They're amazing. I love their spines. I need to get some photos of you with them.'

Samantha took several photos of us with the snowhogs and Sydney the snowman, then said it was time to return to the farm-house to get warm and dry and have some lunch before sledging. The snow had started to tumble again so I was ready to retreat inside for a bit.

Darcie took my hand as we trudged through the snow to the farmhouse. 'That was so much fun!'

'It was, wasn't it?'

'I love it here.'

'Me too.'

Smiling, I glanced across at Samantha but she dipped her head, her mouth downturned, and my tummy sank to the ground. Had Social Services been in touch with bad news? I'd have to get her on her own after we'd eaten but, for now, she probably needed the chance to speak to Josh alone.

'Race you to the house!' I cried, setting off.

Darcie squealed as she gave chase. I deliberately let her shoot past me at the last minute, laughing as she did a victory dance on the doorstep which we'd recently watched on TikTok. I'd never seen her this happy and would be forever grateful to Samantha and Josh for giving us their home, their time and their friendship.

* * *

By the time we came back downstairs in fresh clothes, Samantha was dishing up bowls of tomato soup in the kitchen. There were a couple of baskets of warm bread buns on the table and it smelled so good, my tummy growled.

'What have you been up to?' I asked Rosemary as I sat down beside her.

'Nothing much. Samantha was on her laptop so I had some quiet time.'

There was a clatter at the Aga. 'Sorry,' Samantha said, her cheeks colouring. 'Dropped the ladle. Don't mind me.'

I didn't miss the questioning expression on Josh's face and the slight shake of Samantha's head in response. My initial instinct had been right. Rosemary had said something to her, although I had no idea what it could be. I wasn't going to make an issue of it in front of everyone, especially when we were celebrating Darcie's birthday today, but I wasn't going to stand for Rosemary upsetting Samantha after everything she'd done for us.

Darcie kept the conversation going by telling Rosemary, Paul and Beth all about our snow creations. I kept glancing over at Samantha who sat quietly and barely touched her soup. I knew I'd struggle to get her alone, so I held my phone under the table and quickly texted her.

⬛ To Samantha
Can I speak to you privately when you've finished eating?

I watched her take her phone out and frown at the message but she didn't look across at me, clearly picking up the need for discretion.

⬛ From Samantha
I'll go up to my office if you want to follow in a minute

She pushed her bowl aside and left the kitchen. I gave her a minute then excused myself to go to the toilet.

'This is all very cloak and dagger,' she said when I joined her in her office and closed the door behind me.

'Sorry. I didn't want to make an issue of it. I need to ask you something. Has Rosemary said something to upset you?'

'What makes you ask that?'

If answering a question with a question hadn't already told me 'yes', the guilty expression on her face would have.

'Educated guess. What's she said?'

'I don't want to cause any problems between you.'

'You won't be. I know what she's like. She can have strong opinions and she can be blunt. She clashes with her daughter Andrea and it's not all Andrea's fault. Rosemary gives as good as she gets.'

Samantha plonked herself down on her office chair and sighed. 'It's probably best if it comes from her.'

'I'll ask her too, but I'd really like you to tell me what's going on. Please.'

'Okay. Rosemary can't stay with Celia anymore because Celia's discovered she's allergic to dogs. Andrea's invited her to live in London which is a definite no, but she doesn't want to return to the flat. She wants to sell up and buy a bungalow and...'

'And what?' I prompted.

'I'd really rather she tells you. I've said too much already.'

'You might as well finish it,' I said gently.

She ran her fingers through her hair and winced. 'She wants you and Darcie to move in with her.'

'Really? Since when?'

Samantha shrugged. 'Since she left hospital, I think. How do you feel about the idea?'

My tummy did a somersault as I wrapped a lock of hair round my index finger and unravelled it again, perturbed by the sense of dread rather than excitement.

'You look worried,' Samantha prompted.

'I was desperate to move out of Tina's and in with Rosemary after Dad died, but things have changed now. I've got Darcie to think about. She loves it here – never seen her so happy – and so do I. And it works with stuff like the school run. If we moved in with Rosemary, how would that work? Rosemary isn't getting any younger and she isn't getting any healthier. If it was just me... I have to think about what's best for Darcie. I don't know if living with Rosemary would be best. What do you think?'

'Based on the information you've told me about Rosemary's health, I've got the same concerns. Look, it's not something you have to make a decision on now. If Rosemary asks you later, you can tell her you need time to think about it or that you don't know where things stand with Social Services. Speaking of Social Services, it might be that Jackie doesn't see living with Rosemary as an option for Darcie. It was fairly straightforward letting you stay here because Josh and I are DBS checked, I'm a nurse, I work from home and we're in a position to practically and financially support you both. If you live with Rosemary, they may see that as you taking on additional responsibilities which will diminish the care you can give to Darcie.' She sighed and shook her head. 'I feel awful saying that, but I have some inkling of how these things work.'

We sat in silence for a few minutes, Samantha gazing out of the window towards the meadow, and me hanging my head, twiddling with my hair. I felt completely overwhelmed by it all. Living with Rosemary was the one thing I'd wanted so desperately. But that was before.

'I'd better get back downstairs,' I said eventually, flicking my hair back over my shoulder. 'If Rosemary asks me, I'll say that Social Services have approved us living here but might not approve somewhere else.'

'We can always query it with Jackie if moving in with Rosemary is what you want.'

I nodded and gave her a smile before slipping out of the room but, as I slowly descended the stairs, I knew it wasn't something I wanted to query with Jackie. This morning, rolling out snowballs with Samantha, Josh and Darcie, I'd felt like part of a proper family for the first time ever. I wanted Rosemary in mine and Darcie's lives but as a grandmother figure, just like she'd always been. I wanted Samantha and Josh as my parent figures. I just hoped Rosemary would see it that way because I didn't want to lose her, but if she made me pick between her and Hedgehog Hollow, that might just happen. Staying with Samantha and Josh was without a doubt best for my animal-loving little sister and it was best for me too. For once in my life, what I wanted *was* going to be taken into consideration.

* * *

When I returned downstairs, Darcie was in the hall pulling on her coat and wellies while Josh stood by the door urging her to hurry.

'What's going on?' I asked.

'Fizz is here on a tractor!' she cried, diving for the door.

My heart leapt at the mention of Fizz's name and I swiftly pulled on my coat and boots and ran after them, catching up as a big red tractor pulled into the farmyard.

Fizz waved enthusiastically at us and, when the tractor halted, jumped down, and raced over to us.

'Say goodbye to my brother, Barney,' she said to Darcie.

Barney turned the tractor and waved as he headed back down the track.

'I have a birthday gift I'll give to you after we've been sledging,' Fizz told Darcie when we returned to the farmhouse. 'My brother also has a gift for you – a day at his farm during the Easter holidays.'

Darcie gasped. 'Does he have animals?'

'Sheep, cows, horses, goats, chickens… loads of animals. But it needs to be Easter as the weather will be better then and you'll be able to help to bottle-feed the lambs.'

I smiled gratefully at Fizz. She'd just made a friend for life. Darcie loved Hedgehog Hollow but the farm itself was arable and she was desperate to visit a farm which had animals other than hedgehogs and a cat.

Rosemary decided to settle in front of the log burner with an audio-book while we went out sledging. Samantha offered to keep her company and I noticed her relieved expression when Rosemary insisted everyone went out as she'd probably doze off.

The field behind the dairy shed was sloped so we trudged through the snow, Beth pulling Archie on a sledge, Josh pulling Darcie, and Fizz pulling me.

My heart leapt when Fizz sat behind me on the sledge at the top of the slope, wrapped her arms round my waist and clung on as we sped down the hill faster and faster, giggling hysterically as we tumbled out and into the snow at the bottom. I'd never met anyone who was so excitable and such a laugh to be round. She got us to do races and it was hilarious watching Samantha, Josh and Beth – who were normally pretty chilled – becoming all competitive and desperate to win. I don't think I've laughed so much in my whole life as I did that afternoon.

Darcie was in her element but seeing her so happy and free confirmed that there was no way I could take her away from this to move in with Rosemary. Her world had been restricted to home, school and the scabby playground and now she had woods and fields to play in and so many people giving her the family she'd never had. It was how it should be.

'You look deep in thought,' Fizz said as we pulled the empty sledge back up for one final ride.

'Just thinking about Darcie and how amazing all this space is for her.'

'Growing up on a farm is awesome. Darcie's going to have the best childhood living here.'

I agreed. But would Rosemary?

* * *

When we returned to the farmhouse, we changed into dry clothes and it was time for presents. Everyone piled into the lounge and Darcie's face was a picture, staring open-mouthed at the pile of gifts piled up in the room.

'All for me?' she asked uncertainly, glancing up at me.

'All for you. They're from different people so we need to check the tags.'

When Samantha had asked me what Darcie might like for her birthday, I knew immediately: a Princess Tiana costume from *The Princess and the Frog.* Samantha ordered it online and insisted I gave it to Darcie as my gift. When I protested about the money, she said I should think of it as payment in lieu for the great work I'd done on the accounts.

Darcie squealed when she opened her costume. She pulled it on immediately over her clothes and twirled round the room so we could all admire the pale green and lemon dress.

She squealed again when she opened one of the gifts from Samantha and Josh containing a tiara and shoes – which she put on too – and a Tiana soft doll.

It brought tears to my eyes seeing how grateful she was for every single gift, rushing up to the giver to thank them before opening the next. Samantha's and Josh's family and friends had even sent round presents. These people barely knew us, but they'd welcomed us into their lives and I felt like I had a family for the first time in years. It took me back to the days in Renleigh Court when Dad and I had fish and chips with Rosemary every Friday. We'd been a family then. I hoped Rosemary would understand that me saying no to her kind offer didn't change that. I still wanted and needed her in my life.

Fizz gave Darcie a pink T-shirt with a sparkly hedgehog on it. Protruding from the hedgehog's head was a unicorn horn.

'My friend designed this for me and I called it a hedgicorn. Look! I'm wearing one too.' She lifted up her fleecy jumper to reveal a matching T-shirt. Seeing Darcie fling her arms round Fizz's neck and kiss her cheek touched my heart. Unicorn T-shirts and promises of farm visits had won my little sister over but her kindness, bubbly personality and zest for life had won me over.

* * *

'Is there somewhere I can talk to Phoebe in private?' Rosemary asked Samantha after we'd had our tea and a slice of birthday cake.

'You could go into the lounge while we clear up in here.'

Samantha mouthed 'good luck' to me as I linked Rosemary's arm and led her across the hall to the lounge.

'I've decided not to return to Renleigh Court,' she said as soon as we sat down. 'Sydney and I always planned to move to a village and, even though he's no longer with me, it's time I followed the plan.'

'Sounds great,' I said when she paused, my tummy doing somersaults as I waited anxiously for the next part, hoping she wouldn't be offended by my decision. 'Do you have somewhere in mind?'

'Nowhere specific but I want a large village in this area on a bus route into Reddfield and two spare bedrooms. One for you and one for Darcie.'

'For when we come to visit?' I asked, trying to keep my voice light.

'To live in,' she said sharply, as though it was obvious. 'We've talked about you moving in for years, but Tina wouldn't let you. She has no say in the matter now. So are you ready to start hunting for our new home next week?'

'I can help you house hunt but it's a no to moving in. Darcie loves it here and so do I and—'

'You'd rather live with a stranger than me?' She sounded disgusted by the idea.

'It's not like that. If it had just been me, I'd move in with you like a flash. You know that. But I have Darcie to think of now and—'

'And you think I'm too old and decrepit to offer her a home.'

'No! That's got nothing to do with it. She adores you and I know you'd be amazing with her. It's just that she loves living on a farm and having so many people around and I don't think...'

I tailed off as she stood up. 'I'm feeling tired. Will you ask Josh to drive me back to Celia's?'

'Rosemary! I'm not trying to upset you.'

'I'm not upset. I'm tired and I want to leave. If you don't want to live with me, that's fine.'

'It's not that I don't *want* to live with you. It's just that I need to think of Darcie and what's best for her.'

'Which isn't me.'

I hated it when she got like this, twisting every word. It was rare she did it with me but I knew the pattern, having seen it so many times with her family.

'Social Services have approved Hedgehog Hollow for Darcie's home and the fostering placement is going ahead on that basis. I can't risk messing things up by changing where we live. I can't risk losing Darcie.'

Her shoulders stiffened and she drew in a deep breath and pursed her lips. I braced myself for an objection but she softened and nodded.

'I understand. But I am tired, so please can you ask Josh about that lift?'

When I hugged her goodbye a few minutes later, I felt a distance I'd never felt between us before. Did she understand or had she just said that to end the conversation?

43

I woke up on the morning of my nineteenth birthday, twelve days after our snow day, and felt excitement rather than dread. I hadn't felt excited about my birthday in years because a birthday – or more specifically *my* birthday – was nothing special in the Grimes household.

My first birthday after Dad married Tina was my thirteenth. He was on a 6 a.m. shift start, leaving before I rose, so he'd wished me a happy birthday the night before.

'I'm sorry I won't be here in the morning to see you open your gifts,' he said, sitting down on the edge of my bed. 'But I know you'll love them. Tina chose them this year. I figured she'd have a better idea than me of what a teenage girl would like.'

I wasn't so convinced. After seven months of living with her, Tina knew nothing about me and what I liked, but I smiled and thanked him anyway.

'I told her to spoil my special girl,' he said, kissing my forehead. 'Happy birthday, sweetheart.'

God knows how much money he'd given her to 'spoil' me but she'd excelled herself in doing the opposite: a hoodie that I knew she'd bought for herself which had shrunk in the wash, some knock-off perfume which brought my wrists out in a rash and a couple of DVDs that I knew Cody had nicked. The only new purchase was a bar of chocolate... which had passed its best before date.

More upsetting than the crap 'presents' was that she'd conned my dad yet again. I'd overheard her and Jenny laughing about what she'd spent the money on and she even had the audacity that day to wear the brand new T-shirt and jeans she'd bought.

I knew that Samantha and Josh would make today special. Although I was excited about opening my gifts, the biggest thrill came from knowing that this birthday and all my future birthdays would be spent away from *that* family. A judge had given me the best birthday gift ever when he'd sentenced Jenny and Tina.

I'd loved to have been there when they arrived back at the airport, smug and tanned, and seen their faces fall when they spotted their welcoming party, the handcuffs were snapped on, and they were read their Miranda rights.

'You do not have to say anything...' According to Fizz, they'd said a lot. It was loud and sweary as they were dragged through the airport, their holiday well and truly over.

And now they were on 'holiday' again. Only this time it was a two-by-three-metre cell. No pool, no beach, no room service and, best of all, no company because they'd been banged up in different prisons. That had been an unexpected bonus.

I'd barely slept for the three nights running up to yesterday's sentencing. I'd have preferred never to see them again, but I knew how much stronger the case would be by having me there. As I took to the stand, I could feel their eyes boring into me, the pair of them emanating hate, but then I reminded myself that they'd always been like that and the only difference now was that I was the one who held the power. I was the one who could hurt them. So I did, but only by telling the truth about everything they'd ever done to Darcie and me.

I hated reliving those painful and terrifying experiences, seeing the photos of my injuries flashing up on a large TV screen, but I hated them more. The desire for justice for me, Darcie, Samantha, Hayley,

Idris and anyone else whose life had been affected by their drug dealing or thieving kept me going.

Trigg was also behind bars. He had priors for drug dealing and assault so was given a tougher sentence. And those blue hashtag and yellow bee tablets I'd uncovered had been tested and they'd been the same ones that had killed that student and Idris. All three of them would be on a very long 'holiday'.

So today, on my nineteenth birthday, my life couldn't be more different. After years of struggling, I was somewhere I felt I belonged. Waking up each morning filled me with excitement instead of dread, and I had a renewed sense of purpose in life, knowing I hadn't just saved myself; I'd saved Darcie, too. I had an amazing family who cared about me instead of treating me like an unpaid servant and it didn't matter that we weren't connected by blood.

But there was one family member who'd pulled away from me and it broke my heart. At the start of last week, Rosemary announced that she'd changed her mind about wanting Samantha's help with her house hunt, saying she could manage it with my help only. I didn't appreciate the pressure, but I was grateful she wasn't sulking with me for not moving in with her.

I viewed several bungalows with her after college across the week, armed with a checklist from Samantha and Josh of the sort of things to watch out for. None of the houses struck me as suitable for a severely visually impaired woman with mobility issues living on her own: busy main road, too remote, too many steps to the door, not on a bus route. There were illogical layouts, unexpected internal steps and kitchens and bathrooms needing complete overhauls. The more I looked, the more I was convinced this wasn't the right solution for her.

'Wouldn't you prefer to live in a retirement flat?' I asked as we clambered back into the taxi waiting for us outside the seventh unsuitable property on Saturday.

'You mean a care home?' she responded, her tone curt.

'No. I mean a retirement flat, although one with help on hand. I think it's called assisted living.'

'Urgh. Horrible phrase. Assisting you to the grave, more like, by gradually taking away all your independence.'

'I don't think that's what they're like.'

'You've lived in one, have you?'

'No, but—'

'You sound like Andrea. I'm quite capable of independent living, you know. I've managed it for several years so far.'

'I know that, but—'

'Don't you dare say I'm not getting any younger.'

'But you're not and this way you have the best of both worlds. You get your own brand new flat but you know there's someone on hand if you have a fall or anything.'

'Why would I have a fall?'

'Because you might.' I bit my lip. I was going to have to say it. 'Because you're not as steady on your feet as you used to be.'

She wouldn't speak to me after that. She engaged the taxi driver in mindless conversation about the weather and the news all the way to Hedgehog Hollow. She didn't even say goodbye to me when I got out; just stubbornly lifted her chin.

I'd called her on Sunday and asked if I could visit her at her B&B but she wouldn't let me, saying there wasn't a lobby or lounge area where we could meet. She shut down my suggestion to go to a café instead and made a flimsy excuse to end the call.

I had no idea if she'd get in touch today to wish me a happy birthday and that hurt. What hurt even more was that she hadn't wished me luck in court, either, although I'd kind of seen that coming. It was something else she'd got mardy about. I'd made the decision not to tell her what Tina and Jenny had done to me and to focus instead on the theft, the drugs and the neglect. She didn't need to carry any guilt for not protecting me. I'd talked it over with Samantha and she urged caution because the truth usually came out somewhere down the line but I'd decided to take that chance. She'd been through too much herself and I knew that she was way more shaken by Trigg's attack than she was letting on.

Thing is, to keep the truth from her meant not letting her come to court and she wasn't impressed with that either. 'Oh, I see. You've got Samantha now so you don't need my support.'

It wasn't like that at all but there was no convincing her. Hopefully she'd come round. If I had to turn up at the B&B at the weekend and demand she see me, that's what I'd have to do. For now, I was going to celebrate my freedom.

* * *

My birthday fell on a Thursday and, knowing how chaotic the morning routine could be at Hedgehog Hollow, I'd decided to wait until everyone was home from school, college or work before I opened any gifts.

As I rode my moped into the car park after college, I was surprised to see several cars and vans in the farmyard. I spotted Fizz's mini among them and my heart leapt.

I was about to head to the barn when a text came through:

✉ From Samantha
Your birthday surprise awaits you in the dairy shed xx

Intrigued, I made my way past the barn and meadow and down to the dairy shed. The path was lit by lanterns, which was just as well as the shed itself was in darkness.

'Hello?' I called pushing open the door.

The loud cheers of 'surprise' made me jump. Lights came on and streamers and party poppers exploded in front of me. Darcie ran up to me and leapt into my arms.

'Happy birthday!' she cried before planting a smacker on my cheek.

I glanced round the sea of smiling faces, stunned to see so many people gathered together to celebrate my birthday: Josh's family, Samantha's dad, Rich and Dave, Hannah and Toby with their daughter

Amelia, Fizz, Zayn and some of his college friends. Zayn had become a surprise friend since the start of the college term. He'd spotted me sitting alone at lunchtime on the first day back and invited me to join his table. I'd been wary at first in case he said anything, but he introduced me to his mates as his friend from the rescue centre and it was obvious from their reactions that they had no idea what had gone down.

'We've got something special lined up behind me,' Samantha said.

Several sheets had been hung from the rafters and they dropped to the floor revealing numerous giant inflatables and it was clear from the excited reaction of the guests that they hadn't known what was behind the sheets either.

A woman I didn't recognise stepped forward. 'Hi, everyone! My name's Natasha Kinsella and I run an events company. I was approached recently by a company who specialise in inflatable games. I'm thinking about investing but, when they offered me a chance for a free road-test, a surprise party for Phoebe seemed the perfect opportunity, so happy birthday, Phoebe. Let the fun begin!'

I thought sledging had been fun but the giant inflatables took it to a whole new level. There were four big games: a rodeo bull, giant sumo wrestling, a gladiator duel and a bungee run. As I caught my breath between activities, Samantha joined me, fresh from a sumo wrestling match against Josh.

'Are you enjoying your birthday?' she asked.

'I'm having the best time ever. I've got a stitch from laughing so much. I can't thank you enough.'

'It was actually Fizz's idea. We were thinking of a surprise party but as soon as she heard about the inflatables, she suggested your birthday would be the perfect time for her mum to test them.'

We both looked over at Fizz, who was having a gladiator duel with Zayn, laughing as her jab of her pugil stick sent him toppling off his podium, making her the winner.

The only sounds I could hear were laugher and cheers and I couldn't stop smiling as I took it all in.

'I noticed Rosemary's not here.'

'We asked her but it's not really her thing. She thought the noise might be too much for Trixie. I'm sure she'll have something a bit less loud planned for you.'

She didn't sound convinced and I wasn't either.

Fizz ran over, eyes sparkling, cheeks glowing. 'Sumo wrestle?'

'You're on!'

She grabbed my hand and we ran towards the wrestling ring, giggling. I hated that things were difficult between Rosemary and me right now but no way was I going to let it put a downer on my amazing birthday surprise.

44

SAMANTHA

It was late morning the following day before I had a chance to sit down with my copy of the local paper, *Wolds Weekly*, and I was beyond thrilled with the coverage.

The reporter had been amazingly supportive and had secured the front page and a three-page spread inside. The front-page scoop focused on the court case and sentences issued but inside was full of photos showing our rescue successes alongside the devastation caused by the Grimes family. She'd certainly gone for the sympathy vote and hopefully it would generate plenty of donations as well as some more volunteers. The locations of the donation bins had been printed with a link to our Amazon wish list and the paper had also set up a crowd-funding page, which was a lovely surprise.

I hadn't had a chance to check social media either and logged on to find more than 500 notifications on Facebook. Our feed was full of messages of support and pledges of donations. The *Wolds Weekly* had tagged us into their Facebook post, connecting to their online article and including the wish list and crowdfunding links. That post had been shared hundreds of times.

Clicking into the crowdfunding page, I gasped. No way had they

already raised more than £4,000! Our local community were
phenomenal.

My fingers shook as I shared it on our feed with a huge thank you
for all the support and a promise that I'd get through all the messages
as soon as I could.

⬜ To Josh
We've had hundreds of messages on Facebook and the
paper have set up a crowdfunding page. It's already
past £4k! I'm in shock! xx

⬜ From Josh
That's brilliant news! Word has spread big time.
First customer came in with a collection jar with
£50 in it and the bins are overflowing! The hedgehogs are going to be OK. Which means full steam
ahead for the wedding and honeymoon doesn't it? xx

⬜ To Josh
Yes it does! I'm so relieved, I've had a little
cry xx

⬜ From Josh
Sending hugs and virtual tissues xx

I'd barely made a dent in working through the messages on social
media when an unfamiliar vehicle pulled into the farmyard. I grabbed
my gloves and a crate and left the barn to investigate.

A short, stocky man wearing shorts and a tight Lycra T-shirt lifted a
laundry basket out of the boot of a rusty-looking car. 'I've got three
hedgehogs for you, but one might be dead.'

'Might be?'

'My missus thinks it is, but I can't decide. We haven't seen it move
for a couple of days.'

I glanced into the basket. Three large hedgehogs were curled into balls on top of a ripped towel. None of them were moving, but I could see faeces.

'Where did you find them?' I asked as I hastily transferred them into my carry crate. A biting wind was blowing across the yard and I was anxious to get them inside and warmed up before inspecting them.

'The missus spotted one of them on the way back from the pub on Christmas Eve, lit by the moon, and thought it would make a cute pet and—'

'You've been keeping them as pets?' I couldn't keep the disbelief out of my voice. They were wild animals and should only ever be cared for in someone's home when there was a good reason for bringing them inside and the carer knew what they were doing.

The man didn't pick up on my incredulity. 'Daft bugger thought she'd be able to play with them but all they did was curl up into balls and shit everywhere.'

He released a loud guffaw as though he'd made a hilarious joke. There was nothing funny about this situation. There was a reason wildlife were called that – they belonged in the wild!

I tried again. 'You do know you can't keep hedgehogs as pets?'

'Er, yes you can. I've seen them on Instagram.'

'They'll be a special breed of domesticated hedgehogs like the African pygmy hedgehog but what you have here...' I raised the crate, 'are European hedgehogs and they need to live in the wild.'

He narrowed his eyes at me. 'Then why do you have a barn full of them?'

'Because they're all poorly and need our help but they're released back into the wild as soon as they're well. If you find any other hedgehogs, please don't keep them as pets and if they're—'

He took a step closer and seemed to grow in stature as he stared me down. 'Who the fuck do you think you're talking to?'

I gulped as I took a step back, suddenly aware of how alone and vulnerable I was just now if he struck out. Even if I screamed, Beth and

Paul wouldn't be able to get to me quickly enough. I decided to end it there. I could feel the panic welling inside me and frantically tried to calm myself. I couldn't have a PTSD episode in front of him. No way.

I smiled brightly. 'Thanks for bringing them in. I'd best get them inside.'

He shouted something at me but it got lost on the wind as I hurried over to the barn, trembling. I only released the breath I'd been holding when I heard the roar of his engine as he lurched out of the car park.

'That was fun,' I muttered to myself as I placed the crate on the treatment table and plugged in the heat pads. I'd been lucky so far that I hadn't had much negativity, but there was always going to be somebody who thought they knew best. I just hoped that the three hogs hadn't suffered during their time in captivity and that their captors had at least done some research on what to feed them.

'It's all right, sweetie,' I said as I lifted out the first hog. 'You're safe now.'

The stocky man had got one thing right: one of the hedgehogs definitely hadn't made it. I gently placed it back in the carry crate to check over later, hoping that the cause of death wasn't neglect on their part.

The other two hedgehogs – one male and one female – were dehydrated but I couldn't see any obvious external problems. I suspected his 'missus' wouldn't have kept them inside for long if she'd spotted ticks, flystrike or maggots on them.

One of them had been unceremoniously scooped up at night-time on the way back from the pub. It was very likely a healthy hedgehog in a period of arousal from hibernation, searching for food or perhaps even changing nests – something that could happen if the original nest was disturbed – and should have been left to go on its way. What possessed them to think it was acceptable to keep a wild animal as a pet on a whim?

After both hedgehogs had left samples, I checked them under the microscope and there were no concerns internally. Today, we'd been lucky, but I'd read about far too many cases of hedgehogs being taken in as pets who'd suffered as a result, or poorly hogs being taken in by well-meaning members of the public who hadn't had the expertise to care for them and it had been too late by the time they'd relented and taken them to their local rescue centre. Every story like that made me so sad because those lives could so easily have been saved. I'd put a reminder on social media to always get hogs to a rescue centre where experts could help them and never keep them at home.

Our new theme for naming hedgehogs was 'childhood memories' – characters from TV programmes, films, books or toys we remembered – and was proving great fun. I christened our new patients Tinky Winky and Laa-Laa from the Teletubbies and settled them into their new homes.

After making a coffee, I returned to the comments on social media, which helped restore my faith in humanity.

'Hello?'

I looked up and smiled at Terry. 'I was miles away then. Come in.'

'I've got our Wilbur with me today.'

'That's fine. There are no hedgehogs out.'

Wilbur ran up to me and immediately rolled onto his back so I could rub his belly and scratch his ears. I laughed as he gave me a big lick.

'Lovely to see you too, Wilbur.' I looked up at Terry. 'Time for a cuppa?'

'That'd be smashing. Thanks, lass.'

He nodded towards my copy of *Wolds Weekly* on the table when I handed him a drink. 'I read that last night. Shocked, I were, but not surprised. That family...' He pursed his lips and shook his head. 'The stuff Gwendoline used to tell me.'

'She talked to you about her family?'

'Sometimes. She used to joke that she were adopted 'cause she were nowt like the rest of 'em. She had two brothers and two sisters, all older than her, and they were always in trouble with teachers or the police. Looks like the bad blood passed down through the generations.'

'Looks like it, although hopefully this is finally the end of their vendetta against me.'

'I'm sorry they took all your money. That's low, but it's how they've always operated. Take whatever they want without lifting a finger to earn it, and to hell with who it hurts. How have you been managing?'

'I'd placed a big order before Christmas so we had some stock. My dad and Josh's practice gave us a loan and now the paper have set up a crowdfunding thing, so we're getting there.'

He slid a folded piece of paper across the table. 'This should help.'

I picked it up and did a double take at the figure on the cheque. 'No, Terry, I can't accept this. That's far too much.'

'I'll be offended if you don't.'

'But thirty grand? Terry! That's a fortune.'

'And I can't think of a better use for it. They took it from you and I'm replacing it. It's the least I could do. You've been good to me and it means a lot to me that you've created this for Gwendoline.'

'Because she meant a lot to you?' I posed it as a question.

'She meant everything but, you know, you can't make someone feel what they don't.' He cleared his throat. 'When our Marion died, she left everything to me. I don't need the money and I've no relatives to leave it to. Hedgehog Hollow is already named as the sole beneficiary of my estate when I'm gone, but you need some money now, so here it is.'

I pressed my fingers to my lips, tears pooling in my eyes, unable to form any words for fear of them exploding in a sob.

'I've got summat else I think you'll like.'

He pulled a brown A5 envelope out of his pocket and emptied the contents onto the table.

'Win some, lose some,' he said as he spread out the pile of photos. 'But friends was better than nowt.'

'I'm so sorry, Terry.'

He shrugged. 'She were always honest with me. Never led me on. Never pretended it could be more. Problem is, when you fall for someone like Gwendoline, no bugger else stands a chance.'

'Did you know Thomas?'

'Aye, and I wanted to hate him 'cause he won her heart when I couldn't, but how could I? He was perfect for her and probably the nicest bloke I've ever met. And he got her away from that godawful family of hers and gave her the life she deserved. Some things are meant to be and some aren't.'

The words were positive but I could hear the pain and regret in each one. I knew only too well how hurtful unrequited love was, as I'd been there with James and could clearly remember the tears and heartache. Then I'd met Josh and I fell so much deeper for him, my perfect match. For Terry, Gwendoline had evidently been his one and only match and he'd never been able to find a love even close to it again.

I glanced down at the cheque. 'Thank you for this, Terry. I can see how much this means to you and what it represents. We'll put it to good use.'

'I don't want any fuss making, mind. Don't tell that reporter or put it on your Facebook. Just between you and me and your Josh.'

'Thank you. And I bet Gwendoline's looking down on you and thanking you too.' A couple of tears spilled down my cheeks and dripped onto the table.

'Aye, yeah, maybe.' Terry swiped at his eyes and cleared his throat once more. 'Let me tell you about these photos...'

As Terry talked me through his collection, the love he'd felt for Gwendoline was obvious in every word, every smile, every memory. What an amazing woman Gwendoline Mickleby had been, with two men who'd loved her so passionately that they'd never found love again, a legacy of friendship, a passion for wildlife, and the strength to get away from her bullying family. I wished I'd known her as an adult. I bet I'd have learned a lot from her because, more than twenty years after her death, I was still learning.

Four weeks later

'How are you feeling?' Josh asked, handing me my hedgehog mug. 'Delight or dread?'

I smiled at him as I wrapped my hands round the mug of tea. 'I keep lurching between the two.'

He sat beside me on Thomas's bench and gazed out over the meadow. There'd been a light frost this morning but it had melted away fairly quickly. The clear sky was now baby blue but steadily deepening in tone.

'Good weather for moving day,' he said. 'It bucketed down the day I moved into Alder Lea. Luckily I didn't have much stuff at the time, but my boxes were soaked.'

Chloe and James's house sale in Whitsborough Bay and the purchase of Dalby House in Bentonbray had gone through quickly and today was moving day. The house had been empty and the owners had generously allowed Chloe and James to have a set of keys if they wanted to redecorate on the proviso that they didn't actually move in until the sale was complete. The house only needed a bit of freshening up here and there so Josh, Dad and I had been roped into painting and glossing.

The old Chloe would have found excuses not to wield a paintbrush like having Samuel to mind or having a spot of shoulder pain, but she'd surprised Josh and me by leaving Samuel with Auntie Louise and had done her bit. Okay, so there'd been some drama over paint colours resulting in an emergency trip to the DIY store to return some 'hideous' colours, only for her to return with something that I swear could only have been one shade different. It would be unrealistic to expect the old Chloe to completely disappear!

Today, Josh had taken the day off work and we were meeting them at 11 a.m. to help put beds together. Fizz had a lunchtime finish at university so she'd offered to drive straight over and keep an eye on the hedgehogs for the afternoon. Phoebe had a half-day at college too ahead of the half-term holiday so the pair of them were going to continue with the preparations for Sunday's open day.

It had been Fizz's suggestion to hold an open day as a fundraiser and to push back the Family Fun Day to later in the year so there wouldn't be too events so close together or the pressure of trying to host an event on the same weekend as our wedding. As we were getting married on what would have been Gwendoline's eightieth birthday, it seemed fitting to hold our rescheduled Family Fun Day on what would have been Thomas's eighty-fifth birthday: Saturday 26th June.

'Aren't you cold out here?' Josh asked, bringing my thoughts back to the present as he put his mug down on the arm of the bench and zipped up his coat.

'It's a bit nippy but I don't mind, not when I've got you to cuddle up to.'

He put his arm out so I could snuggle up closer.

'Do you realise that, ten weeks tomorrow, we'll be standing right over there saying "I do"?'

'Oh my gosh! It is! We need to get the invitations sorted. At least everyone's saving the date.'

'It's probably time to go dress shopping, too. I know you were holding out for your mum but there are others who'd love to help you.'

After the New Year's Eve party and Mum's declaration about her New Year's resolution to seek help for suspected PTSD, I'd thought things might improve between us but there'd been little contact and that was down to unfortunate timing. I knew how emotional the support process was and I'd have loved to have reached out to her to offer support and encouragement but there was always something happening connected to Phoebe or Darcie – birthdays, fostering and adoption discussions, plans for Darcie to change schools – that time was never on my side. I hoped I hadn't missed my opportunity – with Mum or with finding a dream wedding dress.

'I'll give Ginny at The Wedding Emporium a call and see if I can get a private appointment next week.'

'You could make a day of it,' Josh suggested. 'Take Phoebe and Darcie and get some lunch.'

'I've been thinking. I know it means even more money for dresses – especially when I've already added Beth and Lottie into the mix – but how would you feel about me asking Phoebe and Darcie to be brides-maids too?'

He smiled. 'I was going to suggest it myself. They'd both love it.'

'And what about Fizz? She's become such a good friend. I'd been thinking about asking her last year when I asked Beth.'

'Remind me who was it who wanted a small wedding?' There was laughter in his tone so I knew he didn't object.

'I know! And I did, but our family's just grown. Plus, the pressure's off now that we don't have to use our wedding savings to bail out the hedgehogs.'

The crowdfunding appeal plus independent donations had raised an eyewatering sum. Added to the generous donation from Terry, I could pay back the loans from Dad and the practice, we could spoil Phoebe and Darcie, and relax knowing we had financial stability for Hedgehog Hollow for several years.

I chewed on my lip as I added up how many bridesmaids I'd have by adding in Phoebe, Darcie and Fizz. 'It's gone a bit far, hasn't it? Eight bridesmaids is ridiculous.'

'Nine would be ridiculous but eight's good. Eight's where to draw the line. And, strictly speaking, Amelia, Lottie and Darcie are flower girls so that's really only five bridesmaids.'

I cuddled closer to him. 'I like your thinking. Thank you.'

He kissed the top of my head. 'You don't need to thank me. This is a once in a lifetime special day and it should be exactly the way we want it to be. Three more dresses won't break the bank and I want you to have the people who mean the most to you to support you.'

I pushed away thoughts of whether Mum, with her newfound acknowledgement that she'd treated me badly all my life, would be there as mother of the bride or whether she'd feel too hypocritical to take the role.

'I *am* chilly now,' I said, standing up. 'I'll go inside to call Ginny.'

* * *

'I want a pink bridesmaid dress,' Chloe said as we cleaned the kitchen cupboards while the men were upstairs putting the bed together after lunch.

'We're not doing pink.'

'Why not? It's my favourite colour.'

'And it's my least favourite colour so I'm not having it for my colour scheme. Besides, you had pink so I'm not going to copy.'

She flung her cloth into the bowl of soapy water and planted her hands on her hips. 'So you're saying you didn't like the colour scheme for my wedding?'

'It was beautiful. For *your* wedding. But you've always known I'm not into pink.'

'But your bridesmaid dress was pink.'

'Which I wore because you wanted me to but, if you cast your mind back, you'll recall that you originally asked me what colour I'd like and I told you anything but pink.'

'I don't remember that.'

'Clearly not, because I wore pink.'

'Well, it's up to the bride what colour her bridesmaids wear and I wanted pink.'

'You're right. It *is* up to the bride which is why *I'll* be choosing the colour for my wedding.'

'You won't dress us in something hideous like snot green or rusty brown will you?'

'Oh my gosh, Chloe! Why would I do that?'

'So we don't upstage you.'

I shook my head. 'You know you said I should call you out when the old Chloe reappeared and started being obnoxious? This right here. This is classic old Chloe behaviour. So can the new and improved Chloe come back and ask me nicely what colours I'm contemplating and be happy for me?'

She stared at me for a moment, eyes narrowed, and I braced myself for an outburst, but she surprised me by shrugging. 'You're right. Sorry. I *am* happy for you and you're right about pink. No point copying me. So what colours are you thinking of?'

'I'd love something that compliments the meadow in May.'

'Buttercup yellow?' She wrung out her cloth.

'Not that bright! I might go for a different pastel shade for each dress. I've got a few ideas in mind but I want to see what Ginny can do, bearing in mind I've probably left it a bit late with only ten weeks to go.'

'Yeah, that is really late. I was beginning to think you'd ditched me and decided to only have your lodgers as bridesmaids.'

And the old Chloe was back!

46

PHOEBE

Butterflies swarmed in my tummy as I rode my moped along the farm track after an early finish at college ahead of the half-term holidays. When Fizz's blue mini came into view in the farmyard, they intensified, and I had to stop and take a few deep breaths.

I'd tried so hard to push away my feelings for Fizz but it was impossible. She was so lovely. She made me laugh and helped me forget about how horrible the last four years had been and to focus on the future instead of the past. I'd never been much of a talker but I felt like I could chat to Fizz about anything. I loved that I could make her laugh too and I finally knew what a close friendship looked and felt like.

The problem was that I wanted more than friendship and I had no idea what to do about that. I'd never had a girlfriend and the only time I'd kissed anyone was best forgotten about.

I didn't know how to tell the difference between someone being friendly and flirty. Fizz had never said or done anything to make me believe she might be gay, which made everything so much harder. I knew she didn't live with anyone, except Jinks the lazy cat, but that didn't mean she wasn't seeing someone.

This afternoon, I was determined to find out. There'd been some drama at college with one of the girls on my course whose boyfriend had dumped her and she'd got her revenge. I thought Fizz would be amused and it was the perfect lead-in to ask her if she had a boyfriend. Which was why I was so nervous. It needed to be done. For some reason, my gut told me she was gay but, if I was wrong about that, I'd need to find a way to stop drifting into a dreamworld where we were together.

Fizz was at the sink when I parked my moped and she waved at me out of the window, making my heart leap. *Must play it cool. Must not burst into tears if she says she has a boyfriend.*

I removed my helmet and shook out my hair as I opened the barn door. Her red hair was tied in low bunches and she wore an oversized cream jumper covered in pink sequin hearts over a pair of deep purple leggings. I loved her quirky style and wished I was more daring, but I'd always gone for plain clothes, longing to blend into the background.

'Hey, you! How was the last day of college?' she asked, smiling brightly.

There'd never be a more ideal conversation opener so I was going to have to dive straight in.

'Dramatic.' I shrugged off my coat and hung it up. 'There's this lass on my course and she came to class in tears because her boyfriend dumped her this morning. He's going to Corfu for half-term and he wants to go on the pull without feeling guilty but, get this, he expects her to take him back after the holiday.'

'That's outrageous! I hope she told him where to go.'

'She bought a chocolate milkshake at morning break and emptied it all over his head in the middle of the canteen in front of the whole college.'

'No way! That's awesome. That girl deserves some serious respect. Unless she takes him back when he returns from his holiday.'

'No chance of that. She's finally realised what a nob he is.'

'Most men are.'

This is it! There'll never be a better moment. Do it!

'You don't have a boyfriend?'

'Nope. Men don't do it for me.'

My heart raced. I had to be sure. 'You've got a girlfriend?'

'Not at the moment. I split up with my last girlfriend, Nadine, about eighteen months ago and there hasn't been anyone since. Probably should get out there again. What about you? Boyfriend?'

'No. I've never had a—'

The barn door was flung open and a woman wearing Lycra running gear dashed over to us, clutching an old-style Quality Street tin. 'I found these in my garden. Shouldn't they be hibernating?'

She plonked the tin on the table. There were three small hedgehogs curled up in one corner.

'Can't stay! I'm late for Zumba.' Seconds later, the door slammed behind her.

Fizz rolled her eyes at me. 'I'm guessing she doesn't want her tin back. Right! Let's see what we have here. Can you grab some of those heat pads and plug them in?'

And that was the end of the conversation about boyfriends while we focused on the three hedgehogs who Fizz said were underweight and dehydrated so we needed to get them warm and some fluids into them quickly.

I couldn't think of a way to return to the conversation. What was I meant to say? *This one's feeling warmer now and, by the way, would you like to go out sometime?*

* * *

We had two more hedgehogs dropped off across the afternoon: a big drenched one who'd been fished out of a village green pond and a smaller one who'd been found stuck in an empty Pringles tube by a public bin.

Watching Fizz working was amazing and I loved how she explained what she was doing and why. I was uploading the details into the Hog Log – the rescue centre's database – when Samantha and Josh returned with Darcie.

'How was your last day ever at Rillings Primary?' I asked Darcie as she ran up to me for a hug.

We'd had a look around Bentonbray Primary School – the closest one to Hedgehog Hollow – at the end of January and Darcie had been offered a place. I'd told her the decision was up to her and she didn't have to move but, as soon as the story broke in the local news, the bullying started. The school had been amazing but that made Darcie's mind up. She loved her teacher but she hated the kids and wanted a new start after the half-term holiday.

'Brilliant! They gave me presents. I got a book and some pens and some sweets.'

'Aw, that's lovely of them. So one week off and then a brand new school. Are you excited?'

'I can't wait. We got my uniform on the way home. It's a boring grey skirt again but the cardigan is red and I love it!'

'Darcie wants to do a fashion parade for us later,' Samantha said. 'She's going to look so smart.' She nodded at the table. 'New arrivals?'

'Five of them,' I told her. 'From three different people. And the last man gave us this.' I handed her £100 in cash.

'Oh, my gosh! That's amazing.'

'Do the new hedgehogs have names yet?' Darcie asked. Naming them was one of her favourite things.

'Two of them do,' Fizz said. 'We've decided on a new theme, which is silly words. We've both named one and we thought you, Samantha and Josh could all name one each.'

'I'm dying to hear what you've come up with,' Samantha said.

'There's a male who'd fallen into a pond so I called him Kerfuffle,' Fizz said.

'And there was a female who'd got stuck in a Pringles tube so I stayed with the crisp theme and called her Wotsit,' I added.

Fizz smiled at Darcie. 'So we have three small hedgehogs – one boy and two girls – who need names. Any ideas?'

Darcie looked up at Samantha. 'What's that word you said on

Saturday when we were baking cakes and you couldn't think of the name of the mixing things.'

'Ooh, that would be oojamaflip.'

Darcie giggled. 'We'll call one of the girls Oojamaflip.'

'I'll say Flippertigibbet for the other girl and Josh will pick Skedaddle for the boy. He loves that word.'

We laughed as we debated the spellings so I could enter their names into the Hog Log.

Samantha pulled out a chair for Darcie and then sat down herself at the treatment table. 'You can tell me more about the hedgehogs shortly but, while I've got you all here together, there's something I want to ask you. As you know, Josh and I are getting married on 2nd May and I've got Hannah, Chloe and Beth as bridesmaids and Amelia and Lottie as flower girls. I wondered if you, Darcie, would like to be a flower girl too and if you two would be my bridesmaids?'

Darcie squealed and launched herself at Samantha and Fizz looked as surprised as I felt. I genuinely hadn't expected that.

'For real?' Fizz asked. 'Me too?'

'I want all my favourite people to be my bridesmaids and you're on that list. Is that a yes?'

'I've always wanted to be a bridesmaid. Yes! Thank you so much.'

'And what about you, Phoebe?'

I was so touched that I couldn't speak. I just nodded then hurled myself at her too.

'I think you can take that as a yes,' Fizz said. 'And if hugs are happening...' She joined us and winked at me as her hand touched my arm. For a moment, I dared to imagine that something could happen. Not yet. But maybe somewhere down the line. Moving to Hedgehog Hollow with Darcie had brought me happiness for the first time in years and I dared to believe that there could be even more in store.

'Will you tell me a story?' Darcie said as I settled her into bed that evening. Misty-Blue jumped onto the duvet and draped herself across Darcie's tummy, purring loudly as soon as Darcie stroked her.

'What about?' I don't know why I bothered asking as the answer was nearly always unicorns or, more recently, hedgehogs.

'About the king and queen of the hedgehogs getting married and Princess Tiana and Misty-Blue being flower girls.'

I pushed a couple of curls back from her forehead and smiled. 'Okay, Princess Tiana of the hedgehogs. Once upon a time...'

I'd only managed about five minutes before Darcie drifted off, no doubt exhausted from the excitement of the last day at school and being asked to be a flower girl.

I put her bedside lamp off, leaving the room bathed in the gentle glow of the unicorn nightlight, and leaned back against her bedroom wall, gazing round the room and thinking about how different it was to what she'd had at Jenny's.

Samantha and Josh had asked whether I'd want to move into one of the holiday cottages with Darcie, emphasising that they weren't trying to move me on but they recognised that I was an adult and might prefer my independence. We hadn't even been there for a month but it was already obvious to me that the farmhouse was best for Darcie. After living in a house full of people who'd ignored and neglected her, I could see how much she thrived on a house full of people who made her the centre of their world.

Each of the rooms on the top floor had already been furnished with a double bed, wardrobe and chest of drawers and, once I confirmed we'd stay in the farmhouse, Samantha ordered a desk/dressing table and bedside drawers which would arrive over half-term. We'd taken Darcie shopping for pink and purple paints, unicorn bedding and soft furnishings – everything a little girl could ever dream of. She told me and Samantha every day how much she loved her bedroom and had promised to keep it tidy.

Satisfied that Darcie was in a deep sleep, I slipped out of her bedroom and across the landing into mine. My room still had cream walls and the original lemon-coloured bedding. When we went shopping for Darcie's room, Samantha asked me how I'd like mine decorated. They'd already bought me a stack of clothes including a thick winter coat that kept me warm and snug when I was on my moped. They claimed they were birthday presents but it was so generous that, even though I'd seen a colour scheme I loved, I couldn't let them spend more money on me, so I pleaded indecision.

I lay down on my duvet, put my earbuds in and listened to a playlist on my phone, smiling contentedly to myself. This time just two months ago, my life had been hell. With just under a week to go until Christmas, Tina and Jenny were drinking even more than usual, which meant they were extra aggressive and, with college finished for a fortnight, I was expected to be at their beck and call while they made increasingly more unreasonable demands.

I remembered 19th December well – exactly two months ago today – because that was the day Jenny had blamed me for the ice in her vodka and coke melting too fast and diluting her drink. I ran my fingers across the scar by my left eye where the tumbler had struck me. As the blood streamed down my face and I'd fought hard not to keel over, she'd apologised.

'I'm so sorry...' then she'd added with a snarl, 'that I missed your eye. Get that cleaned up. Now!'

And I had – too shocked and scared not to.

I'd spent the next five hours at A&E waiting to be patched up, yet another lie prepared about how I'd slipped down the stairs and banged my face on the shoe rack. More photos to add to my 'one day' file. Another tale of abuse to keep secret.

There was a gentle tap on my bedroom door. I pulled out my earbuds and sat up. 'Come in.'

Beth appeared with a mug of hot chocolate. 'I'd just made one for Paul and me and I thought you might like one. It's chocolate orange.'

'It smells lush. Thank you.' I took the mug from her and breathed in the aroma. It was Rosemary's favourite flavour of hot chocolate and it made me yearn for my friend even more. I hadn't seen her in weeks and phone calls were short, as though we were two strangers. I'd heard from a former neighbour that the sale on her flat had completed and her belongings had gone into storage so had asked Rosemary why she hadn't told me herself.

'Didn't think you'd care,' was the frustrating response.

I nearly hung up on her for that. I'd done nothing but care about her. I'd continuously put myself in the firing line with the evil Grimes sisters to ensure no harm came to her or Trixie and this was her attitude? I wasn't sure what to say or do to get through to her. I missed her and I wanted her back in my life and, even if she was too stubborn to admit it, I knew she wanted me in hers.

'Are you okay?' Beth asked, bringing my thoughts back to the present. 'You look sad.'

'Do I?' I shrugged. 'I was thinking about Rosemary. I don't like her being so distant. I keep thinking that, if she'd just let me see her, we could work things out.'

'But she's still refusing to tell you where she's staying?'

I nodded. 'She's annoyed at me for suggesting assisted living but I honestly think it's the best thing for her.'

Beth leaned against the doorframe. 'I'm sure she'll come round with a bit of time.'

'I feel so guilty. I wish she'd realise that I'm not trying to take her independence away. I'm suggesting something that would keep her independence but make her safer.'

'Some people don't respond well to stuff like that. They see it as interfering and being told what to do. She'll eventually realise that she's the one being unreasonable but, until then, you can't help someone if they won't help themselves, so try not to let it eat away at you.'

'Thanks. It's good advice.'

'Enjoy your hot chocolate.' She smiled as she gently closed the door behind her.

I took a sip of my drink then picked up my phone. If Rosemary didn't want assisted living, I couldn't force her, but she couldn't live in a B&B indefinitely. I hadn't searched online for any bungalows recently and a two-bedroom new-build in the centre of Fimberley caught my eye. As I scrolled through the photos and read through the details, I buzzed with excitement. This could offer the perfect compromise. I just needed to persuade Rosemary to meet up with me for a tour.

48

SAMANTHA

'I think that's Celia's car,' Phoebe said as a blue vehicle slowly passed us on Tuesday evening then indicated to pull into Sycamore Mews. 'Yes, it is. She's waving.'

'Do you think she'll have told Rosemary on the way?' I asked.

'I asked her not to. Rosemary's expecting to go to April's Café for afternoon tea so there's no reason for her to be suspicious.'

'Let's hope this works.'

'Me too. I had to try something.'

I squeezed her hand. 'I know you did. And I think this is a brilliant plan.'

I hoped the birthday girl was in a good mood and wouldn't accuse Phoebe or me of trying to ruin her special day.

Celia was as worried about Rosemary as Phoebe was and said she'd known her friend to be stroppy and stubborn but this was extreme even for her. She was very willing to go along with the plan for a birthday afternoon tea with us all and a secret detour via Fimberley first.

We'd left Darcie at Hedgehog Hollow helping Fizz in the barn. If Rosemary was funny with us, there was no need to expose Darcie to it.

If she was willing to hear us out and we made it as far as afternoon tea, we wanted to keep the focus on Rosemary.

Celia parked in front of 5 Sycamore Mews – the corner plot on a development of five two and three-bedroom bungalows. They were being sold privately by a developer who specialised in properties for residents with reduced mobility. Everything was on one level with wider doorways and he could add in handrails and other helpful aids depending on the buyer's needs. I'd viewed it at the weekend with Phoebe and it had seemed like the perfect compromise. If Rosemary would be willing to wear a personal alarm then she'd have all the support that came with an assisted living setting without moving into one. I only hoped Rosemary would view it that way.

The developer, Christian, was waiting inside as we'd warned him we might get pushback from Rosemary and might need a moment... or several! He reassured us that wasn't unusual and he was sure he could help Rosemary see the positives if we wanted him to intervene, having gone through it with his own mother.

Celia got out of her car and smiled at us all but didn't speak. She released Trixie from the back seat and attached the harness as Rosemary exited the passenger side.

'We've taken a slight detour,' Celia announced when she'd handed Trixie over. 'We're still going to April's for afternoon tea but we're in Fimberley first and there are—'

'Why are we in Fimberley?' Rosemary interrupted.

'To look at a bungalow.'

'There aren't any bungalows for sale in Fimberley. You looked, remember.'

'That's right, but this one isn't through an estate agent. This is a private developer. And it wasn't me who found it. It was Phoebe and she's here.'

'Happy birthday, Rosemary,' Phoebe said, looking nervous but managing to keep a smile in her tone.

'Phoebe? What's going on?'

'I found a bungalow in Fimberley that I thought would be perfect for you. Samantha and I looked round it at the weekend.'

'Why's she looking round it before me?'

'Because I wanted her opinion before I mentioned it to you and she's here now too.'

Rosemary pursed her lips. 'Is she now?'

I forced a smile and injected all the brightness I could into my tone. 'Happy birthday, Rosemary. That's a stunning dress.'

She pulled her coat across her body like a petulant child. 'You gave your opinion at the weekend so why are you here today?'

'Rosemary!' Phoebe cried. 'She's here because I asked her to be.'

Rosemary gave a 'humph' sound and put her arm out for Phoebe to link. 'What's so special about this bungalow, darling girl?'

'I'll let the developer tell you that,' Phoebe said. 'He's inside. It's a lovely house. Brand new, quiet cul de sac, no steps.'

She looked across at me for encouragement and I smiled. She was right not to mention the assistance aspects yet. We'd leave that to Christian's expertise.

* * *

Half an hour later, we stepped outside and Christian locked the door behind us.

'Let me know if you have any more questions,' he said. 'I have a second viewing tomorrow so, if you're interested, do bear that in mind. Lovely to meet you, Rosemary, and enjoy the rest of your birthday.'

'Thank you, Christian. Very kind of you.' She was all smiles and I hoped that was a sign it had gone well but as soon as he was out of earshot, the smile slipped. 'I don't feel like afternoon tea now, Celia. Take me home.'

'Rosemary!' Phoebe protested. 'You can't—'

'I can't? *I can't?* Since when did you become my mother, Phoebe Corbyn? You've changed since you moved into that farm.'

Celia gasped. 'Rosemary! That's out of order.'

'What's out of order is you lying to me. I thought you were my friend, Celia. I thought I could trust you of all people, but you've been conspiring with the enemy behind my back.'

'Are you calling me your enemy?' Phoebe's voice was high-pitched and cracked on the last word, her face pale, her eyes wide.

'You haven't exactly been a friend, have you? You let me and my dog get beaten up by your drug-dealing family in my own home so I have no choice but to sell it, you choose to live with a stranger instead of me, you tell her all your secrets and shut me out, and now you're trying to force me into a home designed for someone in a wheelchair when I explicitly said I wanted my independence. What the hell's wrong with you?'

Phoebe burst into tears. Rosemary couldn't see her but she could hear the pain she'd just inflicted and I paused, waiting for her to realise she'd gone way too far, but there was nothing. Not even a look of remorse on her face.

'Are you driving me home or do I need to call a taxi?' she said stiffly.

'I'll take you home,' Celia muttered. Her cheeks were flushed and her head was dipped and I sensed the poor woman wanted the ground to swallow her whole. She opened the back door and secured Trixie in place while Rosemary lowered herself into the front passenger seat.

I've always been the calm one, thinking first before speaking, trying to diffuse any tension. But not today. Rosemary reached to close the door but I put my hand out and stopped it.

'When Phoebe told me all about her friend Rosemary, I couldn't wait to meet her. She described this amazingly strong, kind, generous woman who'd looked after her since she was a baby and been the one person who she could always turn to. I'd love to meet that Rosemary.'

'I have no idea what you're talking about.'

'Yes, you do. I understand you've been through a horrific experience and something like that can change a person. It changed me. I've got PTSD thanks to the Grimes family. But they are *not* Phoebe's family and it's not her fault Trigg assaulted you. Do you have any idea what they put her through?'

'No, because she won't tell me! She's got you now.'

'Phoebe not telling you is nothing to do with having me now. It's about not wanting to vocalise it again, about wanting to move on, about not wanting you to hear something that will hurt you and which you can't unhear.'

'You're being unnecessarily dramatic about this,' Rosemary huffed.

'It doesn't matter,' Phoebe gasped between sobs.

'No, Phoebe, it does. Rosemary needs to hear this.' I gave her a reassuring squeeze on her hand before turning back to Rosemary. 'Phoebe would have gladly moved in with you as soon as her dad died. Probably before that. But do you know why she didn't? Because they threatened her and everyone she cared about.'

Rosemary's eyebrows shot up, as though surprised, and I hoped this drastic approach wasn't going to backfire as I continued.

'Do you know that phrase to take one for the team? Phoebe did that for Team Dad, Team Rosemary and Team Darcie. They beat her up, Rosemary. They threw things at her, scalded her, burned her and slashed her. You won't be able to see the damage but, if you don't believe me, you can run your fingers across that poor girl's arms, legs and face and feel the damage they inflicted. And that's just the physical damage. We're not talking the mental and emotional strain here. But she stayed because, if she left, the people she cared about would get it instead. They kicked her out on the coldest day of the year but told her they'd hurt you and Trixie if she stayed with you, so do you know what she did? Wandered the streets all alone in the dark and slept in your garage when she was sure the coast was clear.'

Rosemary maintained her position, rigid, facing forward, but the tears pooled in her eyes and I knew I'd got to her.

'Phoebe didn't want you to know all of this because she didn't want you to feel even a tiny fraction of guilt that there was something you could have done to stop it, but you need to hear this so you can think again about your accusations. They're a family of criminals and Phoebe is in no way responsible for their actions.

'As for moving in with a stranger, have you heard yourself? Phoebe and Darcie were in danger and we provided them a safe haven and will continue to do so for as long as Phoebe wants to stay. It's the best environment for Darcie and that is the reason for Phoebe choosing the farm over a bungalow with you. She has *not* chosen me over you. This is *not* a competition. This is what's best for a neglected little girl to get to school and back, to have space to play, and to have people round her all the time and it's also the *only* option that Social Services would approve, so Phoebe's hands are tied. And while all the fostering stuff is going on, she's been frantically trying to rebuild your friendship, find somewhere to live that's right for you, continue with her studies, and testify against that family. She needs your support right now. She needs the Rosemary I was looking forward to meeting.' I took a deep breath and straightened my shoulders.

She turned her head away but not before I'd seen tears slip down her cheeks. 'Take me home, Celia.'

Celia ran her hands down her face and shrugged slowly. 'Closing the door now, Rosemary.'

With her body blocking Rosemary, she patted Phoebe lightly on the arm. 'Give her overnight. She'll come round. I'm sure of it.'

'I'm not,' Phoebe whispered.

'But you've only known her for eighteen years. I've known her for fifty-odd. She needed to hear that just now. She really did.'

'I wasn't sure if I'd pushed it too far,' I said, feeling shaky.

'It'll have hurt but it was the right thing to do. She's fond of telling home truths. She needed to hear hers.'

Rosemary knocked on the window.

'That's my cue,' Celia said. 'I'd better go, but don't worry, Phoebe. She *will* come round. I'll make her!'

The car pulled away and I readied myself with an apology, but Phoebe spoke first.

'Thank you for telling her,' she said, her voice weak as she wiped her damp cheeks. 'She needed to hear it. It's up to her now. I didn't escape from the Grimes family only to have Rosemary turn on me. If she wants to cut me off, that's her choice. I've no energy left to fight it.'

We returned to Hedgehog Hollow in silence. I hoped Celia was right about Rosemary coming round when she'd had time to mull things over. If they'd been friends for over fifty years, she'd know Rosemary well, so I was hopeful she'd be right about this. If she wasn't, I'd be there to pick up the pieces because, no matter what Phoebe declared, losing Rosemary was going to hurt.

49

PHOEBE

I woke up on Wednesday morning feeling a strange mix of nerves and excitement. Samantha's dad had taken the day off work to keep an eye on the hedgehogs while we had a bridesmaids' day out in Whitsborough Bay. Darcie and I were excited about our first ever trip there and even more excited about trying on bridesmaid dresses and helping Samantha choose her wedding dress.

The nerves came from a combination of two things: seeing Fizz again and the situation with Rosemary. Fizz was meeting us at The Wedding Emporium. I'd been thinking about her even more than usual now that she'd confirmed she was gay. I knew that didn't automatically mean she'd be interested in me, but it made it a possibility. If we hadn't been interrupted by the hedgehog arrivals, I might have blurted out that I liked her, which could have made things awkward if she didn't feel the same. I valued her friendship and I knew she meant the world to Samantha so I didn't want to mess things up for anyone. The best plan was not to have a plan. We'd continue to build our friendship and see what happened. Maybe the romance of Samantha and Josh's wedding day might bring us together.

As for Rosemary, I hoped Celia was right about being able to bring her round. I'd never seen her so angry. I wanted her in my life but not if it meant her being cold and bitter.

'Phoebe!' Darcie burst into my bedroom and launched herself onto the bed, giggling. 'I'm going to be a flower girl!'

I pushed aside the nervous feelings and focused on the excitement as I tickled her making her squeal with laughter; my favourite sound.

* * *

Whitsborough Bay was even better than I'd imagined. We travelled across with Beth and Amelia and, as we had plenty of time before meeting the others, Samantha took us to an area called Sea Cliff where there were sweeping views of the town and beach.

Darcie stood on a bench so she could see more clearly as Samantha pointed out various attractions and promised visits to the arcades and fair, donkey rides, trampolines on the beach, cliff lifts, fish and chips and ice cream sundaes when the weather improved. Darcie looked like she'd just walked into Santa's workshop, her eyes flicking everywhere and a huge grin on her face. This. This was what childhood looked like and this was what Samantha and Josh could give to her which Rosemary couldn't, and I wouldn't be manipulated into thinking I'd made the wrong choice.

We met Chloe, Hannah and Amelia in a café called The Chocolate Pot next door to The Wedding Emporium, which had a warm and friendly feel. The walls were covered with a mixture of new and vintage metal signs and the wooden chairs were painted different colours.

Darcie tried, and loved, her first ever panini, followed by a white chocolate brownie, washed down with a raspberry milkshake. She couldn't stop smiling and neither could I at seeing her so excited. My face was already aching and we hadn't even done the best part.

We were waiting for the bill when Fizz arrived. My cheeks flushed and my heart raced at the sight of her. The red hair was gone, replaced by candyfloss pink.

'Who's ready to go dress shopping?' Samantha asked.

A petite, dark-haired woman welcomed us next door, giving hugs to Chloe and Samantha before introducing herself to the rest of us as Ginny. There were several plush chairs running alongside the window display so we spread out along them.

'We thought we'd start with the adult bridesmaid dresses,' Samantha said. 'The three flower girls will wear something slightly different. There's no set colour for the adults. Ginny's picked out some dusky shades that will complement each other and the wildflowers and I'd like you all to pick a different colour and style of dress.'

Ginny pulled back a curtain revealing some stunning full-length gowns in shades of blue, grey, lilac, pink and heather. 'Come and have a look.'

'They're gorgeous,' Beth said stroking her fingers down the fabric. 'I'd be happy in any of those colours so I'll take whatever's left.'

'Same here,' Hannah said. 'They're all beautiful.'

'Can I have this shade of pink, please?' Chloe asked.

Samantha smiled. 'I had a feeling you'd say that.'

'That's one happy bridesmaid,' Ginny said. 'Any other preferences?'

'I'm happy with any colour,' Fizz said, 'but this one's awesome.' She unhooked a pale heather dress and held it against her. The colour looked stunning against her pale skin and pink hair, stirring the butter-flies in my tummy once more.

'I love this blue,' I said, 'if nobody else minds.'

Hannah decided on lilac and Beth went for light grey.

'What do you think about this, Darcie?' Samantha asked, holding up a three-quarter length dress with layers of pale lemon tulle for the skirt. 'I know pink's your favourite colour, but you love your Princess Tiana costume so much that I thought you might like this one. Ginny's got the same dress in pink or lilac if you prefer those.'

Darcie's eyes shone with excitement as she scanned her eyes back and forth across the three dresses before settling on the lemon one, leaving lilac for Amelia and pink for Lottie.

An hour later, we'd tried on several dresses and chosen a different style each with Ginny's advice on what looked best with each body shape.

'Your turn,' Hannah said, clapping her hands together.

Samantha bit her lip as her cheeks reddened. 'I'm not really a dress person.'

'But you are wearing a wedding dress?' Chloe asked, sounding shocked.

'Yes, but I'm not sure that a big white dress is me.'

'I see you in something with more of a vintage look,' Beth said. 'Something dreamy with lace and maybe in cream rather than ivory or white.'

'I agree,' Fizz said. 'You look amazing in Gwendoline's vintage dresses.'

'Sounds lovely.' Samantha smiled at Ginny. 'What they said but if the lace has a flowery design, even better.'

'I might just have the perfect dress for you.' Ginny pointed to a display of shoes and sandals. 'Why don't you look at the footwear while Sam's trying the dress on?'

Ginny closed the curtains and we distracted ourselves trying on shoes.

'I think we have a winner with the first one,' Ginny called a little later, pulling aside the curtain.

I gasped and Chloe started crying as Samantha stepped forward, looking prettier than I'd ever imagined in what couldn't have been a more perfect dress. The lacy V-neck bodice was covered in tiny little flowers which flowed down onto the skirt and a long train. Underneath the lace the material was deep cream, giving it a warm vintage look. Fluttery lace sleeves completed the look.

'You look like an angel,' Darcie gushed and I added my agreement to that.

'That's definitely the one,' Hannah said. 'It could have been designed just for you.'

'Eight bridesmaid and flower girl dresses and one of these then, Ginny,' Samantha said, tears glistening in her eyes as she twisted and turned in front of the mirror. 'I can't believe how easy that was or how much I love this dress!'

As we were getting ready to leave a little later, Samantha's phone rang. She turned her back to us as she connected the call but I was closest and couldn't help listening in.

'Hi, Dad, everything okay? ... Oh! Did they say why?' She turned and glanced at me. 'Yeah... we're about done so we won't be too long. You told them we were in Whitsborough Bay, yeah? ... Up to them, I suppose... Yeah, thanks for letting me know. See you soon.'

'Everything all right?' I asked.

'That was my dad. Celia and Rosemary have turned up at the farm wanting to see you.'

'Oh!'

'Dad told them we were here but they wanted to wait.'

'Did they say what they wanted?'

'They wouldn't tell him so they're in the lounge with a cuppa and the TV as he's got a rescue in.'

My tummy lurched. Please let it be that she'd calmed down and come round and not that she wanted to give me a piece of her mind. We'd had such a lovely day out and an argument wasn't how I wanted it to end. If it did, it would be too much like life back in Reddfield and I wanted that to stay firmly behind me.

'Are you sure you don't want me to come in with you?' Samantha asked as she parked in the farmyard back at Hedgehog Hollow beside Celia's car.

'Yeah, I'm probably best to see her on my own. At first, anyway.'

'Okay. Call me if you need me. Darcie, do you want to come into the barn with me and meet the new hedgehog?'

Darcie needed no encouragement. She was out of the car and racing over to the barn before Beth had managed to unstrap Lottie's car seat.

'You've got this,' Beth whispered as we made our way towards the farmhouse.

Pushing open the front door, I heard laughter from the kitchen.

'That sounds promising,' Beth whispered.

I placed our shopping bags by the shoe rack. 'I hope so.'

Archie was in his highchair at the end of the kitchen table, Paul sat adjacent to him and Celia and Rosemary had their backs to the doorway, with Trixie lying by Rosemary's feet.

'We're back,' I announced, a hint of trepidation in my voice. 'Hi, everyone.'

Celia turned and gave me a warm smile. 'Have you chosen your dresses?'

'Yeah. All sorted.' I was too nervous about what Rosemary wanted to expand on that. She hadn't turned round like Celia but that didn't have to signify anything.

Beth squeezed past me and gave Archie and Paul a kiss. I bet they all wanted to escape, but there was little they could do while Archie was still eating.

'Sorry we weren't here. I didn't know you were coming.'

'Oh, that's okay, dear,' Celia said. 'We were in the area and it was spontaneous. Paul's kept us entertained.'

I gave Paul a grateful smile while inwardly cringing at the awkward pause. Rosemary still hadn't spoken. I could hardly blurt out, 'What do you want?' but that was exactly what I wanted to know.

'Should we go into the lounge?' I suggested.

Celia linked Rosemary's arm and led her across to the lounge. Trixie followed us and lay down on the rug in front of the log burner.

'Rosemary has some news.' Celia nudged her friend. 'Don't you?'

'Yes, I do. I... erm... I've found somewhere to live.'

'That's brilliant! Where?'

Celia nudged her again.

'It's the house in Fimberley. The one you found.'

Celia gave me a double thumbs-up and mouthed 'told you'.

I couldn't resist an opportunity to wind her up. 'Would that be the house in Fimberley which was completely unsuitable and an insult to your ability to live independently?'

'Yes, well, I had some time to think about it and we went back for another tour and a chat with that nice young man this afternoon. I liked the feel of it. It flowed well and there was plenty of space. Trixie liked it too, so I decided to go for it.'

'I'm really chuffed for you both. It's an amazing house and the village is ideal for you. Congratulations!'

'Will you stop nudging me, Celia!' Rosemary snapped. 'I'm going to be covered in bruises again at this rate.'

'I'll stop nudging you when you stop sounding like a stroppy teenager and say what you're meant to be saying.'

Rosemary sighed. 'I'm sorry I've been a bit off with you lately.'

'A bit off with her? You've been horrible to the poor girl, and you know it.'

'All right, Celia, keep your hair on! I'm sorry, Phoebe, that I've been horrible to you. I know what happened wasn't your fault and I shouldn't have taken my fear out on you. Those things Samantha said about what that family did to you, were they true?'

'Yes.'

'I'm so sorry. I should have realised. I knew you weren't happy there but I never imagined... are you okay?'

'I will be. You don't just get over these things, as you've discovered. But there are some good people around and I'm lucky enough to be living in a house full of them right now.'

'Which is why you didn't want to move in with me.'

'As I said before, it wasn't that I didn't want to. You're family and, if it had just been me, I'd have said yes. But it isn't just me, and Hedgehog Hollow is the best place for Darcie, and you have to admit it's what's best for you too. She's amazing but she's an excitable seven-year-old who finally has a chance to be noisy and messy, to be a child, and that's not what you need day in, day out.'

'Did they hurt her too?'

'The broken arm was Jenny's fault.'

Rosemary pressed her hand against her throat. 'Oh, my goodness. That poor little girl.'

'She's okay. I'm hoping I got her away from them before they could do any permanent damage.'

'Did you really sleep in my garage?

'Yes.'

Rosemary shook her head and her eyes glistened. 'I'm so sorry, darling girl. I've been far too wrapped up in my own problems and my behaviour has been appalling. Can you ever forgive me?'

'I want to and I can but there's something you have to do first. I'm not the only one you've snapped at.'

She pursed her lips then her face softened. 'You're right. Samantha didn't deserve any of that. Is she here?'

'She's in the barn but I can ask her to come over.'

'Yes, please. But before you do, can I ask a favour of you?' She stood up. 'Can a grumpy old lady have a hug from her surrogate grand-daughter?'

'Of course you can. Coming in.'

A lump burned my throat as I hugged her. What a relief to have her back in my life and even more amazing that she'd gone for the bungalow in Sycamore Mews. The next thing to do was persuade her to wear one of those alarm pendants in case she had a fall, but I'd enjoy this victory for now and prepare for that battle later.

51

SAMANTHA

I felt a little apprehensive when Phoebe rang and asked me to come over to the farmhouse, and even more so when she told me that Rosemary wanted to speak to me alone.

Walking the short distance from the barn, I took several deep breaths as I tried to prepare for Rosemary saying her piece. As long as things were resolved with Phoebe, she could hurl what she liked at me and I'd take it. It didn't mean I was a pushover; it simply made me a peacemaker.

'Phoebe said you want to speak to me,' I said, trying to keep my tone light as I sat down.

Rosemary straightened back her shoulders. 'What you said yesterday hurt.'

She paused and I wondered if she was expecting me to apologise. I would, but she needed to go first as her behaviour towards Phoebe had been unacceptable and I'd never have felt compelled to share some home truths if it hadn't been for that.

'I felt like I'd been ambushed and I was furious with you all, including Celia. I told her to drop me off at the B&B and leave but she followed me inside and said she wouldn't go until I'd seen sense. Daft woman's allergies were wreaking havoc. She couldn't stop sneezing but her putting herself through that helped me realise that you were all right and I was wrong. I'm now fuming with myself for how I've treated that darling girl, and I'm sorry I turned on you because that upset Phoebe even more.'

It was a veiled apology, but I'd take it. 'I'm glad you and Phoebe have sorted things out. I know how important your friendship is to her.'

'As is hers to me. So very important.'

Her voice wobbled and, at that moment, I realised what this was all about. Getting upset about Phoebe not moving in with her and suggesting assisted living wasn't about the fallout from the assault or even the desire to live independently; it was about loneliness. How had I missed that before? It seemed so obvious now. She was worried that Phoebe would build a new life for herself at the farm and no longer have time for Rosemary.

'Just because Phoebe's living here, it doesn't mean she'll spend less time with you. In fact, she'll probably spend more time with you as you'll be so much closer.'

'Do you think so?' The doubt in her voice confirmed my suspicions.

'I know so! And you and Trixie are welcome at the farm any time. Josh or I can pick you up and Phoebe's going to learn to drive over the summer so she'll be able to do that herself before we know it.'

'Thank you. I'd appreciate that.'

'I'm sorry for hurting you, Rosemary. That wasn't my intention.'

'You were right to say it.'

'Perhaps, but I'm still sorry it hurt you. How about we start over?'

'That would probably be wise.'

'Josh and I are getting married on 2nd May, right here on the farm. Phoebe's a bridesmaid and Darcie's a flower girl and we'd all love it if you and Trixie could join us. Maybe Celia could be your plus one.'

'Why would you want me at your wedding after how I've behaved?'

'Because you're part of Phoebe's family and she's part of mine now so, by default, so are you. Although I should warn you that we're a big family and about 160 of us are more than a little prickly.'

She looked momentarily bewildered then smiled. 'You mean the hedgehogs? Have you really got that many?'

'At the moment, yes. I'm sure Darcie would love to take you over to the barn and give you a running commentary on it all.'

'I'd like that. She was so good that day they made the snowman. Most intuitive for one so young. So, tell me more about yourself...'

As we chatted, that cool exterior thawed and I finally got to see the woman who'd been there for Phoebe and I suspected we might even become friends.

52

SAMANTHA

As the half-term break drew to an end, it was a relief to see Phoebe smiling again now that things were back on track with Rosemary.

We had a busy day ahead of us – a pub lunch with Lauren and Dad to celebrate Lauren's birthday, then Josh and I were going out for a drink this evening to celebrate our one-year anniversary.

'Is it too early to FaceTime my mum?' Josh asked as we administered the final round of hedgehog medication that morning.

'It's after nine and you know how much Alex loves his breakfast. They'll definitely be up by now.' Alex had whisked Connie away for a surprise weekend in the Yorkshire Dales.

Connie answered quickly and Josh propped up his phone on the table so we could both see and wish her a happy birthday.

'What did Alex get you?' Josh asked.

Connie had told us that the weekend away would have been more than enough as a birthday gift but Alex had wanted to spoil her on their first birthday as a couple, so he had presents too.

'He bought me a magazine,' she responded, grinning. 'And a planner. Oh, and this.' She held her hand up to the camera revealing a square diamond ring with clusters of tiny diamonds either side on a rose gold band. 'I know we've not been together for long, but we didn't act on how we felt when we first met and now that we've been given an amazing second chance, we don't want to lose any more time.'

Alex appeared beside her. 'When you know, you know,' he said, gazing at her lovingly. I felt dewy-eyed, seeing them both glowing like that.

'Congratulations!' Josh cried. 'And I completely agree with you. Time's insignificant when you know it's right.' He squeezed my hand.

'I'm so pleased for you both,' I said. 'When did this happen?'

'Last night. Alex took me out for the most delicious meal I've ever tasted and the waiter bought out a special miniature birthday cake with a sparkler on it. When the sparkler blew out, I could see the words "Will you marry me?" iced on the cake and one of those Haribo jelly rings. Alex got down on bended knee and asked if I'd like to swap the Haribo ring for a real one.'

'Aw, that's so lovely.'

'Only she didn't swap it,' Alex said, laughing. 'She ate the Haribo one anyway.'

'It was a red one. They're my favourites!'

'Nice one, Mum,' Josh said. 'So when are you thinking of getting married?'

'It depends on you two,' Connie said. 'Hedgehog Hollow's pretty special to us both. If Alex hadn't bought in those hoglets and you hadn't invited him to your barbeque, we'd probably never have crossed paths again. You said you want to hold more events there and we'd love our wedding to be one of them, but we completely understand if you'd rather we don't.'

Josh looked at me, his eyebrows raised in question.

'We'd be really touched if you held your wedding here,' I said.

'I told you they'd be fine.' Alex kissed Connie's forehead. 'Thank you so much.'

Connie blew us a kiss. 'We're not sure when. We're going to discuss it today but we do know we want it to be this year.'

We chatted a little longer about their plans for the rest of the day then congratulated them again and ended the call.

'I was hoping he'd propose this weekend,' I said.

'Me too. I didn't like to say it in case I jinxed it. Alex is a good bloke. He's made my mum so happy.'

'Do you think your dad and Beth will get married?' I'd had several conversations with Beth about the wedding and she'd never once mentioned whether she and Paul were thinking about it or whether it was something she even wanted, and I hadn't liked to pry. Getting married – like having children – could be a sensitive subject and wasn't for everyone.

'I'm not sure. I thought Dad might have wanted to get married when he was ill in case the worst happened. It's possible he asked and Beth didn't want to think like that.'

'I did wonder about that. But he's doing so well now and, with your mum newly engaged, maybe they'll go for it.'

Josh drew me close and gently kissed me. 'I love that you want everyone to find their happy ever after.'

'I can't help it. I want them all to be as happy as we are.'

'I think Dad and Beth are. I've never seen them argue, which is weird because Beth and I used to argue all the time. Shows how badly matched we were.'

'Like my parents.' We sat down at the table and Josh raised an eyebrow questioningly.

'When Dad told us what happened to Mum, he talked about how she was before. Their first two months together were perfect and that's when he proposed to her, but he admitted they had problems when he returned from university. I think they'd grown apart during his studies and neither of them wanted to admit it and call off the engagement. Then Mum was assaulted and understandably a mess. My dad's lovely. No way would he have abandoned her after that, no matter how tough it got. I sometimes wonder if that amazing summer together before he went to university should have stayed just that – one summer romance.'

'I thought your dad loved her.'

'He did, but was he still in love with her? I'm not so sure. I'd love him to meet someone else and experience what he and Mum had that first summer together in a more enduring way. I'd love Mum to meet someone too, someone who isn't part of her history.'

Josh crossed his fingers and smiled at me. 'As I said, I love that you want everyone to find their happy ever after. Just don't be too disappointed if they don't. Being part of a couple doesn't work for everyone. Sometimes happy ever after means being single some or all of the time.'

'That's true. But I still believe in love and romance and weddings.'

'Just as well, or that's one expensive party we're planning.'

53

Phoebe and Darcie had been back at college and school after half-term for nearly a week and it had been non-stop at the rescue centre. With a whopping 168 hedgehogs now in our care, there was a constant cycle of feeding, cleaning and medication.

One of the many benefits of the publicity surrounding the theft was that I now had an army of volunteers who wanted to help out and I'd built up a list of locals who were interested in fostering hoglets when babies season started. Last year had been tough providing round-the-clock feeding but I anticipated up to ten times as many this year now that we were so well known, so help was essential. When the first batch of hoglets arrived, I'd run training sessions for 'hogster parents' who'd take over the feeding and care for the little ones in their homes.

I left June and Barry – a retired husband and wife team – cleaning out crates and took my hedgehog mug out to Thomas's bench around mid-morning on Friday. March had arrived at the start of the week with unseasonably mild weather and the gentle sun warmed my cheeks.

I flicked through my hedgehog wedding planner. When we'd set the date last year, it had seemed so far away, but it was now only eight weeks on Sunday and there was still so much to do. The dresses and shoes were sorted so I could tick that off. The men were also organised. Josh wasn't at home in a suit but wanted to look smart so he'd chosen a shirt sleeves, tie and waistcoat combination which I knew he'd look gorgeous in. His longstanding best friend, Lewis, was his best man and Lewis's younger brother Danny was an usher alongside Tariq, a friend from his veterinary course.

'The invitations are ordered,' I muttered to myself, 'and...' I snapped my head up at the crunch of gravel.

'Only me! Not disturbing anything, am I?'

I forced a smile as I closed the planner and put it to one side. 'No. How's things?'

'Ugh, I'm so bored!' Chloe plonked herself down on the bench and passed me Samuel for a cuddle.

I already knew she was bored because she'd turned up every day so far this week and told me the same thing. She didn't seem to appreciate that I couldn't drop everything for a cuppa and a catch-up and I was starting to feel the pressure of falling behind with my work.

'Have you finished unpacking yet?' I asked hoping it might prompt her into a shorter stay.

'I've done a couple more boxes but it's not as much fun as I expected.' She glanced down at the planner. 'Everything sorted now?'

'Still quite a lot to do.'

'I'd offer to help but you know how useless I am at stuff like that, as I proved at my own wedding.'

Chloe had been so chaotic that I'd ended up organising pretty much everything, which hadn't been easy considering she was marrying the man who, at the time, I still loved.

'You're not useless,' I said gently. 'It's just not your forte.'

'I'm not sure anything's my forte.'

'There's loads of things you're good at.'

She raised her eyebrows doubtfully. 'Yeah, right.'

'What's brought this on?'

She gave a dramatic shrug, reminiscent of the old Chloe. 'I thought it would be different living here. I thought we'd meet loads of people and be invited round the pub or to someone's house for a barbeque but I don't know anyone.'

'Chloe! You only moved in a fortnight ago. Give it a chance! And it's not exactly barbeque season yet, is it?'

'I know, but the people who sold the house said it was a really friendly village and everyone knew everyone. They said there were loads of people our age, especially couples with young families, and I just thought...'

'You thought they'd be knocking on your door and getting you involved?' I suggested when she tailed off.

'Maybe.'

'I hate to break it to you, but it doesn't work like that. You have to make an effort if you want to get to know people. Take Samuel for a walk and chat to people while you're out. Get involved in village life.'

'How?'

'Bentonbray has a village hall so see what goes on there. I'm sure they'll hold events and run clubs. There's a village noticeboard so check that out. Ask around.'

'Is that what you did when you moved here?'

'It was different for me. It's evolved naturally through having the rescue centre. You'll meet people too in time, but you can't sit back and wait for them to come to you. People our age work or they're looking after families or both. You have to be proactive.'

I could almost hear the cogs whirring and I braced myself because I knew exactly what was coming next.

'Can you introduce me to some of your friends?'

'You already know my closest friends.'

'Who?'

I listed them off on my fingers. 'Hannah, Toby, Rich and Dave, Fizz, Zayn, Terry.'

'Not them. Your other friends.'

'Like who?'

'All the people who were at your New Year's Eve party, for a start.'

'Come on, Chloe. They're people I've met through this place. We get on well but most of them aren't people I see regularly. We don't go to the pub or have barbeques together or whatever else you're after. And what do you expect me to do? Knock on their door and say, "This is my cousin Chloe, she's just moved to the area, will you be her friend?"'

'No, but you could be a bit less sarcastic about it.'

'I'm not being sarcastic. I'm being realistic. I can't make anyone be your friend. You have to do that for yourself. But if you want to sign up as a volunteer here, that could be a starting point to meet people.'

She frowned, evidently contemplating the idea. 'What would volunteering involve?'

'Cleaning out the crates and—'

'Mopping up hedgehog shit? Seriously?' She stood up and snatched Samuel from my lap, making him wail. 'Thanks a lot, Samantha. You keep your friends to yourself. Don't worry about me. I'll just stay out of your way from now on.'

She stormed across the gravel and round the corner of the house.

I shook my head, sighing, and chased after her. 'Chloe! Don't be like that!'

'Like what?' She shouted over her shoulder. 'I ask for your help and your only solution is to have me mucking out hedgehogs.'

'That was *not* my only solution. I gave you loads of options.'

She stopped halfway across the yard and spun round to face me. 'Oh yeah, join a club and chat to a random stranger while I'm out. I can't do stuff like that! I'm not you! Why did you suggest I move here if you weren't going to help me settle in?'

'What? I *never* suggested you move here.'

'You did! I was saying how crap our views were back home and you said: "You know what you should do? Move to the Wolds." Remember?'

I *did* remember but it was a passing comment and not something I expected her to take literally. But I knew how Chloe's mind worked and if I said that, she'd think I didn't want her here and the amazing progress we'd made since the summer would have been for nothing.

'I didn't think you'd ever leave Whitsborough Bay.'

'Yeah, well, I wish I hadn't now. At least I had Mum and Dad there and I had a job. Now I've got nothing and it's all your fault.' She turned and flounced back towards her car.

I wasn't having that. She was the one who'd decided to move and the first I'd known of it was the big surprise on New Year's Eve when it was already a done deal.

'Chloe! I've got a hot tip for you. When you make a huge decision about moving area, it's a good idea to check the area first to see whether it's somewhere you'll be able to settle.'

'And you reckon you're not being sarcastic?'

'I wasn't before but I am now and you asked for it. You and James made the decision to move and I knew nothing about it, but even if I'd spent hours convincing you it would be a great idea, it *still* wouldn't be my fault that you're having a wobble. It wouldn't be my responsibility to find you friends. It wouldn't be my job to make you happy here. Only you can do that. Did the summer teach you nothing?'

'Trust you to bring that up!' She yanked open the car door and fastened Samuel into his car seat, releasing a frustrated squeal when she didn't manage to clip in the fastener first time.

Red-faced and frazzled-looking, she turned and glared at me as she slammed the door closed.

'I've got a hot tip for you too,' she snarled. 'Friends are people who help each other in times of need. Looks like we're not friends anymore.'

She scrambled into the driver's seat and started the ignition.

I banged on the window and she wound it down. 'What?'

'This! This pathetic little strop you're having right now is *exactly* what I'd expect from the old Chloe. If she's back, then you're right, we're not friends anymore. I can't keep doing this.'

'So I'm right. It *is* all about you and you hate it that I've infiltrated your perfect little world.'

'No, Chloe, as usual you're making it all about you. You live in a beautiful place in an amazing community and you could be so happy here if you let yourself, but I cannot and will not do it for you. I'm currently looking after a vulnerable child and adult, I'm sharing my home with a cancer patient, I've 168 hedgehogs to care for, I'm embroiled in a fight to recover my stolen money, I'm battling PTSD, trying to plan a wedding, running four holiday cottages, and still hoping for a miracle with my mum, so you'll forgive me if organising your social life isn't my number one priority.' My voice had grown louder with every sentence and ended on a shout so loud that my throat stung.

She narrowed her eyes at me then wound her window up and shoved the car into gear. I jumped out of her way as she wheel span out of the farmyard.

As I watched her race down the track, the sky darkened. I could hear footsteps running across the gravel and through the long grass. Men were shouting. Misty-Blue yowled.

'Leave my cat alone!' I screamed, sprinting across the car park towards the back of the barn. I smacked into something, some sort of fencing blocking my route, and stepped back frowning. What the hell...?

'Are you all right, my dear?'

I turned to see my volunteers, June and Barry, staring at me, their expressions full of concern.

'Yeah. Sorry. I'm... erm...' I rubbed my forehead, feeling totally disorientated. It was light again and I was standing by Hedgehog Dell, our enclosed soft-release garden.

'You look very pale,' June said. 'Should I get you some water?'

'Please.'

'Get her to a seat, Barry.'

'Bench.' I wafted my hand towards the back of the house and gratefully slumped against Barry as he led me to Thomas's bench and I sat down heavily, my head between my legs.

'Here's your water,' June said a few moments later.

I raised my head and took a few deep glugs. 'Thank you.'

'What happened?' she asked. 'We heard shouting.'

I couldn't dismiss it as nothing.

'I've got PTSD and I've been fine for months but an episode was triggered just now.' Normally I recognised the signs and I had coping mechanisms, but this had come out of the blue thanks to that argument with Chloe.

'Is that from what that family did to you?' June asked.

'I'm afraid so.'

'Do you want us to call anyone?'

'No, I'll be fine. Thank you. I just need a few minutes. How are you getting on?'

June gave me a weak smile. 'We're all done so we were about to head off, although we were planning to have a lovely cuppa first, weren't we, Barry?'

'What? Oh, yes! A nice cuppa.'

Clearly they hadn't been planning that, but I appreciated the gesture and I welcomed the company until I was sure the episode had passed.

'I've got a packet of chocolate digestives if you fancy dunking.'

Barry nodded. 'Now you're talking.'

We slowly made our way back into the barn and June boiled the kettle while I settled on the sofa bed, stomach churning, still feeling shaken. I'd unleashed all the frustration that had built up each time Chloe had reverted to the selfish, self-centred version of herself and I'd forgotten all the kind things she'd done like talk my mum into coming across for New Year and... well, that was about it, but it was a big thing.

Would the confrontation with Chloe open her eyes to her behaviour or would it drive another wedge between us? Right now, I didn't actually care either way. What concerned me most was another PTSD episode. With Phoebe and Darcie now in my care, I wanted to be there to support them and not have my own mental health regressing.

* * *

'I'm so pissed off with her.' Josh paced up and down in our bedroom that evening, clenching and unclenching his fists after I'd told him about the incident with Chloe and my PTSD episode. 'I'd really started to like her, but this...'

He stopped pacing, sat beside me on the bed, and adjusted the cool flannel I'd placed across my forehead.

'Sorry. You don't need me getting all wound up. How are you feeling?'

'Pretty pissed off myself. I can't believe she's blaming me for her move to Bentonbray. It was such a passing comment. She laughed and said they'd best get the house on the market but I thought she was joking. How can anyone take a conversation like that seriously?'

'In Chloe World, anything can happen.'

'I'm gutted I had another episode. We'd made such brilliant progress, I genuinely thought it was behind me.'

He took my hand in his and lightly kissed it. 'It was one setback because of an unexpected argument. Don't let it undo all the great things you've done. It might never happen again.'

'But what if it does and Darcie's with me? June and Barry were great, but it would terrify Darcie. It would terrify Phoebe, too.'

'Then I have a suggestion. Let's sit down with them over the weekend and explain all about it. I'm sure Phoebe will get it, but we can Google ideas for how to explain it to a seven-year-old. You can tell her what she needs to do if it happens and reassure her it's nothing to be scared of. What do you think?'

'I think you're amazing. Thank you.'

'Does Chloe know?'

'No. I haven't heard from her and, if I'd got in touch with her, I'd have probably triggered another episode.'

'I think she needs to know.'

'No! Josh! She'll blame herself.'

'And so she should!' His shoulders softened and he stroked the side of my face. 'I know she's a complicated woman and she's faced up to some tough things recently but so have you and she needs to know the affect her behaviour has on you. I'm not saying she needs to know right now. It's best done when she's had some time to calm down and you're feeling better. You still need time and space to heal and having Chloe turn up every day isn't giving you that.'

'I'm not sure. It was just the once and I shouldn't have let her wind me up like that. I should have stayed calm.'

Josh raised his eyebrows at me. 'If you'd broken your leg, would you go for a run?'

'No.'

'If you'd dislocated your shoulder, would you carry heavy shopping?'

'No.'

'So if you have PTSD which is triggered by stress, would you let someone visit you every day who is all about the drama and stress?'

I sank deeper into the pillows. 'Point taken.'

'Chloe in small doses is great. Chloe every day? Not so much.'

He was right. Having her turn up every day didn't work for me and it was doing our relationship no favours. If we were going to remain friends – although that was debatable for the moment after her outburst – then I was going to have to manage her expectations about what that could look like. Visiting every day moaning about being bored and expecting me to resolve that for her wasn't an option and I was going to have to get over how guilty that made me feel, because I shouldn't feel guilty. She shouldn't be placing those demands on me.

Wednesday afternoons had become my favourite time of the week. Fizz had the afternoon off university and spent it volunteering at Hedgehog Hollow and I had no classes either.

I wished I was more like Fizz. She knew exactly who she was and what she stood for and didn't care what anyone else thought. I loved the way her eyes shone when she spoke about animals or her family. Darcie loved hearing her stories about weekends and school holidays spent on her grandparents' farm and was already on a countdown to the Easter holidays when she'd get her tour from Barney and be able to feed the lambs.

On the second Wednesday in March, I hadn't been back from college long when Samantha's phone rang. She was busy removing maggots from a large hedgehog with a badly infected cut.

'Could you answer that, Phoebe?' she asked. 'Put it on speaker phone.'

'Hello? Hedgehog Hollow rescue centre.'

'Hi. My name's Yasmin. I was washing my car and I went to tip the bucket down the manhole when I spotted a hedgehog down there. I've tried to get my hand down but my arms aren't long enough and I can't think of how to get it out without hurting it. Can you come and rescue it?'

I glanced at Samantha, who nodded and indicated I should write down the address.

'Yes. We can do that. What address is it, please?' I scribbled down the details. 'We'll be there shortly.'

'Thanks, Phoebe,' Samantha said when I hung up. 'Fizz! I've got two choices for you. You can either take over with the maggots or you can do a drain rescue in Little Tilbury.'

'Maggots or drain? Such a tantalising choice.'

Samantha laughed. 'It's all about the glamour here.'

'I'll go for the drain and hope it's not full of sewage. Do you want to come with me, Phoebe? Might be a two-person job.'

My heart leapt. Alone time with Fizz? Deffo!

* * *

Little Tilbury was a twenty-minute drive from Hedgehog Hollow. Fizz shared tales of some of the other drain rescues and I found myself hanging onto every word. She had an amazing gift for telling anecdotes in a way that I felt like I was right there in the action.

'You'll have to tell Darcie those stories one bedtime,' I said as we drove into the village. 'They're so much better than my attempts.'

She smiled at me. 'I bet you're great at telling stories.'

My tummy fizzed at the compliment. 'Thank you, but I promise I'm not. Numbers are my thing, not words.'

'Maybe we could tell her a story together?'

'I'd love that.' And suddenly I had a vision of Fizz and me together at Fizz's cottage, tucking Darcie in as we made up a bedtime story together, a happy family of three. A hot flush swept through me, and it was a relief when we stopped outside a cottage at the far side of the village so I could step out into the cool air.

A tall, slim woman wearing a white long-sleeved paint-spattered T-shirt under baggy maroon dungarees pulled open a wide wooden gate and waved at us. She was probably a similar age to Fizz, with long blonde hair pulled back into a loose fishtail braid.

'Yasmin?' Fizz asked as we got out of the car.

'That's me. Hedgehog Rescue?'

Fizz laughed. 'Yeah. I'm Fizz and this is Phoebe. We'll have a look first before we get the kit out.'

We followed Yasmin past a gleaming red mini on the drive and she made a comment about having the same great taste in cars as Fizz. It wasn't particularly funny, but Fizz laughed again.

Down the side of the cottage, a manhole cover had been lifted aside and we peered in. About a metre down, curled up in the middle of a gulley, was a hedgehog.

'I've no idea how it got down there,' Yasmin said. 'It's a solid cover here.'

'It probably fell in somewhere else and made it this far. Have you seen it move?'

'Yes. I was scared it might be dead but it's changed position a couple of times.'

'Awesome. Can you keep an eye on it and we'll be right back?'

I followed Fizz to the car and we pulled on thin boiler suits to protect our clothes as Fizz talked me through her thoughts on the best way to get the hedgehog out. I picked up the carry crate and she took out a net and an extendable pole with a leather pad at the end.

'Phoebe's going to hold the net,' Fizz told Yasmin, 'and I'm going to try to encourage it to move into the net with the pad on the end of the pole. It's a long way down and we don't want to hurt or distress the hedgehog, especially when it'll have already been through quite an ordeal, so it might take some time.'

We lay on our tummies either side of the drain. I was terrified of hurting the hedgehog, but Fizz was so calm and reassuring as she guided me to move the net. It took about quarter of an hour but finally the hedgehog moved a few paces and curled up in the net, allowing me to gently lift it up. Fizz scooped it out and gave it a quick inspection to make sure there was nothing tangled round its body or in its mouth which might cause problems on our journey back.

'It's a girl and we need a name.' She smiled at Yasmin. 'We've just started on singers, so who's your favourite singer?'

'I love sixties soul, so it has to be Aretha Franklin.'

'Nice choice.' Fizz settled Aretha into the crate. 'She's dirty, drenched and exhausted but we'll soon have her clean and dry.'

'That was amazing,' Yasmin exclaimed. She lightly touched Fizz's arm and my heart sank as I saw a look pass between them – eye contact, eyes sparkling, smiles.

'It's all thanks to you for calling it in. There's no way she'd have survived down there for much longer.'

'Good job I was having a creative blank and decided to wash my car.'

'What do you do?' Fizz asked as we walked back to her car with Aretha.

'I'm an artist and a messy one at that, as you can probably tell from the clothes. I dabble in all sorts. Bit of painting, sculpting, ceramics.'

'Sound awesome. I've always fancied a go at sculpting.'

'I've got a studio and a kiln in my garden. You'd be welcome to come round any time and give it a go.'

'You're on.'

'Is this your full-time job?' Yasmin asked.

'This is voluntary. I'm studying to be a veterinary nurse.'

'Aw, that's amazing. I love animals. I've got three cats, a rat, a bearded dragon and a blue-tongue skink.'

'No way! I love reptiles.'

'Then you definitely have to come round. Wait here!'

Yasmin dashed back to the house, and I stole a glance at Fizz. Her cheeks were pink as she watched after Yasmin, a gentle smile on her lips.

'She seems nice,' I said.

'Yeah, she does. Really nice.'

It was a strange sensation, seeing the person I'd fallen for fall for someone else and being helpless to do anything about it. The chemistry between them was unmistakable and Fizz had never looked at me that way.

Yasmin emerged from the house, holding a small piece of card.

'That's my business card,' she said, handing it to Fizz.

Their fingers met and neither of them pulled away.

'I'll put the stuff in the car,' I mumbled.

Without a word, Fizz clicked her key fob to open the car and I willed myself not to cry as I secured the rescue crate in the footwell behind my seat.

I glanced across as I opened the boot and saw them nodding and laughing together. *Definitely missed my moment.*

'I've got a date!' Fizz squealed as soon as we pulled away, waving goodbye to Yasmin.

'That's amazing,' I said, hoping I sounded enthusiastic. 'When?'

'Tonight. Yasmin's going to cook for me and show me her studio.'

'Hope it goes well.'

'Me too! I'm so excited.' She hadn't needed to add that. I could tell.

I stared out of the window as Fizz fell unusually silent, probably imagining what might happen with Yasmin tonight.

'You're very quiet,' Fizz observed as we pulled onto the farm track.

'Just thinking about Aretha and hoping she'll be okay.'

'Aw, that's so sweet. She's in the best place and fingers crossed Yasmin found her in time.'

We unpacked the car and took Aretha and the kit inside the barn. Samantha had finished working on the maggot-ridden hedgehog so was ready to check over the new arrival. Fizz filled her in on the rescue while I started a chart for the hog.

'And you'll never guess what,' Fizz said. 'I've got a date tonight.'

I couldn't do it. I couldn't stay there and listen to her raving about Yasmin.

'I've just remembered. I've got some coursework that has to be in tomorrow. I'd better get on with it. See you later. Good luck tonight, Fizz.'

I had to force myself not to run out of the barn. I was really happy for Fizz, but it was a little too raw for me right now and I needed some space.

Upstairs, I sat at my dressing table, staring at my reflection in the mirror. There was a smear of mud on my right cheek and my hair was tangled. I ran a brush through it and weaved it into a fishtail braid then sighed and pulled it out again. I couldn't compete with Yasmin's beauty and effortless style, her sculpting or her reptile collection.

I closed my eyes and shook my head. 'It's not a competition,' I muttered. 'It's just life.'

Life was full of things we couldn't control and love was another one of those things. I'd get over her. Maybe it wasn't love. Maybe it was just a bit of a crush on Fizz because she was kind and friendly and I'd let it feel like more when I'd found out she was attracted to women.

I was new to this. My only experience so far was four years ago and it had very nearly put me off for life.

55

PHOEBE

Four years ago

There was a reality TV show called *Tropical Heat* on during the summer when I was fourteen. My friends at school were obsessed with it and pretty much every lunchtime conversation was about which of the men were the hottest.

I wasn't a fan of reality TV but, sick of being on the outside of every conversation, I reluctantly tuned into *Tropical Heat* one evening. It wasn't the men who drew my gaze. It was Cara Phelps – twenty-three-year-old cabin crew from Bristol – who had me captivated. All the women were stunning but there was something extra special about Cara.

I wasted all the pocket money Dad gave me on magazines containing articles about *Tropical Heat*, obsessed with reading about Cara. I often dreamed about her and, while I pretended to my friends that I couldn't decide between Luis and Ashton, I knew it was Cara I chose.

It was then that I first suspected that my friendships were superficial. If I'd had a true and genuine friend, I'd have been able to talk about my feelings. Every time I imagined a conversation with any of them, all I could picture was them laughing at me and spreading a rumour that I'd tried something on with one of them. So I gradually pulled away from them. I told myself it was because I was about to start my GCSEs and needed to focus on my studies, but it wasn't that. If I couldn't be me with my 'closest' friends, were they friends at all?

The Christmas holidays arrived and I visited Rosemary on my way back from the final day at school.

'I have some wonderful news, darling girl,' she said as soon as I'd stepped inside the flat. 'Matthew and Morgan are visiting after Christmas.'

'That's great news.' And it was for her. I knew she missed them.

'You'll have to come round to see them.'

'Oh! I, erm... I'm not sure. It's been a long time since... I don't think they'd want to see me.'

'Nonsense! The three of you used to play so beautifully together.'

Yes, we did, but then they grew up and turned into bullies.

'I don't think we have anything in common anymore. Except you, of course.'

But Rosemary could be very persuasive when she wanted something and I found myself trudging up to Renleigh Court on 27th December, trying to decide what was worse: seeing that cow and her brother for the first time in three years or spending another day with the Grimes family.

Christmas had been dire. Dad had been working overtime for most of December and was shattered. When he came off the night shift on Christmas Day morning, he wished us a merry Christmas then headed up to bed, telling us to open presents without him.

I was ordered to make Christmas dinner for Tina's family and Jenny's and, because space was tight with Connor and Cody both having girlfriends round, I had to sit on the stairs to eat mine. By the time I'd chased after them all with extra gravy and top-ups on their drinks, my food was cold.

I'd put my earphones in while I picked at my meal so didn't hear Dad creeping downstairs.

'Why are you eating out here?' he asked.

'Erm, I...' I couldn't think of an excuse.

He glanced down at my phone beside me on the stairs. 'You didn't like your new phone?'

'What new phone?' The words were out before I had a chance to filter a response, realising too late that Tina must have been given money to buy me a new phone and had spent it on herself instead.

I knew Tina would make me pay for the huge row they'd had, and I was still waiting for that moment as I arrived at Rosemary's. I didn't feel comfortable letting myself into her flat while Matthew and Morgan were there, so I knocked on the door.

'Oh. It's you,' Matthew said. He was nineteen now and barely recognisable from the skinny teenager I remembered. 'Grandma said you'd probably show up.'

'Is she in?'

'You've just missed her. She's out with the dog.'

'I'll come back later.'

'She said you should come in and wait.'

Morgan was lounging on the sofa with a mug of hot chocolate. She'd grown even more beautiful and butterflies swarmed in my tummy. I wondered if her beauty was still only skin-deep.

'Happy Christmas,' I said, trying to sound like I was pleased to be there.

'It would have been if we'd been allowed to stay at home.'

I wasn't sure how to respond to that.

'Matt!' she shouted. 'Where the hell's my chocolate orange? Are you picking the cocoa beans yourself?'

'Catch!'

A chocolate orange hurtled across the room straight into Morgan's mug, covering her in scalding hot chocolate.

'Shit! That's boiling.' She leapt up and whipped off her dress, revealing a purple and black plunge bra and, through her sheer tights,

I could see she was wearing matching knickers. I'd never worn posh matching underwear in my life. I realised I was ogling and, cheeks burning, I turned away as Morgan stormed into the spare bedroom, cursing her brother.

I looked up at Matthew who was staring at me, eyes narrowed. I shuffled uncomfortably on the spot then headed into the kitchen for a cloth to mop up the drink.

Matthew left the room while I was wiping up and, a few minutes later, Morgan reappeared wearing a sheer black top. I could see that she'd changed her bra too. It was now a deep red one and I swiftly averted my eyes.

'My brother's such a nob, don't you think?'

I shrugged. 'I don't really know him anymore.'

'You're lucky. Believe me, he *is* a nob. But most boys are.' She released her hair from its clip and shook it out. 'I'd rather be with a girl any day.'

I returned to the kitchen and rinsed out the cloth, my heart racing. Had Morgan just told me she was like me? I had no idea how to feel about that. I peered out of the kitchen window, willing Rosemary and Trixie to walk across the car park but there was no sign of them.

'Come back in here, Phoebe,' Morgan called. 'I won't bite. Unless you want me to.'

My throat felt dry as I stepped back into the lounge. She patted the sofa cushion beside her and I sat down on the edge of it, hardly daring to look at her.

'I'm glad you're here. I wanted to talk to you about something. I'm sorry things weren't great between us before I moved to London. It's difficult, isn't it?'

I eyed her warily. 'What is?'

'When you realise you're attracted to the same sex.'

I gulped as she took hold of my hand.

'I didn't know what to do with my feelings so I think I might have been a bit mean to you.'

A bit? Understatement of the year!

'But now I'm older and I'm comfortable with who I am.'

She shuffled closer, still holding my hand. She placed her other hand on my thigh and, even though I'd grown to despise her, I couldn't control the zap of electricity through my body.

'Have you had a girlfriend yet?'

'I, erm... I'm not...'

She stroked my hair back from my blazing cheeks. 'We both know you are. It's okay. You can be who you are with me. I could teach you a few things.'

My heart raced as she pressed her soft lips against mine. I was too shocked to respond. I'd never been kissed before and here was the most beautiful girl I'd ever seen in real life, now a woman, throwing herself at me and I didn't know how to feel. My head was screaming *she's a cow, push her away!* But my heart wanted to melt into her kiss.

'Come on,' she purred, releasing my hand and running her fingers through my hair as she kissed me again, her tongue teasing as it parted my lips.

My head lost the battle with my heart and I responded to her kiss. She smelled of peach and tasted of cherry.

She lifted my hand and placed it on one of her breasts. I froze momentarily.

'It's all right. Relax. I want you to touch me.'

So I did. Then she shoved me backwards and leapt off me. 'Oh, my God! Matt was right. You're a lezzer. Matt!'

Matt ran into the room. 'I told you!'

I looked from one laughing face to the other.

'You've been lusting after my sister all these years,' Matt cried. 'That's hilarious!'

I shoved past him and ran out of the building, their laughter following me. Rosemary and Trixie appeared round the side of the garages and I ducked round the back of the building, waiting until they'd entered, before I sprinted across the car park and out of sight.

I should have trusted my instincts about Morgan. She was ugly inside and, even if she had been gay, she wasn't worthy of my first kiss.

I'd never get that moment back and I'd never forgive her or Matthew for playing games like that and for making me lie to Rosemary later about why I hadn't visited her that day. She could never know what they'd done to me. She idolised the pair of them and I wasn't about to expose them for what they really were. Once again, I'd take one for the team. Story of my life.

56

SAMANTHA

Present day

On Saturday evening, after we'd cleared up from dinner, we had a production line going in the kitchen with the wedding invitations. Phoebe had beautiful handwriting, so her job was to write the names on each invitation, Beth was adding address stickers to the envelopes, I was folding a directions/information page, Josh was stuffing the envelopes, and Darcie was adding a postage stamp and a cute hedgehog sticker to seal them.

A playlist on my phone gave us some music while we worked. I found myself watching Phoebe, who didn't seem herself at the moment. She'd spent the past few evenings in her bedroom, claiming she had a lot of coursework to do, but I couldn't shake the feeling that wasn't it. All I could do was emphasise that I was there for her if she ever wanted to talk.

'Something's definitely upsetting Phoebe,' I said to Josh when the invitations were all ready and everyone had left the kitchen.

'I agree. She's too quiet. Could she have had a run-in with Rosemary?'

'It's possible but I'd have thought she'd have told us if that was the case. It couldn't be worse than the big fallout.'

Josh made us a mug of tea each while I quickly flicked through the pile of invitations to double check they all had stamps on them. I paused at one and removed it from the pile, staring at it thoughtfully.

'Whose is that?' Josh asked, placing my mug down beside me.

'Mum's. I'm wondering if I should deliver it personally.'

'You could do. What does your gut say?'

'That I haven't seen her new home and it's probably time I did.'

'Will you call her first?'

I pondered for a moment then shook my head. 'It's easier for her to say no over the phone.'

'Do you want me to come with you?'

'I'm not sure. It might send the wrong message.'

'Your dad's on call tomorrow. Why don't we see if he can base himself here with Fizz and Zayn while we drive over to Whitsborough Bay with the girls. We can go to the beach while you're with your mum and we're nearby if she's up for more visitors or on hand for you if it doesn't go well.'

I smiled at him. 'Have I told you lately how amazing you are?'

'Not since this morning. Right back at you.'

* * *

The following morning, Josh dropped me off outside Mum's house – a cosy three-bedroom new-build not far from where I'd been raised. We agreed that they'd wait at the park round the corner and, if I didn't phone within ten minutes, Josh would drive down to North Bay with Phoebe and Darcie and assume that Mum and I were talking but it was best done alone.

My palms were sweating as I rang the doorbell and waited on the step, regretting the decision to turn up without warning. She hated surprises.

'Samantha!' She didn't look or sound angry which was a good sign.

'Hi, Mum.'

She glanced past me, frowning. 'Are you alone?'

'Josh dropped me off. He's taken Phoebe and Darcie to the beach. We didn't like to all turn up without warning. I can go if it's bad timing.'

'I was just making a coffee. Do you want one?'

'That would be lovely, thank you.'

I followed her along the hallway into a bright kitchen diner at the back of the house. French doors opened out onto a deck and a surprisingly long and beautiful garden bursting with tubs.

'Your garden's stunning,' I said. 'Did you do all this?'

'Yes. The garden's what sold me the house. It was only a patch of soil, but it was so much bigger than the others with it being a corner plot and I knew I could do loads with it. Do you want a tour while the kettle's boiling?'

Outside, Mum talked me through the different areas she'd created and which insects the different plants attracted. She'd put a pond in and was even growing her own vegetables. I'd never heard Mum talking so passionately about anything before.

'I had no idea you knew so much about gardening.' She'd looked after the garden at our family home and it had always looked pretty, but this was what I'd expect from a professional.

'I read a lot of books over the summer and got hooked. It was great starting from nothing and creating my dream garden from scratch, but I'm itching for a new project now. There are still things to do here but they're small.'

'You should become a landscape gardener,' I said as we walked back towards the house.

'I've been wondering about enrolling at Claybridge Agricultural College in September, but I don't know. It's been so long since I last studied anything.'

'You studied a few books in the summer...' I paused and swept my hand across the garden, 'and look what you created from that. If you're wondering if you can study and apply it, this is your proof.'

She smiled – a wide, genuine smile – and I felt quite emotional for a moment, knowing I'd said something to evoke that reaction.

We sat with our drinks at a metal table on the deck a few minutes later.

'How's Chloe settling in?' she asked. 'Have you seen much of her?'

I wrinkled my nose. 'Can we start with an easier question?'

'What's happened? Have you fallen out again?' It was clear from her surprised expression that she didn't know, which meant that Chloe hadn't bad-mouthed me to her or Auntie Louise for a change.

'I don't think village life is what Chloe expected,' I said, hoping that sounded diplomatic enough. Chloe and Mum were too close and Mum and I were too distant for me to say anything more.

Mum studied my face for a moment. 'Let me guess. She's been up at the farm every day demanding you entertain her because she's bored and has had a strop because you've got work to do.'

I couldn't help smiling. 'That's our Chloe. I haven't seen or heard from her for over a week now.'

'She'll come round eventually.'

'I'm not so sure this time, but I'm trying to keep so many plates spinning at the moment that I've had to let that one go. For now.'

'You look tired, Samantha. Are you looking after yourself?' The depth of concern in her voice was unexpected and something I'd longed for in so long that a sob escaped.

'You're not, are you?' she said, removing a packet of tissues from her pocket and sliding them across the table.

'I had another PTSD episode the last time I saw Chloe,' I spluttered through my tears. 'I thought I was in control of it and we argued and I was back to square one.'

'What happens?'

I took a deep shaky breath and dabbed at my eyes. 'The sky goes dark – or it seems to – and I'm back to the night they threw eggs at the barn and tried to get my cat. I can hear them running through long grass. I can hear Misty-Blue yowling and there's this gripping fear. The weird thing is that I was more scared when the barn was alight than that night, but my counsellor thinks it's because the Grimes boys weren't there when the barn was burning. It's having a confrontation that's my trigger so, if stress levels rise because of a confrontation with someone, I'm right back at that night when there was a confrontation rather than the fire when there wasn't.'

She wrapped her hands round her mug of tea and took a few slurps. 'I can't walk down narrow streets or alleyways even in broad daylight. The smell of tequila... a couple of songs...' She shook her head then looked up at me. 'I kept my New Year's resolution and there's something I need to tell you...'

I'd already heard it from Dad last year, but hearing about that night from Mum made it all the more heartbreakingly real. I didn't need to feign shock because I felt it all over again, deeper, more powerful.

'Your dad and Louise urged me time and time again to get help, but I refused. I wanted to put it all behind me and just get on with my life but when I lost your sister at seven months, I lost myself. I was so angry with the world and everyone in it, especially myself, when the only person I should have been angry with was him. It shouldn't matter what I was wearing, how drunk I was, that I was alone, that I didn't scream. No woman is *ever* asking for it or putting themselves at risk. The blame lies completely and solely with that one man who chooses to violate her.'

'I'm so sorry, Mum. That must have been terrifying.'

'It was, but so was the fallout from it. The repercussions of that one night have affected me for nearly thirty-five years and they've impacted on my relationships with all the people I care about.'

She drained the last of her tea.

'I'm still working through all of that with my counsellor. Obviously, the biggest impact has been on your dad and on you, and I know it's connected, but we haven't fully joined the dots yet. That's mainly because of me. I'm really struggling with how I treated you. Each session unearths new memories of things I said or did and I know it was me, but I don't recognise that person as me. It's like I've got this film reel of my life playing in my head and I'm the director and it isn't playing out like it was meant to. I'm stood to one side yelling "cut" but the person playing my part just keeps going and keeps hurting you. That probably makes no sense whatsoever.'

She chewed her lip thoughtfully. 'I haven't been avoiding you. I wanted to get this clear in my head before I came to the farm so that I could give you some sort of explanation for my disgusting behaviour. There's no excuse for it. Yes, the anger and hatred were trigged from that night but, every time I picked a fight with you, said something cruel, gave something of yours to Chloe, ignored one of your amazing achievements or any of the long list of offences, he wasn't standing behind me with a knife. I had choices. I made the wrong ones and I have me and only me to blame for my behaviour.'

'Is there anything I can do to help?'

'You've already helped way more than I deserve.'

'How?'

'Look at you! Look how you turned out. It's like you've taken every ounce of negativity I've thrown your way and turned it into an act of kindness. You're a nurse who now devotes her life to rescuing hedgehogs. You've opened up your home to those in need – Josh's family, Chloe and Samuel, and now Phoebe and Darcie. Kids should look up to their parents as role models, not the other way round, but I'm looking at you as the type of person I want to be. I'm so proud of you.'

I couldn't find any words to respond. I'd never in a million years expected to hear a speech like that from Mum, and handed out so freely and enthusiastically. All I'd ever wanted was to know she was proud of me and, after she'd had a tour round the barn in the summer, Josh was convinced that her saying her parents would have been proud was her way of saying that she was, but this was something else. This was a fanfare and flag-waving.

'You look shellshocked.'

'I am.'

'How do you do it, Sam? How do you keep giving when you're not getting anything in return? What makes you keep trying when you're facing a brick wall?'

'Some people might think it's naïve but I believe that everyone has the potential to be kind. There are some horrible, evil people in the world like the man who raped you and serial killers and pretty much every member of the Grimes family except Darcie and her mum. But for everyone else, if they lash out or say hurtful things, there's usually a reason. It could be something from their past or a fear about the future or pretty much anything in between but give them enough time and patience and you'll usually get to the bottom of it and amazing things can happen for that person and also for you.'

'The fragrance stays in the hand that gives the rose.'

'Oh, my gosh! You heard that from Gramps?'

'He used to say it about you. I never saw it before, but I do now.'

'I miss him.'

Her eyes glistened. 'I do, too. Another thing I'm sorry for. I pushed them away. I was too ashamed to have them ever find out what happened.'

'You know there's nothing to be ashamed of, don't you?'

'I do now.' She gazed around the garden. 'A year ago, you asked me if we could work out what was wrong with our relationship and try to move forward. I wasn't ready to face up to any of it back then, but I am now. I can't expect you to forgive me when I don't think I'll ever forgive myself, but if you would still like to try to move forward, I'd really like that.'

'It's all I've ever wanted. But there's something really important you have to do before we have any chance of that happening.'

'What's that?'

'You have to forgive yourself.'

'I can't. That film reel...'

'You can and you will because if you're serious about wanting a relationship with me then you need to put your whole self into it and enjoy it instead of letting guilt eat away at you.'

She gave me a watery smile. 'With help, I'll give it my best.'

'Good. And there's one more thing I need you to do for me.' I removed her wedding invitation from my bag. 'I want you to be at our wedding and I mean properly, as the mother of the bride. No slipping in at the back at the end of the ceremony.'

She opened the envelope, removed the invitation and scanned down it. 'You're sure about this?'

'About getting married or about inviting you?'

She laughed. 'I've met Josh and seen you together. I know there's no doubt about getting married. Thank you, Samantha. I'd love to be there.'

She stood up and wrapped her arms round me and we stood there on her deck for several minutes in silence, clinging onto each other while the birds chirped and a light breeze ruffled our hair. As she tightened her hold and whispered 'sorry', I felt as though she was passing on every missed hug throughout my lifetime and I closed my eyes and melted into them.

There'd be some people who didn't believe Mum ever deserved my forgiveness. If they watched that film reel of our lives, they'd say the relationship was toxic and I needed to walk away and cut her off completely. If I was an outsider, I'd probably advise the same. But that was the thing. I *wasn't* an outsider and that made me the best judge about whether there was a future for us. Mum had hurt me countless times. It didn't matter that she'd never physically struck me, as cruel words and filthy looks could still cause pain. I'd risen above it all and, thanks to Dad, my wonderful grandparents, and Chloe, I'd made it out the other side relatively unscathed. Mum hadn't. She'd battled with pain, guilt, embarrassment, anger and self-loathing for most of her adult life because a stranger dragged her into an alleyway, held a knife against her throat, and raped her. She deserved patience, understanding and empathy. Those were all things in my toolkit to give and I chose to offer them.

I was convinced that seeking professional help was the best thing that Mum could ever have done. I could already see considerable differences in her in a couple of months. By the end of the year, she'd be a completely different person. And if that person started to demonstrate the behaviours I'd seen growing up, that was when I'd make the decision to walk away. Giving her a final chance didn't make me weak. It made me strong because it was all about choice; *my* choice about what I wanted for *my* life.

57

PHOEBE

As I rode up the track to Hedgehog Hollow after college on Wednesday, I felt so wobbly with nerves that I expected to take a tumble off my moped at any minute. When the farmyard came into sight and I spotted Fizz's blue mini, I skidded to a halt and had to take a moment to sort myself out.

I hadn't seen her since the hedgehog rescue from Yasmin's drain last week, even though she'd been to the barn several times. I wished I could dump my moped and go straight to the farmhouse, but that would only worry Samantha. She'd already asked a zillion times if I was okay.

Shaking my hair out after I removed my helmet, I forced a smile onto my face and poked my head round the barn door. Samantha and Fizz were stood up near the treatment table, staring down at a hedgehog on the floor.

'What's—?'

Samantha twisted round and put a finger to her lips before I could finish the sentence, and beckoned me towards them.

I slipped off my backpack and gently placed it on the ground, then tiptoed over.

The hedgehog unfurled itself and twitched its nose, sniffing the air. There was a bowl of food a few paces away and it set off towards it then veered to the left, moving round in a circle a few times before curling back into a ball again.

Samantha scooped it up and placed it on a fleecy blanket on the treatment table.

'I've not seen that before!' Fizz exclaimed. 'Poor Bowie.'

'What's wrong with him?' I asked.

'I can't be certain but I'm thinking ear mites which are causing a balance issue and making him veer to one side.'

'So he's dizzy?'

'Pretty much. I'll need to take him to the practice. Are you two okay to hold the fort?'

It was on the tip of my tongue to say I had coursework, but I couldn't do that to Samantha when she needed me, and it wasn't fair on Fizz either. She'd shown me nothing but friendship, and I had no right to throw that back in her face just because she had a new girlfriend.

I removed my coat and washed my hands while they prepared Bowie's crate.

When Samantha left, there was an awkward silence for a moment and then we both started to speak at the same time which broke the ice.

'You go first,' I insisted.

Fizz smiled. 'I was just going to say I've really missed you this week. Have you got on top of your coursework?'

'Yeah. It was a big piece but I'm fine now.'

'That's good. What were you going to say?'

'I was going to ask how it went with Yasmin last week.'

'Really good. We've been out a couple of times since. Early days but a great start. She's such a talented artist. I'm in awe. I had a go at sculpting with clay. Nightmare! I swear I made better stuff from Play-Doh when I was five. What do you think this is?'

I huddled against her and looked down at the photo on her phone. 'That looks like a cat. Is it Jinks?'

She turned her head and stared at me in amazement. 'It *is* Jinks! You can actually tell from that?'

'I think it's really good.'

'Thank you. That's so lovely.'

We held eye contact for a moment and my heart thudded. Our faces were so close, I'd barely need to move for my lips to meet hers. I wanted it so badly, but that wasn't fair on Fizz, not when she'd started seeing someone and sounded happy about it. But I couldn't seem to make myself move away from her. It felt like there was something sparking between us, but what did I know? It was likely just my imagination.

Fizz cleared her throat and straightened up. The moment – if there had been one – had passed.

'I've got something for you.' She wandered over to the coat hooks, rummaged in her bag and turned to me with a big grin. 'Close your eyes and hold your hand out.'

I rolled my eyes at her then did as she asked. My heart thudded again as she came closer and I could hear her breathing, smell the coconut shampoo in her hair. Her fingers lightly touched my palm, sending a ripple of pleasure up my arm.

'Open them,' she whispered.

I looked down at my hand and gasped. 'Mum's rings!'

'Someone tried to flog them to a jeweller in Hull but he recognised them from the appeal in the paper and called the police.'

I turned them over and gazed at the inscription with my parents' initials for Carolyn Eloise and Vincent Stephen inside the wedding band:

The stars shine for you, CE. Forever yours, VS xx

'They're yours, yeah?'

'I never thought I'd see these again.' I pushed down the lump in my throat. 'I can't thank you enough.'

'I didn't do anything.'

'You returned them to me.' I didn't want to cry, but I couldn't help it.

'Aw, come here.'

I closed my hand over the precious rings and held onto Fizz, the tears trickling down my cheeks and dripping onto her shoulders. I was a little taller than her and my thoughts strayed to how well we fit together. Not going to happen. I stepped away and grabbed a couple of tissues.

'Do you know much about your mum?' Fizz asked.

We sat down on the sofa bed. 'Just snippets. She was killed when I was only six weeks old, so I've got no memories of her. I wished I'd asked Dad more about her but it didn't occur to me until it was too late.'

'What do you know?'

'She was an accountant and I get my maths brain from her. She used to tell me bedtime stories and sing to me before I was even born. She loved cooking but hated tidying up and Dad said the kitchen always looked like an explosion in a supermarket when she'd finished, and Dad and her were really happy together.'

'Do you know how they met?'

'That *is* something I asked about. It was at the ready-meals factory where Dad had his accident. Mum was twenty-four and Dad was twenty-two and they were on their induction together. Dad said it was love at first sight for him, but he was convinced he'd never stand a chance with her. He described her as this beautiful, brainy accountant with a list of qualifications as long as his arm whereas he had three GCSEs to his name, was a bit scruffy round the edges, and his job involved twelve-hour shifts putting handfuls of grated cheese on top of cauliflower.'

I smiled at the deprecating way that Dad had described their differences. 'Mum was engaged at the time so he genuinely didn't stand a chance, but they became friends and would eat lunch together if his shifts fell right. He never told her how he felt. He believed that, if it was meant to be, it would happen. What gave him hope was that Mum didn't have a wedding date set. He told me that, if he'd had someone as incredible as Mum agreeing to marry him, he'd have a date set and the deed done before anyone else could snatch her away.'

'So what happened?' Fizz asked.

'They'd been friends for about four and a half years, getting closer and closer. Dad still hadn't told her how he felt and hadn't tried anything. About a month before Christmas, they met for lunch and he could tell she'd been crying. She told him it was over with her fiancé and she'd moved out, but she wasn't ready to talk about why. It was the moment he'd longed for but he knew he had to give her time.

'They were at the factory's Christmas party a few weeks later and found some quiet seats in the lobby to talk. They spotted mistletoe above them and laughed and kissed each other on the cheek. Mum told him her engagement ended after her fiancé asked her what she wanted for Christmas. The thing that popped into her head was unexpected but, as soon as it was there, she knew it was exactly what she'd wanted for several years but hadn't realised and there was no way her fiancé was going to get it for her. Dad asked what it was but Mum looked up at the mistletoe again and said, "That's a huge bunch of mistletoe and I really don't think we did it justice." They kissed on the lips that time and, when they pulled away, Mum said, "The thing I wanted for Christmas? It's you." They got married four months later, and I came along nine months after that.'

'Aw, that's such a sweet story.'

'I used to get Dad to tell me it over and over. I love the way that Dad never gave up hope and that it was Mum who made it happen in the end.'

I sat back against the cushion, smiling. Dad had waited for Mum, hoping it would happen eventually. I could do the same. If Fizz and I were meant to be, it would happen when the time was right and, for both of us, that time wasn't now. So I'd embrace the friendship and keep the hope but I'd prioritise the many other important things in my life: Darcie, Rosemary, my exams, and Samantha and Josh's wedding. My life had changed beyond all recognition this year. I had so much to be grateful for and so many people to be thankful to and I wasn't going to let my newfound happiness be blighted by a spot of unrequited love.

I unfurled my hand and gazed at the rings. It had happened for my parents and, one day, it would happen for me.

58

'Did you really need to blindfold me?' I asked, laughing as Dave guided me past the barn and down the track towards the dairy shed.

'I want you to get the full effect.'

It was the end of March and five weeks until the wedding. I'd been sent out to the cinema with Beth, Phoebe and Darcie for the afternoon while Dave and Josh constructed our wedding gazebo at the side of the meadow. Dave had been working on it in the dairy shed for the past week and I'd been banned from taking a sneaky peek, so I had no idea what to expect.

He stopped me. 'We're here. I'm going to remove the scarf but don't open your eyes until I tell you.'

'Okay.' The scarf was loosened and removed but I kept my eyes tight shut.

'I'll countdown from three,' he called from a slight distance. 'Three, two, one. Tah-dah!'

I stood there blinking for a moment as my eyes adjusted to the daylight. I pressed my hand to my mouth, a lump in my throat. I was standing several feet away from the gazebo and could see the wild-flower meadow through it and either side.

'It's stunning!'

It was better than anything I'd imagined, with a two-tiered roof and an adorable turret at the top. The deep bluey-grey tiles perfectly complemented the meadow and fields beyond. I didn't peel my eyes away but I was conscious there was a group standing to one side.

'We had a bit of help,' Dave said.

I'd expected to see Rich and Josh and I knew Phoebe, Darcie and Fizz had followed me across but Dad, Lauren and our best man Lewis were surprise additions. Even more surprising were Mum and Chloe. Mum was smiling, but Chloe looked a little sheepish.

Before I had a chance to say anything, Josh ran forward, grabbed my hand and pulled me inside. I ran my fingers across the white wooden pillars as I followed him to the back of the gazebo.

'Look at this.'

Carved into the back railing were a pair of hedgehogs and a garland of flowers and hearts.

'That's gorgeous. Did Dave do that?'

'No, but I think you'll be surprised when you find out who did. So what do you think? Would you like to marry me here?'

'It would be a dream come true.'

'Five weeks today,' Josh said, kissing my forehead. 'I can't wait.'

'Me neither.'

I slipped my arms round his neck and melted into his kiss.

'All right, knock it off!' Dave called. 'Your dad doesn't need to see that.'

Laughing, we broke apart and I gazed round at their smiling faces. 'Thank you all so much. This is beyond anything I imagined, and I love it. I feel like I should have got some prosecco in so we can toast to our new feature.'

'Funny you should say that...' A couple of glasses of bubbly were passed forward.

'To your wedding gazebo!' Dave called and everyone repeated his toast and sipped on their drinks.

I leaned on the railings. 'So who's responsible for the amazing carvings?'

Everyone turned and looked at Mum and Chloe. Josh had said I'd be surprised, and I don't think I could have been more so.

'You really did them?'

'It was Chloe's idea,' Mum said.

'But you did most of the work,' Chloe said, nudging her.

'It was a joint effort.'

'Thank you.' I glanced back at the carvings. 'They're perfect.'

After posing for several photos as a couple and with family and friends, we piled over to the farmhouse so everyone could sit down and grab another drink.

Paul and Beth joined us with Archie and Lottie and it reminded me of Christmas, having so many people I cared about in the kitchen at the same time, the room ringing with laughter. Mum and Dad were laughing together, Phoebe was bouncing Lottie on her knee, and Darcie was cuddling Archie. Not that long ago, I'd felt like the only family I had left was my dad and now look at it, rapidly expanding.

'Can we talk outside?' Chloe asked.

I followed her round to Thomas's bench and sat down. In the distance to my right, I could just see the turret and the very top of the gazebo roof at the edge of the meadow. I wanted to thank Chloe again for the carvings, but I didn't want to be the first to speak. It was her turn to break the ice and apologise. I wasn't going to pave the way this time.

'It wasn't your fault I moved here,' she said eventually. 'I knew as soon as you said it that it was a passing comment, but it stuck in my mind. I kept thinking about how happy and settled you were here and how miserable I was in Whitsborough Bay so I convinced myself that, if I moved here, I'd find what you'd found.'

'Aw, Chloe,' I said gently.

'I know it was stupid. The reason you have what you have is because of you. People gravitate towards you but run from me and I know that's my doing. I find it hard to let anyone in.' She sighed heavily. 'The truth is I'm lonely and I have been for a long time. Moving to

Bentonbray has made that even worse because I don't have Mum and Dad round the corner.'

'I'm sorry. I didn't realise it was that bad.'

'It is, but I shouldn't have expected you to solve it. You were right. I made the decision to move here and it was up to me to make the move work. I should never have put any pressure on you or said any of those things. My apologies probably don't mean much anymore but I really am sorry.'

She sounded it, but I wasn't going to make it that easy for her. 'So what are you going to do about it? Because I can't have this argument again. I had a PTSD episode after you left, and I'm devastated about that.'

Chloe's shoulders slumped and she hung her head. 'I know. Your mum told me. I'm sorry.'

'She did what?'

'Don't get mad with her. She had a right go at me about the way I treat you. Pretty ironic when you think about it, but she was right about every single thing she said. She also told me what happened to her. I had no idea.'

'It explains a few things, doesn't it?'

Chloe nodded. 'And here was me thinking I was the only one with skeletons in my closet. Anyway, she asked what I was going to do about it and she marched me down to the village noticeboard and made me pick a club. Thanks to you two, I'm now doing Pilates and am the newest leader with the village Beavers pack.'

'You aren't!'

'I had my first meeting on Tuesday. Sixteen six-to-eight-year-olds.'

'And...?'

'And I loved it. Pilates, not so much, but I'm sure I will when I get used to it. One of the women from Pilates has a daughter the same age as Samuel and we're meeting for coffee tomorrow.'

'I'm so proud of you. Those are huge steps.'

'I'm not saying the two of us will end up being best friends but it's a start. It'll get easier, right?'

'Definitely.'

We sat in silence for a few minutes before Chloe stood up. 'We'd better go back before they send out a search party. I've got a hot tip. There's a woman in Huggleswick who doesn't just rescue hedgehogs. She rescues people too and she talks a lot of sense. If you're lucky enough to be her friend, hang onto her, because she's the unicorn of best friends. Rare, precious and kind, guaranteed to add sparkle to your world.'

'You sent me a text on your wedding day saying that last part.'

'I remember. And it's just as true today as it was then.'

I hugged her tightly. 'Never be lonely, Chloe. I can't live your life for you or make new friends for you, but I'm still your cousin and your friend. However, I do have a job to do. You're always welcome here but I'm not always going to be able to give you my undivided attention. What I do is important. You're important, too, but I have to balance both things and I have to look after my health. I need to know you understand that or we'll crumble again.'

'I understand. Believe it or not, I do know it's not always all about me.' She giggled as she pulled out of the hug. 'Although sometimes it should be. I am, after all, a genius at carving hedgehogs in gazebos.'

'You certainly are.'

Arm in arm, we made our way back to the kitchen. I caught Mum's eye and, as she raised her eyebrows in question, I mouthed, 'Thank you.'

What an amazing and unexpected afternoon this had turned out to be.

◄ From Chloe

HOT TIP! There's a wedding today between the two
most perfectly suited people in the whole world. A
pair of unicorns who sparkle and shine even round
those who don't deserve it! Happy wedding day from
someone who's learning to be more unicorn! xx

I put my phone down and released an excited squeal.

'It's my wedding day today,' I whispered in the direction of the meadow canvas. 'And it would never have happened without you, Thomas. Thank you for everything.'

I lay there for a few minutes, enjoying a moment's peace before the getting ready frenzy began. Our wedding was at 11 a.m. and we had three local hairdressers booked, two make-up artists and a nail technician for a major pampering session.

Auntie Louise, Uncle Simon and Mum had all stayed in Quilly's Cottage and we'd been out last night for a family meal along with Dad, Chloe and James, Phoebe and Darcie, and Terry. I hadn't been able to eat much for excitement, not just about the wedding, but about having my whole family together for the first time in nearly two years – with a few additions – and without any arguments or hostility for the first time in pretty much ever.

Josh had gone out with Paul and Beth, Connie and Alex, Lauren, Lewis and his brother Danny, and usher Tariq. Josh had then stayed at Lewis's so the next time I saw him, he'd be waiting by the gazebo, ready to say, 'I do'.

✉ From Josh

```
Good morning to my beautiful bride. Can't wait
until 11 a.m. The next step in our amazing life
together. I love you more every day xxxxx
```

✉ To Josh

```
Hey you. Counting down the hours. Can't wait to
become your wife. I love you yesterday, today,
tomorrow and forever xxxxx
```

My door was flung open and Darcie hurled herself onto the bed wearing her Princess Tiana dress, followed by Phoebe.

'I'm going to be a flower girl!' Darcie cried.

'Oof!' I said, pretending to be winded. 'I think somebody might be a little bit excited. You look beautiful, Princess Darcie.'

'She's been up since half five, desperate to put her dress on, so we compromised for the moment. Happy wedding day,' Phoebe said, bending down to hug me. 'Did you manage to sleep?'

'Surprisingly, yes, but I've been awake for about an hour and my face is already aching from smiling. I can't believe I'm getting married today!'

* * *

I stood in front of the cheval mirror, hardly able to believe that the woman in the stunning cream wedding dress reflected in the glass was me. Josh had always told me I was beautiful, but it had been Chloe who'd been blessed with beauty in our family, and I'd always felt very average. Today, I felt completely different.

'I should have brought some more tissues with me,' Mum said, removing the last one from the small packet in her bag.

'There's spare packets in the top drawer over there,' I said, pointing to my dressing table.

'You're a vision in that dress,' she said, dabbing her eyes. 'Josh is a very lucky man.'

I lifted my skirts while Chloe and Hannah each fastened an ankle strap on my shoes for me.

'Are you ready?' Hannah asked. 'Have you got your something old, new, borrowed and blue?'

'The dress is new and the necklace borrowed.' I smiled at Mum as I lightly touched the vintage pearls that Nanna had worn on her wedding day – an unexpected surprise from Mum. 'I just need my something old and blue, so I'll meet you downstairs in a minute.'

Mum, Chloe and Hannah left the room and I lifted the lid of my jewellery box. When I'd cleared the farmhouse after Thomas died, I'd kept Thomas and Gwendoline's wedding and engagement rings and a silver bangle with a hedgehog etched onto it. I picked the bangle up and slipped it onto my wrist – my something old – and I opened up a drawer and removed a pale blue handkerchief of Thomas's. I have no idea what had prompted me to keep it but I was glad I had because I now had something of both of them on my wedding day. There was a little pocket sewn into the skirt especially for it, so I kissed the fabric and slipped it inside.

My shoes were embroidered with a rose design which made me think of Gramps and his phrase for me so, along with Nanna's necklace, I felt like I had a piece of both my grandparents with me too.

I paused at the top of the stairs and smiled down at Mum, Dad, my five bridesmaids and three flower girls.

Dad ran up, kissed me on the cheek and offered his arm. 'Beautiful,' he whispered. 'So proud.'

He sniffed and cleared his throat as we ascended together. I thought I'd cry. I could feel a whirlpool of emotions bubbling so close to the surface but the strongest by far was sheer joy.

Beth handed me my bouquet made from wildflowers, some of which had been picked from our meadow. I breathed in the fragrance as Phoebe, Darcie and Fizz lifted up my train.

Outside, I looked up at the cornflower-blue sky, peppered with fluffy clouds. The weather couldn't have been kinder. We strolled across the farmyard towards the barn and I paused by the barn window and blew a kiss to the hedgehogs.

Josh and I had chosen a 'white lights and woodland' theme. White lanterns and a curtain of white fairy lights had been hooked along the wall of the barn to be lit later, and a woodland-style signpost stood at the edge of the farmyard, directing guests to the gazebo and dairy shed, which now had a new name thanks to Darcie: Wildflower Byre. She'd suggested it after finding the word 'byre' in one of her books and discovering it meant cow shed. It couldn't be more ideal.

The guests were seated on benches made from tree stumps and reclaimed wood. Across their heads, I could see Josh and Lewis standing by the gazebo. Lewis spotted us and whispered something to Josh, and I knew it would be taking all his willpower not to turn round. He wanted to wait until the music started before he turned, catching his first glimpse of me at the end of the aisle.

Mum took her place at the front next to Auntie Louise and Uncle Simon while the bridesmaids and flower girls arranged themselves into height order with Darcie holding Amelia's hand at the front as they scattered rose petals; another nod to Gramps.

A string quartet struck up. I'd been expecting them to play a classical piece, but it was Bruno Mars's 'Just the Way You Are'. My heart leapt as everyone, including Josh, turned round and looked in my direction. I caught his eye and he nodded at the quartet, pointed at me, placed his hands across his heart and smiled so tenderly that my heart raced even faster.

Dad squeezed my arm and we set off behind the bridesmaids. The music had reached the first chorus and I fought back tears as I heard the lyrics in my head. When we'd first got together, I'd been so full of doubts about my appearance and Josh had been stunned at my insecurities and instructed me to listen to this song any time I had a moment. He'd even changed the ring tone on my phone so that it played it whenever he rang me.

I'd planned to look at the guests and smile in welcome, but I couldn't take my eyes off Josh, my heart bursting with love for him for changing the music.

Hannah took my bouquet and Dad kissed my cheek then handed me over to Josh, who squeezed my hand as he looked deep into my eyes. He didn't need to whisper that he loved me because I felt it emanating from him. Mum had said he was a lucky man, but it worked both ways. I was a lucky woman and would be forever grateful that he'd come into my life.

'Good morning!' the registrar called. 'And a very warm welcome to you all, whether you're a friend, family member or a hedgehog.' She paused for a ripple of laughter. 'I'm delighted to be here on such a beautiful day in the most stunning of settings for Joshua and Samantha's wedding.'

Josh and I stepped up into the gazebo and faced each other. He looked even better than I'd imagined in his shirt sleeves and waistcoat. I'd have to see if I could convince him to wear waistcoats more often.

'Let's begin...'

The service was beautiful and the setting was so magical. When we were about to exchange rings, a pair of Adonis Blue butterflies flitted into the gazebo. Our ring holder was a slice of log with our wedding date burned into it and a wooden heart with our initials on tied round it. The butterflies momentarily rested on the wood, one next to each ring, before taking flight and settling on the railings, as though wanting to watch the rest of the ceremony. Josh caught my eye and nodded. I'd often felt that Thomas and Gwendoline sent me signs that they were there, proudly watching over me, and this felt like another.

'It is my pleasure to pronounce you husband and wife,' the registrar said when we'd stated our vows and exchanged rings. 'You may now kiss your bride.'

Josh gently cupped my face and lowered his soft lips to mine in the most tender yet sensuous kiss. 'I love you.'

'I love you too.'

We turned and faced the guests, hand in hand, and laughed as someone – Dave I think – released a loud whistle and the guests all clapped and cheered. We'd done it!

As we walked back down the aisle, hand in hand, Misty-Blue trotted beside me and I smiled at her – an extra special flower girl.

Natasha and her team had spent yesterday dressing Wildflower Byre and the transformation was breath-taking. There were white lights everywhere, inside and out, in assorted glass jars, around pillars and strung across the rafters.

Outside in the field we'd used for last year's Family Fun Day were several games to keep guests of any age entertained, including space hoppers, hula hoops, a ring toss, oversized versions of Jenga and Connect Four, and a trio of wigwams.

Inside were rustic-looking wooden tables and chairs. Each centre-piece was a log slice with the table number on it, a glass jar of white lights and a bottle of wildflowers, with additional jars of lights and flowers on log plinths round the barn.

Our wedding day was everything I'd ever dreamed of and more. Sitting beside Josh at the top table as he made his speech, listening to him relaying the story of our first few disastrous encounters and how everything had changed on the night of Connie and Lauren's fiftieth birthday last February, it was hard to believe that there'd ever been a time when he hadn't been in my life.

I glanced over to the wooden steps set up across the room where framed photos of those who were no longer with us were set amongst jars of lights and flowers. I focused on the photo of Thomas and Gwendoline on their wedding day, then Nanna and Gramps on theirs. James had broken my heart, and Harry before him, but I'd needed to experience that to know how different Josh was and I was convinced ours was a match made in heaven by four very special people.

* * *

Shortly after we'd cut the cake – a stunning design of three stacked logs with a bride and groom hedgehog on the top – we were invited onto the dance floor for our first dance as husband and wife.

I rested my head on Josh's shoulder as we shuffled to Christina Perri's stunning 'A Thousand Years'.

'Enjoying yourself, Mrs Alderson?' he whispered.

'Having the best day ever.'

'So, tell me about the hedgehogs...' he said.

I smiled up at him. 'Just think, if you hadn't said that, today might never have happened.'

His lips lightly brushed mine. 'We were meant to be together. Two troubled souls united, just like Auntie Lauren said. A team forever.'

The wedding party and other guests were invited to join us as the song changed. Dad took my hand and Connie took Josh's.

'You look radiant,' Dad said. 'It melts my heart to see you so happy.'

'I've got everything to be happy about. How are you doing?'

'My little girl has married a man who I have no hesitation in calling my son, she has her mother here today, and there's peace. I always knew you'd find your perfect match, but I'd given up hope on any progress with your mum.'

'I hadn't.'

'I know. You really are the most remarkable young woman.'

'And who do you think I learned that from?'

Dad hugged me close. 'Thank you.'

Terry asked if he could cut in shortly afterwards. Dad kissed my cheek and was about to leave the dance floor when Lauren stopped him and the pair of them waltzed around the floor, giggling like schoolchildren. Perhaps the romance of the wedding would get to them and tonight would be the night when they finally took a step beyond friendship. I hoped so. They were so good together.

'I saw the photo of Thomas and Gwendoline,' Terry said. 'That were lovely. She'd have been right touched by that.'

'I know I never met her, but I always feel her presence.'

'Oh, aye. She's here, all right.' He tapped his heart. 'And in here.'

'I'm sorry it didn't work out for you, Terry.'

'I'm not. It's the way it was meant to be. It's what led us to today. Without them being together and their vision, none of this would have happened. Those two young lasses…' He glanced over at Phoebe as she twirled Darcie. 'Doesn't bear thinking about.'

The music changed to a more upbeat number so Terry shuffled off the dance floor to get a drink and more guests joined us. I stayed for a few dances, surrounded by my bridesmaids, my heart bursting with joy as I watched Josh spinning Darcie round the dance floor and then letting her step on his feet as he danced.

'I used to do that with Rosemary's husband Sydney,' Phoebe said. 'It's lovely seeing Darcie have someone to do it with. He's so good with her.'

'Isn't he? He loves children.'

'I can't thank you and Josh enough for everything you've done for Darcie and me. You saved us both.'

Tears sprung to my eyes and I wrapped my arms round her, reminded of what Chloe had said that I didn't just save hedgehogs; I saved people. Why wouldn't I? I had enough love to go round and I had a home that was meant to be filled with people, like Thomas and Gwendoline had always dreamed.

Having Paul, Beth and the kids, and Phoebe and Darcie stay with us had helped them all in a time of need, but it had helped me too. I'd found new friends, new family, new purpose with them all. Gramps was right. The fragrance really did stay in the hand that gave the rose.

I glanced across at Thomas and Gwendoline's photo again and

smiled. Terry was right too. It had all started with their vision and so many lives had been changed and hedgehogs saved because of them. And I knew exactly what the next step needed to be.

* * *

'Where are you taking me?' Josh asked as I led him out of the barn later that evening.

We could still hear the music but the chatter and laughter faded as we walked further from Wildflower Byre.

'I wanted to give you your wedding present,' I said.

'But you already gave me this.' He pointed to a silver pocket watch dangling from his waistcoat which I'd had engraved.

'There's something else.'

'Very mysterious,' he said, laughing.

Fairy lights strung across metal poles beside the benches illuminated our way to the gazebo. Natasha had placed a pedestal in the middle of the floor where we'd stood earlier, with a beautiful floral arrangement on it.

I led Josh round the back of the pedestal and rested against the hedgehog carvings. Confident that we were hidden from sight, I slid my arms round him and pulled him into a deep kiss. My heart raced with longing as he responded with passion and I was half tempted to grab his hand and run to Meadow View where we were staying that night to give us some privacy, but that could wait.

'Mmm, I liked that wedding gift,' Josh murmured when we came up for air.

'That's not your real gift,' I said. 'That's just something I've been dying to do all day.'

'Mrs Alderson, you're spoiling me. What's my real gift?'

'It's something I've been thinking about for a while and I'm 100 per cent certain about it now. Once your dad and Beth are settled in Alder Lea and Phoebe's got her qualifications and has found a job, I'd like us to start trying for a baby.'

He gasped. 'Sammie! You're sure?'

'I couldn't be more sure. I've seen how amazing you are with Archie and Lottie and now with Darcie and Phoebe. You should have an opportunity to be a dad—'

Josh opened his mouth to object and I gently placed my finger over his lips.

'I was about to say but, as we'd agreed, it had to be right for both of us. It's right for me now too. I love having babies and children in the house. I love playing with them, bathing them, reading them bedtime stories. I want to do that with our children. I'm not my mum. I'm me and that's a badass hedgehog saviour who's deeply and forever in love with the future father of my children. What do you think?'

Josh took my hands and held them against his heart. 'I think you've already made me the happiest man alive by marrying me today and saying yes to children is an amazing gift but, as I've always said, the best gift of all is having you in my life.'

'You say the loveliest things.'

'I mean them. And yes to children. You'll be the best mum in the world. You already are.'

I kissed him once more, so full of love for him. We broke apart at the sound of voices and Josh peeked round the flowers.

'It's your mum and dad,' he whispered.

'Really?' Surprised, I peeked round the other side. They were sitting on a couple of the benches, Dad with his back to the gazebo and Mum facing him.

I didn't like to spring up from behind the flowers and make them jump so I indicated to Josh that we should stay where we were, hidden from sight. I wondered if they were having a heart to heart or whether Dad was thanking Mum for accepting the white flag I'd been waving for years, helping make my wedding day extra special.

Several minutes passed and I started to regret my decision to stay hidden. I was itching to get back to the party but it was going to be awkward suddenly springing from the gazebo now.

'We might just have go for it,' I whispered to Josh.

I peeked round the flowers again and did a double take. Mum and Dad were slow dancing in the aisle. I recognised the song coming from Wildflower Byre as one they both loved. Dad was holding Mum very close with his head rested against hers.

I indicated to Josh to take a look and we both took a sharp intake of breath as Mum tilted her head to look up at Dad and their lips met. It wasn't just a brief kiss. It was a full-on passionate one.

'Shit!' Josh muttered. 'Look!'

I looked beyond my parents. Lauren was standing behind the rows of seats. There was a string of lights right beside her illuminating her face and there was no disguising the expression of devastation as she watched them. She pressed her hand across her mouth, hung her head, then took off in the direction of the holiday cottages.

Josh and I glanced at each other, wide-eyed. Moments later, Mum and Dad pulled apart, exchanged a few words, then headed in the direction of the holiday cottages, holding hands.

I slumped back against the railing and Josh did the same.

'That was unexpected,' I said. 'Do you think they've gone to...?'

'Looks that way.'

'And do you think Lauren...?'

'We always suspected it, but...' He ran his fingers through his hair. 'They say weddings can have a strange effect on people.'

Misty-Blue jumped onto the gazebo and weaved round Josh's legs before disappearing into the meadow.

'I was hoping that the romance of the day would sweep Dad and Lauren away, not Dad and Mum.' I looked up into the night sky. 'I think things might be about to get a bit messy.'

Josh took my hand and kissed it. 'Ready to throw some more shapes on the dance floor?'

'You're on.'

Laughing together, we returned to Wildflower Byre, and I pushed aside what we'd just witnessed. It didn't need to mean anything. It had been a snapshot moment during the romance of a wedding. Mum and Dad might have gone to the cottages to talk and the expression on

Lauren's face could have been a worried protective friend rather than a woman seeing the man she loved kissing someone else. They were all grown-ups and, if there were any repercussions, they could deal with them.

In the meantime, there was a dance floor calling and much to be celebrated. On what would have been Gwendoline's eightieth birthday, there'd been a wedding at Hedgehog Hollow – the first of many celebrations in this wonderful place born from her vision of saving the most adorable but vulnerable creature – and the next stage of my wonderful life with Josh.

AUTHOR'S NOTE

Although my settings and characters are fictional, the stories I tell do represent real life. I therefore undertake significant research to ensure that what I write about is accurate.

However, some information is not freely available and, for *A Wedding at Hedgehog Hollow*, banks are understandably not forthcoming about the way they handle fraud. The way I have chosen to play out this scenario is based on a combination of significant research, conversations with current bank employees, my own experience working for a bank for a decade, and some helpful case studies shared by the Financial Ombudsman.

It may not be how some readers think a bank would deal with it or how their own bank would respond, but please be reassured that it is representative as to how a bank *could* respond, bearing in mind I have created a fictional one.

Thank you
    Jessica xx

ACKNOWLEDGMENTS

Oh, my goodness, I can't believe I've just written the fourth book in the Hedgehog Hollow series! What started out as an exercise on my Master's in Creative Writing to put a character in an uncomfortable setting – a woman being bridesmaid for her cousin's wedding when she was secretly in love with the groom – has certainly taken on a life of its own! I hope you've enjoyed reading it as much as I've enjoyed writing it.

I've been overjoyed and overwhelmed with the love from readers for the series so far. Every time I receive a message from a reader/listener telling me they've discovered the Hedgehog Hollow books and can't put them down, it makes me so happy. What makes me even more happy is that, alongside the love for the story and the characters, I hear tales of readers who've fallen in love with hedgehogs, have made their gardens hedgehog-friendly, and have even rescued hedgehogs or hoglets when they'd previously not have known they were in danger.

This is a fictional series, but I undertake a considerable amount of research to ensure I accurately capture the plight of hedgehogs and the many dangers they face. I love that, in a work of fiction, it's possible to learn so much too. Thank you to everyone who has taken hedgehogs to their heart and who has been inspired to help in whatever way they can.

When a new book is released – particularly one in a beloved series – it's nerve-wracking wondering what reception it will get and whether readers/listeners will like it as much as the previous one. I was especially nervous about book three in the series – *Family Secrets at Hedgehog Hollow* – because I'd chosen to tell Chloe's story. I knew from reviews and comments on social media that Chloe was not popular and quite rightly so; she hadn't treated our lovely Sammie well at all. How would readers react to her being the second narrator? I was relieved to discover that it was overwhelmingly positive. Some still didn't like her but loved the story, some didn't like her but felt they understood her, and others completely changed their mind and found themselves wanting to give her a big hug. I didn't think it was realistic for Chloe to change completely so, as you've seen in *A Wedding at Hedgehog Hollow*, she still has her moments but she learns from them and each episode is essential for Sammie's ongoing development, hitting the point where she won't accept any more of Chloe's shenanigans and puts the job of peacemaker firmly in Chloe's hands.

So it turns out I didn't need to be worried about the reaction to Chloe but there was a negative reaction to something most unexpected. I had no idea that a cliff hanger could be so divisive! I'd already used one at the end of book two – *New Arrivals at Hedgehog Hollow* – without much reaction but the one at the end of *Family Secrets* caused some uproar! Okay, so I'll admit that the *Family Secrets* one was a whopper, throwing Hedgehog Hollow into complete disarray, but I had no idea some readers would get quite so angry about it, especially when the complete story being told in that book had already been told and the cliff hanger was only there as a tease to what was coming next. Oops!

You'll notice that this book still ends on a cliff hanger, but it's not quite such an enormous drop off the cliff; more of a little jump down onto the sand. I promise this is nothing to do with the backlash I received from some and is simply down to the story coming in book five. I felt it required more of an 'Ooh, that's intriguing' lead-in than an 'OMG! I can't believe it!' moment.

I'd better move on to thanking a few people. Firstly, let me talk about my dedication. In *A Wedding at Hedgehog Hollow*, the community rally around Samantha when the Grimes family do their worst again. As an author, I'm part of two invaluable communities: a community of writers who are exceptionally supportive and a community of readers whose enthusiasm for a particular book and/or author can make such an incredible difference.

In early 2020, I set up 'Redland's Readers' – a closed Facebook group for readers/listeners who might like to learn a little more about the writing process and the worlds in which I set my stories (Whitsborough Bay as well as Hedgehog Hollow). I was amazed at how quickly it grew and was honoured when a couple of members asked if I'd like to join a new group they'd just set up called 'The Friendly Book Community' with a purpose of doing exactly what the name suggests – being a warm and friendly space to discuss all things book-related. They've absolutely achieved that and I'm so proud to have been a part of it since the start. While the group has rapidly grown in membership, they have remained true to their roots and it genuinely is a happy place to be. As a reader, I've discovered new authors and, as an author, I've been so grateful to everyone who has discovered my books thanks to the group. Adrienne, Hazel, Louise, Marie, Michelle and Sarah, you are amazing and I'm so thrilled to have met you virtually and hope to perhaps meet you in person one day. Same goes to Meena, who came on board as a moderator. Thank you all xx

While on the subject of Facebook communities, a huge thank you also goes to 'Heidi Swain and Friends – A Facebook Book Club' for all the book love and support there. I love Heidi's books, so it's a privilege to be part of a group celebrating her amazing books and those by authors who might also appeal to her fans. Thank you to Sue and Fiona for the amazing work in running that group.

Thank you also to all these amazing people who have given their time and expertise:

- Jo Bartlett, fellow Boldwood author (do check out her fabulous books) and friend of many years for the expertise on fostering and adoption.
- Helen Phifer, another amazing author and good friend for all the police-related information.
- Nicola Cornick, another talented author, for information about guide dogs.
- Sarah Kingsnorth, one of the founders of 'The Friendly Book Community' and now a lovely new friend, for guidance on visual impairments and guide dogs (a shout out to Ozzie, Sarah's gorgeous guide dog) and the genius behind Josh's dad joke about 'A Room With a Moo'.
- Caz, Tim, Emily Coltman, Lizzie Sparkes, Bella Osborne, and a whole host of others who work or have worked in financial services for helping me with the fraud scenario.
- The social media pages, websites and blogs of umpteen hedgehog rescue centres – too many to name – for so much invaluable information and inspiration, particularly Wolds Hedgehog Rescue – a rescue centre in the real Hedgehog Hollow country.
- Members of Redland's Readers for their ideas for a name for the dairy shed and specifically Rachel Maile, who suggested using 'byre', prompting the final name of Wildflower Byre.

I undertake a copious amount of research for every book I write but this is a piece of fiction and occasionally an author needs to bend how something will happen in the 'real' world to move a story on or they discover that there have been changes in thinking which occur after a book has been written, so a novel may not always be 100 per cent accurate, but it's pretty close. Please therefore do forgive any elements that may not fully match your knowledge or experience.

We ran another 'name the hedgehog' competition for this book and our randomly selected winner was Mrs Pricklypants, courtesy of

Rachael MacKay. Congratulations Rachael! Absolutely loving that name.

Thank you, as ever, to the team at Boldwood Books. This is the fourteenth book my fantastic editor, Nia Beynon, and I have worked on and I have learned so much from her with each. I'm so grateful for all the advice and guidance on what to cull, ditch or expand, strengthening my writing and improving the story.

Thank you to Cecily Blench for copy-editing, Sue Lamprell who has also worked on all my books for the proofreading skills, and Debbie Clement for another stunning cover. This is my favourite so far. I love it so much!

Rachel Gilbey organised another fabulous blog tour, so thank you to Rachel and all the book bloggers and reviewers for their kind words and support.

Emma Swan has provided her brilliant narration and has, for the first time on one of my audiobooks, been joined by Kitty Kelly. Thank you both for bringing this story to life, to ISIS Audio who make the recording, and to Ulverscroft for the distribution.

Mum and Sharon, eternal gratitude as always for being there with a pick-me-up and encouragement when I have a crisis of confidence, and to Mark and Ashleigh for never moaning at the endless hours I spend welded to my office chair, absorbed in my fictional world.

Finally, I couldn't do any of this without you, the reader/listener. I truly hope you loved your fourth trip to Hedgehog Hollow and thank you for buying or borrowing this story. If you've sent me a message, left a review, recommended any of my books to friends or family, I'm so very grateful to you. Recommendations make such a difference.

The hedgehogs look forward to welcoming you back for book five and, if you've not taken a trip to Whitsborough Bay yet, they'd encourage you to do that. Who doesn't like to be beside the seaside?

Big hugs

Jessica xx

HEDGEHOG TRUE/FALSE

Hedgehogs are born with spines

FALSE - Imagine poor mum giving birth if they had spines! Ouch! When hoglets are born, their skin is covered in fluid and, after a few hours, this is reabsorbed and soft white spines erupt from the skin

Hedgehogs are good swimmers

TRUE - They're really good swimmers and, perhaps even more surprisingly, can climb trees. They do sometimes drown, though. It's not the swimming that's the problem; it's the getting out again and they can perish due to the exhaustion of trying to escape. It's therefore important that ponds have the means for a hedgehog to get out if they accidentally fall in

Baby hedgehogs are called hoglets

TRUE - Isn't it cute? They're sometimes known as piglets, pups or kittens but the official term is hoglets

Hedgehogs are nocturnal

TRUE AND FALSE – We tend to think of hedgehogs as being nocturnal which would suggest they're only out at night but, while they are most active at night time, the technical term for hedgehogs is 'crepuscular' which means they can be active at twilight too. We often see hedgehogs moving around in summer when it's still light because the days are longer and they need to search for food

Hedgehogs can run in short bursts at speeds of up to 3mph

FALSE - They're even faster than that. They are surprisingly nippy and can reach top speeds of 5.5mph in short bursts. Go hedgehogs!

Hedgehogs lose half their body weight during hibernation

FALSE - It's actually just over a third but that's still a significant amount and hedgehogs fresh from hibernation are going to need some major feasts to build up their strength quickly

Hedgehogs got their name in the Middle Ages from the word 'hyge-hoge' which translates today as 'hedge' and 'pig' combined

TRUE - The name does what it says on the tin! They snuffle round hedges for their foot and this snuffling/grunting is just like a pig

Hedgehogs have good eyesight

FALSE – Eyesight is the weakest of the hedgehog's senses and they are very susceptible to visual conditions. They have a keen sense of smell, taste and hearing and it's these senses they will use far more than their eyesight so one-eyed hedgehogs and even blind ones can survive in the wild thanks to their other senses

Hedgehogs are quiet eaters

FALSE - They're very noisy when they eat. They love their food and will slurp, crunch and lip-smack with their mouths open. Not the ideal dinner guest!

HEDGEHOG DOS AND DONT'S

Food and Drink

DO NOT give hedgehogs milk to drink. They are lactose intolerant. Dairy products will give them diarrhoea which will dehydrate them and can kill them

DO give hedgehogs water but please have this in a shallow dish. If it's in a deep dish, the risk is that they'll fall in and be unable to get out again

DO give hedgehogs dog or cat food - tin, pouch or biscuit format - they can eat both meaty and fishy varieties. It's a myth that they can't have fishy varieties of food but they may prefer meaty varieties because they prefer the smell

DO try to create a feeding station for a hedgehog so that other garden visitors (including cats) don't beat the hedgehog to it. You don't need to buy anything expensive. There are loads of tutorials and factsheets online around creating your own simple station

Your Garden

DO avoid having fences with no gaps under them. Hedgehogs can travel a long way in an evening and they rely on being able to move from one garden to the next. Or you can create a hedgehog highway in your fence

DO place a ramp by a pond so that, if a hedgehog falls, it can easily get out

DO NOT let your dog out into your garden without checking it's hedgehog-free. This is especially important during babies season (May/June and Sept/Oct) when there may be hoglets out there

DO build a bug hotel and DO plant bug-friendly plants. It will attract all sorts of delicious food for your hedgehogs

DO NOT use slug pellets. Hedgehogs love to eat slugs so pellets reduce their food supply and/or poison hedgehogs

DO have a compost heap or a messy part in your garden. If you can have some sticks/wood piled up in a safe corner, this makes a perfect habitat for hibernating

DO check your garden before strimming or mowing. Garden machinery can cause horrific accidents or fatalities

DO NOT leave netting out as hedgehogs can become trapped in it. If you have football goals in your garden, lift the netting up overnight and secure it safely to avoid injury or fatalities

DO always check bonfires before lighting as there may well be hogs nestling in there

Finding Hogs

DO NOT assume that a hedgehog out in the daylight is in danger. They usually are but watch first. It could be a mum nesting. If it's moving quickly and appears to be gathering food or nesting materials, leave it alone. If this isn't the case, then something is likely to wrong. Seek help

DO handle hedgehogs with gardening glove - those spines are there to protect the hogs and hurt predators - but keep handling to a minimum. Stay calm and quiet and be gentle with them. Transfer them into a high-sided box or crate with a towel, fleecy blanket or shredded news-paper (and a thick layer of paper on the bottom to soak up their many toilet visits). This will help keep them warm and give them somewhere to hide. Make sure there are plenty of air holes

DO NOT move hoglets if you accidentally uncover a nest but, if mum isn't there, do keep an eye on the nest and seek help if mum doesn't return. Hoglets won't survive long without their mother's milk. Put some water and food nearby so mum (assuming she returns) doesn't have far to travel for sustenance. If the hoglets are squeaking, this means they are hungry and you may need to call help if this continues and there's no sign of mum

MORE FROM JESSICA REDLAND

We hope you enjoyed reading *A Wedding at Hedgehog Hollow*. If you did, please leave a review.

If you'd like to gift a copy, this book is also available as an ebook, digital audio download and audiobook CD.

Sign up to Jessica Redland's mailing list for news, competitions and updates on future books.

http://bit.ly/JessicaRedlandNewsletter

ABOUT THE AUTHOR

Jessica Redland writes uplifting stories of love, friendship, family and community set in Yorkshire where she lives. Her Whitsborough Bay books transport readers to the stunning North Yorkshire Coast and her Hedgehog Hollow series takes them into beautiful countryside of the Yorkshire Wolds.

Visit Jessica's website: https://www.jessicaredland.com/

Follow Jessica on social media:

 facebook.com/JessicaRedlandWriter

 twitter.com/JessicaRedland

instagram.com/JessicaRedlandWriter

bookbub.com/authors/jessica-redland

ALSO BY JESSICA REDLAND

Welcome to Whitsborough Bay Series

Making Wishes at Bay View

New Beginnings at Seaside Blooms

Finding Hope at Lighthouse Cove

Coming Home to Seashell Cottage

Other Whitsborough Bay Books

All You Need is Love

The Secret to Happiness

Christmas on Castle Street

Christmas Wishes at the Chocolate Shop

Christmas at Carly's Cupcakes

Starry Skies Over The Chocolate Pot Café

The Starfish Café Series

Snowflakes Over The Starfish Café

Hedgehog Hollow Series

Finding Love at Hedgehog Hollow

New Arrivals at Hedgehog Hollow

Family Secrets at Hedgehog Hollow

A Wedding at Hedgehog Hollow

ABOUT BOLDWOOD BOOKS

Boldwood Books is a fiction publishing company seeking out the best stories from around the world.

Find out more at www.boldwoodbooks.com

Sign up to the Book and Tonic newsletter for news, offers and competitions from Boldwood Books!

http://www.bit.ly/bookandtonic

We'd love to hear from you, follow us on social media:

facebook.com/BookandTonic

twitter.com/BoldwoodBooks

instagram.com/BookandTonic